# His Fifth Kiss

## HAMMOND FAMILY FARM ROMANCE

### IVORY PEAKS ROMANCE
#### BOOK FIVE

## LIZ ISAACSON

# CHAPTER
## One

A PIECE that had been knocked loose inside Michael Hammond found the right place to be as the familiar pine trees lining the road went by. "I've missed Ivory Peaks," he said.

"Mm." His father drove, and Mike's memories ran at him fast and hard. He'd come to work this farm every summer since the age of twelve. He'd met a pretty girl here —Gerty—and he'd kissed her. His first kiss. Hers too.

They'd been real friendly for years, but the past two times he'd come back to the family farm, she hadn't been here. The first time, he'd tried to find out where she'd gone. Her father, who still worked for Uncle Gray, had said she was down in Texas, doing farrier school.

Gerty would always work with horses, Mike knew that. For some reason, he'd expected her to stay right here in Colorado, on his uncle's farm, and wait for him to get out of the military.

She hadn't, unless she was waiting at the familiar farm-house around the bend in the road Mike knew by heart. His pulse jumped, but he told himself she wouldn't be there. Why would she be there? He hadn't spoken to her in thirteen and a half years, after that last summer after his senior year, when he'd gone to college and then enrolled in the Marines.

He'd become a helicopter pilot, just like he'd told his father he wanted to become. Now, at age thirty-one, he had to have his daddy drive him home after his honorable discharge from the military.

"Looks like they've got everyone in off the farm," Dad said as the big red barn where Molly, Mike's cousin-in-law, ran her children's equine therapy program. Stables and more barns, horse rings, paddocks, and pastures ran to the west, and across the wide pasture sat the farmhouse, as well as the generational house where Mike's grandfather had once lived.

He'd come back to the farm for his grandfather's last few days on earth, and then the funeral. Forty hours later, he'd been back in the Middle East, with completely different people and a completely different climate.

Oh, how he missed Colorado.

Dad rolled down his window, and the cheers and whis-tles of the cowboys and cowgirls gathered along the fence came in through the window. Mike's face heated, and he wanted to turn away.

"I don't need this," he murmured.

"They miss you," Dad said. "Be nice."

"I am nice, Dad." Mike used to swallow his tongue when his dad told him to be nice. Now, he didn't have to. He wasn't fifteen, or even twenty-five. He was a grown man, and just because he had a hurt shoulder right now didn't mean he needed to be lectured by his daddy about how to be nice. "I just don't know any of them that well."

"You know Matt," Dad said, his voice aged and gravelly. Mike hadn't gotten married yet, but his younger brother Easton had. Mike had come home for that too, and he'd been back in Coral Canyon for about four months, recovering. But now that summer had arrived, Dad had brought him to the farm.

Always the farm.

"Oh, there's Elise," his mom said from the back seat.

Mike saw his Aunt Elise, and she'd aged gracefully. She was far younger than Dad or Uncle Gray, and she still wore pretty sundresses that made her seem more youthful than she was. None of Uncle Gray's younger kids had gotten married, though Jane had been engaged for about eight months last year.

He caught sight of Hunter, and a dose of extreme guilt punched Mike in the gut. "Dad," he said, but he couldn't get his voice to say anything else. He knew he'd disappointed his father by joining the military instead of coming back to the greater Denver area to take over the family company.

Hunter had been running it for close to seventeen years now, and he and Molly had four children. Mike had looked up to Hunter for his entire life. He couldn't see himself anywhere near Hunter's stature in only thirteen more years, which was how many years older Hunt was than Mike.

He wouldn't be married with four kids in even fifteen years. He wouldn't be running the huge family company, with a beautiful wife running her own business. He wouldn't own this farm, live in this beautiful farmhouse, or have any of the serenity or happiness Hunt had.

In truth, Mike was absolutely miserable.

*That's not the right word*, he thought as Dad brought the truck to a stop. He rolled up the window, and Mike waited patiently for his mother to come help him unbuckle his seatbelt. He hated this part, and he locked his jaw while Momma opened the door.

Their eyes met, and Mike did his best to put a smile on his face. "Thanks, Momma."

"I know you hate this," she said, reaching across his lap to undo the belt. "But I have a really good feeling about this summer." She gave him a smile. "Easton and Allison will be here in a couple of weeks, and Opal has a week or two off from her residency, and she just told me she'd come to the farm."

She smiled at Mike like this was just fabulous news, and Mike supposed it was. He really just wanted to be shown to his cabin; he wanted to close the door behind him; he wanted to be alone.

As the cowboys who'd cheered for him crowded around the truck, Mike didn't think he'd be alone for at least a few hours. Aunt Elise had likely been cooking for hours—days, even—and Mike stayed in his seat as his mother stepped back.

*Lord*, he thought, but he couldn't finish the prayer. He didn't know what to say anyway, and he realized that he wasn't miserable.

He was lost.

"Come on, son," Daddy said, and Mike slid out of the truck and landed on his feet. He could walk just fine. His right shoulder just didn't work anymore, and no amount of therapy, painkillers, surgery, or prayer had healed him.

He hadn't given up, but he didn't know where else to turn. Thus, when his parents had suggested they come to the farm for the summer, Mike hadn't had any reason they shouldn't.

"Mikey," Uncle Gray said, and Mike didn't have the heart to tell him he didn't go by that nickname anymore. He was an officer in the Marines, and he hadn't been Mikey for over ten years.

Uncle Gray grinned at him, every strand of hair on his face and head the color of his name. He pulled Mike into a hug, and Mike put his good arm around his uncle. For some reason, his eyes burned with tears, and he clung to Uncle Gray so no one would see until he could compose himself.

"Welcome home, son," Uncle Gray said, and when he stepped back, Mike actually felt like he'd come home. His cousins came to greet him, and then the cowboys. Mike did his best to smile and laugh with all of them.

Cord Behr was still here. Travis Thatcher. Cosette and

Boone. Matt and Gloria. Keith and Britt hugged him simultaneously, and Mike felt a new kind of kinship move through him with the Whettstein kids. Keith was only a year older than him, and Mike looked him in the eye.

"You're here," he said.

"Yeah." Keith nodded. "Been back about two years?" He looked at his father. "Almost three, I guess."

To Mike's knowledge, Keith wasn't married either, and he suddenly didn't feel so alone.

"I'm a counselor here now," Britt said, her absolutely bright personality exactly the same as it had been as a child. She was tall and billowy, with long, thin limbs, and bright blonde hair, a pair of blue eyes to go with it.

She reminded him slightly of Gerty, and Mike found himself looking around for her. It seemed like the news of his return to the Hammond Family Farm had reached far and wide, and perhaps Gertrude Whettstein would be here.

He didn't want to ask Keith or Britt, so he walked with them toward the steps that led to the porch. Aunt Elise hugged him and put an arm around him. "Come eat," she said, smiling all the while. Aunt Elise was the epitome of kindness, and his mother had been best friends with her for decades.

He didn't want anyone to feel sorry for him, but he couldn't hide the sling his arm sat in. He didn't want eyes on him, but everyone stared at him. He did his best to talk to everyone, eat everything his aunt and mother put in front of him, and laugh with as much authenticity as he could muster.

After an hour, he met his father's eyes, and Dad stood up from the table where he'd been sitting with Hunt and Uncle Gray. "Let's go see the horses," he said, and he opened his arm for Mike to step into.

He nodded and did just that. Dad went outside with him, but he didn't come down the steps with Mike. "You go on," he said, and Mike didn't hesitate. He walked the length of the fence alone, his steps somewhat halting because he couldn't swing his right arm.

"Mike!"

He turned and found Jane jogging toward him. She made him smile, and he laughed as she reached him and threw her arms around him. She wasn't careful with him, and Mike appreciated that. Sometimes his parents looked at him like their eyes alone would shatter him. Jane didn't treat him like that, and he hugged her hard with his left arm.

"There's so many people inside." She exhaled and ran her hands down the front of her body. "So many questions."

"Tell me about it," Mike said. They started walking again, and he didn't want to start in on the questions for Jane either. "Are you staying here for the summer?"

"Uh, yeah," Jane said, her voice pitching up. She exhaled again. "I just quit my job actually. I'm starting at HMC next week. Accounting."

"You're kidding." Mike felt like someone had hollowed out his chest. "That's great, Jane."

"Do you really think so?" She looked at him, and Mike cut her a glance out of the corner of his eye.

"I mean, it makes me feel like a loser, but yeah. It's great."

"You're not a loser," she said quietly but with plenty of emphasis. "You're an amazing pilot, and you served your country for almost eight years." Every word she spoke filled him with more confidence. "Just because you don't get a check from HMC doesn't mean you're not amazing."

Mike wanted to show her his dysfunctional arm; he wanted to argue; he wanted to tell her all his fears. He didn't say anything as they continued toward the barn.

"You datin' anyone?" he asked.

"Oh, now you sound like my mother," Jane said dryly.

Mike laughed. "At least she's askin'. My momma knows everything I do, all day long. Every day." He needed space, and the wide open sky, and to get lost in these mountains. His soul settled as a pretty bay horse looked his way.

Jane's phone rang, and she said, "Speak of the devil." She answered the call and said, "Yes, Momma, I just got here." She rolled her eyes at Mike and went back the way she'd come. "I'll be right in."

Mike smiled at her back, because Jane could be a touch overdramatic sometimes. She was a genius with figures and numbers, and she knew exactly who she was. That was why she'd called off her wedding only five weeks before the I-do's, and why she could quit a good job and go to work at HMC.

He went down the footpath between the administration barn and the pasture, his goal the very last stable. He surely wouldn't know any of the horses here at Pony

Power now, but his pulse settled into a slower rhythm as he approached the bay at the fence.

"Hey," he said, reaching to let the horse smell him. The animal ducked his head and nosed Mike's shoulder. "Yeah," he said. "It's not really working right now. I can't ride you or anything." He gave the bay a sad smile. Mike couldn't drive. He couldn't ride a horse. He couldn't do a lot of things, and he had the distinct thought that he needed to start learning how to do things one-handed, because his shoulder wasn't ever going to be all the way better.

He didn't want to accept that, and he left the bay at the fence and headed for the far stables. Maybe he could lead a horse out to the remote cabin where he'd first kissed Gerty.

The pasture beyond the last stable held several horses, all of them spread out and dotting the area. He put one foot up on the bottom rung and watched them graze. A couple of them looked at him, and a deep, dark black horse came plodding toward him.

Mike smiled at it, but the horse didn't seem to be looking at him. It nickered and called, and Mike twisted to look over his shoulder.

"Mikey."

When Gertrude Whettstein said his teenage nickname, Mike didn't mind at all. He could only stare at the woman standing twenty feet from him. She wore jeans, and she was just as straight up and down as she'd always been. Thin and lithe, strong and sexy, and he wasn't embarrassed he'd thought that.

She wore her dirty blonde hair in a ponytail high on

top of her head, and she tucked her hands in her back pockets, her bony elbows poking out to the sides as she studied him.

He turned fully and stumbled toward her. "What are you doing here?"

Something hard crossed her face. "Am I not allowed to be here?"

"No, it's just—just—" He couldn't find the words. "I—the last couple of times I've been here, you haven't been."

"I've been in Texas," she said. "Montana. Up in Calgary. Around." She shrugged one shoulder, and Mike sure did like her blue and white tank top. It was simple and beautiful, which was Gerty through and through.

"How long are you going to be here?" he asked.

Gerty looked across the pasture, her shoulders and chest lifting with a big breath. "I don't rightly know."

Mike grinned, the world suddenly brighter and more open than it had been five minutes ago. "You don't *rightly know*?" he teased. He'd never heard her talk like that before.

She faced him again, a smile flickering against her lips. Gerty fought against giving him that grin, something she'd done in the past. She'd present him with it eventually, and Mike moved toward her until he stood only a pace away.

"Go out with me," he said, feeling braver and stronger than he had since his helicopter had gone down.

"You don't even know if I'm single," she said, raising that chin he'd once held in one hand just before he kissed her.

"Are you?" he asked.

Gerty pressed her teeth together, and Mike had his answer. He wasn't going to let her off the hook, though, and he waited. And waited. A smile came to his face as he…waited for her to tell him she was, in fact, single.

# CHAPTER
*Two*

GERTRUDE WHETTSTEIN COULDN'T RESIST the gravitational pull to Michael Hammond. She hadn't seen him in thirteen years, but the tether that had always drawn her toward him had not diminished. Not even a little bit.

Did he know he stood over six feet tall? He must.

Did he know he exuded passion, charm, and confidence all at the same time? Probably not, as he'd never been arrogant about his handsomeness or his brains—and he had plenty of both. So much, in fact, that Gerty had only passed her math classes in the early years of high school because she could send Mikey the problems, and he'd call her and work through them with her.

After he'd left and gone to college, she'd felt too insignificant to call him. He hadn't reached out to her either, but because of the farm that connected the two of them, she'd known he'd gone to officer flight training and then become a pilot in the Marines. A helicopter pilot.

Did he know that was the sexiest job a man could have? She doubted it. To him, he'd just wanted to first, fly, and second, serve. He'd done both, and she could hardly believe he was standing right there in front of her.

"Gerty," he finally said, chuckling. He dropped his gaze to the ground, and she knew he didn't have any idea how adorable that was. She'd asked him about it before, and he'd said he had no idea being more submissive made him more attractive. He looked up at her without truly moving his head, his eyelashes fluttering. "You know how to make a man wait."

And a man now, he was. She supposed she wasn't the same thirteen-year-old who'd met Michael Hammond out near these stables for the first time either. He'd filled out in the shoulders and chest; he'd grown a couple of inches since she'd seen him last. He had to shave every day now, and it was obvious that this morning, he hadn't.

She'd added a few inches to her height since they'd met for the first time, but her spirit felt just as wild as it always did. She hadn't gained any curves as she'd matured, and she folded her arms and cocked her hip just to give herself some shape that wasn't straight up and down. "Fine," she said. "I'm not seeing anyone right now."

"Then we can go out."

"No," Gerty said instantly. She wasn't sure why she couldn't just give into the fire raging between them. "I'm…." She swallowed hard. "I just got out of a relation-ship with someone I really…liked, and I'm not ready to start dating someone again."

Mikey nodded, though he didn't look convinced. "Well,

I'll be here all summer," he said, and with that, he stepped past her. Actually went by her like the conversation was over. Done. Like he had nothing else to say to her.

"I'm sorry about your grandfather," she blurted out.

He turned back to her, his face showing shock. He cleared it quickly, swallowed, and said, "Thank you. It's been a few years, but yeah. Thanks."

Gerty missed Chris Hammond greatly as well. "He was my favorite person here," she whispered.

"Oh, don't be sayin' that, Miss Gerty," he said, and he sounded like the men in Texas Gerty had known. He'd never drawled like that before, and she had the distinct impression that he was teasing her. He took a step back to her and reached out with his left hand, the one that wasn't in a sling. He brushed his fingers along hers and finally caught the very tip of her pinky before bringing his hand back to his side. "All this time, I thought I was your favorite person here."

Gerty swallowed, her throat suddenly as narrow as a drinking straw. "You weren't here that much, Mikey."

"I go by Mike now."

"Okay."

"You're still Gerty?"

"Yes, sir," she drawled out.

He chuckled and shook his head. "You know I don't like it when you call me sir."

She couldn't help smiling with him, and with that action, he brightened like she'd made his day. "You'll only be here for the summer?"

He shrugged his good shoulder. "There's a specialist

here my parents wanted me to see. They're hoping I can get some more mobility in my shoulder." He sobered, and Gerty switched her gaze to the sling.

"I'm sorry about the accident."

"They happen," he said as if he really was okay with his physical condition.

"You can't ride, I suppose," she said.

"Not yet," he said. "The best I can do is walk alongside the horse."

She looked over the pasture again, drinking in this farm. This place she loved with her whole soul. This place where her father and step-mother lived and were raising Gerty's two half-siblings. She'd always felt at-home here, and that hadn't changed despite her absence.

She wasn't sure if she'd regret spending the afternoon with Mikey—oops, Mike—or not. Her daddy wouldn't be happy about it, but Gerty had come to terms with not being able to please everyone. Sort of.

Her heart ached at the blueness of the sky, at the way she and James used to lie in the fields and laugh, kiss, and watch the world roll by. Then they'd get up, dust off, and go take care of the horses.

Gerty loved horses with her whole soul. They loved her back. Behind her, Tennessee—who she'd originally come out here to see—nickered and called to her. She twisted and looked at him, giving him a look that said, Give me a minute, you rascal.

She looked at Mike again. "What's your schedule like today?"

He swept his good hand in front of him. "This."

"I have to take Tenney out," she said. "Maybe you'd like to walk alongside him."

Mike grinned, those straight white teeth dazzling her. Everything about this man dazzled Gerty, and it always had. "Depends on how far you're goin'," he said. "I think my momma gets nervous when I'm more than fifty feet from her."

Gerty's heart ached for him too. She wasn't great at expressing her emotions, but once Daddy had married Cosette, she'd gotten a lot better at talking about them. She loved her step-mom with her whole heart and soul, as her biological mom had been gone so long, Gerty could hardly remember her. She called Cosette "mom," and she loved her younger brother and sister. Her absence had been hard on all of them, and Gerty regretted that it had taken her so long to see James for who he truly was.

"You decide," she said to Mike. "I think I'm gonna ride him out to the retreat cabins and back. It's a good couple of miles."

"I can call Hunt if I need a ride back," he said. "I haven't been doing much physical activity since I've been home."

Gerty wanted to ask him everything. Thirteen-plus years was a long time, and they hadn't kept up. She suddenly had a mouthful of words to tell him, but she managed to turn toward the stable first. "I'll get his tack."

"I'll text my momma so she doesn't worry."

Gerty walked away, her heart pounding beneath her breastbone. Once inside the shady stable, she shook herself. "What are you doing? You vowed you would not date for a solid year. To find yourself. To figure out where you should be."

She'd ended things with James only a month ago. One month. A single turn of the moon through its phases. She'd stayed in Montana with her maternal grandparents for a few weeks, and had she known Mike would be here on this farm when she arrived, Gerty...well, Gerty didn't know what she'd have done.

Daddy had questions she didn't want to answer. Cosette watched her with dark eyes, biding her time. Her siblings didn't much care why Gerty had come back, but Walter wanted to show her his stunt tricks all day long, and Amy had definitely inherited their daddy's penchant for talking and laughing. And laughing and talking. And then talking some more.

She sighed and reached up to rub her forehead. She'd just wanted some peace and quiet, and she'd made an excuse about Tennessee and left the cabin as her parents both watched, each with a very different expression on their face.

Mom had smiled her out of the house and would likely text her a couple of questions, and Daddy had frowned mightily, which meant he'd stay up until Gerty came home, and then he'd make her sit next to him on the couch while they talked it all out.

She honestly didn't mind either of those, but she just wanted solace. "Dear Lord," she whispered as she looked up into the rafters of the stable. "I just need to find some peace. Please."

Everything in her life had been shocked, blitzed out of

place, turned around, and then shaken up. She'd quit her job in Montana when she'd discovered James's infidelity, and Molly had been more than willing to take her on this summer.

So she'd come back.

Mike had a specialist to see in the city. So he'd returned.

Was it serendipitous? Should she go out with him?

Her heartbeat ricocheted through her body, as if it were three distinct pieces, each trying to beat on its own. She wasn't sure how to be in a relationship with a shattered heart, and she'd told Mike the truth.

She wasn't ready.

Her phone buzzed, and she looked down at it. Mom: *What time do you think you'll be back? Do you want me to hold dinner, or are you riding for a while?*

*A while*, Gerty thumbed out. She wanted to tell her mother that she was twenty-eight years old and certainly knew how to feed herself. She owned a truck, and a horse trailer, and four horses of her own. Gray and Hunter had been more than gracious to allow her to house them here, and she heard Tenney calling for her again.

Mom: *I'm worried about you.*

"Join the club," Gerty grumbled under her breath.

Mom: *Will you at least tell us about your stay with Carrie and Kyle? Your daddy wants to know.*

*Yes*, Gerty sent back. She'd have to tell her parents everything, she knew, but some of it she didn't know how to put into words quite yet.

Thus, her need for a horseback ride. In Gerty's experience, they could fix almost anything. Maybe not a cheating fiancé, but a lot.

Gerty collected Tenney's tack and took it outside, her arms straining with the weight of his saddle. She was strong, and she knew it. People everywhere had underestimated her, and Gerty had almost gotten used to it. She didn't call attention to herself, and she'd worked two ranches in Texas while simultaneously becoming a barrel racer before she'd gone to Calgary to compete in the Stampede there.

She wasn't rodeo queen material, but she could ride a horse that was for dang sure. She'd won second place, and then she'd gone to Montana to work at a ranch there. She'd met the owner at the Stampede, and he wanted someone to train his horses to carry riders the way hers did. She'd worked at the Johnson Manor Ranch for the past five years, where she'd met her boss's son, fallen in love, and had expected to get married atop two horses and ride off into the sunset.

She should've known her life wouldn't be that easy. Her own mother had died of a rare blood disease when Gerty was only seven years old.

"Gerty," Mike said, and she looked at him. He reached out and touched her cheek. "Where were you?"

Gerty didn't know how to answer. "I just…I need it to just be quiet," she said. "It's so loud inside my head."

He nodded, his eyes harboring a serious edge. She'd seen it before, right before he kissed her that first time. And the last. He was a fun guy—now a man—and a hard worker. Everything he did seemed effortless, even with his arm in that sling.

Tenney took the bit easily, almost reaching for it, and Gerty swung into his saddle. "You're okay to just walk?"

"Yes'm," he said.

"Oh, boy," she retorted. "You're not a cowboy, Mikey."

"I'm wearin' the hat," he said.

She scoffed and shook her head. "That doesn't make you a cowboy."

"I'm working for Pony Power this summer," he said. "I'll figure it out. It's like riding a bike." They started off, and Mike didn't say anything. Gerty appreciated that, as well as the lilting breeze that kept the worst of the summer temperatures from overheating her. She'd been wearing copious amounts of sunscreen since birth, and her skin didn't seem to know how to hold a hue.

One of her farrier trainers had dubbed her The Pasty Gangster, because Gerty could shoe a horse better and faster than anyone, even the most finicky of equines. She'd loved wearing the leather aprons and working on horse's hooves. She'd told Molly she could do all of that here, and Molly had readily agreed.

The grasses waved around them, making soft swishing noises. Mike's feet on the ground added to they symphony, as did the heavy snuffle of Tenney's breathing. He wanted to go faster than Mike could, and Gerty held him back. He finally gave in to her after about five minutes, and he settled into a slow walk.

Gerty could relax then too, and the world around her turned soft. She loved the blues and greens together, only broken up by brown wooden fences and the occasional puffy white cloud. "Everything in Montana is a bit washed out compared to here," she said.

"Mm?" Mike didn't ask a full question, but then, he'd never had to. Gerty remembered everything with him, and her heart played leapfrog with itself. He'd been good and kind. He'd been helpful and respectful. If anything, the years he carried now had only added to his allure and his charm and his stunning spirit.

"Yeah," she said, deciding it wouldn't be so bad to talk if he was the one listening. "I worked there for the past several years. There's a lot of beige and yellow in Montana."

"It's not fall here yet," he said.

"Then there's only more color," she said, looking west to the Rocky Mountains. They punctured the sky, and the memories of her and Mikey in Coral Canyon when she'd gone with him for a few weeks in the summer flooded her mind. "The trees are pretty in Montana. Lots of color then, but it's just like that here."

"I bet."

"You ever been to Montana?" she asked.

"No," he said. "Just Wyoming and Colorado. I did college here in Denver, and then Officer Training in Georgia. After that, I did the flight training on a base in Florida."

Gerty hadn't been to any of those places, and she knew Mike had been all around the world. Her doubts piled on top of each other, the inner voice in her head whispering, *Why would he want to go out with you?*

He'd served his country. He'd listed his dreams and done them.

She'd hopped around, grabbing at any opportunity that came her way. She'd learned what she needed to learn whenever the situation called for it. She'd enjoyed her life, and she told herself she couldn't get down on herself for not owning her own farm.

"It's cold in the winter," she said. "My daddy used to tease the cowboys here that they didn't know cold, that they'd never really farmed in the winter." She gave a light laugh. "He was right."

"But you liked it there?" Mike looked up at her.

Gerty gazed down at him, that fire licking up the tether between them. She actually wanted to reach for it and see how badly it would burn her. Daddy had always told her she played too close to the fire, but Gerty didn't know how to be someone else.

"I did," she said. "My mom's parents are there, so I got to see them a lot. I'd go talk to my mom whenever I was just...lost."

Silence fell around them again, and Gerty couldn't help wondering if Mike felt lost right now too. "What are you going to do after the summer ends?" she asked. "Work at HMC?"

"I don't know." His voice reminded her of something haunted, and it came out too low. "I have a business degree, but I...don't know."

"I understand that," Gerty said quietly. And she did.

They reached the retreat, and Gerty slid from the saddle. She looped Tenney's reins over the fence and looked at Mike. Something zipped and arced between them, and Gerty got transported back in time about fifteen years.

Her first kiss. Right here behind this cabin, where later, Gray had arranged summer camp retreats for teens. Gerty had helped with those too, and she had loved her life here at the Hammond Family Farm.

"Do you remember my favorite food?" she asked.

"Assuming your taste buds haven't changed," Mike said, grinning and putting a bit of swagger into his voice. Oh, the man was a flirt when he wanted to be. "It's a good, sloppy, barbecue brisket sandwich."

For some reason, the way he described it made Gerty laugh. She tilted her head back and faced the heavens, feeling freer and lighter than she had since learning about her fiancé's misdeeds.

"You got it." She leveled her gaze at Mike. "Guess who put one on their menu, courtesy of my daddy?"

"Hilde?" he guessed.

Gerty nodded, feeling quite flirtatious herself. She took a step toward him and ran her fingers up the front of his shirt, bumping them over the straps of the sling. "Maybe we should go get one sometime."

"Yeah," he said, his voice somewhat hoarse. "Maybe we should."

She grinned at him, danced ahead of him, and turned around. "All right. I'm gonna go check the cupboards for some of those gross granola bars. You find us a shady spot to sit, and I'll come find you." They'd done this before, because Gerty could open cabinets and sneak through a house without leaving any evidence that she'd been there.

Gerty hurried off to do that while Mike laughed at her, and as she entered the cabin which had sat dormant for the winter and spring, she couldn't help feeling like a new door had just opened in her life. Sure, maybe she was like this cabin. Maybe she needed some TLC after a long season of darkness. Maybe she needed to be aired out and cleaned up. Maybe she needed to get a coat of fresh paint and some new curtains.

Maybe then, she'd be all fixed up to fall in love again.

As she searched through the empty cupboards, she wondered how many other women Mike had kissed. She wondered if he'd ever been in love. She wondered if God had really brought them back to this farm, at this time, so they could have their second chance.

Empty-handed, she left the cabin and started looking for Mike. There was only one thing to do—well, two really.

Heal. Gerty needed to heal first.

Then, she'd find out if she and Mike could take the fire between them and hold it in their hands without getting burned.

# CHAPTER
## *Three*

MIKE MANAGED to get to the ground, the long grass softening the blow to his knees when he dropped. Thankfully, Gerty wasn't here to see that. Quick humiliation ran through him as he rolled onto his hips and scooted backward until he could lean against the trunk of the thick cottonwood tree.

In only a few months, the leaves would turn the hills where the farm sat a vibrant rainbow of gold, orange, pink, red, and everything in between. His favorite trees were aspens; he loved the white-barked trunks and their leaves couldn't be beat in the autumn.

A sigh slipped out of his mouth. How he'd missed the mountains and the trees. They settled something in his soul and spoke to him in a way a cot and a tent and a helicopter couldn't. He'd felt at-home in the cockpit too, whether he was pilot or co-pilot. This was just…different.

Slower. Calmer. More peaceful.

"Nothing," Gerty said, and Michael opened his eyes to see her walking through the grass toward him. It seemed to part for her as if she were Moses himself, leading the children of Israel through the Red Sea to save them from certain death.

He smiled up at her, wondering if she could rescue him the way Moses had rescued his people. "Whatcha got in your hands then?"

Her sigh wasn't as peaceful and slow as his as she got to the ground and folded her long legs under her cross-wise. "I always have a snack in my saddlebag." She looked at the wrapped items in her bag. "I think these are actually from a flight I took at some point."

She looked up, and Mike wanted to push pause on his life and live inside this moment for a very long time. Gerty wore an expression of vulnerability, and he didn't get to see that very often. She was somewhat of a hothead, and she'd always been crystal clear on what she wanted from him and what she expected from him, even as a teenager.

He couldn't pause life, so her face changed in the next moment, and he took the bar from her. "Pumpkin seeds and sea salt chocolate?" He frowned. "This sounds like a punishment, not a snack."

She started to laugh, the sound light and airy at first, then gaining strength as it morphed from giggling to laughter. Still, she ripped open her package and took a bite. "I like them."

He watched her take a bite, and she didn't grimace or wrap up the bar again. Instead, Gerty gave him that smile that reminded him of when he was a teen, working this farm and missing his parents and siblings so very much.

He suddenly felt lighter than he had in a decade, and he relaxed back into the tree. She slid closer to him and said nothing as her leg touched his. He gripped the bar in his right hand and ripped it open with his left. Gerty didn't watch or offer to help him, the way his momma would've.

She simply sat with him, and she only turned toward him when he said, "Okay, here I go."

That beautiful smile returned, giving him courage to take that bite. The chocolate and salt hit his tongue first, and the seeds actually had a really nice, creamy texture against the oats and granola, which was packed together tightly so it didn't crumble the way some other bars did.

He nodded as he chewed, pleasantly surprised. "This is great."

"See?" Gerty took another bite of her bar. "I think I got them when I flew home from Calgary. Or to Montana." Her face fell. "When I flew from Calgary to Montana."

Mike's heartbeat skipped and stuttered. He didn't like seeing her unhappy, and he couldn't do what felt natural: reach over and hold her hand. She sat on his left, so he could definitely touch her easily—if he didn't have the granola bar in his hand.

He quickly stuffed the rest of it into his mouth and lifted his arm around her shoulders. Gerty melted into his side as easily as she always had, and they took a deep breath together.

She'd said things were so loud inside her head, and

Mike didn't want to add to the noise there. Her momma and daddy probably had a lot of questions for her, the same way he did. He figured he had all summer to get the answers, and probably longer.

He finally finished chewing the granola bar, and he pressed his shoulders as far back as he could get them. Gerty shifted, but he said, "Don't go."

"Does it hurt?"

"Not really," he said. "I just don't like hunching forward over it." He looked down at her to find her gazing up at him. He'd kissed her under this tree before, from this exact position, and he wondered if she was thinking about that.

He sure was.

Heat raced through his veins, and Mike told himself he couldn't kiss her. Not within an hour of being reunited with her after they'd promised to stay in touch and they hadn't. "So." He cleared his throat. "Thirteen years. Do you want to start with something easy?" He looked away from her, out at the softly rolling landscape in front of him. A fence sat a dozen or so yards away, and then the fields expanded for a while.

Gerty settled back into his side, one hand resting lightly on his thigh near his knee. "I graduated at the top of my class from farrier school."

A smile popped onto his face. "I bet you did."

Her horse snuffled nearby, snacking on the delicious grass back here. "What about you? I assume you were top of your class at flight school."

Mike let his eyes drift closed, his memories of flight

school right there in his head. "I enjoyed it," he said. "But I wasn't the best."

"Second then," she said.

"Third, if you must know."

"Mm, I figured."

They fell into silence then, and Mike found he didn't have much else of consequence to tell her. "I saw some rodeo pictures of you."

She groaned and buried her face in his chest, moving closer to him to do it. Hip to hip they sat, and Mike's old feelings for Gerty roared back to life in colors of blue, white, and yellow.

"I hate those pictures," she said. "They make you wear so much makeup—and false eyelashes. I dang near ripped out my real eyelashes once after a competition."

He chuckled and said, "Not everyone is as beautiful as you, Gerty."

She let several beats of silence go by, but she didn't tell him that his line was cheesy. He knew it was and he didn't care. She *was* beautiful, and he'd always thought so.

"I think I'm still washing the hairspray out of my hair," she whispered.

Mike turned his head and took a deep breath of her hair. "Mm, I don't think so. Smells like sunshine and horses and leather." She hadn't been wearing a cowgirl hat when he'd encountered her at the paddock, but he still wore a hat, the brim of which created a private bubble for him and Gerty. Not that they needed it. There probably wasn't a human soul for a mile, and Tennessee wouldn't care if he kissed her.

"Are you going to miss flying?" she whispered.

"Yes," he whispered back. "There's nothing like flying, Gerty. Nothing."

"You'll have to take me sometime."

"All right." He couldn't drive a car, let alone fly anything right now. Not even a kite. It wasn't a promise. It was just easy conversation with someone who felt like an old friend when Mike needed one of those very, very badly.

The silence stretched, and he relaxed and closed his eyes again. Gerty grew heavier against his side, and he looked down in time to watch her head droop. He had no idea when she'd arrived on the farm. He hadn't seen her at his welcome-home party, but her parents had been there.

He gently eased away from her and let her head settle into his lap. She breathed in and out in long strokes, and Mike couldn't look away from the softness of her face while she slept. She wasn't just beautiful; she was stunningly gorgeous, and Mike wondered what the eighteen-year-old version of himself had been thinking, leaving her here in Ivory Peaks while he went off to college and then flight school.

He gently stroked his fingers along her hair. It felt like silk against his skin, no signs of hairspray at all. Gerty had never been very girly, and that hadn't changed much. Her skin held very little color, though she'd obviously been outdoors a lot. His eyes ran from her bare shoulder and down her arm to her long fingers. Hands he'd held before. Hands he wanted to hold again.

His hormones shot through him, and he whispered, "I

missed you so much, Gerty," to the sky, the grasses, and her horse as he grazed nearby.

He couldn't believe this was where he was right now. After all he'd seen. All he'd done. All the places he'd visited. All this time.

Sitting with his back against a tree, listening to the country stillness talk to itself, while the gorgeous Gertrude Whettstein took a nap with her head in his lap.

A sigh filled his soul, and again, it spoke of peace and quiet. "Thank you, Lord," he whispered. "Thank you for this farm, and thank you for bringing me here when I needed it." Then he leaned his head back and closed his own eyes.

He had appointments coming up, and surely his momma had sent out a search party for him by now, but for this moment, Mike forgot about the heap of troubles he faced so he could simply enjoy being alive, even if he wasn't quite whole.

Yet.

————

MIKE WOKE the next morning and let himself come to consciousness without moving. His shoulder ached, which his doctors in the Marines and up in Coral Canyon told him was a good sign. The numbness was bad, and that usually only came when he did his physical therapy.

He opened his eyes and looked straight up, the summer sunlight already coming in through the blinded windows in this new bedroom of his. Uncle Gray had given him a cabin to himself, because he had it to spare. Momma and Daddy were staying in the generational house, which only had one bedroom. Mike could sleep on a couch, but he didn't want to if he didn't have to.

He groaned as he used his core muscles and good arm to get himself into a seated position on the edge of his bed. Hunter had brought him out here last night, and he'd said the bed was brand new and really nice, and he hadn't lied. Mike would be sure to text his cousin and tell him he'd slept great.

"Great" might be an overstatement, but Mike wasn't going to make Hunter's life any harder than he had to. No matter what the mattress was, Mike would be up a couple of times in the night.

Carefully, he lifted his left hand high above his head and stretched over to his right side, feeling the pull all down the left side of his body. He rotated his neck in a figure-eight pattern, leading with his chin.

He needed to move to the right side, and wow, he didn't want to. He gritted his teeth, and using his left hand, he lifted his right, pressing up against his elbow until he made it past the point when his socket pointed down.

Up here, he could hold his arm above his head. He timed his breathing, puffing out his breath as he held his arm straight up for as long as he could. He rarely moved his arm and shoulder this way, and he swore he could feel and hear tiny things popping and adjusting in his body.

He reached over with his left hand and grasped his right fingers, tugging gently to get the stretch going on this side. He once again inhaled, held his breath, and then huffed it out, over and over until he couldn't take the pull any longer.

He couldn't just drop his arm either, as his shoulder couldn't slow the fall of it and it jarred too much when it reached its limit. He used his left hand to get his right back to his side, and then he got to his feet with one final exhale.

A heartbeat throbbed down his right shoulder and bicep, but he ignored it and moved to open the blinds so he could greet the day. "Doctor at ten this morning," he said as he pulled the string to flip the blinds open.

He yelped as he found a face there, hands cupped around eyes as they peered in. The woman on the other side of the glass screamed and fell back too, and that was when Mike recognized Gerty.

He bent closer to check and make sure it was really her. It was, so he hastened to open the window. That was quite the feat with only one arm strong enough to really pull on something.

Thankfully, the Good Lord Above saw fit to allow the window to open with the first yank of his left hand. It had no screen, and he stood only a few feet from Gerty now. "Are you spying on me?"

She stared at his chest, and Mike realized in that moment that he wasn't wearing a shirt. Embarrassment flooded him, especially at what she might see on his right shoulder. All the scars and lines and patchy skin.

He stared at her while she drank him in, and she wore another pair of jeans today, these paired with a bright pink tank top that once again showed off the muscles in her arms and shoulders. She didn't have an overly large chest, but enough of a swell to make a man swallow a couple of times, and Mike pulled his gaze away from her body and back to her eyes.

Her gaze met his, her cheeks flushed. "Not spying. Looking." She grinned next and held up a brown paper bag. "My daddy said you got your own cabin, but there are two empty ones here, and I didn't know which one."

He leaned his left shoulder into the window frame and grinned at her. "Why didn't you ask your daddy which one?"

"Oh, he...." She shook her head and didn't finish. "I have breakfast if you want it. I know you're going to the doctor's later, but I figured you had a little time this morning, same as me."

He wanted to ask her a lot more about why she couldn't ask her daddy which cabin Mike lived in, but he decided to do it when he had breakfast in his hand and a shirt covering his scars. "C'mon in," he said. "I didn't lock the door."

# CHAPTER
## *Four*

GERTY HAD WORKED with a lot of cowboys. She'd seen some shirtless before, and they had muscles in their abs, chests, and shoulders.

She'd never seen muscles like Mike's. "They must make them different in the military," she muttered to herself as she opened his front door and entered his cabin. Her mood sweetened, but only slightly. Mike hadn't made her answer anything hard yesterday, and Gerty had gotten out of talking to her parents too by claiming she was just so exhausted from traveling.

She hadn't lied. She'd fallen asleep in Mike's lap yesterday for crying out loud. She should've been exercising her horse and figuring out what to do with her life, and she'd literally taken a nap while the sun set.

When she'd woken up, she'd apologized profusely, but Mike said he didn't care. He'd had to walk back to the farm in twilight and then dusk, and his momma had been waiting along the fence where Gerty had found Mike hours before.

Bree Hammond was a nice woman, but she could put on a fierce Mama Bear face, and Gerty had seen it last night. Mike had told her he was fine, and he'd defended Gerty in his low, quiet voice to the point that Bree had backed down.

Her daddy had too, both last night and this morning, though she owed that miracle to Uncle Matt. He'd come by right when Gerty was putting together the breakfast sandwiches and saying she had to leave to get to a client's barn for a re-shoeing.

Again, not a lie. Just not the whole truth. The re-shoeing wasn't until noon, and Gerty certainly didn't need to leave before eight o'clock with four breakfast sandwiches made with all of Mike's favorite things.

A sigh tugged against her ribcage, because Gerty had a lot of explaining to do, to a lot of people. She'd just set the bag of sandwiches on the counter when footsteps told her Mike was coming.

She turned and found him approaching with a dark gray T-shirt in his hand. His face shone like an overripe tomato, and he practically threw the shirt at her. "Can you help me?" He'd never used that voice with her before, and Gerty didn't know what to make of it.

She fumbled the shirt, but managed to grip it with the very tips of her fingers so it didn't fall to the floor. "Sure," she said, her word as blunt and forceful as his. "I don't really…." Her brain misfired again as she took in his bare torso.

Did he know he was absolutely beautiful? He had to.

His right shoulder slumped a bit more than the left, and Gerty's eyes tracked the lines along the front of it. She swallowed and didn't dare look him in the face. After quickly closing the distance between them, she practically stood toe-to-toe with him and reached up to touch his shoulder.

She hesitated and asked, "Can I?"

"It won't hurt," he said gruffly.

"What happened?" she asked. "I mean, I know what happened. What's wrong with your shoulder?"

"I lost half of my rotator cuff in the accident," he said. "What's left isn't great, and I'm here to meet with a shoulder specialist to consider a complete shoulder replacement."

Gerty did switch her eyes from the pink, puckered scar to his gorgeous, dark eyes then. She had no idea what to say, because he held her captive with something as simple as his gaze. She couldn't say she was sorry, because that was so trite. She couldn't act like she knew he'd be okay if he got the shoulder replacement, because she knew from personal experience that surgeries didn't fix everything.

Fire blazed in his eyes, and she could suddenly see the alpha Marine officer flying helicopters inside this man in front of her. "I can't lift my arm," he said, the words hard in his mouth. "If you can thread my hand and arm through the sleeve of the shirt, I can then pull it on."

Gerty's mouth felt like she'd eaten the paper bag for breakfast. No amount of saliva would moisten it, and she looked down at the shirt in her hands as if she didn't know what it was. She backed up one step and put her hand against Mike's chest, right where his heart beat.

He pulled in a breath, reaching with his good hand to cover hers.

She had no idea what she was doing, only that she wanted to touch him there. The heat from his skin seared hers, and she once again looked up at him. He stood a good six inches taller than her, but she could tip up and he could lean down.

Gerty did just that, but Mike's grip on her fingers increased. "No," he ground out from somewhere in the back of his throat.

The word slapped Gerty back to solid ground, and she tried to pull her hand away. He wouldn't let her go, and her own fire got ignited. "Mike—"

"I want to kiss you," he said next, silencing her. "But I'm not going to do it when I'm so broken—or when you are."

She'd normally lift her chin to challenge such a state-ment like that, but with Mike, she dropped it instead. The fight left her body, and his grip on her fingers relaxed. He'd known she wasn't whole, and she hadn't even told him anything.

"When I kiss you again, I'm going to be able to lift both of my hands to your face," he whispered now, actually stepping closer to her until their hands barely fit between them. "And hold you right where I want you."

Gerty's nerves buzzed with want, with energy, and she could scarcely believe she was even *thinking* about kissing him.

She'd been engaged only thirty-four days ago. Engaged to another man. She wasn't sure how to simply turn off the love she'd developed for James, and she knew she had nothing to give Mike.

Yet.

She pulled her hand back again, and he let her go this time. Keeping her head down, she bunched up his shirt so that she could thread his non-moving hand and arm through it properly. With it almost up to his armpit, he reached up and took the bunched hem, ducked his head through the hole, and then maneuvered his good arm through the other sleeve.

"Thank you." He still spoke as if he had a handful of rocks in his mouth, and he turned away from her before she could see his expression. Even when he was in pain and embarrassed, he was polite.

"Of course." Her voice sounded too high, and she took a deep breath in the hopes of calming it. "I brought sausage, egg, and cheese sandwiches." She practically lunged for the paper bag. "On biscuits, not muffins. They might not be hot anymore, because I had to drive here from my parents', but I figured you'd probably ate worse in the military."

"I'm sure they're fine." Mike sounded more normal now, and he pulled open his fridge, then promptly shut it again. "I don't have anything to drink here."

"There's water in the faucet," she said easily. She produced two sandwiches for him and smiled, thankful when he met her eyes.

"Mike, listen." She took a big breath and pushed it out

with a rush of words. "We shouldn't be embarrassed with each other, okay? So you have a hurt shoulder. So what? It's me. We've been friends for practically my whole life, and I wouldn't care if you could never use your shoulder again."

She swallowed, her eyes feeling so, so round. He stared at her, neither one of them looking away. "I'd help you put your shirt on every day, and I wouldn't even think twice about it." Her face heated now, and she was sure she looked one step away from a boiled lobster. Thankfully, the filtering part of her brain kicked in and told her, *do not say another word.*

Mike ducked his head as he picked up a sandwich. "Thank you, Gerty. I know I have a lot of people who care about me and are willing to help me." He looked straight at her again. "That doesn't mean I don't feel weak. I do, and I hate it."

She wanted to tell him he wasn't weak, but he wouldn't appreciate it. "I don't see how you can possibly be weak," she said nonchalantly, cocking her head to the side. "Have you *seen* the muscles in your chest?" She shook her head and whistled appreciatively. "Because, wow." She picked up a sandwich and wished it was big enough to hide behind. "Definitely not weak." Then she took the biggest bite of her life and prayed that the Lord would help her censor herself better moving forward.

Mike blinked at her and then burst out laughing. They both knew his "weakness" came in a different form than muscles, but Gerty sure was glad to hear that laugh again.

She grinned and grinned, which made chewing her

monster-sized bite hard. As he sobered, Gerty swallowed. A drink would be great, but she didn't say that. She said, "Promise me we can just be ourselves this summer. I really need it."

He gazed at her. "You'll have to tell me why."

She nodded. "I think I can do that." She wasn't entirely sure, but this was Michael Hammond, and she wanted to try.

"And you won't be embarrassed, because it's me, and we've known each other our whole lives."

"*Practically* our whole lives," she clarified.

He grinned and lifted his breakfast sandwich as if toasting her. "Practically our whole lives."

Except for the thirteen and a half years when she hadn't spoken to him. And the first thirteen years of her life before she'd met him. But she'd had almost four years with him, and she really felt like she knew him. He hadn't changed that much, though there were some distinct differences in him that had nothing to do with the muscles she'd never seen before.

"I'm shoeing a horse at noon at the Palmer's farm today," she said. "You'll call me when you're back from the doctor? I want to hear all about it."

"Yes, baby doll. I'll call you when I'm back from the doctor."

*Baby doll.* Gerty had thought she hadn't forgotten anything about Mike or their time together from before. She'd been wrong, because she'd forgotten how it felt to be called *baby doll* in his deep, delicious voice.

————

GERTY FILED BACK AND FORTH, back and forth, straining with what felt like everything she had to get the hoof right. She finally managed it and straightened enough to wipe the sweat from the side of her face.

The horse didn't move, and she'd have corrected him if he had. She only had this one hoof left, and she expertly nailed in the new shoe and finally let the horse's leg down. "Good boy," she said to the beautiful creature. "Now you're all ready for the summer." She smiled at him and ran her hand along the side of his neck.

It had to be close to one o'clock by now, because a re-shoeing usually took at least an hour, and this horse had had some issues with one of his frogs on his back right foot. Feeling dirty and sweaty and hot, Gerty pulled her phone from her back pocket.

Mike had not called or texted.

She wasn't sure why she was so disappointed, only that she was. She reached for her water bottle and gulped the cold liquid. Then she started cleaning up her tools, folding everything together neatly into her leather apron, before she went to find Mr. Palmer.

He checked his horse, smiled, and said, "Mighty fine work, Gerty. Thank you." He paid her, and Gerty said she'd come back any time if he needed her.

She didn't officially start at Pony Power until the weekend, when they were having their summer opening social for families. That was always a busy time at the children's equine riding facility, and Gerty paused as she arrived at her truck to consider the feelings running through her.

"Gratitude," she whispered as she identified it. Tears came to her eyes, which for Gerty, said a lot. She rarely cried, and it took extreme pain, strong emotions, or pure humiliation to make her eyes water.

Right now, it was strong emotion.

"Thank you for alerting me to James's infidelity before I married him," she whispered. She couldn't even fathom how she'd have felt if she'd then had to figure out if she wanted to save her marriage or let it go.

She didn't want to think about giving herself to him, body and soul, only to find out he hadn't been faithful. It was bad enough to think about it when they hadn't been married yet.

Not only that, but she knew their marriage wouldn't have survived the infidelity. He hadn't been repentant, and his words still struck her like a whip to her back.

*You're no fun, Gerty. You work all the time, and I swear, you love those horses more than you do me.*

She'd cried when he'd said that too. Not in front of him. Then, she'd stood strong, with her fingers clenched into fists, as she'd fired back at him that he got to make his own choices. Never once had he complained about her work schedule. Never once had he told her to come in from the stables so he could see her.

He didn't need her, because he had two other women in town ready and willing to fill in any gaps Gerty left in him.

She brushed at her eyes and shored up her strength.

God gave her that too, and Gerty once again felt pure gratitude for her Heavenly Father in her life. Without Him, she honestly didn't know where she'd be.

The anger and shame she'd felt at the dissolution of her relationship with James left as quickly as it had descended upon her, and Gerty opened the back door of her truck and tossed in her tools.

The slamming of the door ended the memories, and Gerty straightened her shoulders and pushed her ponytail off of the right one. The grumbling of an approaching truck met her ears, and she glanced over to it, expecting it to go past her and down the lane to the farmhouse.

She did a double-take when the big, black behemoth pulled in beside her, Mike in the passenger seat and his father behind the wheel.

Mike wore a smile the size of Texas, and Gerty felt it infuse inside her, driving out any remaining melancholy, anger, or resentment. At least for now. She knew she still had a long way to go to be completely healed, to truly grieve the death of the life she'd thought she'd have with James, but she felt like she'd taken the first step.

She stepped over to the truck and opened the door. "What are you doin' here?" she drawled out. He wore a pair of jeans and that same dark gray T-shirt she'd helped him put on that morning. He wore a big, black cowboy hat that made her pulse pound out several loud beats, and even if he wasn't a full-time cowboy who trained horses, he sure looked the part.

Mike lifted a big white bag with the Hilde's logo on it.

"Daddy and I just went to lunch, and I brought something for you, because I figured you wouldn't have eaten yet."

"Michael Hammond," she said, her eyes now glued to that bag. "Is that a brisket sandwich?"

He chuckled as he nodded. "Now, take this so I can unbuckle and get out."

# CHAPTER
## *Five*

ONCE MIKE HAD GOTTEN out of the truck, he turned back and faced his father. "I have my phone, okay? I'm gonna be a couple of hours, I'd imagine."

Daddy nodded, his eyes skating past Mike to where Gerty was putting her lunch in her truck. "Michael," he started, drawing out the name in a long drawl Mike had heard before.

"I know," Mike said quickly. "I'll be careful with this girl, Daddy."

His dad's dark eyes scorched him. "Son, she's no girl. You best be careful with that woman."

Mike swallowed and leaned further into the cab, because he didn't know where Gerty was. "I like her, Dad," he whispered.

"Obviously," Dad said, also keeping his voice low. "It's not a crime, but you've already got a lot on your plate." So much more was said than just those words, and Mike heard them all. His father had always spoken like this, and Mike had learned to interpret from an early age.

*Son, you're moving into a new phase of your life here.*

*You have shoulder surgery in a few weeks, and a major healing phase after that.*

*You're starting to train as the CEO of the family company, literally next week. You think you can add a girlfriend to that?*

*Maybe you're not thinking clearly, Michael.*

Yes, Daddy had said a whole lot more than "you've got a lot on your plate."

"I know," Mike said again. "Daddy, can you lecture me later, please?"

His dad smiled and nodded. "I'll get Momma in on it with me," he said with a chuckle. "So you best enjoy your afternoon with Gerty while you can."

Mike backed out of the cab and shut the door. He turned to find Gerty waiting only a couple of paces away, smudges of dirt on her jeans and tank top. She wore thick-toed boots and the brightest smile in the universe.

"My daddy thinks I'm a fool," he said, unable to straighten his own smile.

Gerty's slipped. "He does? Why?"

"Because I'm literally going to have shoulder surgery in three weeks." He moved closer to her as his father backed out and drove away. "And I told Hunt this morning I'd start working with him at HMC a couple of days a week, and I don't even live here in Ivory Peaks."

When he stood right in front of her, he took her hand in his. "And here I am, standing with this gorgeous woman, bringing her lunch, and hopin' to start something with her." He lifted her hand to his lips, touched her skin to his for a moment, and kept his head down as he lowered her hand. "I'm definitely a fool."

"You're having shoulder surgery in three weeks?" she asked.

"That's what you got out of what I just said?"

"It's a big piece."

Mike met her eyes, and they both grinned again. Hers once again fell away quickly. "Mike, I'm—I—I told you I just got out of a relationship. I wasn't lying. I'm...."

"Not ready to date," he said. "I think I remember you saying that too."

She nodded, her throat working as she swallowed. Mike wanted to erase her anxiety, and he leaned closer to her until she tilted her head back and he could press his cheek to hers. With his mouth right at her ear, he whispered, "You set the pace, baby doll. Okay? If you wanna go slow, we go slow. If you just want me to bring you lunch sometimes, I'll do that. If you don't, you just say so, and I'll bow right out of your life for however long you want me to."

"I don't want you to bow out of my life."

He wasn't sure if they started swaying or if that was simply the earth hurtling through space, but he felt lightheaded and drunk on this woman. "You can be yourself with me," he said. "I know you will, but I'll say it anyway: Tell me what you want and what you need, okay?"

He didn't say she could tell him she just wanted to be friends, and he'd be her friend. He wasn't even sure how to just be this woman's friend. He could be her boyfriend, or he wouldn't be with her. Those were the only two options in his mind, and even a very slow, very long relationship while they both dealt with what needed to be handled was fine with him.

Being only friends with Gerty wasn't.

"I will." Her hands slid up his back, and he tensed his right side involuntarily. She didn't apologize for maybe hurting him, and she didn't pull back. Mike appreciated that more than he knew how to express, and shivers ran down his spine as her fingers played with the ends of his hair that stuck out below his cowboy hat.

"All right." He finally stepped back and opened his eyes. It took a moment to adjust to the brightness of the sun—or maybe that was Gerty's shine. Either way, he blinked a couple of times before he could see her properly. "I'll be working to get better physically and mentally and emotionally and spiritually. If you need time to do that too, I'm really okay with it."

She nodded, her eyes wide and full of fear, like a deer that's just been caught in a hunter's spotlight.

"Will you tell me about him?" he asked gently.

She turned away from him quickly, but Mike saw the pain etched on her face before she did. "Maybe," she said. "Not today."

"Okay," he said easily. "How about how long it's been since you broke up with him?"

She walked over to her truck and opened the driver's door. "Who says I broke up with him?"

"Did you?" Mike followed her, still unable to read her

expression because she kept her back to him. She didn't answer, which was her answer, and Mike detoured to go around the bed of the truck so he could get in the passenger seat.

He managed to do it with as much grace as he could, which was about that of a hippopotamus getting out of a mud hole. He was sweating by the time he got his buckle lined up with the attachment. "Could you?" he asked, glancing over to her.

He held the belt in place, but he couldn't line it up and push at the same time with his non-dominant hand. Gerty helped him buckle, and the simple act of service broke the tension in the cab.

"We only broke up a month ago," Gerty said as she looked out her side window, her face turned completely away from him. "I was *engaged* to him, Mike." She practically slammed the truck into reverse, and Mike reached for the handle above the door, thinking she was about to take them on a wild ride.

"I'm so sorry," he said, but he didn't mean it.

She looked over to him, her foot still firmly on the brake. "You are?"

"No," Mike said. "I mean, yes? It's difficult to explain."

She nodded to where he gripped the overhead handle, having to stretch across his whole body to do it. "I'm not going to kill us."

"I'm injured," he reminded her. "Don't throw me around." He added a smile so she'd know it was a joke. Kind of.

She visibly relaxed and eased her foot off the brake so

the truck moved gently. He let go of the handle and said, "I'm really sorry that a relationship that meant a great deal to you ended the way it did—however that was. You're obviously hurting from it, and that makes me hurt."

It actually made him want to hunt down the man who'd hurt her and make him suffer the way she was. Sometimes the dormant commanding officer side of him rose up, and this was definitely one of those cases. He'd make the man who made his Gerty unhappy apologize until he was sobbing, and Mike shook the thoughts from his head. There would be no hunting and no apologizing.

He glanced over to Gerty, who still watched him, the truck barely moving. "Am I sorry that you're single now? I mean, my momma taught me not to tell a lie, so...." He left the words there and smiled out the windshield.

Out of his peripheral vision, he saw Gerty shake her head. She was hopefully smiling again, and Mike reflected on all he'd said to her that day.

Stuff about kissing her while he held her right where he wanted her with two hands. He cringed internally just thinking about this morning. At the same time, he'd done his momma proud, because he hadn't lied. He also hadn't kissed Gerty when neither of them were ready. So he could easily tell his daddy that he was being careful with this woman.

He'd just told Gerty she could set the pace for their relationship. She'd need to go slow, he knew, and he needed the exact same thing. He'd literally told her she could dictate to him what she needed from him, and he'd do it. Did that make him pathetic?

*More than you already are?* he wondered. He stole a glance over to Gerty, and she drove with both hands on the wheel, at ten and two, clearly somewhere inside her own mind.

She'd told him a lot that morning too, and he appreciated that she'd said she'd help him every day with his shirt and not even care. That his worth wasn't dependent on how well his shoulder worked.

He wanted to be whole again, though, and he once again wanted to be a strong, safe place for Gertrude Whettstein.

As she turned right, away from the Hammond Family Farm, he asked, "Where are you takin' me, baby doll?"

She didn't even glance over to him, though when Mike had called her that as a teen, she'd cocked her head and challenged him. He liked both versions of Gerty just fine, and he grinned to himself as he took in her profile.

"First, there's this place my daddy used to take us for Sunday afternoon picnics," she said. "It's like, five miles down the road here. Is that okay?" She switched her gaze to him but didn't wait for him to answer.

"Second, baby doll?"

He burst out laughing, and that felt so incredibly good that Mike thought for the first time since he'd woken up in a hospital in Germany that he'd be happy again. "Hey, it worked for that guy on *Criminal Minds*."

"I don't watch that show," she said.

He reached over and took her hand in his. "You should."

"We've had this conversation before."

"Yes, we have." He couldn't stop grinning about it too, and he didn't care if that made him look like a fool. He'd likely already sounded like one, and Gerty hadn't told him to get back in the truck with his father and get on home.

"Tell me about the doctor's appointment," she said.

Mike's smile tapered then. "My momma took notes, but the long and short of it is I need a shoulder replacement. They went over all the risks, what the surgery is like, the recovery, all of that."

"And?"

"And I'm having a shoulder replacement in three weeks."

Gerty looked over to him again, this time holding his gaze for a lot longer than a breath of time. Her eyes rounded, and surprise shone deep within. "Really?"

He grinned again, because a shoulder replacement could be a new life for him. A new beginning, one that wasn't full of pain and scar tissue and endless drugs. "Yeah," he said. "They had an opening as someone had literally canceled that morning and the surgery scheduler hadn't had time to call anyone and move them up. So I slid into the spot."

"Mikey, that's so great," she said, her surprise dissolving into a cheerful smile. "I mean, I'm assuming it's great."

"It's great," he said. "But, Gerty…Mikey?"

"Oops, I'm—"

His laughter cut off her apology, and she dang near swerved them into the ditch on the side of the road as she swatted at his chest.

"Hey, hey," he said, still laughing. "I'm injured, baby doll. Don't be driving so crazy." He grinned at her and then out the windshield, and it just felt so...good to not be worrying about every little thing all the time. "You said I didn't need to hold on."

"You don't." She settled her fingers between his again, and Mike brought her hand to his lips and kissed the back of it.

"I don't care if you call me Mike or Mikey," he said. "Either is fine, but don't be tellin' anyone else that."

"My lips are sealed," she said. "And I suppose baby doll isn't so bad...if it's only you callin' me that."

"Deal," he said.

"Deal," she repeated, and then she yanked her hand away and applied the brakes in a very hard fashion, once again telling him he should've held on to the handle above the window, no matter what she said.

"Sorry, sorry," she said. "This is just...our...turn." She made it while he employed all of his abdominal muscles to hold him in his seat, and then added, "It snuck up on me."

Once they settled back onto four wheels and the world wasn't so drenched in centrifugal force, Mike said, "You mean you haven't been out here for a while."

She glanced over to him, an edge in her eyes. "No...I haven't."

"Mm," he said.

"Mm?" she repeated. "What does that mean?"

"It means your daddy was waiting for me when I got back from my appointment, and he wanted to know how he could get you to talk to him."

Gerty clamped her mouth shut, her jaw jutting out. Fire danced in her eyes, which she quickly focused back on the road. He wasn't complaining about that, but Mike had seen this tactic from her before.

He could wait, and he settled in to do just that.

# CHAPTER
## Six

GERTY PULLED UP TO HER PARENTS' house and sighed. She'd been gone far longer than it took to re-shoe a horse, and Daddy would know it. Cosette too, and they were both home from the farm already.

She wasn't used to accounting her time to anyone besides James, and even then, he'd never given her a hard time about what she made a priority in her life.

She swallowed, because that had been a problem, hadn't it?

"He didn't tell you," she whispered to herself. She couldn't change what she didn't know about, and it wasn't her fault James had cheated. It was *not*.

*You work all the time, and I swear, you love those horses more than you do me.*

Gerty hadn't apologized for loving the horses. She did love them, but she'd loved James too. If she'd have known he wanted her to come in off the ranch earlier, she'd have at least made an effort to do so. Half the time, he hadn't even been home—and now she knew why.

Her parents were home, and Gerty smelled evidence that she'd be up late talking tonight in the form of spice cake. Cosette had been baking, and that had always been her way of dealing with her thoughts. Then, everyone got to benefit while they had hard conversations.

Gerty reminded herself that she'd had plenty of those over the years. Her life had not been stress-free or perfectly easy, though she didn't have a whole lot to complain about either. Maybe her mother dying when she was so young, but she'd made her peace with the Lord on that one.

She pulled open the front door and went inside with the words, "I'm back."

"I was just about to send out a search party," Daddy said from the kitchen at the back of the house. He turned toward her, his trademark smile on his face. He was larger-than-life in everything he did, and Gerty had always loved him with her whole soul.

When she was a little girl, she'd run to him and say, "Swing me up, Daddy!" and he would. He'd toss her so high, a twinge of fear would strike her behind the ribs on the way down. He'd laugh with that big voice of his, and he'd always, always caught her.

He'd been the one to tell her about her mother's illness. He'd held her while she cried when her momma had died. He'd had hard conversations with her about leaving Montana, dating boys, and becoming a farrier.

They hadn't always gotten along, but one thing Gerty

had never, ever doubted was how much her daddy loved her.

She found she couldn't move very far into the house. She'd moved here with Cosette after she and Daddy had gotten married, and Gerty had come to feel like this was her home. She should be able to walk in at any time, any day, of any month and feel welcome—and she did.

But she didn't know what to say right now, and Daddy knew it. He reached for a hand towel to dry his hands at the same time Gerty's eyes started to burn with unshed tears.

"We're having cake on the deck," he said.

"Great. I'll see you out there," Gerty managed to say before she spun, whipped open the front door, and left the house.

"Gerty," he said behind her, but she kept going. He'd catch up, she knew. She made it down the front steps and across the lawn before he came huffing up beside her. "Gerty," he said again.

"I can't, Daddy." She burst into tears then and turned into him. He wrapped her up in his strong arms, the way he always did, and let her cry against his chest.

"Hey," he whispered. "Hey, it's fine. It's okay. You're home, and we love you." He held her tightly against his chest, and she loved that about him. Maybe if he held everything together for her, she wouldn't fall apart.

She hadn't told her grandparents much, either, other than she and James weren't getting married anymore and that she'd let her parents know. She had, and then she'd taken her sweet time coming back to Colorado. She hadn't given them any more details than she'd given her grandma and grandpa, and literally no one knew why she'd ended things with James.

*No wonder the world feels so heavy,* she thought. In her mind, she saw the Savior, and she felt strongly that she didn't have to carry her burdens alone. He could help her, but He'd also given her people right here on earth to help her.

She sniffled and pulled away from her dad. "I'm sorry," she muttered. "There's just all this stuff going on, and I'm confused, and I'd really rather just saddle up and ride away or file hooves down so I don't have to think about it."

"Yeah," Daddy said. He didn't let her get too far from him. "I figured, because that's how you are, Gertrude."

She wiped her face and looked up at him. "James cheated on me."

Her daddy's eyes widened, first in surprise and then with pure anger. "I—your mom will be upset if you tell this story without her there." He took her hand, his way too tight around hers. "Come on. We'll have the kids go inside." He started back to the house.

Gerty stumbled slightly as she tried to orient her body in the right direction and walk at the same time. "They don't have to go in," she said.

"Amy is ten."

"Then she's old enough to know that some men aren't honorable."

Daddy paused and looked at her. "You want her to know?"

"I don't care if she knows," Gerty said. "It's up to you and Mom."

He looked like he needed a minute to think on it, and he stayed silent—quite the feat—on the way back inside. Mom turned from the kitchen sink, worry etched in every line on her face, and Gerty's tears reared again.

She should've come home sooner. She shouldn't have stayed away from Ivory Peaks for so long.

"I sent them outside," she said, hurrying toward Gerty and her father. "They wanted to have their cake on the trampoline."

"It's okay," Daddy said.

"My Gerty-girl." Cosette drew Gerty into her arms, and Gerty experienced true, maternal love, and it was strong and beautiful. "Why have you been crying?"

"I'm so sorry," she whispered. "I should've come home more. I should've come straight here after."

"You're fine," Mom said. "It's fine." She pulled back, her eyes seeing and searching. "After what, Gerty?"

"After I broke up with James." Gerty hung her head. To her surprise, Daddy didn't jump in and tell Mom what was going on. She looked over to him, but he gestured for her to speak up. "He cheated on me, and when I found out, I ended things with him. Called off the wedding."

Gerty looked up and blew out her breath. "I left Coldwater and went and stayed with my grandparents for a while. I don't know, I was just...."

She didn't know what. Lost.

Part of her had hoped that it would all be a mistake, and she hadn't wanted to put too much physical distance between her and James. But it hadn't been a mistake. He hadn't called or texted her once since, and she'd finally deleted his number from her phone the night before she'd driven here.

"I'm—I don't know what to say," Mom said. She exchanged a glance with Daddy, who still wore one of the darkest looks on his face that Gerty had ever seen. "I should've made the apple cider doughnuts."

For some reason, that made Gerty smile, and then she started to laugh. "I don't think doughnuts can fix infidelity," she said between the giggles.

"Oh, now, that's where you're wrong." Mom grinned at her. "Come sit down."

"We can go out on the deck," Gerty said. "I don't care if the younger kids know." She drew in a big breath. "Everyone will find out eventually." She thought of Mike and how closed off she'd gotten the very moment he'd mentioned James and wanting to know about him. She'd told him she was engaged to him and that it had only been over for a month.

Mike hadn't gone anywhere. He hadn't even acted concerned.

"I'm okay if they hear," Daddy said. "They're not babies."

"Okay," Mom said cautiously. "Just remember that they're young."

Gerty knew, so she nodded and said, "He'd been cheating on me for at least a year, with at least three different women. Two of them I knew."

"I am going to find him and kill him," Daddy said, his fingers curling into fists.

"Boone," Mom said, her eyebrows drawing down. "You definitely can't go outside and say stuff like that in front of your children."

"Who does that?" Daddy raged. "Not a man. A coward."

Gerty let her father say what he wanted, because she didn't disagree. Her so-called friends had been complicit in things too, but it hadn't hurt to walk away from them as much as it had James. Even now, part of her still loved him. She wasn't sure how to simply turn off that feeling.

She'd had many times where she wanted to do exactly what Daddy had just said—hunt James down and kill him. And in the very next moment, she'd be sobbing because she missed him so much. None of it made sense, and Gerty didn't know how to unravel it all.

"I don't disagree," Mom said. "But you can't say stuff like that in front of Amy. She'll say it to everyone at school."

"School just got out," Dad said back. The two of them went into the kitchen, and Gerty followed. "I just can't even believe it. We met James only eight months ago. He was cheating then? How could he have looked me in the face—the father of his girlfriend—and *lied* to me?"

He'd been doing the same thing to Gerty too, and she knew how deep that betrayal stung.

"He lied to you; he lied to my dead wife's parents!" Daddy yanked open the silverware drawer, sending the utensils into angry rattling.

"Boone," Mom said again.

He didn't even seem to hear her. "And worst of all, he broke my daughter's heart. How dare he? I mean, just...*how dare he?* Who does he think he is?" His eyes met Gerty's, and she shrugged one shoulder. The rage she understood. She'd been where her father currently was.

"Did you tell Grandma and Grandpa?" he asked.

She shook her head. "I just told them we broke up."

"Honey, you don't—"

"Boone," Mom said again. She handed him the cake. "Go outside and calm down. Let me talk to Gerty for a minute alone."

He gave her a dark look too, but he did what she said. When the back door slammed closed, Gerty let out of a sigh. "See why I didn't want to talk?"

Mom gave her a sharp look. "I get one minute to lecture."

Gerty lifted her chin. "Fine."

"He's right—you don't need to hold everything inside yourself. You should've told us immediately, so we could help. Secondly, I'm as upset as he is, and if I hadn't already told him he couldn't act like that, I'd be on the computer, buying a ticket to Montana to find that man and give him a piece of my mind."

Gerty's eyebrows practically flew off her face. "Mom," she said, completely shocked.

"Third, you should've come home sooner, but I'm not going to say another word about it. Heaven knows you've already been beating yourself up about it."

Gerty dropped her chin toward her chest again. "And

worse, Mom, Michael Hammond is at the farm, and I held his hand today."

"Okay, we are not telling your father about that," she said. "Give him one more day, Gerty, please. He's going to have a heart attack as it is."

"He already knows," Gerty said.

"I'm sure he does." Mom sighed. "What with you running off this morning the way you did." Their eyes met, and Gerty didn't know if she should start crying again or smile.

"I'm not a teenager anymore," she said.

"We know," Mom said. "But that doesn't mean we worry any less about you, honey." She gave Gerty a warm smile, her own eyes welling with tears. "I'm so, so sorry about this. You know I know what relationship pain is like, and I can't even imagine carrying it alone."

Gerty started to weep again, and she had trouble maintaining eye contact. She looked away again, glad when her mom pulled her into a hug. "Lecture's over," she whispered. "You get to cry as much as you want, and be mad as much as you want, and if you want to see if you and Mikey have a chance again, that's okay too."

"Is it?" Gerty asked. "Because what if I'm just not worth loving?"

"That's simply not true," Daddy said, and Gerty opened her eyes to find him standing only a few feet away. "It's not, Gerty, and I don't ever want you to feel like that."

She stepped out of Mom's arms and nodded.

"Amy asked if they could go over to Joann's to see the puppies, and I said yes," he said to Mom.

"Great," she said. "That's perfect."

"There are puppies next door?" Gerty asked. "Can I go over too?"

"No," Daddy growled. "You're going to come tell us everything about James, your grandparents, and Michael Hammond."

Gerty swallowed. So he'd heard. "Daddy," she said, planting both hands on her hips. "I never once got myself in trouble with Mike, and I'm not going to start now."

Daddy gave her a smile, some of his usual charm returning to his face. He'd definitely grayed a little in the past year, something Gerty was just now noticing. "Obviously, sugar-pie," he said. "It's not you I'm worried about."

"Hey," she said. "Mike's a great man." In her opinion, she'd be lucky to end up with him. Fear gripped her lungs. Would he find fault with her when she told him about James and what he'd said?

"Maybe," Daddy said.

"There's someone good enough for Gerty," Mom said. "Come on, Boone. You need a lot of sugar right now."

"I won't talk you out of the doughnuts next time," he said.

Mom gave her a grin over his shoulder as they walked toward the back door, and Gerty smiled her way after them. She definitely thought Mike was good enough for her; the real question was whether she was good enough for him.

––––––––

A FEW DAYS LATER, the weekend arrived and that meant so did Gerty's first day back at Pony Power. She drove over to the farm in her own truck, her younger brother in the front seat and her younger sister in the back.

"...and then they'll get to go home with their forever families," Amy said. She hadn't stopped talking about the puppies for longer than it took to breathe in the past fifteen minutes.

"That's great," Gerty said. "You didn't talk Daddy into taking one?" She smiled at her little sister in the rearview mirror.

"No." Amy pouted. "He says we can't have a dog, because we're never home, but I just *know* he could bring it out here to the farm."

"Maybe," Gerty said. She glanced over to Walter, who'd been fairly quiet. He didn't usually try to interrupt Amy, but he'd add to her stories too, and he'd not said more than five words since they'd left the house.

"Hey," she said to him. "You okay?"

He looked up from his phone, his face instantly turning the color of a terrible sunburn. "Yeah." He shoved his phone under his leg. "Fine."

"Who are you texting?"

"No one," he said. He turned away from her completely then, and Gerty recognized a lie when she heard it. Was this how her father felt, raising her? She'd started dating Mikey the summer she'd turned fourteen.

"What do you want for your birthday?" Amy asked, not even realizing that Walter had obviously been texting someone he didn't want anyone to know about.

"A huge birthday cake," Gerty said. "Chocolate on the inside and sprinkles on the outside."

Amy cheered in the back seat, and Walter gave her a scathing look. "It's too loud, Amy," he said.

She didn't care about his eardrums at all, and Gerty smiled at them both. "Are you going to do your stunts today?" she asked her brother.

"Yeah," he said. "The kids like them. I always—"

"Have you met the new Pony Power therapy dog?" Amy asked. "You have to, Gerty. She is so cute."

"Baby, you cut off Walt." She looked over to him. "You always what?"

"Nothing. I just always do the stunts for this event."

Gerty nodded as she made the final turn to go down the dirt lane to the farm and Pony Power. They were arriving early so they could help get set up for the event, and soon enough, the place would be full of cars, parents, and kids for this annual event. She'd been gone long enough not to know if their classes were full or not, but she'd also been hired to run horseback riding lessons this summer, and she imagined Molly would have sign-ups for those.

"When's your next competition?"

"End of July," he said. "It's down in Colorado Springs. You'll come, right?"

"Sure," Gerty said. "Of course I will." She smiled at Walter and pulled into the employee lot, which hadn't been there when she'd lived on the farm as a teen. She parked, and Amy jumped from the truck almost before it had stopped moving.

"Hey," Gerty said after her, but the girl was gone. She figured she couldn't get into too much trouble, as Daddy and Mom were already here. She shook her head and turned off the ignition.

"So," she said to Walter. "What's her name? The girl you've been texting."

Walt instantly turned into a tomato again. Gerty giggled and said, "Walt, it's fine to like a girl." She held out her hand. "Let me see."

He made no move to hand her the phone. "No way."

"You have to work on not turning bright red whenever you talk about her," Gerty said. "Or Daddy will find out faster than you can blink."

"Don't you dare tell him."

Gerty sobered. "*You* better tell him, Walter. Daddy doesn't like being lied to, and he *will* find out. He always does."

Walter nodded, and he looked absolutely miserable. "Yeah, I know. I just don't know how."

"It's not too hard," Gerty said. "You could even just hand him your phone and say, 'Dad, I've been texting this girl, and I need help asking her to the summer ice cream social at church. Do you think I could do that? Will you help me?' and he'll read all the texts, growl about having another kid going on dates when they're only fourteen, and then he'll help you."

Walter's face drained of color now, which was saying something as he had their father's dark coloring. Both he and Amy did, as Cosette had dark hair and eyes too. Gerty stood out among the four of them, but she absolutely belonged to them too.

"I'm not asking Ashley to the ice cream social at church."

"No? Why not? I was thinking of getting a date and going."

"You don't have to have a date to go," he said, rolling his eyes.

"Great, then you can meet Ashley there, and Daddy will find out in public. Seems like *such* a better plan than what I said." She unbuckled her seatbelt and started to get out of the truck.

"Gerty?"

She turned back to Walter. "Yeah, bud?"

He pushed his glasses up on his nose. "Will you read these and see if she likes me? Like, really likes me?" He held out his phone, and Gerty took it.

She didn't look at it though. "Why wouldn't she like you?"

"Because I'm a total geek," he said. "I run the robotics club at school, Gerty, and I stunt-ride for fun."

She frowned. "So what? Those are both totally cool."

He shook his head. "No, they're not."

Gerty leaned toward him, the fire inside her licking upward. "Well, if she doesn't think they're cool, then you don't have time for her, okay? You deserve someone who thinks you're wonderful *because* you run the robotics club and stunt-ride for fun. Do you hear me?"

He searched her face and nodded, a hint of fear in his eyes. "Yeah," he said. "I hear you."

She handed his phone back. "I'm sure she likes you. You texted her for a solid fifteen minutes on the way here."

He took the phone, still nodding. "Gerty?"

"Yeah?" She was tired already but didn't want to show it.

"Do you miss James?"

She sucked in a breath, her eyes suddenly searching Walter's. "No," she said. Her mind raced, and she worked to slow it. "I mean, sometimes." She sighed. "Yeah, sometimes."

"Why'd you break-up with him?"

Gerty looked out the window, trying to find the right answer. The side of the big, red-barn administration office stared back at her. "Because, bud," she said. "He didn't think I was wonderful because I love horses and love working with them." She gave him a sad smile. "You gotta trust your gut on these things, okay? Ashley either likes you for you, or she doesn't, and if she doesn't, then she's not for you."

Walter accepted her answer, finally reaching to unbuckle his seatbelt. Gerty reached out to stop him, and he looked at her again. "And James cheated on me, Walter. That's the real reason I broke up with him and called off the wedding. He wasn't who I thought he was, and it really had nothing to do with me and horses."

Walter's eyes turned big and round. "Oh, Gerty, that's —why would he do that?"

"I don't know," Gerty said instead of calling James a name. "But I want you to know the truth."

Walter's face clouded as he nodded. "What a jerky thing to do to you."

Gerty grinned. "Now you're starting to sound like Daddy." She gave a light laugh. "Come on. Let's get going or all the good jobs will be gone."

They got out of the truck and Walter asked, "Are there good jobs with this? Because last year, I had to stand next to the lemonade dispenser, and it was terrible."

Gerty laughed fully then, slung her arm around her brother, and said, "Yeah, bud, there are good jobs. Stick with me, and I'll make sure you aren't handing out cups of lemonade for the next three hours."

As they rounded the corner, a couple of cowboys were already setting up folding tables, and Gerty smiled and said hello to Mission and Cord, as well as Keith.

Jane came out of the barn next, and she said, "Gerty, praise the heavens." She reached for her hand. "I've got to show you something."

"What is it?" Gerty stumbled after the other woman, one of Gray's kids that she'd been friends with growing up. Jane was a couple of years younger than Gerty, but they'd gotten along just fine.

Inside, the air conditioning blew, and Jane didn't seem to have a job yet. She towed Gerty down the hall and into a nearly empty room. "What is going on, Jane?" she asked.

"Nothing," Jane said, somewhat out of breath. "I just didn't want to be outside with Mission and Cord."

Gerty cocked her head. "A statement like that has a story behind it. Probably more than one."

Jane tossed her fine-as-silk hair over her shoulder. "Yeah, it does."

"Gerty?" Walter called.

She poked her head out into the hallway. "Right here, bud. Give me two seconds." She looked at Jane again. "You and Cord?"

Jane didn't duck her head or hide it. "I can't help liking him," she said. "We're adults now, Gerty. Do you think it would be weird?"

"How much older than you is he?"

"Eleven years," she said with a monstrous sigh. "He won't even look at me. He scampers away every time I'm within a half-mile of him."

Gerty grinned. "A half-mile, Jane?" She'd always been an exaggerator. "You were within five yards of him, just now."

"Yeah, and if I hadn't dragged you in here, he'd have made some excuse and ran for the farmhouse." Jane cocked her hip and folded her arms. "What do you think I should do?"

"Do?" Gerty asked with a laugh. "I have no idea what you should do. I just called off my wedding, so I'm in no position to tell you how to deal with a man."

Jane watched her for a moment. "I'm sorry about the wedding."

Gerty swallowed, because she was tired of talking about James and her relationship with him. "Don't be," she said. "There's a reason I called it off."

"Yeah, and there's a reason I came home," Jane said. "It doesn't mean it was what you necessarily wanted to do."

Gerty nodded, wishing this room had something for her to pick and fiddle with. "You didn't want to come home?"

"It's not that I didn't want to," Jane said, another sigh following the words. "It's complicated."

"I understand complicated," Gerty said. "Now, I promised Walter I'd get him a good job, so I better go see where Molly needs us."

"Yeah, all right," Jane said. "But we need to go to lunch."

An idea popped into Gerty's head. "Do you think your dad would let me cook in the generational house?"

"Yeah, maybe," Jane said. "I'll ask him."

"Then we can eat there," Gerty said.

"I'm starting at HMC on Monday," Jane said. "Who's 'we'?"

Gerty turned to leave the room. "You're starting at HMC? Since when?" She'd rather get Jane talking than tell her that if she didn't come eat lunch in the generational house, then Gerty and Mike could dine alone.

# CHAPTER
## *Seven*

MIKE REFUSED to sit at the front table and greet people as they arrived at Pony Power. In the end, Hunter had convinced Molly to let Britt and Gloria do it, as they actually worked directly with parents and their kids, and Mike had escaped to the training rings.

He hadn't been able to set up any of the tables or coolers on them. He'd carried a bag of plastic cups in his good hand, and Hunt's oldest son, Ryder, had set them all out.

Cord Behr and Mission Redbay still worked here, as did Matt and Boone Whettstein and Travis Thatcher. They'd taken all the horses out, and Mike had seen Gerty and her brother Walter helping with the animals too.

Keith, Matt's son, worked at Pony Power right now too, and he'd been taking people on tours of the place for the past hour, as had Deacon, Mike's cousin. Everyone seemed to be in high spirits except for him, but he couldn't get himself to go back to the farmhouse where his parents were.

Uncle Gray and Aunt Elise would be there too, and they'd host a huge luncheon on the back deck and in the backyard once the event ended.

Mike left the training rings, where a couple of horses went round and round, and headed for the back paddock again. If he just kept walking, he'd get back to the cabin, and maybe then he wouldn't feel so useless.

*It's only a few weeks until your surgery,* he told himself. In the spiral where he currently existed, his next thought was, *Yeah, and then you have months of recovery and physical therapy to get through.*

He wasn't going to be magically fixed in one day. The truth was, now that he knew he could have the surgery, he'd become impatient. He wanted it now, and then he wanted to be healed magically in one day too.

The stark reminder that such a thing wouldn't happen, and while he hated that it hurt, that didn't make it hurt less.

He arrived at the paddock, and the same black horse he'd walked beside earlier this week came to say hello. "Hey, Tenney," he said to Gerty's horse. "She's busy this morning, but I'm sure she'll be out here to ride you this afternoon."

He wasn't sure what Gerty's plans were this afternoon. He hadn't asked her out again since he'd taken her a brisket sandwich earlier in the week. He'd texted her a few times, and she'd texted back.

He'd gone into the office with Hunter yesterday, and while it hadn't been terrible, it also hadn't been Mike's idea of a grand time. Everything in his life felt unsettled, and he didn't want Gerty to be one of those things.

"Let me text her, okay?" He pulled out his phone and sent her a quick message. *I know you're working the event this morning, but then what? Do you want to go see a movie and get dinner with me?*

He'd said she could set the pace. She could decide everything, and her response would tell him if she was ready to go out with him or not. Maybe it would be better to simply hang out around the farm. He could make lunch in his cabin, and they could eat there together on days he worked the farm.

He knew lots of people who had relationships without really dating. Mike had had a couple of those himself, but it wasn't really what he wanted to do with Gerty. He wanted to take her out, get her away from the farm and their regular lives, and get to know her again.

*I'm starting at Pony Power today*, she replied. *So I have to work this afternoon. But I'd love to go out tonight.*

A smile filled his face and then his soul. *I'll see what's playing.*

*Where'd you escape to?* she asked, and he could just hear her teasing him. *Probably somewhere with air conditioning.*

He turned around and took a selfie of him and Tenney, the horse looking very unenthused, and sent the picture to Gerty. He didn't get a response from her right away, and he didn't know what job she'd ended up with for the event. Maybe she'd gotten called away to do something, and he turned back to her horse.

"We're goin' out tonight, and did you know she has to work this afternoon? I'm sure she'll come see you though."

Tenney nickered, and Mike grinned at him. He stroked his hand down the side of the horse's neck, seeing and feeling why Gerty loved him so.

He called again, and Gerty said, "Oh, hush, you."

Mike turned and found her sauntering toward him. Well, as much as a woman like Gerty could saunter. She didn't just walk for fun. Everything she did, she did with a purpose, right down to walking.

She moved right into his left side and reached for her horse too. "Is he telling you secrets?"

Mike put his arm around her. "Nothing I haven't told you already."

"Mm, I don't believe that."

"It's true."

She looked at him, and she possessed a glow today he hadn't noticed before. "You're hiding back here."

"Not really," he said, though he sort of had been. "I just —didn't want to be out front."

Something blazed in her eyes, but she didn't ask him to elaborate on what he'd said. "I guess I'm driving tonight?" she asked.

"If you could," he said with a swallow following the words. "I can pay you for the gas."

She gave him a kind smile. "I can pay for gas, Mike." She leaned into his chest, and he adjusted his hand on her waist, keeping her tight and close against him.

He wanted to stand here with her in peace and silence for a good, long while, the scent of the peach in her shampoo just underneath the dirt that also came from her. "I went to work with Hunt yesterday," he said.

"Yeah? How was it?"

"It wasn't terrible."

"That doesn't mean it was good."

"It was all right," he said. "I think I'd like it, once I know what's going on."

"That's good, then."

Mike watched Tenney make room at the fence for another horse, this one gray. "What's this one's name?"

"Stella." Gerty spoke with a smile in her voice. "Gloria thinks we can train her up to use with the kids."

"Is that right?" Mike asked. That sounded like Gerty would be here for longer than a summer, but he didn't vocalize that.

"Yeah." Gerty stroked her neck too, and the horse leaned into her touch like it was made of magic.

"Gerty," he said quietly.

"Hmm?"

"I'm probably gonna be the next CEO of HMC."

She turned to face him and stepped back. Surprise danced across her face. "You are? Is that what you want?"

He didn't say it didn't matter what he wanted. "Yeah," he said. "Like I said, it wasn't bad, and the more I learn, the more comfortable I'll be."

"Wow."

"Why does that surprise you?"

"I don't know," she said. "Just, when we were kids, you said you weren't sure that was for you."

"I got to go do what I wanted," he said. "Hunter's ready to retire and do what he wants to do, and I think I'd be a decent CEO."

She kept stroking the horse, almost absently now. "Of course you will be."

He cleared his throat. "I've got to figure out what to do with my money too."

Her eyes came back to him, another round of shock in them. "Your money?"

"Yeah." He ground his voice again. "Uh, when I turned twenty-one, I got a bunch of money from my parents. I got this huge lecture too—apparently everyone gets it. But I'm supposed to use the money for something good. Hunt's started two charitable organizations. My Uncle Colt did a ton of research on the Human Genome Project. Uncle Cy still builds a couple of really expensive bikes and donates them every year."

Gerty simply stared at him, like she didn't comprehend. Maybe she didn't. Even Mike couldn't conceptualize what two billion dollars looked like, and it had been sitting in his bank account for almost a decade.

Surprisingly, it hadn't been his father to remind him of his duty to do something good with it, but Hunter. He'd asked Mike yesterday what he'd done or planned to do, and Mike hadn't had anything to tell him.

Hunt was such a good friend and a good person that he'd said, "You'll figure it out," and then he'd just moved onto the next thing.

"How much money are we talking?" Gerty asked.

"A lot," Mike said. "What would you do if you had enough money to do anything in the world?"

Her eyebrows went up. "Anything in the world?"

He nodded and turned to the horses. Gerty seemed to only own jeans and tank tops, as today's was brown with a star in the middle of it.

"I'd buy my own farm," she said. "Where I could have as many horses as I wanted."

He smiled. "That does sound like you."

"I love horses," she said. "And farming and ranching. I've always wanted to be a cowgirl and own my own horse ranch. So yeah. That's what I'd do with it."

"What sounds like me?" he asked.

She didn't blurt out the first thing that came to her head, but a few seconds went by as she thought about it. "You've always wanted to fly, and you made that dream come true. Now? I'm not sure, Mikey. Maybe you should buy a restaurant like your daddy."

He shook his head, though he smiled. "Nah, I don't think I'm cut out for that." And his father hadn't bought the restaurant for himself, but for someone else. Not only that, but it had been funded through a special outreach program which his father had implemented at HMC. Hunter still ran the program, and Mike had known about it for years and years. He imagined he'd do it once he took over at the family company.

"You've always loved hiking," she said. "The National Parks. The great outdoors." She spread her arms wide, which her horses did not appreciate. Tenney nickered at her and Stella backed up a few feet. "Oh, you guys are such babies." She grinned at her animals, and Mike swore they grinned back.

"Yeah," he said. "The great outdoors." The very beginnings of an idea percolated in his head, but he didn't say anything else.

An alarm on Gerty's phone went off, and she said, "All right, Mister, you're coming with me." She took his hand, and they turned around.

"I am?" But he already was. "Where are we going?"

"It's time for me to talk to a group of people about horseback riding lessons, and that means my brother needs someone to help him with Denver."

"Denver? He got the job of babysitting Denver?"

Gerty grinned at him. "Are you jealous of a fourteen-year-old?"

"Heck yes," Mike said. "Molly almost made me work the front table, and now I find out I could've been babysitting a therapy dog who's better behaved than half the people I know?" He shook his head as Gerty sent a peal of laughter into the sky. He liked the sound of that, and he couldn't wait until their first real date that night.

————

MIKE REACHED for a chip from the bowl that had just been placed in the middle of the table. "I love chips and salsa."

Gerty grinned at him and let him scoop up a whole chip-full of the spicy variety in one of the bowls next to the chips. "I do too, but not that hot stuff." She plucked a chip from the bowl as he put his entire one into his mouth.

She didn't dunk hers in salsa at all, and Mike wasn't that surprised. She'd never liked spicy food all that much, and he'd been surprised when she'd suggested this Mexican restaurant on the tail end of Main Street in Ivory Peaks.

He'd commented that he'd never been here before, and she'd told him that her daddy told her it was new in the past couple of years.

He chewed and swallowed and looked at her. "How long have you been back in town?"

"I came back the day I met you by the horses." Something invisible slipped between them, but Mike felt it.

She wore a sundress tonight, the wide straps in blue and pink going over her strong shoulders and leaving enough skin for him to admire. She'd let her hair down, and it fell over her shoulders in soft waves.

"Have I told you how pretty you look?" he asked, adding a smile as he reached for another chip.

She rolled her eyes, but her smile widened. "You have."

"Funny, I didn't hear it from you." He put his loaded chip in his mouth and looked at her with his eyebrows up.

Gerty had never been very free with compliments, and that hadn't changed about her. It took effort for her to talk about how she felt, but once she started, she didn't hold back.

"You look amazing tonight, Mike," she said, her voice barely loud enough to make it past the mariachi music piping into the restaurant through speakers in the ceiling.

He swallowed again, a delicious burn across his tongue and down his throat. "Thank you, Gerty." Mike looked down at his button-up shirt. "I had to wash this today so it would be presentable. I didn't bring a lot of dating clothes."

She folded her arms on the table and leaned into them. "Didn't think you'd meet anyone here this summer?"

"No," he said honestly. "I didn't. But if I'd have known you'd be here, I'd have packed differently."

"Mm." Her eyes danced with a bright blue flame. "I think you have enough money to do a little shopping if you find your wardrobe lacking." Her right eyebrow went up while the left stayed down, and Mike laughed.

"I suppose you're right," he said.

She grabbed another chip, and this one she dipped in the mild salsa, but didn't scoop any of it onto the chip. She actually shook it a little before putting it in her mouth, as if trying to get rid of as much of the salsa as possible. He couldn't stop grinning, and he didn't even know why.

"What are you afraid of?" he asked, and that brought surprise to her expression.

She chewed quicker and reached for her water glass. "Getting a spicy bite of salsa."

"If you don't like it, you don't have to eat it." He wondered if she needed permission not to eat it. It sort of seemed like it.

"I *want* to like it," she said. "But I don't think I do." She smiled and shook her head, and she said nothing more about what she might be afraid of. When they'd dated as teens, they used to ask each other questions like this all the time.

"I'm afraid I'm going to let someone down," he said as he sat back in the booth. His right arm ached, but not because he'd moved it, but because he hadn't in so long. It felt so stiff, and he just wanted to stretch it and rotate it and have it move the way it was supposed to.

"Mike," she said. "You never let anyone down."

He looked away from her then, the images in his mind not any he wanted to tell anyone about. "Everyone has expectations for me," he said.

"Like what?"

"My momma wants me to check in with her every half-hour," he said. "My daddy expects me to be the CEO at HMC. The military says I have to go to therapy for a certain number of sessions." He shrugged one shoulder, actually surprised that he'd brought up his counseling requirements.

Gerty didn't even blink strangely. "What expectations do you have for yourself?"

He hadn't been expecting that question, and he gave himself a moment to think about it. "In flight school, we were told over and over that everyone was relying on us. As a pilot, it was your job to keep your head in crazy situations. Keep your aircraft in the air. Keep the men on the ground safe. Keep your crew together."

She sat very still, listening.

Mike swallowed. "I didn't exactly do that. I didn't meet the expectations."

She shook her head then. "That's not true."

The scent of flesh, flames, and fuel filled his nose, though they weren't there in the Mexican restaurant. The phantoms of his accident followed him everywhere, even to Ivory Peaks, where he'd been hoping the beauty and good feelings he'd always had here would keep the demons at bay.

"I didn't keep my bird in the air," he said quietly. It didn't matter that his co-pilot had been shot and wounded. His men had all been on-board, all shouting, all clamoring for his attention.

"Do you want to tell me about it?" she asked. "It's not like we get reports on things like that from the US military."

He shook his head. "Another time." He painted a bright smile over the melancholy mood he'd brought. "Wow, sorry. I was just wondering if there's anything you're afraid of."

"Lots of things," she said casually. Far too casually for it to actually be casual. She brushed something off the table on her side and kept her eyes down.

"Not going to share?"

She looked up and right into his eyes. He found her stunning in absolutely every way, and he wondered what her expectations for him were. "I'm afraid I won't be able to be myself and manage to get married."

Mike didn't miss a beat as he said, "Oh, I think you're wrong about that, baby doll. I'm having a hard time staying on this side of the table, and you're being your beautiful, blunt self just fine."

A blush colored her face, and she couldn't hold his

gaze. He slid to the end of the booth and stood, feeling very much like a penguin with his arm glued to his body. She looked up in surprise as he came to her side of the booth.

"Well," he said. "Scoot over and make room for me. This is even my good side, and that means I can hold your hand while I tell you how wrong you are."

# CHAPTER
## Eight

GERTY FELT like she'd fallen down a rabbit hole and entered some fantasy dimension. Michael Hammond—the very handsome, strong, tough, and now she knew, rich, Michael Hammond—wanted to sit right next to her and hold her hand.

She slid over.

No woman in their right mind would tell him to get on back to his own side of the booth. She wasn't entirely comfortable sitting right next to him instead of across from him, because she'd never eaten like this with a man before.

He sat down beside her, squeezing in nice and close, his body heat kissing her bare arms and making her shiver. He did take her hand, and then he let out an exaggerated sigh. "Yeah, this is better."

Gerty loved his compliments. She loved hearing him say how much he liked her. She adored the crackling energy between them. She couldn't be imagining that, and as she turned and looked at Mike, she *knew* she wasn't. What existed between them could not be faked.

"I'm scared I'm going too fast," she said next. She wanted to swallow to get her voice to turn off, but even when she did, she had more to say. "With you. I want to get to know you all over again, but I want to kiss you right now. It's scary, because I also know I'm still in love with my ex-fiancé, and it's absolutely insane that I'm even on a date right now."

She did manage to stop talking then, but only because she ran out of air. Mike gazed down at her, his eyes moving between hers and her mouth. "I can't hold your face in both hands yet," he whispered. "So no kissing. Sorry."

She nudged him with her shoulder and ducked her head. "You're going to take that seriously, huh?"

"Yes," he said. "Because you want and need to go slow, and I want to be whole before that happens."

"What if I just lunged at you right now?" she asked, looking up at him again. A challenge rose through her. "You'd reject me?"

"Are you going to lunge at me? Because if so, I need to brace myself. I'm an *injured man*, Gerty. There should be no lunging." His dark eyes danced with a teasing quality, and Gerty reached up with her free hand and cradled his face.

He leaned into her touch, and she stroked her fingers down his strong jaw to his neck. "I won't lunge at you." She wasn't ready to kiss him, even if she'd been thinking about it a lot tonight.

"What was the name of your ex?" he asked.

"James," she murmured before she knew to censor herself.

"Terrible name," Mike said. "So biblical."

Her memory fired hard at her, and she burst out laughing. He'd once told her that his name was too biblical, and he hadn't liked it much growing up. As she quieted, she leaned further into his chest. "He wasn't biblical in how he acted, that's for sure."

"How long did you date him?"

"A year before we got engaged," Gerty said. Maybe having him sit on this side of the booth was better, because she could talk to him without looking at him. "We were engaged about six months before I called it off."

His fingers in hers tightened, then released. "And why'd you call it off?"

"I found out he was cheating on me," she whispered. "I was so humiliated, Mike. I can't even describe it. Even now, I'm embarrassed to tell people, as if it's my fault, you know?"

"I don't know, baby doll." He brushed his lips along her temple. "But I'm real sorry. I can't imagine why anyone would do that to another person, least of all you."

"You don't see me clearly," Gerty said.

"Of course I do," Mike said. He pulled away, but Gerty didn't want to look at him. "Gerty."

She reached for a chip instead of turning to face him.

"Gertrude."

That got her to look, and she glared at him. "I hate that name."

He leaned closer. So close, his forehead almost touched

hers. "I have always seen you clearly, and just because we're older now, with some history behind us, doesn't mean that's changed. Okay?" He spoke in his military voice, and it was low but oh-so-commanding.

Gerty found herself nodding, though she wanted to argue. "Okay," she whispered. She closed her eyes against the power in his. "You don't think I'm pathetic for getting cheated on?"

"Absolutely not," he said. "I don't see how that's your fault."

"He said I wasn't any fun." Gerty's eyes burned with tears, and she couldn't believe this was what she was talking about on her first date with Mike. "He said I worked too much."

"Then he didn't know you at all," Mike said, his breath washing softly across her cheek. He pressed his lips there. "You're one of the funnest people I know. Who figures out how to give their brother a job babysitting a dog, so he doesn't have to do any work? Someone who knows how to have fun."

He touched his mouth to her jaw, and Gerty pressed into him. Apparently, he only meant kissing on the lips wasn't happening until he could hold her face with two hands, and that only made Gerty want to kiss him solidly on the mouth all the more. "And anyone who knows you knows work is like play to you. You love it. I haven't even been around you for thirteen years, and I still know that."

His next kiss landed on the side of her neck. "Do not let this man fill your head with lies." The warmth of his mouth on her collarbone made Gerty weak in the knees. "Promise me, Gerty."

"I promise," she whispered.

"Good." He lifted his head, and Gerty's swam a little bit at how quickly he'd heated her up and then withdrawn.

"Have you two decided?" someone asked, and Gerty opened her eyes, trying to remember where she was. A Mexican restaurant probably wasn't the best place to have her boyfriend kiss her everywhere but on the mouth.

*Boyfriend?* screamed through her head.

She wouldn't let just anyone touch her the way Mike just had, but Gerty definitely couldn't have a *boyfriend* only a month after abandoning her wedding plans and breaking up with her fiancé.

Could she?

"I want the chile verde pork enchilada," he said. "I think she's gonna want the taco salad." Mike glanced over to her, no ruddy blush on his face at all. Gerty's felt like she'd just pressed her cheek against the surface of the sun. "Yeah, baby doll? Taco salad?"

She nodded, and he confirmed the order. "Oh, and we both want one of those citrus sunrise drinks. I want the ice cream in mine, but she won't."

"You got it," the waitress said, and she walked away.

Mike chuckled as he lifted his left arm around her. She sure did try hard not to immediately melt into him, but he made her feel like chocolate out in the sun. "Your face is on fire, sweetheart. Was it something I said or something I did?"

"I'm going to drive so crazy on the way home, you'll wish you'd been nicer to me tonight."

He laughed, the sound sexy and satisfying at the same time. "This is as nice as I get," he whispered. "But I'll behave myself now, okay?"

"That would be great," she said, because while she sure did like how Mike made her feel alive, and worthwhile, and sexy, and desirable, she didn't like feeling so out of control. She didn't like losing track of where she was, and most of all, she didn't like that he hadn't kissed her some-where that she could kiss him back.

────────

"COME ON," she said to Stella and Hodges, the gray horse plodding along but the palomino ignoring her completely. She whistled, and that got Denver to come with her. That meant the horse would too, and once they'd all started to follow her, the little girl Gerty had come to pick up from the counseling cottage would too.

Denver trotted up next to Gerty's boots, and she looked down at the golden retriever. "Go back by Kayla," she told the dog, and Denver did it.

Kayla adored animals, and it had been Gerty who'd realized that she needed the comforting presence of more than one horse during her sessions. Gerty had also seen how much she adored Denver, and now the ten-year-old never had a session without the dog with her. She didn't like talking to the counselors much, but Gerty had gotten her to go if the horses led her there and brought her back.

On the walk across the pasture, Gerty's thoughts traveled to Mike. His surgery was in only three more days, and the past two weeks had been some of the best of her life. She'd never imagined she'd find him here, or that he'd be interested in her again, or that their relationship would develop so quickly.

She'd always been able to be herself with him, and he'd kept that promise perfectly. He'd become her friend—her best friend—in a world where Gerty's only friends were family or had hooves.

She'd left everything and everyone behind in Montana, and she didn't make new friends extremely well in the first place.

Mike asked her on dates, and they'd been out a few more times since the Mexican restaurant. He'd never teased her with kisses the way he had then, and she wasn't sure if she should be glad about that or not.

"He's probably just behaving himself," she murmured to the dandelions that had already bloomed and gone to seed. "Right?"

They talked every day. Mike came and found her wherever she was around Pony Power, and she'd talked to Gray about using the generational house to make and serve lunch the way his father used to.

Unfortunately, Mike's parents were living in the generational house right now, so Gerty couldn't get in there to cook. She'd met them, of course. They knew Mike was seeing Gerty again, but she'd never been introduced to them as his girlfriend. She'd not done that for him and her parents, as she didn't feel like it was necessary.

"Look, Kay," she called over her shoulder. "Your mama is waiting by the car."

"Mama!" The girl started to run, and Denver kept pace alongside her. Kayla's mother grinned and wrapped her daughter in a hug as she arrived. She spoke to her, but Gerty was still far enough away not to be able to hear her. Her mom straightened and waved to Gerty, who waved back.

With that task done, Gerty turned toward the stables and barns. Her horseback riding lessons would be starting soon, and that meant she'd get to see Mike for a few minutes as he brought the horses to her that she'd be using that day.

Before she got to the barn, her daddy appeared. "Hey, Gerty-girl."

"Hey, Daddy." She grinned at him as he wrapped her in a big bear-hug. Her soul quieted, because she knew no matter what, her daddy would always love her.

"I need you to come look at this horse." He stepped back, most of his joviality gone. "Have you got a sec?"

"My lessons start in about twenty minutes," she said. "But yeah."

"He won't let me look at his right hoof."

"You?" If anyone was better with horses than Gerty, it was Daddy.

"Or Gloria."

"What?"

Gloria practically had equine blood in her veins. *And she still got married*, Gerty thought, not sure why that thought had popped so readily into her mind. She'd been trying to keep her promise to Mike to not let James's lies fill her head, but it was still hard. She still found herself chasing away negative thoughts almost every day.

She dwelt on the one she'd just had. It wasn't exactly negative, but it spoke to how Gerty felt about herself. Because she loved horses so much, she wouldn't be able to get married and love a man as much as them.

But Gloria loved and worked so well with horses, *and* she had married Uncle Matt and built a strong family unit with him. Gerty suddenly wanted to talk to her aunt about so much more than her tasks around Pony Power that day, and impatience built in her chest.

She told herself she had time, because she'd been at the Hammond Family Farm for three weeks, and she wasn't going to be getting engaged again any time soon, not even to Michael Hammond.

"Yeah, she's whinnying and side-stepping everyone," Daddy said. "I said maybe she's got something under her shoe, but she won't let anyone near her."

"Why do you think I can get close to her then?"

"Because you're good with stubborn horses," he said matter-of-factly.

Gerty wasn't so sure about that, but she followed Daddy down the aisle to a stall with only a half-high wall and door. Travis stood there, and he held a rope that had been attached to the bit in the horse's mouth.

"What's her name?" she asked.

"Beauty," Gloria said. "It's the back left leg, Gerty."

Gerty didn't enter the stall right away. Beauty's nostrils flared, and she possessed a wild look in her eyes. She put no weight on her back left leg, but Gerty couldn't see any gashes or wounds.

"All right," she said with as much courage as she could muster. "I weigh maybe one-ten soaking wet, so don't let me get killed in there, okay?"

"We've got her head up now," Travis said.

Gerty didn't like the audience, but she had no other choice. "Daddy, you have my tools?"

He handed her the bag of farrier tools without a single word. Gerty shouldered them and entered the stall. "Hey, there, Beauty." She held out the back of her hand for the horse to smell. She didn't but tried to toss her head.

Gerty took that moment to dart into the back corner, and she crouched down and put her bag on the ground. She didn't open it. She didn't make any noise at all.

"All right there," Travis said. "You're all right, Beauty."

Gerty still couldn't see any blood or issues. Beauty wore shoes that didn't look that old, which meant the nails had to be pulled out before the shoe could come off. She got out her pull-offs, and as the horse limped to the right, Gerty stood and grabbed the left leg. She twisted and lifted her leg over Beauty's, and then she had the horse's leg resting on her thigh—all in less than a second.

"Hold her still," she called, but Beauty didn't move at all. She knew this position, as she'd been shod plenty of times in the past. Gerty worked quickly, her curtain of blonde hair falling down on her right side, to remove the nails and get the shoe off.

Something didn't smell right, and the moment the shoe came off, Gerty knew what it was.

"Oh, boy," she said when she saw the mess underneath. "She's got a bad infection. An abscess about the size of a quarter. It needs to be drained."

"I'll get the supplies," Daddy said, and his bootsteps left in a hurry.

"You okay, Gerty?"

"Fine." Gerty had held much heavier horses, for a lot longer. Beauty didn't even move, but the moment Gerty drained the abscess, she would. "I'm going to check her hoof." Horses didn't just get infections for no reason.

"Her hoof is hot," she said. "We need a vet out here. I can drain the abscess, but I don't know if I should."

"I'm calling now," Gloria said.

Gerty didn't see any puncture wounds, which would be the biggest thing that would introduce an infection to a horse's hoof. She hadn't gone to vet school, but she knew to check for wounds or a hoof crack. Beauty didn't seem to have anything she could see.

"Got a kit," Daddy said.

"I can't do it," Gerty said. "It's too much."

"Gloria's callin' the vet," Mike said, and Gerty was surprised to hear his voice. He hadn't been standing out in the aisle when she'd come into the stall.

"Come on out then," Daddy said. "You don't have to hold her, Gerty."

"She's in a lot of pain," Gerty said. "But she doesn't seem to be if I hold her leg up like this."

"You're not standing there for the next hour until the vet comes." Daddy chuckled. "I know you would, but no. You have lessons in a few minutes."

"Can you guys give her something?"

"Gloria will when she's off the phone," Daddy said. "Come on, now, baby. Let her go and get out of there."

Gerty stroked her fingers softly down Beauty's leg. "Sorry, girl," she whispered to the horse, and then she released her leg and hoof.

She ducked out of the way, collected her bag, and hurried out of the stall to safety.

"Forty-five minutes," Gloria said with a sigh. "Thankfully, he's already out this way, or it would be longer."

"She needs antibiotics or a pain reliever now," Gerty said. "Then see if you can't get her to lie down until he comes." She handed her farrier tools to her father. "Can you take those, Daddy? I have to go get ready for lessons."

"Yep," he said.

"Thanks, Gerty," Gloria said. "Travis, hold her tight. I'm going to give her the pain meds."

"I got most of the horses out," Mike said. "Then I realized you weren't around, but Hodges and Stella were in the main pasture, snacking on all the good grass." He smiled at her as they left the others behind. "So I came to find you."

They reached the end of the aisle, and he put out his hand to pull open the door. "Wow, Gerty. Seein' you in that stall, in complete control of that horse? Mm, talk about sexy."

He opened the door and in a very ungentlemanly move, walked outside ahead of her. She stared after him, wondering if her ears had malfunctioned. The men she'd

been out with in her twenties had called her *beautiful.*
*Gorgeous. So pretty it hurts to look directly at you.*

She'd heard compliments on her clothes, on her work
performance, on her hair, eyes, or shoes.

No one had ever, *ever* called her sexy.

She knew she wasn't sexy. She barely had any curves at
all, and even then, only in her chest. She was too skinny
and too tall, and the combination of the two gave her the
figure of a twelve-year-old instead of a grown woman.

"Come on," Mike called over his shoulder. "You're
already late, and I'm not saddling these beasts with one
hand."

# CHAPTER
## *Nine*

MIKE TOOK a deep breath and looked at himself in the only bathroom in the generational house. His parents had left already, telling him to come around to the deck when he was ready. He didn't think he'd ever be ready to have the spotlight shined on him as intensely as it was about to be.

Uncle Gray and Aunt Elise wanted to have a big family party the night before his surgery, and who was he to tell them no? They'd invited everyone who worked on the farm or at Pony Power, and Mike knew everyone on the guest list.

Gerty and her family would be there. Her uncle Matt, who'd been running Uncle Gray's farm for decades now, would have his whole family with him, all of whom worked at Pony Power with Mike. He liked Keith a whole lot, and it was a good day when he got to be paired up with his best friend.

Hunter and his family would be at the party, of course. Travis and his. Cord, Mission, and Vince, who worked at Pony Power with Mike too.

Not only that, but Mike's brother had arrived that afternoon with his wife. Easton and Allison seemed to be made of shiny diamonds and stars, and Mike felt very dull compared to them. He was older than Easton by a couple of years, but he felt small in his brother's presence.

He'd taken his money at twenty-one and gone into pharmaceuticals. While Mike took college classes and attended flight school, Easton had been funding research on stem cells, forward-thinking cancer treatments, and more.

He'd met Allison in the laboratory, and their romance had been a whirlwind of intensity that had culminated in an engagement after only three weeks.

Mike had known Gerty since he was fourteen years old, and everything in his life seemed to be moving backward while Easton rocketed forward.

He sighed, said, "Don't compare yourself to him," the way his momma had said to him his whole life. The older brother was usually the one with all the popularity and amazingness, but somehow, God had skipped him and given all those traits to Easton.

He'd dated in high school too. He'd gotten decent grades. He wasn't a complete loser, but he wasn't Easton. He kept to himself while Easton would absolutely adore the party already happening on Uncle Gray's back deck and in the backyard.

"Mike."

He jumped at the sharp tone of his sister's voice. She rapped on the door in an equally harsh fashion, and then she opened it.

"Hey," he protested. "I could've been naked."

She looked down to his feet and back to his face. "You're not, and besides, I've seen far more naked bodies than I care to admit."

He scoffed and gave her a look he hoped conveyed his disgust. "Not mine." He reached up with his good hand to smooth his hair.

"You're just going to put on a hat." Opal took his arm as he lowered it and towed him out of the bathroom. "Come on. Everyone's waiting for you."

"Stop it." Mike pulled his arm away, his heartbeat moving too fast. Opal was twenty-six and in her final residency program before she could sit for the boards and be an official, licensed doctor. How he'd come to be in this family of brainiacs, he was still trying to figure out.

Opal looked a lot like Mike—plenty of dark hair, dark eyebrows, dark eyes. Right now, those eyes fired at him as she folded her arms. "You're stalling."

"Of course I am." He gave her another dirty look. "I don't want to go out there and have everyone stare at me. Ask me how I'm feeling. Offer to carry my blasted plate." He turned away from his sister. "You don't get this, but this is really hard for me."

"I get it," she said softly. "Momma's just worried about you."

Mike stared out the window beyond the dining table. He could see his cabin to the left, and he wondered what the fallout would be if he went that way instead of toward Uncle Gray's backyard.

Huge, that's what. He couldn't skip this, and he knew it. Part of him didn't even want to. Aunt Elise and Poppy Thatcher were excellent cooks, and the food would be delicious. Gerty would be there, and maybe he could just stick beside her and everything would be okay.

The thought calmed him, and he turned back to Opal. "Momma's always worried about me," he said. "No matter what I do, that's not going to change."

Opal nodded, and Mike, stepped over to her and engulfed her in a one-armed hug. "It's good to see you, sis. Thanks for coming here on your only week off."

She was doing her residency at a hospital in California, as she'd attended medical school at Stanford. Top of her class too. Her specialty was emergency medicine, and Opal had the cool head and swift hands to make quick decisions in an emergency situation.

She hugged him back, hard, and Mike didn't mind at all despite the twinge of pain in his shoulder. He ignored it, because he loved his sister with everything he had.

"I miss you," she whispered. "Maybe I worry about you too."

"You're too much like Momma," he whispered back. "I'm fine."

She pulled away and looked at him. Really looked. "No, you're not," she said. "I can see it in your eyes. There's pain there, and it's not all physical."

Mike dropped his gaze from hers. "I'm seeing a counselor here. I'm okay."

"Getting better, at least," she said.

"Yeah," he agreed. "We can't really expect more than that, can we?"

"No," she said thoughtfully. "Am I bad if I want more than that, though?"

He looked at her. "What do you mean?"

"I mean, I want you to feel as awesome as you are. Right now. And I can't do that for you, and it makes my heart hurt." Her voice broke on the last word, and Opal shook her head as her eyes grew watery. "It's fine. I know you're going to be fine." She gave him a shaky smile. "I wouldn't be anywhere but here right now."

"Thank you, Opal." His words barely had the oomph to leave his mouth, but he pushed them out and reached for her again. One moment into their hug, someone knocked lightly on the door.

They turned toward it together, and Opal swiped at her eyes. She was a strong woman, and Mike admired her on a lot of levels.

"I'm sure it's for you," she said. One sniffle, and she was calm and composed. Mike felt like his emotions had been put in a blender and someone had switched it to liquefy.

He went to answer the door as it opened. His gorgeous Gerty peered around the big, heavy, wooden door, apprehension in her gaze. "Mike?"

"Hey," he said, everything in his life brightening. "I'm coming. Just talking to Opal for a minute." He moved right into Gerty, who straightened as she entered the house and stepped around the door. He hugged her tightly too, taking a deep breath of her hair. "Mm, you're looking and smelling good tonight."

She held him tightly for only a moment, said, "Thank you," as she stepped back. She looked up to the top of his head. "No hat?"

"I've got one." He turned and walked over to the kitchen counter, where he'd set his hat earlier. He positioned it on his head and faced the women. "Yeah?'

"Totally a cowboy now," Opal said in a deadpan. "Introduce me to your girlfriend, Mikey."

He scrambled to do that while Opal approached Gerty. "This is Gerty Whettstein," he said. "You've met her. I brought her to Coral Canyon one summer for the Fourth of July."

"Yeah," Opal said. "I remember." She smiled at Gerty. "It's good to meet you again."

"You too," Gerty said, a smile also fixed to her face. They shook hands, very formal-like, and Mike wasn't sure what to do with the awkwardness.

She looked at him again, and Mike catalogued the color of her tank top tonight—a bright coral. She wore jeans—no surprise there—and cowgirl boots. Again, not a surprise. Tonight, she also wore a pair of earrings that didn't dangle, as she'd told him she hated feeling them bump against the side of her neck.

"I just came to see if you were coming." She tucked her hands into her front pockets, pushing her shoulders up. "Elise is ready to serve dinner, but they didn't want to start without you."

"I'm coming," he said. He indicated she should leave first. She did, and he nodded Opal after her.

His sister stayed put. "What?" he asked.

She grinned at him and placed one hand against his chest. "You're incredible, Mikey, really, but she is out of your league." She giggled a little and started to leave.

"At least I date," he said after her, which caused Opal to spin back to him.

"I date," she said.

He scoffed again. "Right. When? Who? That guy you went out with twice before he told you about his *other* girl-friend? Five years ago?"

Opal wore a murderous look on her face. "For your information, Mister Nosy, I've been seeing another doctor at the hospital."

His eyebrows went up. "Oh? What's his name?"

"Miles," she said without missing a beat, so maybe it was true. "I just haven't said anything to Momma and Daddy about him yet."

"Why not?"

Opal sighed, the fight leaving her body and face simultaneously. "Probably because he's a little older than me... and has two kids."

Mike's surprise couldn't have been more complete. "Wow, Opal. How old?"

"Six and three." She sighed and ran her hand through her hair. Her bangs sprang right back into place, some wisps sticking up on the side. "He's been divorced for two years, and he's.... Let's just say I don't want to shock Daddy into a heart attack. The man's eighty years old."

Mike grinned at her. "He's not the type of man you bring home. Opal, how *scandalous*." He put his arm around his younger sister, and they left the generational house together.

"Yeah," she muttered. "Kind of like you falling for the girl you loved as a teenager. Who does that?"

"Plenty of people," he said, keeping his voice low too. "And hush up. Gerty and I are going really slow right now, and she doesn't need to hear you saying things like I love her."

He didn't love her. Yet. He sure did like her though, and when he reached the bottom of the few steps leading from the porch, he dropped his arm from his sister's shoulders and took Gerty's hand in his.

"Ready?" he asked.

Her fingers tightened in the spaces between his. "Yeah," she said. "You?" She searched his face too, and Mike wondered what she saw. Did she know he hated this? Could she tell he felt like throwing up?

She tipped up onto her toes and whispered in his ear, "They're just people, right?" As she settled back to her feet, her eyes found his, and Mike could only stare into those gorgeous blue pools.

He'd told her that once when she'd been nervous about working with her very first group of kids taking horseback riding lessons from her, when she'd been sixteen years old.

"Yeah." His voice came out hoarse.

"And your people," Gerty said as Opal went ahead of them toward the backyard. "I was just there, Mike, and they all love you so much."

He managed to pull his gaze from Gerty's and watch Opal go around the trees separating them from the party. Laughter rang in the air, and Mike's urge to flee kicked up a notch. He said, "Yeah," again anyway, and then he took the first step toward the party.

"Don't get too far from me tonight, okay?" he asked.

"I won't," she assured him. "It's really going to be okay."

They went around the trees hand-in-hand, and he took in the three long tables that had been set up on the lawn. People had brought blankets and camp chairs too, and Cord worked by the fire pit, getting the flames nice and high and hot.

Mike swallowed as his mother's eyes found his, and she smiled. She'd always loved him for exactly who he was, his lack of medical and pharmaceutical knowledge notwithstanding. He couldn't disappoint her, and he'd do everything in his power to make her happy.

Daddy turned when she touched his arm, and though Mike's father was up there in age, he'd not missed a moment of his children's lives, Mike's included.

He left the table with all the desserts piled at one end, and that was saying something as Daddy loved sweets. Not as much as Uncle Colton, who'd made the trip from Coral Canyon to be at this party. Mike's other two uncles hadn't made the trip, and he didn't mind a bit. He loved Uncle Cy and Uncle Ames, and he knew they loved him, whether they were here at the party or not.

He released Gerty's hand to give his momma a hug, and she said, "You okay?" in his ear.

"Yes," he whispered back.

"All right," Daddy boomed into the crowd. "We're ready to start. Gray?"

Uncle Gray stood on the deck with his wife and a couple of other people, including Travis and Poppy Thatcher from next door. He smiled at Mike and his father, who put his arm around Mike's shoulders and looked at his brother.

"We have a couple of announcements," Uncle Gray said. "Then where's Cord?"

"Out here, sir," he called, and almost everyone turned toward the fire pit.

Gray waved at him to come in. "Cord's gonna pray for us."

Mike had twisted to look at Cord too, and he noticed Jane hovering close by the fire pit too. He turned to get his uncle's reaction to that, but Uncle Gray had no emotion on his face that Mike could discern.

He stood sandwiched between his parents, with Gerty next to his mother, as Uncle Gray said, "Boone has something to say."

Mike looked over to Gerty, who wore an expression of surprise. He raised his eyebrows, but she shook her head. "No idea," she murmured.

Boone climbed the wide steps to the deck and faced the crowd. "It's my daughter's birthday in a couple of weeks."

"He is not doing this," Gerty hissed.

But her daddy so was doing this, and he grinned straight at her. "She's turnin' thirty, which is a pretty big year, and we're gonna have a party for her at Pony Power.

Well, a lunch. Gerty's not much into parties, but she loves having a hot lunch every day."

Mike reached past his momma and brushed his hand along Gerty's. Momma shifted back and slid Gerty over so she stood next to Mike. He took her hand in his again, and she glanced at him.

"It's lunch," he whispered. "You love lunch."

Boone said, "July seventh, noon. Everyone is welcome." He nodded, clearly done, and came back down the steps. He stopped in front of Gerty and hugged her, and Mike let go of her hand so she could embrace him back.

Her father whispered a few things to her, and she nodded against his shoulder. The love between the two of them radiated from them, and Mike grinned at Boone as they separated. He nodded at Mike and went to join his family as Uncle Gray said, "And Easton has something to say."

His eyes flew back to the deck, his heart doing somersaults in his chest now. "Easton?" He looked over to his father. "What's Easton got to say?"

"I don't know." Daddy barely moved his mouth, and he narrowed his eyes at his second son. He glanced over to Momma, and so did Mike. She wore plenty of anxiety in her eyes as she shrugged.

Easton took center stage, his perfect Hammond features not marred by helicopter crashes and hard physical workouts. He was still tall and trim, without much body fat at all. He took his wife's hand and looked at her, his smile so contagious, Mike felt it filling his soul.

"Allison and I are going to be parents."

Momma sucked in a breath so hard it sounded painful. "She's due right about Thanksgiving." He looked out at the crowd, and because he didn't know everyone there and they didn't know him, the response was delayed.

In fact, it was Mike who whistled first, yelled, "Congrats!" and started clapping. That got everyone else to join in, and Momma rushed the deck. Daddy followed slower, leaving Mike to stand alone with Gerty, his chest turning more and more hollow with every congratulations offered to Easton and Allison.

His feelings made no sense, but Mike had been through enough in the past year to know that things didn't have to make sense for them to be real. He could feel pain in his leg sometimes, though it had healed completely. He could wake up in a cold sweat, the images in his head absolutely real but not there at all.

"Mikey," Gerty said, and he turned toward her. She tried to pull her hand away from his and couldn't. He realized then how he'd been crushing her fingers.

He quickly released them. "Sorry."

She wore questions in her eyes, but Mike didn't want to face them. He couldn't answer them anyway. He moved away from her, thinking he better say congrats quickly, before his throat would be so tight he wouldn't be able to.

His eyes met his brother's, and Easton simply emanated goodness and happiness. Mike wondered in that brief moment before Easton took him into a hug and laughed, if he could possibly ever feel the way his younger brother did.

Right now, it didn't feel like it. His world didn't exist past tomorrow, and even then, he knew he'd wake up with pain and a long road of recovery in front of him.

"Congratulations," he said to Easton.

"Thanks, bro." He lightly bopped Mike's left shoulder. "Surgery in the morning, right?"

"It's at two, actually," Mike said.

"Can you eat?" Allison asked, and she was a pretty blonde, the same as Gerty. In Mike's eyes, she wore too much makeup and tried too hard with curling irons and jewelry and fashion, but she adored Easton and he loved her, so that was all that mattered. Gerty was more his type, and he found her ten times as attractive as Allison.

"Until midnight," Mike said. "So let's get this party started."

"Yes," Uncle Gray said. "Let's do that. I think we've reheated the mac and cheese four times."

Mike looked over to him, their gazes locking. "I didn't mean—" Uncle Gray said.

"It's okay," Mike said. "It's my fault. I'm sorry."

Aunt Elise swooped in between them. "Don't you dare apologize," she said, wrapping an arm around him and making him feel safe. "I have told absolutely everyone not to help you with your food, okay? I know you won't like it."

She gave him a warm smile, and Mike did his best to return it. Something quivered inside his chest at how much she loved him, and he said, "Thank you, Aunt Elise."

"Oh, here's Gerty." She grinned at her and said, "He's all yours, honey," before turning back to the food.

"Quiet down," Uncle Gray yelled. "Cord, up here, son."

The man came up on the deck and stood next to Gray. He swept his cowboy hat off his head and held it in front of him with both hands. He gave the men in the crowd a moment to do the same, and Mike clumsily removed his hat. Gerty took it from him, and they exchanged a look. For some reason, when she helped him, he didn't mind.

Then Mike bowed his head and closed his eyes, trying to find a safe center inside himself.

"Lord," Cord prayed. "We are indeed grateful for Thy bounty in our lives. From the beauty of these mountains to the abundance we have here on the farm, we are thankful for it all. Bless this food and bless those who've prepared it with whatever they stand in need of."

He paused for a moment, and Mike had gotten to know him over the past few weeks at Pony Power. He was a good man, with plenty to say if someone got him talking about baseball or cattle, and Mike knew he wanted his own hobby farm, the same as this one he'd worked for fifteen years.

"Father," he said, his voice a touch higher. "We ask for Thy favor on Mike. He's goin' in for a big surgery tomorrow, and we don't want him to be afraid. Bless the doctors to have steady hands and knowledge in anything they might see or encounter. Bless his family and all of us, his friends, to feel comforted." Cord cleared his throat, and the only sound Mike could hear was the distant crackling of the fire.

He hadn't felt the Holy Spirit this strongly since he'd

talked to his daddy about joining the Marines and learning to fly helicopters. That had simply been right, and Mike had felt it with every ounce of his spirit.

"Bless all the Hammonds," Cord said next. "Amen."

"Amen," chorused through the crowd, but it wasn't as loud as Mike would've expected it to be. Someone nearby sniffled, and he glanced over to his mother, who stood with her arm wrapped around Aunt Elise's waist.

They both wept, and Cord turned to Uncle Gray and shook his hand. Gray pulled him into a hug and said something right in his ear. Cord nodded, and they separated.

He faced Mike and said, "Sorry, buddy."

"It's fine." Mike hugged him quickly. "Thank you, Cord. It was mighty fine to hear you pray for me."

Cord ducked his head and practically ran off the deck. Chatter picked up again as people came up onto the deck to get their dinners, which Mike had delayed by at least fifteen minutes.

He backed up, because he didn't want to go first and slow everyone down. Gerty leaned into him and whispered, "Mighty fine?" She giggled. "You keep that up, and you might just become a cowboy yet."

With that, she reached up and positioned his cowboy hat back on his head. Her eyes skated down to his, where they held. She exuded life, and if Mike had the use of both of his hands, he'd have taken his new first kiss with Gerty right then and there, all the onlookers notwithstanding.

Her eyes danced, and she grinned at him. Before he could unfreeze his thoughts enough to say or do something, she swept her mouth along his cheek in a quick yet sizzling kiss. "I know you don't want my help," she said. "But I could bring you some food if you wanted."

"All right," he said, deciding not to fight this. "You do that, and I'll attack the desserts for us."

"Good plan," she said. "Meet up in five?"

He eyed the line for the food. "Better make it ten."

# CHAPTER

*Ten*

WESLEY HAMMOND LOVED DRIVING his family somewhere in his truck. The mood today wasn't the same as when they'd done road trips as the kids grew up, that was for sure, but his heart only experienced joy as he looked in the rear-view mirror and found all three of his kids sitting on the back bench seat.

Mike sat behind Bree, his eyes out the window as the miles rolled by from the farm to the city hospital, where he'd have his shoulder replacement surgery today. Wes marveled at modern medicine, because it only took two hours for his son to get a brand-new shoulder.

He and Bree were taking Opal and Easton to lunch while Mike was under the knife, and his stomach growled. He'd been fasting since last night's dinner, simply to try to pull more of the Lord's favor onto his son.

Opal rode in the middle, the same way she always had as a girl. She looked out the windshield, her eyes coming up to meet his. He smiled at her, and Opal returned it. She was an interesting mix of him and Bree. She had the brains required to excel in medical school, but she knew how to laugh and have fun too.

She worried too much, like her mom, and she didn't hold anything back, like him.

"Anything new in California?" he asked her.

That drew Easton's attention from behind him, as he'd been looking at his phone. Probably a baby name website or something, as he and Allison had not stopped talking about names since their announcement last night. He looked from Opal to Wes, and Wes knew instantly there was something new.

"No," Opal said, delivering the fib without a flicker of an eyelash or any pitch in her voice.

Mike didn't look over from whatever held him captive out the window, and Wes cut a glance at Bree before looking back to the road.

"Whatever happened with Steven?" she asked, clearly picking up on what Wes had put down. He wasn't sure if Opal was dating someone new or not, but there was something afoot with her.

"Ugh, Steven." Opal rolled her eyes. "He moved to another hospital, thankfully. He made everyone so uncomfortable."

"I thought you went out with him," Bree said.

"No, Momma. I haven't been out with anyone in years." She folded her arms, and that was the key.

Wes grinned, because there was the lie. He'd expected it to be personal, because Opal didn't seem to have a filter when it came to co-workers and her job. She loved emergency medicine, and she was really, really good at it.

"Oh, you're a liar," he said with a chuckle.

"I am not, Daddy."

Bree twisted in her seat to look at her daughter. "What's his name?"

Opal pouted, her eyebrows drawn down. "It's very new, and I wasn't going to say anything."

"Miles," Mike said without looking at any of them. "His name is Miles, and he's a doctor on her floor."

"Mich-ael." Opal looked like she might hit her brother but pulled back at the very last moment. "He's not a doctor on my floor. We don't have floors. We work in the ER."

Mike said nothing, and that did not sit well with Wes. His concern for his son seemed never-ending these days, and he let Bree handle the news that Opal was dating again. Everyone knew it had been years, so this was big news.

His youngest dating.

His middle child about to be a father.

His oldest undergoing a life-changing surgery.

Wes had never been able to say his life was dull, that was for sure, even as old as he was. He didn't say a whole lot on the rest of the drive, letting Bree, Easton, and Opal fill the silence with their voices.

At the hospital, all five of them went in, and Mike checked himself in for the surgery. Wes had spent some time in the hospital over the years, and nothing ever happened quickly. But they came for his son too soon.

He wasn't ready to let him go. What if this surgery wasn't the answer?

He stuffed down his doubt and called on his faith. He grabbed Mike in a hug and whispered, "I love you, son."

That was all. He couldn't make promises that might not come true, and he simply wanted his son to know that he was lovable no matter what. Whether this surgery helped or it didn't. Whether he never got better or he was miraculously healed.

Easton and Opal hugged Mike, and then Bree clutched him tightly for a long, long moment. Finally, Mike said, "Momma, they're going to give my spot to someone else if you don't let me go."

The boy had never been much trouble in his life, even as a teenager. Wes had shipped him down to Gray's farm summer after summer, and Mike simply went. Even when he wasn't overly enthused about going, he went.

Gertrude Whettstein had been a big part of that, and Wes could admit that they sure did look good together now that they were older. He and Bree had held countless conversations about their oldest son and how he was easily overshadowed by Easton's shininess and Opal's strong personality.

Mike could be strong if he had to be. He did amazing things no one knew about, so he could shine too. He simply felt like he didn't always have to voice his opinion, and as long as he knew who he was and what he'd done, he was fine staying out of the spotlight.

He would've never made an announcement last night like Easton had, and he'd told Wes and Bree the very evening he'd returned from the fields with Gerty that he liked her and wanted to start dating her again.

Mike followed the two nurses who'd come to get him, and Wes reached for his wife's hand. She'd been crying a lot lately, and Wes sent up another silent prayer that this surgery would be the solution they'd been searching for and praying for.

The door closed behind them, and that was it. For a moment, Wes felt like weeping too. He didn't know any of these doctors. They'd only seen the shoulder specialist one time before scheduling this surgery.

*You felt good about it then*, he told himself. *Nothing's changed.*

"Let's go to lunch," he said, because he didn't want to stand there staring at an empty hallway, fighting off demons when he should be relying on his faith. He'd had to do that so many times in his life, and it had never ended badly for him.

He turned away from the hallway and put his free arm around Opal's shoulders. "Why'd you not want to tell us about Miles, honey?"

She sighed as the four of them headed for the exit. "He's got kids, Daddy, okay? I haven't met them yet. I told you, it's new. But he's got kids, and I wasn't sure how y'all would react to that."

Wes wasn't quite sure how to react to that. Bree asked, "How old are they?"

"Six and three," Opal said, and she sounded absolutely miserable. "I don't think you'll like him."

"Why wouldn't we like him?" Bree and Wes asked together.

"He's a decade older than me," Opal said. "He's finishing up his residency, because he got a late start on medical school. He's been in a drug rehab facility, and it was there that he decided to turn his life around and become a doctor."

Wes once again found himself unsure how to respond.

Praise the heavens for his wonderful wife, because she said, "It sounds like we'd absolutely love him, honey. A man who's turned his life around and is trying to do better every day? What's not to like?"

"He has tattoos."

"So does Uncle Cy," Wes said. "I don't care about that."

"Uncle Ames has tattoos too," Bree said.

"He's only been divorced for two years," Opal said next.

Wes looked at Bree as he opened her door for her. The kids started to get in the back while he had a silent conversation with his wife. He rounded the truck and got behind the wheel, getting the ignition going so the air conditioner would start to stave off some of the summer heat.

"Baby," he said to Opal, who now rode where Mike had been. "It sounds like you're trying to convince yourself that you like him, not us."

"I—" Opal set her jaw. "Maybe I'm unsure."

"Maybe you are," Wes said.

"Wes," Bree said quietly. He glanced at her, and then closed his mouth. He hadn't said anything wrong, but in situations like this, Opal needed the silence to think and absorb, process and then come to a conclusion. She always had, and he sometimes forgot.

He switched on the radio and turned the truck toward a restaurant he hadn't frequented in a long time: Salvadoro's. Mike could eat after the surgery, and he loved their chorizo and mushroom pizza.

Wes drove while the country music played. No one said anything, and he tried to listen to his gut. To the spirit of the Lord. He didn't feel the antsy, jittery feeling he sometimes did when things weren't right, and he looked over to Bree.

"He's going to be okay," he said quietly.

She nodded, her dark hair streaked with silver. She was as gorgeous as ever, and Wes thanked the Lord every night for his wife. "I think so too." She wrapped her hand around Wes's and smiled with a slightly shaky bottom lip. "He's going to need so much help, Wes. I don't know how we're going to go north with Gray and Elise next week."

Wes pressed his teeth together. He wasn't sure either. Opal would be gone by then. Easton was planning to stay for a couple of weeks, but part of that would be up in Coral Canyon with them.

Gray and Elise normally summered in the mountains in Wyoming, where Wes and Bree lived full-time. It was cooler, and they had their Fourth of July traditions up there.

"He'll come with us," Wes said.

Bree shook her head. "I don't think he will, baby."

Wes didn't think so either, and that was due to a beautiful blonde who'd always drawn Mike to Ivory Peaks.

"It's going to work out," he said. After living on this earth for eighty years, if there was one thing Wes knew, it was that things always worked out.

He didn't know how, or what would take place to allow him and Bree to drive away from their son only ten days after a major surgery, but he knew God had a plan. Wes trusted in that plan, even if he didn't know what it was, and he'd taught his children to do the same.

"I'm going to go out with Miles again when I get back," Opal announced, breaking into Wes's thoughts. "See how I feel then. Maybe it's just because…I don't know why I feel a little unsettled about him right now."

"Maybe it's still too new," Bree said, turning to give Opal a smile.

"Maybe." Opal frowned at her phone and said, "Daddy, you missed the turn for Salvadoro's. Now you're going to have to go all the way down to Thirteenth, because this next street is a one-way."

Wes nearly rolled his eyes at her backseat driving advice, but he caught himself. "Yes, ma'am," he said. "Sorry, I was thinkin' about something else."

# CHAPTER
## Eleven

JANE HAMMOND GOT up from the sewing machine. "I can't sit inside anymore," she said to her mother.

Aunt Annie looked up from the table, where she'd been ironing. "Are you going to go horseback riding?"

"Yes." Jane decided on the spot, but neither of the other women in the farmhouse needed to know that.

Her mom looked up at her, her needle slowing. "Get someone to help you with the tack, Jane. Last time, you nearly separated your shoulder trying to lift it onto the horse's back."

"I will," Jane said. A pinch of guilt nagged at her stomach. She had not been an easy teenager for her parents to raise, and she'd fought with her mother a lot. Her father too. She'd found them out-of-touch with young people and old-fashioned in their rules. She'd hated leaving Ivory Peaks every summer, as she'd had to start over in friendships many times because of it.

Now, she leaned down and kissed her mother's cheek. "Love you, Momma."

"Love you too, sweetie." The sound of the sewing machine accompanied Jane as she left the main room at the back of the house and headed for the front door.

Worry gnawed at her, and she wanted to run until she couldn't breathe anymore and then scream into the sky. She and Mikey had been close to the same age growing up, and he'd been a calming influence on her many times.

Even now, Jane felt like she ran so hot, everything either annoying her to the point of snapping or so wonderful she was almost crying. Honestly, she felt like she needed medication, but she didn't even know who to go see to find out why she was the way she was.

One of her younger brothers, Tucker, had been diagnosed with ADHD as a kid, and once her parents had gotten him on the right medication, he'd excelled at everything. Right now, he was touring with the biggest name in rodeo, doing an apprenticeship with the manager so he could learn how to manage a champion's schedule, their animals, their travel, all of it.

He loved the rodeo, but he'd never been good enough to compete in it. Deacon was almost the opposite of Tucker, in that he wanted a simple life, right there on the farm where he'd grown up.

Jane knew Hunter would retire from HMC as soon as he could, and that Mike would take over as soon as he was well enough. After that, Deacon would run the farm for Daddy, and all the shifting of positions left Jane's stomach sour.

"Why though?" she asked herself.

The answer came to her as she reached the end of the fence and turned right. She had nowhere to belong. As the only girl, she'd always felt a little bit like she was on the outside looking in in her family, and she'd never wanted to be a cowgirl. The small-town life didn't bother her, but it didn't feed her soul either.

Jane wanted excitement. She wanted the freedom to twirl under the blue sky, laughing until she was so dizzy she fell down. Then she'd laugh some more, and a strong, handsome cowboy would gather her close and whisper how much he loved her.

She wanted romanticism, and larger-than-life birthdays and holidays. She wanted someone to think she walked on water and treat her that way, and she wanted to fall in love with someone so deep that she'd never get out.

Her mother had often told her such things only existed in fiction, but Jane wanted them in her real life.

She'd dated a couple of men in college, but she'd never had a boyfriend in high school. She went to dances, and she'd even kissed Ryan Wellington after a football game once. He hadn't called her back and never asked her out again, and that was not the type of romance Jane wanted.

A sigh gathered and gathered in her chest, but Jane refused to let it out. She wasn't going to be one of those women who sighed their way through life because it wasn't going her way.

She'd hated her job in Colorado Springs, so she'd quit. She'd come home. She'd started at HMC a couple of weeks ago. She actually liked it there, and people in the accounting department liked her.

One of the receptionists had even said, "I've never met an accountant with a sense of humor, Jane. It's refreshing."

The problem was, Jane felt everything to the extreme. Happiness. Sadness. Worry. Guilt. Fear.

Right now, she just wanted to know Mike was going to be okay. She'd tried to go over to the hospital, but her daddy had said that Uncle Wes didn't want the whole family there. When Jane had tried arguing, he'd said, "It's not actually Uncle Wes, Jane," in that perfectly even tone that drove her bananas. "It's Mike. He doesn't want us all there, okay?"

That had shut her down, because Daddy was probably right. Mike would be mortified to see a dozen Hammonds sitting in the waiting room when he came out of surgery. He wouldn't even want them to come visit him once he came home. With his siblings here, he was probably over-loaded already.

Jane loved Opal with her whole soul, but the woman had only gotten more intense as she'd gotten older. And Mike felt overshadowed by Easton in every way, so he tended to withdraw even more.

She entered the stable, the whoosh of air around her ankles bringing with it the tell-tale scent of horses. Jane did love horses. They just didn't always love her. She didn't trust them as much as she'd like, and she'd never worked at Pony Power the way Mike and her brothers had. She'd slung burgers like most high schoolers, and she'd been perfectly happy doing so.

It helped that Liam Newcomb had worked at the fast food joint too, because he'd been oh-so-dreamy.

No one seemed to be working this afternoon, and Jane got down the tack herself. She struggled under the weight of it, but she managed to get it in the stall with Hershey, a horse she'd ridden before.

"Shoot." She remembered she didn't saddle the horse in the stall, and she left everything on the floor and led the pretty bay horse outside to a fence. She threw the rope around it, half-thinking Hershey would wander off.

Jane even checked over her shoulder before dashing back into the stable again. This kind of work kept her mind off Mike in a way the sewing machine never could. She'd learned to cook, clean, can vegetables and fruits, and sew from her mother. She did love spending time with her, but Jane wasn't all that interested in a domestic life.

She wanted housekeepers and personal chefs, and she'd even used some of her two-billion-dollar inheritance to fund a female-owned company called She Cooks. The three women who owned it trained personal chefs and placed them in homes in the greater Denver area.

Jane sat on their board when they had meetings, and she loved that she'd been able to help another woman's dreams come true. She'd decided that she didn't need to start her own foundation or company to do good in the world. She knew Hunter found small businesses or floundering businesses or businesses that weren't even businesses yet, and helped them financially through Hammond Manufacturing Company.

She was doing the same with her own money, because

she didn't have the genius ideas others did. But she could fund them and make those dreams a reality.

Relief sang through Jane when she found Hershey still standing at the fence where she'd left her. She started to saddle the horse, but it had been a while since she'd done it, and she couldn't quite remember if she'd done all the steps.

She stood back and looked at her work, the heat of the afternoon making her forehead sweaty. She didn't wear a cowgirl hat, and she was probably burnt already.

"Stay there," she said to Hershey as if the horse were a dog. "I need a hat." They kept extras in the stables for the kids who came to ride, and Jane intended to get one of those.

Instead, she spun and ran straight into a very solid chest.

"Whoa," a voice said, and oh, she knew that voice. It rumbled in her head, her eardrums, her throat, her chest, her stomach, and then her heart.

Cord Behr.

The man had been the fantasy of Jane's childhood. Just because almost fourteen years had gone by since she'd gotten herself and him into a heap of trouble in the family shed, didn't mean that had changed.

She still had a mega-crush on the man, and as he put his hands on her elbows to prevent her from falling down, stars shot through her veins. She blinked, and she got stars set against black plaid.

He backed up a step, but he kept his hold on her. "You okay? You're not going to fall down?"

"I'm okay."

Only then did he pull his hands away, and Jane didn't like that at all. She looked up at him, his dark blue eyes almost black in the shadow of his cowboy hat. He gave her that lopsided smile that she wanted to kiss so badly. She wanted to know if her straight lips would fit against his slightly crooked ones, and she was willing to bet the rest of her inheritance that they would just fine.

So, so fine.

"Howdy, Miss Jane." He tipped his hat at her. "You goin' riding?"

"I was hoping to," she said. "I just needed a hat."

"It's real hot today." He nodded like getting a hat was a good idea.

She wanted to reach out to him and run her fingers up his forearm and suggest he come riding with her. He wouldn't, though, as he was at work, and she'd only get rejected. Painfully.

Besides, she knew now not to play her cards so openly. She could flirt in more subtle ways. "Are you almost done with work?" she asked.

"Yeah, almost." The work never really ended on a farm, but neither of them said that. "Keith and I are gonna head in to see Mike when we're done."

Jane's interest piqued. "You are? My daddy wouldn't let me go."

Cord reached up and rubbed the back of his neck. Though he was almost forty years old, it was absolutely adorable. "Keith said Mike might not let us in, but that we ought to try. The thought counting and all that."

Jane wanted to invite herself along, but she didn't. "I'm sure my uncle will text how he's doing soon," she said. "He should almost be done." She started to move past Cord, because she wasn't sure how much longer she could suppress her flirting.

She went into the stable to get a hat, and it took her several tries to find one big enough for her head. They were for the kids who rode, after all.

Outside, she found Cord standing next to Hershey, adjusting the strap on her saddle. "Did I do it wrong?"

"Just a little," he said over his shoulder. He moved away from the horse as Jane approached, a grin forming on his face. "Nice hat."

She put one hand on top of it and stuck out one hip. "Right? I'm like, totally ready to ride now."

Cord swept his gaze down her body and back to hers. If she wasn't mistaken, pure heat lived in those gorgeous eyes, and the breath left Jane's body.

"I'd love to see you get in the saddle," he said, his voice sounding rusty and overused.

Jane looked down at herself—and that was when she realized she wore a skirt. She jerked her head up again, her eyes wide. Cord simply looked back at her, and she had not been mistaken.

The man looked at her with pure interest in his eyes, and Jane couldn't help opening the box where she'd stored the fantasy of him and her together...and letting it bloom right back to life.

# CHAPTER
## *Twelve*

"WELL, DON'T JUST STAND THERE," Jane said, her voice more vibrant now. "Go get me a stool so I can get on Hershey."

Cord Behr had plenty of other things he should be doing. But he dipped his head, wondering how much of the electricity arcing through his bloodstream Jane had been able to feel. "Yes, ma'am."

"Do not call me ma'am," she barked at him, and he simply scurried for the stables. This woman was off-limits, and she always had been. He hadn't been interested in her when she was younger, but he'd been a big flirt. In most regards, he still was.

He'd gone out with a woman here and there over the years, but he'd wanted to focus on becoming the man he wanted to be. He'd lived here on the Hammond Family Farm for just over fourteen years now, and he loved Gray Hammond like a father.

"And she's his daughter," he muttered to himself as he picked up the stool she needed. "Keep your cool. Do *not* flirt with her again."

He couldn't help it if her skirt made him smile. It wasn't tight at all, but it did end at her knees, with plenty of swaying fabric he'd perhaps admired as she'd gone into the stable to get her hat. That was a hideous thing that didn't match her blouse or skirt or ankle boots, but somehow, the mismatch was totally Jane.

"Here you go, Miss Jane," he said when he arrived back outside. He positioned the stool for her, and she put her hand on his shoulder to boost herself up.

"Like this?" she asked.

"When's the last time you rode a horse?"

"It's been a while," she said.

"And you're going to go out on your own?"

"My mother knows I'm going," she said, plenty of venom in her voice. "Why does everyone act like everything I do is wrong?" She pushed off with the wrong foot, but he kept his mouth shut, and that meant she put far too much pressure on his shoulder.

He grunted, held his position, and couldn't help seeing a little too much leg as Jane flopped herself into the saddle. She quickly pulled the dark blue fabric over her thighs, her face nearly the color of a ripe tomato.

"There."

There indeed. Cord wanted to ask her out, and he hadn't felt like that about anyone in...ever. He'd *never* felt like that about a woman. The few he'd been out with had come about because someone had set them up, or the woman had asked him or suggested they go out, and he'd flirted on back and taken her to dinner.

But Jane Hammond—yes, he wanted to ask her out. He crowded into the horse, pretending to check the reins, and looked up at her. "I think maybe someone should come with you."

"I'll be fine. Hershey won't get lost."

Cord moved back and said, "All right," just as Keith said, "Hey, there you are."

He bent to get the stool and round the horse. "Hey, you done?"

"All done." He looked at Jane sitting on the bay. "Hey, Jane." He grinned at her. "Where you goin'?"

"Just around," she said. "I needed to get out of the house until I hear about Mikey."

Keith sobered, but Cord couldn't look away from Jane. Her nearly white-blonde hair spilled down her back and over her shoulders, making her angelic as she hovered above them on the horse. She had blue, blue eyes, almost like she hadn't come from her daddy at all. Her two brothers had gotten more of him than she had, and Tucker came outside at that moment too.

"Oh, you're going riding? Can I come with you?"

Jane flicked her gaze over to Cord's for a brief moment. He knew she'd been avoiding him for the past few weeks since she'd returned to Ivory Peaks. She claimed she wasn't staying on the farm for long, that she just needed time to find an apartment in the city.

He wasn't sure how hard she was looking, though, because she left the farm every weekday to work at the

Hammond family company, and Cord hadn't seen her for longer than a few minutes at the big party they'd had in the backyard last night.

"I guess," Jane said. "But I just want it to be quiet, Tuck."

"Fine by me," he said. "You're the one who talks too much."

"I do not talk too much." Jane looked at Cord again, and he only smiled at her.

Tucker left to get his horse, and Cord stood there, utterly transfixed by Jane. The connection between them felt like it was made of steel, and it wasn't until Keith stepped right in front of him and said, "I'll help you finish up so we can get going," that Cord realized time had slipped away from him.

"Yeah," he said, the tether between him and Jane broken now. He and Keith left her sitting on Hershey so they could go get the pasture combed, because Gloria didn't like it looking like horses lived there.

"So," Keith said, not casually at all. "You like Jane Hammond?"

"No, sir," Cord said automatically. "I just came out of the stables to head over here, and she'd saddled that horse completely wrong. I fixed that, and then she couldn't get on her. So I got the stool. Just helping her."

"Right." Keith really drew the word out. "You know, I've thought about asking her out." He looked back toward the stables, but Cord would not allow himself to do that.

"Great," he said, the word sticking in his throat. "You should do that. You're not related."

"Neither are you."

Cord looked up and found Keith watching him. He stared right at him. "I'm not interested in Jane Hammond."

Keith looked slightly taken aback, and Cord pressed down on his attitude. His parole had ended eight years ago, and he hadn't spoken to anyone from his former life since coming here, including his parents. Sometimes, the version of Cord who'd lived a much harder life than this one emerged, and he tamped him back into submission.

"All right," Keith said, and the two of them got back to work. "It just sure looked like the two of you had something going on, that's all."

"We don't," Cord muttered. He kept his head down and got the job done, the same way he'd been doing for years now. He did glance over to the stables a couple of times, feigning the need to wipe his face with his handkerchief, as the temperatures had reached a high so far this summer. But he never saw Jane or Tucker return.

He told himself it wasn't his business, and he agreed to be at Keith's in thirty minutes so they could make the long drive into the city to see their friend. Then he got in the shower, his mind still stuck on the blonde-haired beauty he'd never let himself think about...until now.

———

CORD LAUGHED with Keith as they walked into the hospital, glad the intensity from earlier had disappeared. He'd decided he'd simply be more careful whenever he was around Jane, if he ever got himself into that situation again.

The last thing he needed was to alert Gray to his little, maybe-attraction to his daughter.

He and Keith took the elevator to the second floor, and the moment they rounded the corner, Cord's heart sank into his stomach. Gray himself sat there, looking like the cowboy billionaire he was in a clean pair of jeans, a dark purple polo, cowboy boots, and a deep, dark black cowboy hat.

He didn't look up first, but his brother, Colton did. "Hey, guys." Colton got to his feet, his smile genuine. Out of all the Hammond brothers, Cord found Colton the most happy-go-lucky. He always had a smile and a quick laugh, and the man knew more jokes than anyone else on the planet.

Wes had always been warm and welcoming, and he was no different now, while waiting on a couch for his son. "Fellas." He groaned as he got to his feet. "My wife and the kids are back there with him now. We'll see what he says when they come back out."

"If we can't see him, it's okay," Keith said. He shook Wes's hand, and Cord followed suit. Gray didn't get up from the couch, but his smile felt kind enough. He'd been exceptionally kind to Cord over the years.

He nodded to his boss, his mentor, his friend, his father-figure. "Sir."

"How'd things go with the new horses?" he asked.

"Good enough," Cord said, words he'd said many times

in the past. He'd learned that Gray didn't need details unless things were really, really bad. Anything else went through Matt, and he would deliver any news to Gray. "She'll fit in with the other horses as soon as Gloria gets her settled."

"Great," Gray said. "Keith, how's your daddy?"

"Getting better," Keith said. He sighed as he sat in a chair kitty-corner from the couch. "It was so hot today, and I think it's getting to me."

Gray reached over and patted his leg. "Get Gloria to keep you inside tomorrow."

"Yeah, sure," Keith said dryly. "My stepmom gives me special treatment. I'm sure she'll do that."

Cord smiled as he sat down opposite of Keith. "No one has ever thought she gives you special treatment."

"Good." Keith leaned his head back and closed his eyes. "Because she doesn't, and today was proof."

Cord met Wes's eyes. "You guys didn't have to come. It's a long drive."

"I feel great," Cord said, fighting a yawn. He failed, and that caused all the men on the couch to laugh, Gray included. Cord chuckled with them, adding, "I'm fine. Really. I've had way less sleep in the past."

"Yeah?" Colton asked. "When?"

"When I was studying for my mechanic certificate," he said. He never wanted to do that again. He wouldn't have been able to do the assignments, the tests, any of it without Travis. The man had sat with him at night, reading the required texts with Cord and helping him study. Book work had never been Cord's strong suit.

He'd earned his certificate, though, and he worked on all the machinery around the farm.

"That was tough," Gray agreed. He gave Cord a fatherly smile. "But you passed and earned that."

"And then I slept for a week." Cord chuckled. "I have tomorrow off, so I'll be fine."

"You'll be out in the maintenance shed," Gray said. "No doubt."

"I just have a little filing to do," Cord said. The Hammond brothers smiled knowingly, and Cord didn't want to argue with them. He lived alone, and the cabin didn't exactly hold a lot of allure for him. He'd lived in the same small place for years, and Poppy, Travis's wife, had sewn him curtains.

When the walls had needed to be repainted, Gray had organized everyone on the farm and they'd done the whole cabin in a couple of hours. He'd gotten new carpet in his bedroom last year, and the place always had hot water, kept the wind and snow out, and welcomed him home.

But he could only watch so much TV and sleep so late on his days off. It wasn't a crime to go out to the maintenance shed and putter around.

Keith wasn't doing Cord any favors by taking a catnap, as he wasn't super gifted with small talk. Thankfully, Colton was in the room, and he kept his brothers—and Cord—entertained.

Several minutes later, Bree, Easton, and Opal exited through the double-wide wooden door, and they all looked like they'd been crying.

"Cord," Opal said.

"Yes, ma'am." He got to his feet, thinking she likely had something she wanted him to go do.

She gave him a bright smile. "Mike was talking about you. It's great to meet you."

"Oh." He shook her hand. "You too."

"Do you think we can go back?" Cord asked. "Or is he too tired?"

"You probably have a few minutes," Bree said. "They're bringing him dinner, and then when the doctor comes around again, they'll probably start the physical therapy."

"Yeah?" Wes asked.

Colton got up to give Bree his spot on the couch, and she took it. Keith tapped Cord on the shoulder, nodding with his head toward the door. Cord turned to go with him, nearly ramming into a woman for the second time that day.

To be fair, Jane had slammed into him, because he'd snuck up on her. He'd been watching her saddle that horse incorrectly, finding it adorable and cute enough to stay silent.

*No*, he told himself. *You do not find her adorable and cute.* Those weren't the right adjectives for Jane. Beautiful. Smart. Talented. He'd choose any of those any day of the week.

*Which is why she'll never want to be with you*, he thought as he sidestepped Opal. "Sorry," he muttered. "Excuse me." He followed Keith, and together they went through the door and down the hall to Mike's room.

Cord pushed on the partially open door, and it swung inward. Mike lay in the bed, his eyes closed, and part of Cord wanted to leave. Then Mike opened his eyes, saw them, and grinned. "Hey, guys."

"Mike," Keith said. He moved over to the bed first, and Cord hung back. "Wow, look at you. No sling."

Mike didn't move his arm or shoulder at all. An ice pack had been formed over his shoulder and upper arm. "For right now. The physical therapist is coming in a few minutes, so the nurses took it off."

He looked exhausted, and Cord had never had surgery and couldn't even imagine what Mike was going through. "You have to start physical therapy right away?"

"Yeah." Mike sighed. "They don't give you a moment to breathe at all." He tried another smile, but he wasn't very happy.

"Are you in less pain, at least?" Keith asked.

"Well, everything is numb right now," Mike said. "So I feel great."

"Dinner's here," a woman chirped, and Cord pressed himself against the wall as she brought in a tray that seemed twice as big as her. She set it on the shelf and wheeled it in front of Mike. "Doctor Stone is on the floor, and if you don't finish before he gets here, you can finish after."

"Okay." Mike tried to sit up, and Cord lunged forward to grab the remote to get the bed to support him.

"Once the doctor goes, we'll get you walking around the floor."

"Sure," Mike said as if he was super-jazzed to take a walk around this hospital floor.

"We'll go," Keith said. "We just wanted to see you."

"You don't have to go," the nurse said. "Mike might want you to when the physical therapist comes, because there's usually a lot of cursing when that happens."

"Mike?" Keith asked, chuckling. "I don't think I've ever heard him say a bad word."

"I've said them," Mike said. "Things didn't always go perfectly in the cockpit." He picked up his roll with one hand and slowly moved his right hand to pick up a knife.

"Look at you," Cord said. "Using two hands."

"It's hard," Mike admitted. It looked hard, and Cord wanted to jump in and help him. That was the last thing Mike wanted, so Cord stayed against the wall and watched him struggle.

Keith had found his voice after his mini-nap, and he told Mike all about the new horse that had arrived that day. Cord was content to stay quiet, and then Keith said, "We ran into Jane this afternoon. She's worried about you, but Cord—"

Then their eyes met, and Keith covered it up with, "Cord helped her saddle her horse so she could take a ride to clear her head."

"I've called her," Mike said. Thankfully, he hadn't seen the exchange between Cord and Keith, and Cord's jaw clenched. He was suddenly grateful Jane had stayed away from him, because that had made everything easier for both of them.

*Lord*, he prayed. *Bless me to make the right decisions.*

He wasn't sure what those were right now, but he wanted to stay at the Hammond Family Farm, and he wasn't willing to jeopardize that.

*Not even for Jane?*

The question rang in his head, and he had no idea where it had come from. He reminded himself he barely knew her, so no. He wasn't willing to jeopardize his place on the farm—and with Gray—for a woman he barely knew.

Maybe if he got to know her better….

# CHAPTER
## *Thirteen*

GERTY BUSTLED around Mike's cabin, spraying the countertop with cleaner and wiping it until it shone. The turkey pot pies he'd requested for his welcome-home meal baked in the oven, and she wanted everything to be perfect for him the moment he walked through the door.

He'd texted a little over an hour ago that he was on his way down to the parking lot, so he should be home at any time. She wasn't sure if he'd get delayed over at the farmhouse, but that was likely.

Everyone at the farm had been into the city to visit him, herself included. She'd gone the first night and again the next morning. She hadn't seen him yet today, but it wasn't even noon yet. She'd been up since dawn, getting her work done at Pony Power so she could have a few hours with him before her riding lessons.

"Okay." She drew in a deep breath. "What next?"

He'd told her about his physical therapy. How he

needed to ice his shoulder. How much he still had to wear the sling. His meds had worn off after twenty-four hours, and he'd been in quite a bit of pain then. He hadn't wanted to take too much, but he couldn't do the exercises without the medication, and if he didn't do the exercises, his new shoulder would never get out of the sling.

Gerty had seen the pain in his eyes, and she had not liked it. Not one bit.

"Lemonade." She mixed that up and put the pitcher in his fridge. She'd vacuumed the rug in his living room, brought in a new blanket—one of her favorites—a heating pad, and the ice packs her mother had researched for her.

Karo syrup in a zipper bag, she'd insisted. It froze easily, but it stayed flexible and slushy, so Gerty would be able to form it to Mike's shoulder straight from the freezer.

She'd spoken to his parents, and they had plans to leave town in a week. Gerty had assured them she could take care of Mike. There had been some discussion of having someone move in with him, and it had been Gerty who'd finally said, "No. He won't like it, and just no."

They'd all looked at her with wide eyes. His father and mother. His uncles and their wives. His brother and his wife. His sister.

Finally, Opal recovered and said, "I agree with Gerty. Mikey's thirty-one years old. He has a phone. He lives literally three minutes away from this house, and there are tons of people on this farm, including Gerty. He doesn't need anyone living with him."

Together, the two of them had convinced everyone else, and Gerty had asked to move into one of the empty cabins here on the farm, just to be closer to Mike should he need help.

Gray had said, "I'll do you one better. Wes and Bree are leaving. You can have the generational house."

She'd only been able to stare at him while he'd chuckled. "Then you can have your lunches there too."

So Gerty was packing up her stuff again, and she'd move in once Mike's parents went back to Coral Canyon. She fully expected them to come visit their son as often as they could, but Gray said he and Elise had no plans to return to Ivory Peaks until September. So Wes and Bree could stay in the main house.

Molly and the kids sometimes stayed there too, while Hunter worked in the city, and Gerty had learned that the housing conditions here on the farm were a touch more fluid than she'd prefer. She wouldn't want anyone living in her house while she was out of town, but Gray and Elise didn't seem to mind at all.

Gerty brushed something that didn't exist off the counter and wondered if she had time to put together a salad to go with the pot pies. She'd brought a truckload of groceries with her, and she could definitely throw something together quickly.

The front door opened, and Gerty turned away from the fridge. "I can open my own door, Momma." Mike did not sound happy, and Gerty curled her fingers around one another.

"I know," she said. "I just wasn't sure if it was locked."

"Why would it be locked?" He entered the cabin at a normal stride, his right arm in its sling. It was a navy blue, and it wasn't as bulky as the one he'd worn before the surgery.

She smiled at him as their eyes met, and he softened. "Welcome home," she said.

"It smells good in here," he said.

"I made lunch." She watched as his mother gave her a smile and left the cabin. She closed the door gently behind her, and Gerty couldn't help wondering if Mike could remove that sling and kiss her while holding her face in both of his hands.

"You are my favorite person on this farm," he whispered as he closed the last step to her. He sure looked and acted like he was going to kiss her right now, and she put one palm against his chest.

"Whoa, what is happening here?"

"You make turkey pot pie," he said. "Cleaned my cabin." He slid his hand along her waist. "Brought me a new blanket. Got rid of my momma." He swayed with her, bringing her close to him. "I'm going to kiss you."

"Mm, I don't think so, cowboy." She ducked her head and played with the collar on his shirt. "You set the rules, and now you have to live by them." She couldn't stop smiling, especially when he started to chuckle.

The timer on her pot pies sounded, and while she didn't want to step out of the circle of his arms, she also didn't want to burn their lunch. "Hold that thought," she said.

She turned to get the pot pies out of the oven, and she slid the tray onto the stovetop. "I didn't make a salad, but I can, if you want me to."

"I don't think I've ever asked for a salad," he said. "I mean, if it's there, I might eat it, but it's fine."

"All right." She turned around and found Mike draping his sling over the counter. Alarm pulled through her. "Hey, hey. Can you take that off?"

"Sure," he said easily. "I need to do my therapy." He started to lift his right arm. "I have to make sure I use it sometimes, but it does need to be in the sling to heal too." His arm went all the way up, and then he lowered it out to the side. He lowered it to his side, puffing out his breath like the motion hurt.

"Mike," she said.

"I'm fine."

"Your face is turning a little red."

"That's because you're so pretty." He smiled, but it didn't quite cut through the pain.

"Mike."

He stepped closer to her, using both hands as he took hers in his. They didn't stay there, but drifted up her arms to her shoulders, then her face. "You are really pretty," he whispered.

Gerty's world swayed, because there was no barrier keeping them apart anymore. Her eyes drifted closed as Mike drew closer, and the anticipation of having his lips against hers again nearly overwhelmed her.

His hands radiated heat, and she was just about to open her eyes to see what was taking him so long when his breath whispered against her lips. Then his touched hers in a gentle, kind kiss.

She pulled in a breath, and Mike changed the kiss into

something beyond soft. He *kissed* her, and Gerty had never been kissed with as much passion and feeling as Mike poured into his touch.

She did her best to hold on and keep up, because her cinnamon roll of a wanna-be cowboy had just turned into the military alpha hero she imagined he'd been when he'd gone down in his helicopter, injuring himself in such a way that had prevented him from kissing her like this for so long.

———

A FEW DAYS LATER, Gerty sat in a swing with Mike, her feet curled beneath her as her cowgirl boots lay on the front porch. Her riding lessons had just ended, and because his parents were leaving in the morning, they were having a family dinner at the generational house that evening.

She was starving, and she had offered to help his momma in the kitchen. Allison was still here, however, and Bree had shooed Gerty back outside with Mike. He toed them back and forth, the view in front of them one of Gerty's absolute favorites.

The mountains. Fields forever, a barn in the distance, and those great, glorious Rocky Mountains. She loved them here in Colorado, and in Montana, and in Calgary.

"How many girls have you kissed?" she asked.

Mike looked at her, but he had his arm around her, and she lay against his chest, her arm across his stomach. "We're goin' there?"

"Yeah," she said. "I told you about that boy I dated as a senior."

"No one else," he said. "Not James."

Gerty's teeth didn't immediately clench. "Yeah, not James...yet."

"How many boys have you kissed?"

"Just you and Brady," she said, her voice not very loud tonight. "After that, I kissed men."

"Yeah, all right." The smile on his face carried in his voice. "How many men then?"

Gerty didn't have to count too high. "Including you?"

"Yeah," he said. "Including me."

Since their kiss the day he'd come home from the hospital, Gerty had wanted to kiss him like that again. She hadn't, because his momma was a bit of a hoverer, and Gerty still had a job she had to do. Mike had taken time off from Pony Power so he could heal, but he still came out to the stables every day.

Pony Power was a bustling place, though, and it wasn't like she could kiss him with the same passion and precision as they had in his cabin. She wasn't sure a kiss like that could be replicated anyway.

"Six," she whispered.

"Wow, Gerty," he said. "Two boys and six men?"

"I'm almost thirty," she said. "That's not too many. It's like, one man every two years."

"More than me," he said.

"You were kissing men?" she teased.

"No." He ran his fingers up and down her forearm

gently, causing the hair there to stand at attention. "Last week, in my cabin, that was my fifth kiss."

That surprised Gerty, but she said nothing. "Flying helicopters kept you busy, I suppose."

"I'm not the outgoing one in my family."

"You don't have to be outgoing to kiss a woman."

"Yeah, but you have to talk enough to ask someone out."

Gerty watched the sun sink lower in the sky, the gold really starting to come out. "The very day I arrived on this farm, some of the first words you said to me were, 'Go out with me.'"

"That's because you're not a stranger," he said. "I knew you from before."

"Mm." Gerty let her eyes drift closed, satisfied that Mike had told her all she needed to know about his romantic past. He'd never been very serious with anyone, and she'd have to tell him about James sooner or later.

"Are you going to fall asleep?" he whispered.

"Only if you tell me a story in that sexy voice of yours," she whispered back.

He chuckled—that was sexy too—and drew in a breath. "Once, I had to fly a mission with this guy whose nickname was Stonewall. Funny guy and a heckuva pilot. He used to say that...."

# CHAPTER
## *Fourteen*

MIKE'S GIDDINESS increased as Daddy put the last of their bags in the back of the truck and closed the door. His momma had already hugged him four times, and Easton and Allison had left in their fancy SUV an hour ago. Opal had left a few days ago, her residency in California a busy and vibrant thing she couldn't just leave whenever she wanted.

Mike didn't have a vehicle here, but he and Hunter had plans to go shopping to get one. He figured he'd get a truck, because everyone at the farm had one, and he wouldn't be a real cowboy if he bought an SUV.

"Michael," Daddy said.

"I'm going to be fine," Mike said. "I'm off the narcotics now. There's hardly any pain from the surgical site."

His daddy shook his head, a smile playing with his lips. "I wasn't going to say any of that."

Mike wasn't wearing his sling right now, because he'd

been advised to have periods of time where he used his arm as normally as possible. He slept with it on, so he didn't accidentally hurt himself in the night by rolling over or something similar. He always put it on after his physical therapy, because that hurt and the sling held everything in place.

Most other times, Mike didn't wear it, and he had another appointment to see the doctor and they physical therapist next week. He'd have to drive himself to it, and a certain nervousness accompanied the excitement over such a thing.

He was a small-town boy and driving into the bigger metropolitan area of Denver would be new for him. He told himself he'd done plenty of new things in his life, and this would just be another one.

Daddy hugged him, and Mike lifted both arms to return the embrace. He smiled as he did, because having the use of both of his arms was such a miracle. "I love you, Daddy," he whispered, well-aware of his father's age. He hadn't met and married Momma until he was fifty, and they'd had Mike as quickly as they could.

But that meant Daddy was over eighty already, and while he was still quite spry, he was definitely slowing down more and more. "I love you too, my son," he whispered.

"Is Momma gonna be okay?"

"It'll take her some time, and she'll probably call you every day, but yeah. She'll be okay."

She'd been fretting about leaving him, and Mike had

told her over and over he'd be okay. He wasn't alone here, though Uncle Gray and Aunt Elise were going north to Coral Canyon too. Jane still lived in the farmhouse, and four other cowboys lived out in the cabins. The Whettsteins came to the farm every day, two whole families worth of people.

Gerty would be moving into the generational house, and Mike couldn't wait for their first lunch date there.

Hunter's family stayed out at the farm quite often in the summer. Mike definitely wasn't going to be alone here in Ivory Peaks.

Daddy stepped back and smiled at Mike. They stood almost the same height, with Daddy just an inch or two taller. "You take care of that girl," he said.

"Daddy." Mike rolled his eyes. "How many times do I have to tell you Gerty isn't a girl anymore?"

"Seems like one more," Daddy said. He looked past Mike, and he knew without looking that Gerty sat on the front steps of the homestead. She'd been trying to get a little boy to go to his counseling session, but the child wasn't having it today. So Gerty had brought him to the homestead to play with marbles, and he'd happily done that instead.

"She's somethin' special."

"We're going really slow, Daddy," Mike said.

Daddy looked at him. "Why's that?"

Mike didn't quite know himself, other than the fact that Gerty had told him she needed to go slow. "Because she wants to," he said simply.

"But you've kissed her, right?"

Mike ducked his head, though he certainly didn't need to be embarrassed about kissing Gerty. "Yes, sir," he said.

"Then you best take care of her," Daddy said.

"I think she's the one who's going to be taking care of me," Mike said. The thought didn't settle completely right in his head, but he didn't hate it either.

"You let her then," Daddy said. "Don't be stubborn, okay?" He lifted his eyebrows, and Mike nodded.

"Yes, sir," he said again.

Daddy grinned at him and pulled him into another hug. "If you need me to come back, you do *not* hesitate to call me. Understand?"

"Yes," Mike said, leaving the *sir* off this time.

"All right," Momma said from behind, and she sounded out of breath. Mike stepped out of his father's arms and into his mother's. She sniffled, which made no sense. She wasn't leaving Elise here this time. "I love you."

She stepped back and cradled his face in both hands. "If you need anything—*anything* at all—you call us."

"I will, Momma."

"The man has help here, Bree," Wes said, though he'd literally just said the same thing to Mike.

"I know," she said without missing a beat. "But sometimes a boy just needs his mother."

She wasn't wrong about that, so Mike hugged her again and then watched as his parents got in the truck. Gerty came to his side, her long, slender fingers slipping between his.

He waved with his free hand, glad Gerty had a hold of the right side so he didn't have to lift that arm, and his parents waved back as Daddy started backing away from the farmhouse. Gerty waved to them too, and then Daddy turned the truck around, and they started away from the farm.

He watched until the black beast went around the bend in the road, and then he exhaled every last ounce of air out of his lungs. "They're gone." He looked over to Gerty, who wore her cornsilk hair up in a ponytail, as usual.

"Yes, they are."

Mike grinned like a fool. "It feels good to be here by myself."

"Does it?"

He turned into her fully and wrapped her in his arms. She giggled as she stumbled, his weight making them shift together to find their footing. "Yeah," he said. "You wanna go out with me tonight?"

"Mm, I was thinking of a night in." She played with the buttons on his shirt. "I'll bring pizza back from town, and you can help me unpack my seven boxes. Sounds like a hot date, right?"

"With you there?" He leaned down and took a breath of her skin. She smelled like sweat and fabric softener and fresh rain. "It does sound hot."

She giggled again and pushed against his chest. "I might have ten or eleven boxes."

"You just want to watch me work while you eat pizza."

Gerty danced away from him, such light in her eyes. Her shirt today was actually a sleeveless blouse in cream, with lots of pine trees all over it. He loved it, and he loved the feel of her in his arms. "It's payback for you coming to my riding lessons and watching me work while you sip lemonade."

"Oh, honey, I wasn't sipping it." He moved toward her, but she shrieked and jumped away from him. He laughed as he followed her, quickly catching her despite her long legs. He pressed her into the fence that ran along the pasture separating the farm from Pony Power.

She looked into his eyes, and they both sobered. "I just want to remind you that we're not alone," she said.

"He's not watching us." Mike didn't even check the front porch.

"Anyone could walk by."

"Mm, yes, they could." That was half the fun, in his opinion. He didn't want to wait another second to kiss her, as they'd had very few moments alone for a really great kiss. Of course, every time he touched Gerty, a new part of him came alive. Every time he saw her, it felt like another angel in heaven started singing.

He touched his lips to hers, looking for and receiving that stunning shock. It made everything male inside him come to life, and he pressed one hand into her back while the other moved to her face.

They moved in sync, breathed in sync, and as Mike slid his hand into her hair on the back of her head, she moved both of her hands into his hair. He wasn't wearing his cowboy hat, and sparks slid up and down his spine from the feeling of her fingernails along his scalp.

He could kiss this woman forever, and he continued as long as he dared. No one interrupted them, and he broke the kiss first. Mike kept his eyes closed, wanting to keep the world at bay for just a little longer.

Gerty touched her mouth to his again, surprising him. He didn't mind at all, but her kiss was quick and fleeting. He opened his eyes then to find her looking at him. He had no idea what to say, and he found he didn't have to say anything.

"I'm done at five-thirty," she said. "I have to get home and shower, then load up the boxes, and then pick up the pizza. I'll probably be back around seven-thirty."

Mike dropped his hand from her hair to her waist. "Can I come with you?"

"You'll have to talk to my parents while I shower." Her eyebrows went up.

"I can handle that."

"Can you?"

"Sure," Mike said, not liking the challenge in her tone. "Why wouldn't I be able to? I work with your daddy. He likes me."

Gerty sighed and looked toward Pony Power. Mike sensed some unrest inside her, and he didn't like it. Gerty wouldn't talk about it until she was good and ready, he knew that. He tried anyway with, "Hey, what's in your head?"

She shook it slowly. "Nothing."

"It's something," he said.

"Mama and Daddy…." She trailed off, her eyebrows forming a V. "They do like you, but they don't think we should be dating."

Shock blitzed through him. "Why not?"

"They think I'm not ready."

"Are you ready?" Mike backed up and released the hold on her body. He honestly wasn't sure what he'd do if she said she wasn't ready. She kissed him like she was ready to be doing that. They had a great time together, and he wasn't half as comfortable with anyone else like he was with her.

Maybe Keith, but they'd also been friends for a long time.

"I feel like I am, yes," she said quietly. Her gaze came back to his. "I know there's so much you still want to know about James and me."

"Hey." He slid one hand along her jaw and reached for her ponytail with the other. He ran it through his fingers and looked at her. She almost seemed apologetic. "You'll tell me when you're ready, okay?"

"Like you'll tell me about your accident when you're ready."

His jaw tightened, but he didn't disagree. Gerty saw the movement and lifted her eyebrows. "Mike?"

"There are some things about my military service I can't tell you, Gerty."

"Is the accident one of them?"

It was his turn to look away, and he did, once again pulling his hands away from her. "No," he said honestly. "But I'm sure you can imagine that I don't want to relive it very badly."

She put one hand on his chest. "Mike, you relive things whether you want to or not."

"I guess."

"I heard you the other afternoon," she said. "When I found you asleep in the stall with Chorizo? You were having a nightmare."

He whipped his attention back to her. "What? Really?"

She nodded, anxiety in her eyes now. "I might not have known, but you said, 'No, Stonewall! We're banking too fast!' and when I woke you, you nearly hit me in the face."

Mike sometimes had dreams of the things he'd experienced on his flights and missions. Some were okay. Some were not. He swallowed, but his throat stuck together it was so dry. "Stonewall wasn't the co-pilot during the crash."

"Okay," she said. Gerty didn't push him, not on this. She could speak her mind on other things, and she was usually a no-nonsense woman. But she could also exude kindness and grace like she was now, and Mike liked both versions of her.

He pulled her into a hug and kissed her temple. He looked out over the pasture, not really seeing it or anything beyond it. "I'll tell you when I'm ready," he whispered against her ear.

"Then we have a deal," she whispered back. "When you come tonight, don't let my daddy pressure you into talking and don't ask him about James, okay?"

"Okay," he agreed.

She nodded and stepped out of his arms. "Come on, Davy," she called to the little boy on the front porch, and he poked his head around the pillar.

"Time to go?" he asked.

"Time to go," she confirmed, extending her hand

toward him. He came down the steps and slipped his pudgy hand into hers, which only made Mike smile. He had no idea if Gerty wanted to be a mom or not, as she'd never mentioned it. She was so good with horses, and she'd let life blow her about a bit, from ranch to ranch and even into the rodeo. He still hadn't heard all of those stories, and he couldn't wait to learn more about her through them.

"See you in a bit," he said to her.

"Yeah." She smiled, and Mike loved the way it brightened her face. "Can't wait until tonight."

# CHAPTER

## *Fifteen*

GERTY WAITED for Mike at the front of her truck, though they were already late. Their plans had been blown up by her parents, and familiar irritation itched at her. She told herself—again—that everything was okay. She didn't need to show up, shower, and hurry out as fast as possible.

She loved her family, though she had a suspicion Daddy would say something to further annoy her during dinner, or he'd flat-out embarrass her. He loved her to the core, though, so Gerty would forgive him.

"I feel like I need five minutes alone with them," she said as Mike took her hand in his. It suddenly felt scandalous to be holding hands with him, but she didn't pull away. Coming home had been amazingly cleansing for her, and she hadn't anticipated that.

She went days without mourning James now, and then sometimes, she'd find herself weeping in the shower over the loss of the life she'd thought she'd have in Montana. Then she'd straighten her shoulders and as she dried her hair with one of the most powerful blow dryers on the planet, she'd talk to herself.

*You can have a great life anywhere, Gerty. It didn't have to be in Montana.*

*There's land here, sweetheart. You can still have your own farm. You're not even thirty yet.*

*It's not bad to be dating Mike. You should probably tell him more about your life.*

"I can let you go in first," Mike said.

"No." Gerty sighed. "It's fine. You've met my daddy, and you know he's going to say something." She led the way down the front sidewalk to the house.

"I haven't been here in forever," Mike said. "They took out all those evergreen bushes in the front."

"Daddy hated them," Gerty said, a smile touching her lips. "One day, he went to the hardware store and bought a chainsaw. Hacked them all down in a single afternoon. When my mom got home, she was horrified at the carnage." She giggled, remembering how Daddy had called her to tell her the story. She'd been working at a ranch outside of Butte, and she'd needed his weekly calls to make it through each day.

"He said he'd never felt more powerful than when he used that chainsaw. It's still one of his favorite power tools."

Mike chuckled as they went up the steps to the porch. "That's a good story."

"Daddy then put in all the rose bushes for Mom. She loves roses."

Mike paused and gave her a quizzical look. "And you call her Mom."

"Yeah." Gerty didn't know how to explain this to him. "My mom died when I was so young, you know? Cosette has been a good maternal figure for me, and I don't know. I don't look anything like her or Daddy or any of the other kids, but I feel like I belong to them. Most of the time, anyway."

"When do you not feel like that?" He looked down at their joined hands, and she noted he was using his right hand.

"You took off the sling," she said. She hadn't noticed until this moment.

The front door opened before either of them could answer, and Walter stood there. "It is them," he yelled over his shoulder. "Gerty, you have to see this video Amy found of me." He grabbed her free hand and towed her inside.

The energy here never dulled, and Gerty didn't usually mind it. With Mike at her side, she already felt a little nervous, and Amy's enthusiasm over the video of Walter doing his stunt riding from a few years ago almost put her over the edge.

"It was on the *Riding Magazine's* website," Walter said, clearly enjoying the attention. "Isn't that great, Gerty?"

"It's amazing." She gave him a smile. "You guys remember Mike Hammond, right?"

Walter turned toward him as if seeing Mike for the first time. "Oh, sure. Hey, Mikey."

"He goes by Mike now," Gerty said before Mike could. She exchanged a glance with him, where she got the impression that he didn't mind if Walter called him Mikey. "We're dating."

Amy looked up from her device, her ten-year-old eyes wide. "Do you kiss him, Gerty?"

Shocked by the question, Gerty's mouth fished open and closed once. Heat rose to her face. "I mean—"

"Because my friend Lana has an older sister. Her name is Holly, and she has a boyfriend named Shawn, and they kiss all the time. Lana says it's *so gross*."

Gerty managed to gather her wits and emotions during Amy's speech. She smiled at Amy. "It's not so bad."

"I think it's disgusting," Amy said, her nose in the air. She picked up her tablet and started for the kitchen. "Daddy said to come out when y'all get here. He's got the Dutch ovens out of the fire already."

"Right behind you," Gerty called after her.

"I'm taking the plates," Walter said from the kitchen. "Can you guys get the sodas?""

"Sure thing." Once Walter had gone outside too, she looked at Mike, about to explode with laughter.

He raised his eyebrows. "It's not so bad?" he repeated.

"I don't think it's 'so gross'." She grinned at him and moved right into his personal space, planting both palms against his chest and looking up at him. "Maybe you should kiss me so I can decide how good it is."

His hands easily rested on her waist and back, but he blinked at her. "With your parents right outside?" he asked in a mock scandalous tone. "Your daddy already has the Dutch ovens out of the fire. You're going to get me in trouble." He stepped back, turned, and followed the kids toward the back door.

She giggled and followed him, because she didn't want him to have to face her parents alone. She slipped her hand into his on the deck, and they went past the set picnic table to the graveled area where Daddy's fire pit waited.

"Daddy," Gerty said, and he looked up from stirring the cheesy potatoes. "Mike and I are here."

Daddy's smile filled his whole face. "I see that. We're almost ready."

"Oh, the soda," Mike said. "I'll go grab it."

"No time for me to shower?" Gerty asked as he left.

"If you want," Daddy said, straightening. He looked after Mike for a moment, and then he met Gerty's eyes.

He started to say something, but Gerty moved faster. "Daddy, please don't make tonight weird."

"Why would it be weird?"

Mom arrived with a plate of cubed Velveeta. "Here you go, baby."

Daddy took the plate. "Gerty thinks I'm going to make things weird tonight."

Gerty worked not to roll her eyes. "I just know you're not happy about me moving back onto the farm."

"I'm fine with it," Daddy said, but he wasn't.

Gerty looked to Mom for help, but she didn't give any. "You're mad when I stay too long at Mike's at night," she said. "I don't fit here."

"Don't say that," Daddy and Mom said together.

"You are always welcome here," Mom said.

"You fit with us," Daddy added as he dropped the cubes into the Dutch oven. He used a tool to get the hot lid from where he'd propped it against the fire pit and put it back on so the cheese would start to melt.

"My room is an office," Gerty said. "It's fine. I know you don't mind me here. I know that. I just...I don't want to live at home when I'm thirty years old." Behind her, the kids laughed, and she turned to see Mike entertaining them.

"Good thing you're only twenty-nine then." Daddy gave her a dark look and turned around. "We're ready, kids. Everyone." Gerty did roll her eyes then, and Daddy caught the tail-end of it. "What?"

"Nothing." She leaned into the comfort and safety of Mike's side while Daddy said grace, and when he finished, he took off the lids to the Dutch ovens. "We've got barbecue chicken," he said. "And cheesy potatoes with bacon. You get a plate and dish yourself some food. We eat on the deck."

Gerty waited for the kids to run off to get their plates, and it seemed like Mom and Daddy would eat last.

"You've met my mom," Gerty finally said into the silence. "Cosette, this is Mike Hammond. I'm sure you know him."

"Of course I do," Mom said with a smile. She leaned into Mike and gave him a fast hug. Being affectionate didn't come naturally to her, and she'd worked hard over the years to show how she felt more. "It's good to have you with us tonight."

"Thanks for inviting me," he said.

The kids returned with their plates, and that was Gerty's cue to leave. She and Mike went to get plates, and he leaned down and whispered, "What happened when I went to get the soda?"

"Nothing," Gerty muttered. Then she decided just to tell him. "They're not super-jazzed I'm moving out." She picked up Mom's and Daddy's plate too and took them with her. "But they're mad when I'm out late. It's just better for everyone."

Mike said nothing, and they went back to the fire pit to get their food. Mom smiled at Gerty kindly. "Thanks for bringing my plate, honey."

Once everyone sat at the table, the salad got passed around, and lemonade or water or sweet tea poured, Gerty thought things might actually be okay. She sat across from Mike and between Amy and Mama. Daddy and Walter sat on the other side of the table, with Walt between Mike and Daddy.

Her boxes were already packed, and all she had to do was haul them out to the truck. Then Mom could take down the sofa bed and have her office back.

Gerty had left a lot of her big items like her bed and couches in a storage unit in Montana, and she had no idea when she'd get back up there to retrieve them. Maybe she wouldn't. Maybe she'd call her Grandma and ask her to go get them out and sell them in her next yard sale.

"So, Mike," Daddy said, and that brought Gerty's head

up. She first looked at him, then Mike, then Mom. They all seemed to be on pins and needles, waiting for what Daddy would say next. Gerty included.

"You're going to work with Hunter? Going to take over HMC?"

Mike flicked a glance toward Gerty. "Yes, sir," he said. "That's the plan. I'm working at Pony Power part-time too, mostly while I recover from the surgery."

"You're looking really good," Mom said. "You're not even wearing a sling."

"Aren't you supposed to wear it?" Daddy asked.

"Sometimes," Mike said at the same time Gerty said, "Daddy."

He gave her a look too and went back to his dinner. "Never pictured Gerty with a CEO," he said a few moments later.

Gerty sighed, not sure what to say to salvage the conversation. Mike kept his gaze on his plate for what felt like a full minute. Gerty had no idea. Even Amy wasn't talking, and that meant she could feel the tension at the table too.

"Well, sir," Mike said. "I don't rightly know if Gerty and I will end up together, at least not right now. We've been getting to know one another again, and I've sure enjoyed that."

Daddy looked up and right at Mike. Gerty couldn't take her eyes from him either. He hadn't spoken loud or fast, but his words and demeanor held her captive. They held power she could not ignore.

"I don't know how long I'll be CEO at HMC. I know

Hunt's been doing it a long time, and he wants to retire to the farm. I don't have a farm. I don't have much of anything right now, but I know how to work hard, and I try to listen to what God tells me to do."

Gerty started to smile, because he was just so perfect.

"When I come to a fork in my road, I take the path I think I should." He reached across the table and covered Gerty's hand with his. "I hope your daughter and I stay on the same path for a while, and maybe that will mean we get married and have a family. I don't know. I don't even know if she wants a family, because we're goin' pretty slow, and we've got time to do that."

"There you go, Boone," Mom said softly. "Now leave it be."

Daddy nodded and looked past Walter to Mike. "You're a good man, Mike. I've never doubted that."

"Thank you, sir."

"My daughter has dreams of having her own farm someday."

"She's told me, sir."

"You don't have to call me sir." Daddy rolled his eyes then, and that made Gerty's grin all the wider. "What are you smilin' about?"

"You tryin' to be all grumpy," she said. "It doesn't really work for you."

Daddy tried to keep his frown in place, but in the end, Amy and Walter cajoled him until he let his smile fill his face fully. They all laughed then, and the tension that had accompanied them until now dissipated completely.

Gerty met Mike's eyes across the table, and she wanted

to tell him so much. She did want kids. She wanted the farm. She wanted as many horses as she could have.

And she wanted him.

Oh, yes, she could see the perfect life with Michael Hammond, and it was just out of her reach.

# CHAPTER
## Sixteen

MIKE GRUNTED THROUGH THE EXERCISE, fire starting in his shoulder. The doctor and physical therapist both had told him there'd be some pain with these new exercises. Boy, they hadn't been kidding.

Everything seemed so hard in that moment, and Mike dropped his arm, determined to wrap it in the sling and leave it there for the rest of the day. He could make up the lost progress later.

"When later?" he asked, completely disgusted with himself that he wanted to quit. But his shoulder and upper arm ached, and the fire had moved along his back. Tears filled his eyes, and blast it all, the front door opened and Gerty walked in.

"Morning," she said in her cheery, pre-seven-a.m. voice. She went to work at seven to avoid the heat of the day and have a few hours off before her lessons started, and that meant Mike had been getting up early to do his therapy so Gerty could then help him get dressed, do a few of his household chores, and he could walk to work with her.

Today, he wasn't staying at Pony Power, but he'd head into the city to the highrise building that housed the HMC corporate offices. Hunter was expecting him by nine, and Mike couldn't be a blubbering mess.

"Hey, hey, hey." Gerty arrived in front of him, and Mike quickly tried to turn his back on her. She wasn't a big woman by any means, but she was strong, and she gripped his left arm and stopped him. "What's wrong?"

"Nothing." He sniffled and lifted his healing arm to wipe his eyes. "I'm fine. The therapy is just hard today."

"The new exercises?" Gerty frowned. "Are they supposed to hurt that bad?"

"I don't know," he admitted. "Collin said there's always going to be pain when a new motion is introduced." He looked at her, their eyes finally meeting. "I'm sorry, Gerty."

"Don't you dare," she said, her voice hard and unyielding. She took his face in both of her hands. "You are the strongest, sexiest man I've ever met."

Before he could protest, she kissed him, nearly crushing her mouth to his. He didn't mind that at all, and in fact, it gave him the jolt he needed to get outside his head, outside his pain, and outside his humiliation that she'd seen his tears and his pain.

She saw it every day.

He wouldn't let anyone help him but her, and she served him graciously and gladly. He kissed her back, matching her stroke for stroke, trying to take control from her. She finally gave it to him, and he slowed the kiss, turning it more toward passion than abandon. When he finally pulled away, she'd pressed herself flat against him and had both hands buried in his hair.

That meant she couldn't go far, and they breathed in and out together. "Sorry," she whispered.

"I'm not."

She looked at him, searching his face. "I'm scared," she whispered.

"Of what?"

"Us."

"Why?" He held her close, not letting her put a single centimeter between them. He felt closer to her than he ever had another human being outside his family, and he didn't want to lose that. Not yet.

"Because I'm falling for you," she admitted, letting her eyes drift closed again. "I'm thinking about what our life could be like together, and it's this. It's me helping you in the morning, and you walking me to work on our very own farm before you drive into the city."

Mike started to sway with her. "And that's a bad thing?"

"Not necessarily," she said. "I just…I was going to take time to find myself after everything with James." She swallowed and laid her head against his chest. "I'm still working on believing that someone can love me."

Mike wouldn't say he loved her when he didn't. He'd never been in love before, but he had the distinct feeling that he wasn't quite there yet. "Your parents love you," he whispered. "Everyone at Pony Power loves you. Your brother and sister. There are so many people who love you."

"It's different," she said. "You know it is."

He didn't argue the point, but said, "In your thoughts, are there kids, baby doll?"

She nodded against his chest. "Yeah, there are kids. Do you want kids?"

"I'd be happy with kids," he murmured, ducking his head so he could breathe in the scent of her skin and hair. They stood there together for a long time, her breath washing over his chest with every exhale, and the scent of eucalyptus and pomegranate in his nose.

He finally stepped back and said, "You're going to be late."

She nodded and wiped one hand across her face. He wasn't sure if she'd been crying, but if she had, no tears had actually escaped her eyes. His hadn't run down his face either.

"I'm overwhelmed today," he admitted as he picked up his shirt. He handed it to her, and she snapped it a couple of times, a loud *crack!* filling the air between them. Then she helped him thread his good arm through one hole, and then she did most of the work on his injured arm.

"Why's that?"

"I need an ice pack already," he said. "I'm going to call Collin and find out if this is normal or not." Frustration built inside him, and he didn't want Gerty to see it. "I feel like I should be further along than I am."

She said nothing as she picked up his tie and looped it

around his neck for him. The things that took two hands astounded him, because he'd never thought something as simple as putting on a tie and tying it would be so difficult for him.

He pressed his teeth together, making his jaw jump, while she got the job done.

"There," she said, patting his chest and smoothing the tie down. "Why are you upset?"

"I'm not." He turned away from her, because he didn't want to look her in the face and lie to her. "We can skip the chores so you're not late."

Gerty glanced into the kitchen and back at him. "All right," she said without putting up a fight. He draped his jacket over his forearm, because he wouldn't put it on until he got to Hunt's office and could have his cousin help him. She stepped right in front of him when he turned, and he caught the fierce look in her eyes.

"This surgery can take a year to recover from, Mike."

As if he hadn't heard that before. "So I've been told."

"It's been what? Two weeks?"

Two and a couple of days. Her birthday was this weekend, and Mike simply didn't want her to come dress him in the morning when he should be making her day as easy and as fun as possible.

He didn't answer her and instead, stepped around her to leave. She didn't come with him, and he turned back once he'd reached the porch and hadn't heard the clunking of her cowgirl boots behind him. "You comin'?"

"No," she called from inside. He returned to the doorway and found her at his kitchen sink, the water running. She lifted the coffee pot and poured the water into the machine, then set it to start.

"Gerty," he said, definitely loud enough for her to hear. She didn't even flinch toward him. He'd seen her stubbornness before, but usually with a horse or her daddy. Never directed at him.

A sigh moved through his body. He couldn't very well walk her to work if she didn't come with him, and he re-entered his cabin. He joined her in the kitchen, and she handed him a plate she'd rinsed without a word.

He took it and put it in the dishwasher, and they worked around the house like they normally did. Then she picked up his sling, which he always left on the kitchen table, and finally looked at him.

"I'm sorry," he said. "I'm allowed to have bad days."

"Yes, you are," she said simply. She helped him get his arm fitted in the sling, and she tightened all the straps, checking with him like she usually did. When she stood in front of him again, she swept her lips along his cheek and kept her mouth close to his ear as she said, "I'm sorry today is a bad day."

That made him want to break down and cry again, but he pulled in a tight breath to stop himself. She settled flat onto her feet again, nodded at him once, and said, "Okay, now I'm ready."

They left his cabin together, and she walked on his left side so he could hold her hand. She'd never made a big deal out of that, but he knew she did it deliberately. "You know," he said casually as they started down the dirt road that ran straight to Pony Power from the cowboy cabins.

"My sister told me that you were out of my league, and I wasn't sure what she meant."

Gerty didn't say anything, which left Mike to continue with, "I do now. You're an amazing woman, Gerty." He lifted her hand to his lips. "Thank you for helping me today."

She glanced up to him. "Thank you for telling me how you feel."

He focused on the horizon, because he had something hard to say. The fact that she'd confessed some of the things she'd been thinking about gave him courage and strength. "I think you're very lovable, for the official record and all that."

"Mike, you don't have to say that."

"I don't say anything I don't mean," he said. "The Marines taught me that, and Hunt's said it a time or two this month too." He looked at her, but she kept her gaze on the barns in the distance, a thoughtful look on her face.

"I *want* to be the strongest and sexiest man you know," he said. "It makes me feel weak when you walk in on me when I'm about to cry."

"When I need to cry," she said without missing a beat. "I hope you'll be the one who rescues me." She whispered the last few words, and Mike pulled her closer and dropped her hand so he could put his arm around her. Their steps stumbled for two or three strides, and then they evened out.

They fit together, and Mike hadn't really acknowledged it or felt it until this moment. He kept his feelings to himself, because six weeks into their relationship didn't feel slow to him, even if they'd known each other before.

At the stable where he usually kissed her and told her to have a good day, he pulled her against his chest and touched his lips to hers. After a slow, meandering kiss, he pulled away and whispered, "Have a good day, baby doll."

She held onto his shoulders, his arm in the sling sandwiched between them. "I am not out of your league, Michael." She looked up at him, her eyes somber but just as fierce as when she got mad and let the blue fire burn in them. "Promise me you don't really think that."

"I promise," he whispered.

"That's a weak promise."

He rubbed his nose against hers. "I like it when you use my full name."

"Michael," she said, this time a chastisement.

He grinned anyway. "Gerty, I'm fine. You're fine. We're fine." He pulled back and studied her. "Right?"

"I'm going to call Opal and give her a piece of my mind." Gerty stepped out of his arms, the fire in her eyes.

"Gerty, don't do that." They couldn't seem to get on the same page today, and Mike didn't know what to do about it. Maybe nothing. Maybe this was just how relationships were. He hadn't had too many serious ones, and never with anyone as headstrong and capable and talented as Gertrude Whettstein.

"We'll have dinner tonight," he tried. "I'll pick you up like a gentleman, and we'll go to Hilde's." He reached out and touched her chin with two fingers when she kept her gaze out in the pastures instead of on him. She swung her head toward him. "All right? Hilde's tonight?"

"All right," she agreed with a heavy sigh. "Have fun at the office."

"Baby doll." He grinned and shook his head. "There's never any fun in offices." He kissed her again and went back to his cabin, where his new truck waited in the dirt driveway out front.

"Lord," he prayed. But no more words would come. He had no idea what to talk about, and it felt like God had already leant him an angel in Gerty, so how could he ask for more?

"This is hard," he whispered as he backed out of the driveway. "I'm trying to be brave. I'm trying to lean on my faith, but I feel lost. How can I still feel lost?"

He'd been given so much. His life, when others had lost theirs. An amazing surgeon, when others couldn't afford it. An opening in the schedule, when others waited months for treatment. A good family, friends, a job.

He had nothing to complain about, and yet pure misery streamed through him as his shoulder continued to throb while he drove off the farm and onto the highway. Another wave of helplessness crashed over him, and Mike gripped the steering wheel as tightly as he dared.

"Help me," he begged, and in that moment, his phone rang. He glanced over to the screen in the middle of the dashboard, and it said "Daddy" there. Mike pulled to the side of the road, because he couldn't see through the instant tears in his eyes.

God had answered his prayers, and he didn't care if he

was late getting to HMC. He needed to talk everything through with his father. He swiped on the call and said, "Daddy," in a broken voice.

His father didn't hesitate for one second before he said, "I'll be there by three."

———

"AND THAT'S MISTER ELLORY," Hunter said from the doorway of his office. His smile hadn't hitched in the last two hours since the stuffy corporate lawyer had come in, clutching an armful of folders and making an email from a company in China sound like the biggest deal on the planet.

Hunt had known what Mr. Ellory was talking about, and he'd asked heaps of questions. Mike had no idea— absolutely no idea—what most of it had been about, and he didn't want to ask. Exhaustion tumbled through him, and he really just wanted to go home.

His head ached, and he hadn't found any time to call Collin and ask about the physical therapy.

"I don't know if I'm cut out for this job," he blurted out.

Hunter turned back from the doorway, took one look at Mike, and closed his office door behind him. "Sure, you are," he said with plenty of confidence in his voice. "You were born to do this job."

He gave Mike a hearty smile and instead of clapping him on the back and continuing to his desk, Hunter pulled him into a hug. "It's a lot to take in, I know that. That's why you'll come to work with me over the next several months, and you'll start to take on tasks of your own while I'm still here."

"Hunter," Mike said into his cousin's shoulder, but he didn't have anything else to say.

The older man stepped back, wisdom and laughter in the lines around his eyes. "Michael, I don't care what anyone says, and I know how you feel about yourself. *You* are the man for this job."

"You should call Easton," Mike said miserably. Since he'd broken down on the phone call with his father that morning, his tear ducts had thankfully stayed dry.

"This office would eat Easton alive," Hunter said with a laugh. "Nope. It's you, and I've known it since last year." He did move over to his desk then, but only to stand behind it and look out the floor-to-ceiling windows.

He wore dark brown slacks with a pale yellow dress shirt. It stayed buttoned to the throat all the time, and his navy blue tie stayed snugly done up around his neck. "It's a beautiful day for fishing," he said.

Mike moved to stand beside him, once again feeling like the ugly duckling in a room full of swans. Hunter was so...good at what he did, and such a good man and a good father. Mike looked up to him in a lot of ways, that was for sure.

"Who do you take fishing?" he asked.

"Ryder," Hunt said with a smile. "Sometimes Lisa, but she doesn't like baiting her own hook, and I won't do it for her anymore." He chuckled but sobered just as quickly. "I love taking her, though. It's a treasure to spend time with the kids, away from the house, their homework, the chores, their mother, all of it."

Mike's eyebrows lifted in surprise. "Their mother?"

"Oh, kids are different for their mothers," Hunt said knowingly. "Molly likes the break too."

"Do you ever take her?"

"Molly?" Hunter grinned and shook his head. "No. Fishing is for fathers and their kids, at least in my family."

Mike nodded and looked out over the greater Denver area. "It's a beautiful view."

"How about you and Gerty?" Hunter asked almost on top of Mike's statement.

Mike shrugged like he wasn't sure. Truth be told, he wasn't. "We had a little argument this morning. Nothing too bad. I just—don't—know.... I don't know."

"You like her, right?"

"Oh, I like her. I like her too much."

"What does that mean?" Hunt abandoned the view now.

"She's...She just ended a relationship—a serious relationship—with someone else."

"Ah." Hunter nodded like he'd heard this tale before. The phone on his desk chirped, and he stepped over to it and pressed the button. Mike could at least do that now. "Yeah, Rach?"

"There's an older gentleman here to see you, sir," she said. "He doesn't have an appointment."

Hunter looked at Mike, who stared back, blinking. His mind flashed, and then he said, "It's my daddy," at the same time the voice through the speaker phone said, "I used to be CEO of this company. Trust me, I can go back."

"Your daddy's comin'?" Hunter asked, but Mike was already moving toward his door. He opened it to find his father striding down the hallway.

Emotion clogged Mike's throat. "You came."

"I said I would." He practically bulldozed Mike to the ground, but he managed to keep his footing.

"I told you you didn't need to," Mike said against his chest.

"Yeah, well, I've been recognizing your lies for thirty years," Daddy whispered in his ear. He held him tightly for several long moments, and then he released Mike and stepped into Hunter. They laughed together, and Wes looked around the office.

"Wow, Hunt, this place is amazing."

Mike suddenly wanted to know what the office had been like while his daddy was here. "What did it look like when you were CEO?" he asked.

"I didn't have family pictures, for one." Wes picked up one of Hunter's pictures and smiled fondly at it. "Or artwork from my kids on the back wall. Or a blanket on the couch that looks like my wife might use it."

"She does sit there when she comes to work with me," Hunter admitted. "She likes to read and look out the windows, but it's right under the air conditioning duct."

They all looked up to the ceiling, and sure enough, the couch sat right beneath the duct.

Daddy faced the desk, Hunter, and Mike. "It was very dull, indeed."

"You're really giving me something to look forward to," Mike said dryly.

Daddy cocked one bushy, gray eyebrow. "You don't think you and Gerty will make it?"

"I think I'm going to be taking over here before Gerty will be ready to get married, yes," Mike said. "Probably before *I'm* ready to get married."

Daddy didn't say anything, but he clearly absorbed that information. He looked over to Hunter again. "Can I steal my son?" he asked.

"I think he can be done for today, yes." Hunter sighed as he sank into his chair. "I wish I was." He flashed a tired smile and woke his computer. "Unfortunately for me, I have a report to read, and then about six thousand emails to respond to."

"You can never keep up with the emails," Daddy said. "You're still trying?"

"A little bit every day," Hunter said. He grinned then and lifted his arm as if tipping his cowboy hat. He kept two on the coat rack beside the door, and when Mike had asked him why, he said he sometimes went straight from this office to the farm, a play for Lisa, his ten-year-old, a soccer game for Charlotte, his eight-year-old, or some other family or church event.

Daddy put his arm around Mike and said, "You got anything you need to bring with you?"

Mike nearly dove for the folder Hunter had put on the corner of his desk that morning. "Yes." He collected it and said, "See you on Monday, Hunt."

"I'll be at the farm this weekend," he said. "I'm sure I'll see you then."

"All right." Mike then led the way out of the office, knowing his father would take him to a restaurant he'd funded during his time as CEO, and they'd have to have a talk about why Mike felt like his world was falling apart one breath at a time.

# CHAPTER
## *Seventeen*

HUNTER HAMMOND LOOSENED his tie as he stepped off the elevator. A few steps down the hall sat the only apartment—the penthouse suite—where he'd lived for the past eighteen years. Molly and the kids came all the time, and they also had a house on the outskirts of the city, closer to Ivory Peaks.

The kids went to school out there, and Hunter made that drive any time it was feasible to do so. Sometimes a storm would keep him in the city, and sometimes his workload kept him behind his desk until late in the evening and neither he nor Molly saw any point in him making the forty-minute drive just to collapse into bed and leave again the next morning before anyone else got up.

If he simply came to the city apartment, he could video-chat his wife and kids, and he'd actually get to spend a little time with them.

In the summer, Hunter worked four days during the

week and took a three-day weekend. Molly's busiest time at Pony Power was in the summer, and they loved having family time on the farm.

"A few more months," he said to himself as he entered the apartment and turned to lock the door behind him. He opened the fridge and pulled out a protein shake—about all he kept in terms of food in the apartment.

He was so ready to retire. Seventeen years as the CEO of the Hammond Manufacturing Company. He'd thought he'd run it for maybe eight or ten years. Just long enough for Mike to get a degree and take over.

But his cousin had gone into the military after college. He'd been an amazing pilot, and Hunter had pulled some strings and gotten eyes on the official report about his accident overseas. The man was lucky to be alive, as was everyone who'd been aboard his helicopter. The reason they'd all survived?

Michael himself. He'd taken them down in the safest place possible, laying them on the tail to slow them down before the belly crashed into the hard, dry, baked desert.

He tapped to call Molly, noting the time. Just after six. The only thing happening right now would be cleaning up after the riding lessons, and then she'd have to herd all of the kids into their enormous SUV to make the drive home for dinner.

At least they didn't have homework in the summer. Not only that, but Molly didn't have to be at Pony Power until noon most days, so she and the kids had time to sleep in, go to breakfast or an early lunch, take in movies, and a whole slew of other family things.

Hunter was tired of missing them.

"Hey, baby," Molly said, and his soul quieted.

"Mols," he said as he sat down at the dining room table.

"You staying in the city?" she asked, peering at the screen.

"No, I'm going to drive home," he said. "I had to get out of the office, though, or I might never have made it."

"Revolving door today?"

"You got it." He twisted off the top of the protein shake. "Do you want me to get dinner on my way home?"

"I always want you to get dinner on your way home." She smiled at him but quickly looked away. "No, those go in stable two. Thanks, Britt." Her attention came back to Hunter. "Not Mexican and not fast food."

"Pizza?" he asked just as she said, "And not pizza."

Hunter grinned, though he yearned for a pair of basketball shorts, a lot of food, and his family to be piled all around him. His youngest was only three years old, a caboose baby he and Molly hadn't been expecting. Five years sat between Clay and Charlotte, and Hunter adored each of his children, though they were all different.

"Maybe sandwiches from that place that Joel told us about?" Molly suggested. "Stop it, Charlotte. You like sandwiches." She looked down, and when her pretty hazel eyes came back to meet his, she wore irritation there. "She is going to be the death of me this summer," she said through a smile of clenched teeth.

"What does she want for dinner?"

"Hunter, you can't stop at fifteen places."

"I won't," he promised, though he'd been known to stop at three or four and get different things for the different members of his family.

"She wants one of those turkey bacon club sandwiches from that place Joel told us about," Molly said. Her eyes flashed, and Hunter got the message.

"I'll leave here in just a couple of minutes," he said. "I sent the car to get gassed up."

In the beginning, Molly couldn't believe he couldn't stop and get his own gas. "It isn't about that," he'd told her. HMC employed people to do that job, and if he did it, they might not have a job. It was a company car too, so why should Hunter have to take it to the gas station?

"I'm leaving here right now too," Molly said. "So we'll beat you, but not by much." She turned to someone Hunter couldn't see. "Have you seen my son? Ryder?"

"No, ma'am," a cowboy said, and that caused Molly to sigh like the world was coming to an end.

"He keeps disappearing," Molly said. "Then, when I finally find him, he won't tell me where he's been." She wore a genuine look of worry. "Do you—could you talk to him about it?"

"Sure," Hunter said. "I'll take him fishing in the morning."

"No, we have that Girl Scout Camp bake-off in the morning."

Hunter had no idea what that was, but he said, "Right, okay. So we'll go to that and then take a cake out onto the lake." He grinned as his wife shook her head, a tiny smile playing at her lips. "I can take Lisa and Charlotte too."

She lit up, and Hunter realized then that she needed a break. "And I'll call your mother on the way home and ask her if she can take Clay for the day."

"Hunter," Molly said quietly.

He checked the clock on the microwave back in the kitchen. "I think I can get Suzie on the phone before she closes too."

"No," she said.

"Yes," he argued back. "Mols, I see the look on your face right now, and I don't like it." He leaned closer to the phone as if he had to whisper his next words. "You help me when I get like this. Why can't I do the same for you?"

She didn't answer, and Hunter got to his feet. "I'll see you at home in an hour."

"Hunt."

"Love you, baby." He hung up in a rare showing of not wanting to talk to his wife. He suddenly had other calls to make, and some of them were time-constrained, that was all. He started with the masseuse, because she'd be the hardest to get for tomorrow, and to his relief, Suzie picked up on the second ring.

He hadn't even left the apartment yet. "Suzie," he practically bellowed. "Tell me how much I need to pay you to get my wife in tomorrow for an eighty-minute massage, hot rocks, that aromatherapy she loves, and access to the spa."

"Hunter Hammond," she said in a tired voice, and he could only laugh.

"I'll tip you two hundred percent," he said as he sobered. "I need this to happen."

"You only call when it needs to happen," Suzie said. "And God must be smiling down on you, because I can get her in at ten-thirty."

He had no idea how long the Girl Scout Bake-Off would last or even what time it started. But he could take the kids if required. "Great," he said. "She'll be there. Anything she wants. You have my card on file?"

"Yes, sir," she said.

"Thank you, Suzie."

"Try to call me a week in advance next time, Hunter."

"Will do." He hung up, knowing he wouldn't do that. He loved his wife with his whole soul, and he always had. But he was busy, and she was busy, and sometimes—all the time—he didn't see how much she needed an escape until the night before.

"Dinner," he muttered to himself as he left the apartment. "Call her mom from the car." He looked up the name of the sandwich shop in the elevator ride on the way down to the parking garage, and he thanked Robert for filling up the SUV before he got behind the wheel.

A little over an hour later, he pulled up to the gate at his house and tapped in the code to get it open. His driveway curved around a pond and back to the house, and Hunt loved the feelings of peace and serenity that came every time he came home.

Molly's SUV sat in the open garage, and Hunter parked on the other side, behind his motorcycle and his family truck. He'd have to move in the morning to hook up the boat, but that was tomorrow, and this was tonight.

He gathered the bags of sandwiches and headed for the

garage entrance. Music pounded behind the closed door before he even opened it, and when he did, a smile instantly popped onto his face.

Ryder gyrated in the kitchen to the beat, his little brother's hands in his. The two of them laughed and laughed as they danced, and Hunter couldn't help joining in. He slid the food onto the counter and yelled, "Where's Mama?"

"She left," Ryder yelled back.

Alarm pulled through Hunter. He reached on top of the fridge and turned down the music. "She left? Her car is in the garage."

"Daddy." Clay toddled over to him, and Hunter swooped the little boy into his arms. He wasn't potty-trained yet, as he'd just turned three a couple of months ago. Hunter would get the charts and stickers and put on his happy face every time his son went in the potty once Molly decided it was time for him to be out of diapers.

"Where's Mama, baby? Her car is outside."

"She went to the Stephens'," Ryder said. "She said she'd be back in a few minutes."

Hunter looked out the window above the kitchen sink. It showed him the backyard, which was immaculately landscaped and mown. They had a swimming pool, a hot tub, trampoline, and a swing set, as he had so much money he didn't know what to do with all of it.

In the back corner, a gate led from their yard into the Stephens' yard, and he wondered what Cindi needed.

"I have dinner." He tore his gaze from the fence when his wife didn't walk through it. "Where are the girls?"

"Upstairs," Ryder said. "Charlotte wouldn't stop

crying on the way home from the farm, and Mama lost it on her."

"Lost it?" Hunter looked at his oldest son. "Define that, please."

"She was yellin' a lot," Ryder said with a sigh. "Charlotte was being super annoying." He looked disgruntled for a moment, and then he started pulling out the sandwiches.

"Get plates," Hunter said, brushing his hands away from the food. "Clay, you're going in your seat." He strapped the boy into the booster seat at the table and went to the bottom of the stairs. "Girls," he called. "Come eat dinner."

Ryder put plates on the table, and Hunter passed out the sandwiches. "Can we have soda?" his son asked.

"Sure," Hunter said, though he didn't know what other sweets and treats Molly had allowed the kids that day. "I got chips for everyone too." He dumped the single-serve bags into the middle of the table. "Fishing tomorrow?"

Ryder's face lit up, and Hunter thanked the Lord every single day for his son. That he had someone who loved fishing as much as he did, so he could continue the legacy his father had started with him.

"The girls are coming too," Hunter said just as they arrived in the kitchen.

"Coming where?" Lisa asked.

Hunter grinned at her and pressed a kiss to the top of her head. She had her mother's freckles, but his dark, dark eyes, and he thought she was so beautiful. "Fishing," he said.

"I don't want to go fishing," Charlotte said.

"Too bad," Hunter said, giving her a look. "Come talk to me." He looked at Clay and Ryder. "You guys eat without us. Ryder, make sure everyone gets the chips they want before you take seconds, okay?"

"Okay, Daddy."

He motioned for Charlotte to go with him into the living room. She hiccuped as she did, and he told himself to be patient. Molly had already gotten upset with the girl, and she'd feel bad about it. He'd hear all about it as they got ready for bed that night, he was sure.

He sank onto the couch and pulled his eight-year-old onto his lap with a grunt. "Wow, you've gotten big."

"Daddy." She curled into his chest, and she wasn't so big that she couldn't do that. She had long, dark hair and lighter eyes like Molly. She had the Hammond intensity that had skipped over him but had really been prevalent in his Uncle Ames and in his half-sister Jane.

"Baby, you have to listen to Mama at the stables."

"I know." Charlotte's voice sounded like she'd inhaled helium.

"You can't cry out there, and you can't cry the whole way home."

"I know."

"If you can't do it, I'll have to take you to work with me." He didn't want that to be a punishment, but it really was. He had nothing for little girls to do for ten hours each day.

Charlotte sniffled in his arms, and Hunter stroked her soft hair. "Tell me what happened."

"I just wanted to ride Brownie, and Mama wouldn't let me."

"Honey, Brownie is a therapy horse. Only the equine therapy students ride her."

"She's so pretty. I asked if I could feed her, but Mama said she'd already eaten."

"Then she'd already eaten."

"I didn't want a sandwich for dinner."

"Then you can go to bed right now."

Charlotte started to cry again, a soft sniffle that broke Hunter's heart. "Sh, sh, sh," he said. "Stop crying, Char. If you don't want to eat, you can just sit with us, okay? But you can't argue with your mother about it. She has to feed all of us every night—every morning and every day for lunch too—and sometimes, you just get a sandwich. You can't throw a fit about it."

Charlotte had always been the most sensitive of his kids, and Hunter glanced into the kitchen to check on the other kids. They'd all opened their sandwiches just fine, and everyone had chips the way he'd asked. No one would clean up after themselves without being asked, but Hunter would ask them.

Lisa looked over, and Hunter smiled at her. She smiled back, and he noted how good her heart was. She loved her little sister, and out of all of them, she couldn't stand the contention the most.

"Do you want to at least try the sandwich?" he asked Charlotte.

"Okay," she said.

He let her slide off his lap and then he tucked her hair

behind her ears and lifted her chin until she looked him in the face. "Baby, you have to apologize to your mother."

Charlotte's chin wobbled, but she nodded her head. "Okay, Daddy."

"The moment she walks in."

"Yes, sir."

"Good girl. Give me a hug and a kiss right here." He tapped his cheek, his smile growing. Charlotte wrapped her spindly arms around him and hugged him, and then she gave him a smacking kiss on his cheek. They both laughed, and Hunter let her go into the kitchen and sit down at the table next to Lisa before he got up.

He took his seat at the head of the table and started to unwrap his sandwich. He didn't want to call Ryder out in front of his sisters, but they were all going fishing tomorrow too. "Ry, your mama says she can't find you sometimes around the farm." He took a bite of his sandwich and looked at his fourteen-year-old.

Sometimes he didn't feel old enough to have a fourteen-year-old, and sometimes his body felt creaky and quite old enough to have a fourteen-year-old, thank you very much.

Ryder's face turned a violent shade of red, which Hunter had not been expecting. He chewed slowly while his son sat there silently.

Hunter swallowed and asked, "Where are you?"

"Just around," he said.

"Yeah, that's not gonna fly with me, young man," Hunter said in a much harsher voice than he'd just used on Charlotte. "You make her late to leave to come home, and it's stressing her out that she doesn't know where you are."

"I know where he is," Lisa said.

"Lisa," Ryder hissed. "Shut up."

"No, go on, Lisa." Hunter put down his sandwich and looked at his daughter. She and Ryder sat across from one another down the table a seat, with Clay and Charlotte closest to Hunter. "If Ryder doesn't want you to tell me, he should tell me himself."

He cocked his eyebrows at his son, hoping he was doing this right. There were no manuals on how to raise kids, and most of the time he followed Molly's lead.

Ryder shifted in his seat, clearly at war with himself. Everyone remained silent, and only Clay and the girls kept eating.

"Ryder," Hunter said. "Tonight, please."

"Fine," he bit out. "I'm over at the Thatcher place."

"Travis's place?" Hunter's eyebrows crinkled. "Why?"

"Really, Daddy? I have to spell it out for you when you started dating Mama when you were eleven?"

"Hey, we broke up for a long time," Hunter said automatically. Pieces clicked around in his head. "Travis and Poppy have a daughter your age, don't they?"

"Clementine is almost thirteen," Lisa said matter-of-factly. "In fact, we got an invitation to her birthday party a couple of days ago."

Hunter looked from his daughter to his son, with no clue what to say or do next. He thought of his own father and the many, many, many talks they'd had about girls.

Hunter had already done several of those with Ryder, and his own face started to turn a little hot.

"Ryder, tell me we don't need to have another talk about girls," he said.

"No," his son mumbled as he ducked his head. "I'm not doing anything wrong."

"Other than upsetting your mother," Hunter said gently. "Does Miss Poppy or Travis know about your visits to their farm?"

Ryder kept his face practically against his plate. "No."

"Ah, so maybe you are doing something wrong."

"We stand there and talk by the donkey pen," he said. "It's nothing."

"Why can't you do that and then get back to Mama on time?" Hunter asked.

"Because Clementine doesn't go out to do her chores until five-thirty," he said.

Hunter picked up his sandwich again, determined to find out more. He wouldn't ask Ryder if he'd kissed this girl in front of his sisters, but that question *would* be answered before Hunt went to bed tonight. Oh, yes, it would.

"What do you talk about?" he asked instead, and Ryder sighed the sigh of the century. He was saved by the back door getting slid open and his mother entering the house.

"Oh, good," she said. "You didn't wait for me."

Hunter wasn't sure if that was good or not, but he twisted and gave her a smile. "Hey, hon."

She leaned down and kissed him, and he didn't sense

anything too wrong with her. Of course, he wasn't the best at sensing emotions—his or his wife's—but he watched her as she sat down and started unwrapping her sandwich.

"Mama, I saved you these." Ryder passed her the sour cream and chive potato chips she liked, and she gave him a beaming smile.

"Thank you, baby."

"What was goin' on at the Stephens'?" Hunter asked.

Molly met his eye from across the table, and he *saw* her then. She was tired but okay. "Not much. She just needed help with something real quick." That was code for *I'll tell you later*, and Hunter nodded.

"Great," he said. "Well, me and the kids are going fishing tomorrow."

"You are?" Molly's surprise hit him from fifteen feet away. "All of you?"

"All of us." Hunter grinned around at his kids. "So everyone will have to be on their best behavior, and maybe we'll be able to get desserts on the way home."

"Can we have ice cream, Daddy?" Charlotte asked.

"Only if there is no crying," he said, reaching over to boop her nose. She seemed to have made a complete recovery, and Hunter smiled at her and then Molly. He wouldn't want to be raising a family with anyone but her, and he hoped she knew it.

————

HUNTER SIGHED as he finally entered the master suite. Molly sat up in bed, looking at something on her phone. She immediately set it aside. "Well?"

"He hasn't kissed her." He groaned as he reached up to pull off his T-shirt. He unceremoniously flung it aside and pulled down the covers on his side of the bed. "I'm tired, baby."

"Same."

He crawled into the king bed and all the way across it to her. He laid his head in her lap, where she played with his hair. "Your hair is getting long again."

"Mm." He closed his eyes. "Your mama couldn't take Clay tomorrow. It'll be fine. We'll do river fishing, so it'll just be on the bank. The kids can throw in rocks and we'll pack a picnic."

"Hunter, you don't have to do that."

"You have a spa appointment at ten-thirty, and Gloria and Cosette know you're not coming in tomorrow."

She said nothing, and Hunter took that as her acceptance. When she did speak, it was to say, "Ryder and Clementine. Who knew?"

Hunter smiled and pushed himself up to a near-sitting position. "Remember when I first asked you to be my girlfriend?"

She gave him that soft smile he loved. "Yes, I remember."

Hunter kissed her, the feelings of nostalgia mixing with pure love for his wife. "We made it, baby," he said. "He'll be okay. He said he wouldn't be late anymore."

"He'll still go over there," Molly whispered. "Should I talk to Poppy?"

"Probably," Hunter said. "I can call her tomorrow."

"No." Molly ran her hands along his shoulders. "I'll talk to her on Monday when I'm at the farm."

"Sounds good." He leaned in to kiss her again.

"Hunt?"

"Hmm?" He dropped his mouth to her collarbone, so she could keep talking.

"Are you really going to retire?"

He smiled against her neck as he slid his lips along the smooth skin there. "Yes, ma'am," he whispered in her ear. "With a little luck and a lot of prayer, I'm going to be done by the end of the year."

His wife wrapped both arms around him, her fingers clasped on the back of his neck. "And we'll move out to the farm?"

"Yes," he said. "My father said he and Mom would move into the generational house whenever we want them to."

Molly nodded and kissed him again, and Hunter recognized the vibrancy in her touch. He kissed her back, ready to make love to his wife after a day that had been stressful for both of them.

# CHAPTER
*Eighteen*

GERTY SAT on her front porch, shucking an early crop of peas for her mother. She glanced up every few pods, looking for Mike. She'd been given strict instructions not to come over to the administration barn without him, but by her clock, they were late for her birthday luncheon.

His daddy had been in town for a couple of days before returning to Coral Canyon. He'd taken Mike to lunch and then the physical therapist, and Gerty hadn't walked in on her boyfriend weeping again. She reminded herself that Mike hadn't been weeping in the first place. He'd been in a lot of pain and he'd been cranky, and Gerty could understand that.

She felt like that right now, and she thumbed the peas out of the pod and into the bowl and said, "It's lunch, and Mom's going to have all of your favorites there."

Denver looked up from his spot at her feet, and she gave the dog a quick smile. "Just talking to myself again."

She hadn't gotten any presents yet, but everyone she'd seen that morning at Pony Power had wished her a happy thirtieth. She didn't need a lot of gifts anyway, but she knew her siblings would have something for her. They hadn't missed a year of her birthday while she'd been off learning how to shoe horses, barrel race, and work ranches.

She glanced toward Pony Power, but Mike's footsteps approached from the other direction. She nearly dropped the bowl of peas at the sight of him, but thankfully, she caught it before it fell.

He wore dark jeans, a bright blue polo, and that deliciously black cowboy hat. A belt looped around his waist, and the buckle wouldn't pass muster in the rodeo, but for a family farm, it did just fine.

Mighty fine indeed.

"You ready?" He kept his hands in his pockets as she put the bowl aside and stood.

"I guess," she said. Denver got up too, did a big stretch that made her smile, and trotted down the steps to greet Mike.

"Hey, buddy," he said, leaning down to scrub the golden retriever around his ears. "You keepin' Gerty company, huh?" He smiled, and Gerty loved how he interacted with Denver. She'd always thought she could tell a lot about a person by the way they acted around animals, and she felt herself falling for Mike in that moment.

He looked up at her, those dark eyes asking her so many questions. She went down the steps and right into his arms.

"Happy birthday, baby doll," he whispered in her ear.

Gerty smiled against his chest. "You got any presents for me?"

"Just this right now." He leaned down and kissed her, and a floaty, out-of-body feeling encased Gerty. She also felt grounded here with Mike, and she held onto each moment, memorizing it and how she felt.

He pulled away finally, and whispered, "We're already late."

"Whose fault is that?" she teased.

"All mine." He draped his arm around her and grinned toward the big red administration barn. "I'm sure your daddy is goin' crazy."

They started the walk toward the barn, and sure enough, Gerty did see Amy open the door and peek out. New, quiet excitement built inside her.

She'd find everyone she loved—and those who loved her—in the barn, and she *was* starving.

"I did get you something," Mike said about the time they passed the walking rings. "But we have to drive to it."

Gerty's mind raced. "Drive to it?" She slowed her step and looked up at him. "Explain that."

He grinned and took her hand, tugging her along. "After work," he said.

"Mike," she protested. "Tell me."

"You're late to your own party."

Gerty knew then that he'd come to get her late on purpose. He'd waited to mention this mysterious gift until they were steps away from the barn. She pulled her hand away. "I'm not happy with you."

He only laughed, and that ignited the fire in her chest. "Mike." His name almost sounded like a whine.

He faced her, his grin glorious and complete. "Gerty, you have to let me surprise you sometimes." He took both of her hands in his, and she nearly melted right then and there. "I just didn't want you to think I'd forgotten or didn't get you anything."

"No one could've forgotten," she grumbled. "Daddy sent about five hundred texts."

Mike burst out laughing, and any woman who heard him would surely fall head over heels in love with him. Gerty smiled, because his joy was so complete.

He swept a kiss along her hairline. "Come on. Let's enjoy your party." He opened the door to the barn, and the scent of sugar and burning candles met her nose. It wasn't a surprise party, so Gerty heard chatter and laughter coming down the hall before she even made the turn.

She walked past the offices at the front of the building, including where her mom worked, and into the front entrance.

"There she is!" Daddy boomed. "Everyone, one, two, three!"

The crowd assembled there began to sing *Happy Birthday*, and Gerty grinned around at each of them. Keith and Britt stood right beside the desk—and the huge, pink-frosted birthday cake. As un-girly as Gerty was, she did love pink frosting for some reason.

Mom stood behind the cake, lighting a couple of candles that had burnt out while she sang with everyone else. Molly and Hunter stood arm-in-arm, their kids at various places around the room. The other cowboys were there—Mission, Travis, Vince, and Cord.

Poppy had come from next door, and she stood behind the table full of food with Aunt Gloria and Uncle Matt. Steele Thatcher helped put out cups at the end of the table, and right behind him stood Jane and Deacon Hammond.

Gerty loved them all so much, and she raised her hands in clapping as the song ended and the cheering began. "Thank you," she yelled into the fray. "Thank you."

Daddy stepped into her and hugged her tightly, and Gerty wondered why she'd been cross with him. He simply wanted her birthday to be fantastic, and he always had. She sometimes got sad on her birthday, thinking about her birth mother, and he'd worked hard over the years to make it a special day for her.

"Thank you, Daddy," she said into his ear.

He beamed at her as he pulled back. "All right," he said as he turned to face the crowd. "Gerty loves appetizers, so we set up an appetizer bar. Baby?"

Mom came out from behind the cake. "She needs to blow out the candles first, Boone."

"Oh, right." He laughed. "Candles, Gerty, before Molly calls the Fire Marshall."

Gerty left Mike's side and took the two steps to the cake. She drew in a huge, puff-her-cheeks breath, and blew out as hard as she could. She didn't quite get all thirty candles, so Britt and Keith helped her, and the three of them laughed together.

"Gerty, Gerty!" Amy said. "Come see your presents." Her sister grabbed onto both of her hands.

"Not yet, Amy," Boone said to her. "We're eating first, remember?" He looked over to Poppy. "Gerty's mom is going to tell you about the food."

Gerty didn't see why it had to be explained, but she kept her mouth shut as Mom joined Poppy at the table. "Gerty loves finger foods," Mom started. "And anything miniature, so one year for Halloween, I made these 'ghoulish' mummy dogs, and she loved them. So we have those."

Gerty's memories of that night flowed through her head. She'd dressed up as a cowgirl and called herself Apple Jack from the My Little Pony cartoon. If she could pass off her regular clothes as a costume, she was all for that.

"Her mother had a recipe for this sweet kielbasa," Mom said. "She and her father used to make it every year on New Year's Eve to ring in the New Year." She smiled fondly at Gerty and Daddy, who put his arm around her.

They both smiled back at Mom. "Poppy? What's down by you?"

"Gerty came to my wedding when I married Travis," she said. "And we had these miniature—" She swept her arm toward Mom with a grin. "—veggie kabobs. I remember Gerty talking about them for days. She doesn't like carrots of any kind, so these are cucumber, cauliflower, and grape tomato skewers, with ranch dressing—her favorite."

A warm hand slid into hers, and Gerty looked over to Mike. "You still don't like carrots?"

"No, sir," she said.

"We needed a main course," Poppy continued. "And

Gerty loves beef with her whole soul, at least according to her daddy. So these are sliders, with just the bun, the burger, and cheese."

"Keith is cutting the cake right now," Mom said. "And the last thing you'll all want to try is one of Gerty's favorite things that she happened upon by accident. Boone?"

"Fried mashed potato balls," he said. "They're fantastic straight-up, but I made a cheese sauce that has a slight kick to it, because Gerty doesn't like anything too spicy, but she loves cheese." He clapped his hands together. "All right. Tables outside in the shade. Let's eat."

Gerty wanted to stay out of the way, but Daddy insisted she go through the line first. She did, getting some of everything, because these were all of her favorite things. She paused to hug Poppy and said, "Thank you," and when she reached the end of the table, she could only smile at her mother.

Tears filled her eyes, and she didn't have words for how well this woman had loved her over the years.

"Don't," Mom said, her own eyes growing watery. "We're just so happy you're here this year."

"I'm sorry," Gerty choked out. She'd been on the road for some of her birthdays, and simply living somewhere else for others. She hadn't realized how much she needed to be with her family until this very moment.

"I've got the cake, Gerty," Mike said from behind her, but she couldn't answer as she stepped into her mom's arms and let her hold her.

"I love you, Gerty-girl," Mom said. "Happy birthday."

"Thank you." She smiled at her as she released her, and Gerty blinked the tears back into her eyes.

"Presents in like, ten minutes?" Amy asked as Gerty went by Daddy again.

"Amy, everyone has to eat," Daddy said. "If you ask me one more time about the presents, I'm sending you to the farmhouse while the rest of us enjoy the party."

"You can't do that," she said.

"Amy." Gerty turned back to her. "Come sit by me, okay?" Her sister turned toward her with unrest in her eyes. "Don't make Daddy mad on my birthday." She glanced at her father, who did look one breath away from dealing out a punishment.

"Fine." Amy moved away from Daddy, who looked relieved.

"Walt," Gerty said as she moved through the door Cord held open. "You come sit by me too, okay?"

"Be right there," he said, though he hadn't joined the line yet.

Gerty sat with Mike, and as people came outside, they crowded around her. Finally, Amy, Walt, Daddy, and Mom arrived, and they brought a huge, brown barrel of ice cream with them.

"Gerty's favorite flavor is cookies and cream," Daddy said. "I'm going to start dishing it up, and Amy or Walt will bring you a bowl."

Gerty wasn't sure how she'd hit the Father Jackpot, but she knew she had. She leaned into Mike, who put his arm around her and whispered, "Should I go get the presents and bring them out here too?"

She giggled as she watched Amy start to serve the bowls of ice cream. She was probably going crazy inside her skin. "I think that's Amy's job," she said. "Better let her do it."

"Mm." He pressed his lips against the tender spot below her ear, and the hum from his voice strummed through her bloodstream. "Maybe you want seconds of something?"

She handed him her plate. "All of it," she said.

"Your wish is my command," he said, and he stood, picked up her plate, and headed around the corner to get her more food.

Gerty could handle being at her own birthday party without him, but with him gone—even just to get her more food—she realized how much she wanted him at her side. She wanted to hold his hand on every major holiday, all the minor ones, and just on an ordinary Tuesday. She wanted him to be the one to go with her when she was interested in buying another horse. She wanted to make hot lunches for him, so they could eat together after working in the stables.

*He's not going to work in the stables for much longer*, she thought, and boy, wasn't that the truth? He'd already started going into the city more and more, and she hadn't realized how much she missed seeing him at Pony Power until that moment.

# CHAPTER
## *Nineteen*

BOONE WHETTSTEIN COULD WATCH his daughter laugh with her younger half-siblings all day and all night. Once the ice cream had been dished and served, people had made room for Walter and Amy around Gerty, and she'd been entertaining everyone with tales from her time in the rodeo.

She'd only rode for a single season, and because she possessed a bit of a hot streak, she'd become a barrel racer on a dare. He'd learned quickly raising her not to dare her to do something, because she'd do it. No matter what, she'd do it.

His heart felt fuller than it ever had, because while he and Gerty had been close over the years, he knew things had shifted when he'd married Cosette. Gerty loved her too; they'd made a strong family unit together, the three of them.

Then, Boone and Cosette had gotten pregnant, and

Walt had been born only a few months before Gerty's sixteenth birthday. She'd never called it his second family, but Boone had often thought about his younger kids that way. He'd kept them separate from Gerty, because they were. She was his; she always would be. But she'd come from someone else, no matter how completely and perfectly Cosette loved her.

Just looking at the three of them would tell anyone that. Gerty, with her white-gold hair, and then Walt and Amy with their darker locks. With Cosette being a brunette like him, their family existed in shades of dark red, brown, and black. Gerty was the opposite of that, and anyone with eyes could see it.

Still, they fit together, and Boone knew that families came in all shapes and sizes. They didn't even have to be related by blood to feel like family, a fact he knew every time he looked at Gray Hammond or Travis Thatcher. He loved those two men and their families as if they were Matt and his.

He glanced over to his brother now, noting how tired Matt looked. He still put a smile on his face and raised his eyebrows at Boone.

"Presents," Boone said, reaching over and slapping the table near his kids. "Amy, go get the presents and bring them out."

"Yay!" His ten-year-old scampered away from the table like it had caught on fire, and Cosette and Gloria went to help her.

He then eyed Michael Hammond as he leaned down and whispered something in Gerty's ear. Boone hated whispering in public, especially when it made his daughter turn twice as bright as before.

"He's not a bad kid," Matt said as if he could read Boone's thoughts.

"No, I know." In fact, Mike was a very good kid. And not a kid at all anymore. He'd been over to the house a few times since both he and Gerty had arrived at the farm on the same day. He could speak intelligently and easily to Boone and Cosette. He'd had a decorated career in the Marines, and he was currently training to be the CEO of the Hammond's multi-billion-dollar company in downtown Denver.

He was a very, very good man, and Boone wasn't sure why he didn't simply embrace Gerty's relationship with him.

"Why are you so sour on him then?" Matt asked. "I've been begging Keith to find someone to settle down with."

"I'm not sour," Boone said, finally turning away from Gerty right as she looked his way. "You realize she was engaged only a month before she returned to the farm, don't you? I just think she might not be ready for this relationship."

Matt nodded, and he looked over to the pair of them. "She's got a good head on her shoulders, Boone. She'll figure it out."

Yeah, she would. Boone knew that too—intellectually. His father's heart still worried that she'd be hurt in the process, and she'd already been through something terribly painful. He wanted to wrap her up in his arms and keep the world out for just a little while. Just until she remembered how amazing she was.

He'd known she hadn't wanted this birthday luncheon, but Mike had told him it would be great. *Gerty will come around, sir,* he'd said.

He'd been right, of course. Boone's chest burned with a feeling that he'd had trouble identifying at first. He knew it now. Jealousy. He was actually jealous of Mike Hammond, because he got to spend so much time with Gerty, when time was all Boone wanted.

*No,* he told himself. *What you want is for your daughter to be happy.*

As she laughed with Mike and Walt, she sure looked happy. Cord sat down next to them, joined in with their conversation, and Boone felt his jealousy ebbing away. It didn't make sense to him, but Cosette said she understood.

They'd been so thrilled to hear Gerty's voice telling them she was finally leaving Montana and coming back to Colorado. They'd waited for her all day, each leaving work early to be home when she arrived.

Cosette had spent time and energy baking her favorite cookies, and Boone had picked up barbecue from her favorite place. She'd said little when she'd arrived, less during dinner, and then run off the moment she could.

She'd returned very late, and since then, all she'd been able to talk about was Mike-this, and Mike-that.

He told himself that wasn't true, because she talked about her horses a lot too, and Pony Power, her riding lessons, and Denver. The therapy dog had taken a shine to her, and Boone thought that only testified of her broken spirit and how much it needed mending.

He got up to help Amy and Cosette start to pile the presents in front of Gerty, the thought that perhaps Mike was helping Gerty heal faster than she would've otherwise. He'd never felt that way before, but he let the idea swim around in his head while the rest of the gifts got brought out.

Amy ran the presents, and Boone stayed out of her way. He'd been in charge of getting Gerty there, and he'd asked his wife to be in charge of the food, Amy to be in charge of presents, and Walt to be in charge of the animals.

He'd once bought Gerty a horse for Christmas—her very first horse—and she'd loved that animal endlessly. This year, he'd gotten her another pony, as well as a dog of her own, and he couldn't wait to present her with them. They'd both come from a farm on the brink of collapse, rescued by an operation Boone had been volunteering at for several years now.

Mike had asked him about his service there every other Saturday, and Boone had told him about Rescue Ranches and the work they did. This was the first time Boone had brought any of the animals who'd been rescued from a farm or ranch in the west back to the Hammond Family Farm, but he'd gotten permission from Gray, Molly, and Gloria before anything had been final.

They'd been here on the property for about three days now, and the fact that Gerty didn't know yet was a miracle all its own. Boone had sworn everyone to secrecy, and he'd worked here longer than Gerty. Otherwise, he was sure they'd have spilled the beans by now.

"This is the last one," Amy said, shooting Boone a huge smile that everyone in the near vicinity saw. Gerty too looked at Boone, her eyebrows high.

She took the package, which wasn't much bigger than a shoebox. He'd put a collar with an un-engraved tag, as well as a bridle with room for a name on the side of it, in the box, wrapped that, and hoped she'd be excited.

"What is it?" she asked.

"Open it and see," he said with a smile.

He glanced over to Mike, who knew about the horse and the dog. He'd been the only other one besides Boone and the kids who'd been taking care of them. In fact, Mike had been late bringing Gerty over tonight, because he'd been putting a bow on the horse and dressing the pup in a sweatshirt that said *Happy Birthday* on it.

So Boone clearly didn't dislike the man. He was simply worried about his daughter—and no one could tell him to stop doing that. He'd talked through everything with Cosette at least twice, and she'd be a liar if she said she wasn't a little nervous about Gerty picking things up with Mike so fast.

In the end, however, Cosette said she trusted Gerty to know how she felt and what she should do, and they must too. Boone was trying. He was just a lot slower at such things than his wife.

The paper came off, and Gerty opened the lid on the box. She removed the collar, her brow puckering. "This is for a dog." She looked up then, her eyes bright and round. "Daddy."

"There's more in there," he said, leaning over as if he needed to check. "Isn't there?"

Gerty didn't dive back into the box. "Did you get me a dog?" She held up the collar, which was blue, white, and green. "It looks like a boy dog."

"Maybe," he said evasively.

She got to her feet without even looking in the box again, and Boone knew—he *knew*—he should've done two presents. It wouldn't have mattered. Whichever one she'd opened first would've stolen all of her attention, just like the collar had.

"Where is it? What breed is it?"

"There's more in here." Boone picked up the box and shoved it back at her.

Gerty practically growled at him, and both Keith and Mike chuckled.

"Baby doll, finish opening the present," Mike said.

She gave him a glare that wasn't as powerful as the one she'd given Boone and looked back into the box. "This is just a bridle. I have—" She cut off when she saw the bright orange sticky note that Boone had put on the name plate.

Her eyes once again blitzed back to his. "Daddy, where is the horse this belongs to?"

Boone wished he'd timed things better with his son. He couldn't know how long it would take Gerty to go through each present, and Walter had slipped away right after Gerty had opened his gift. Amy had given it to her first, and that had been about twenty minutes ago.

"Right here," Walt said, and everyone spun, Gerty the very fastest.

The equine Boone had bought for his daughter stood next to Walt, the two of them looking like the gangly pair they were.

"Daddy." Gerty didn't even look at him as she gasped out his name. "This horse is not okay."

"He's fine," Boone drawled as he got to his feet too. "We rescued him a week ago is all. He's still recovering." He followed her the handful of paces to the animal, where she was already stroking both of her hands down the side of his neck. "I figured there wasn't anyone better on this planet to fix 'im up than you."

"And Gloria," Gerty said. "And you, Daddy."

"He's yours," Daddy said. "You'll have to pay the boarding fee here, but only after the first six months. Cosette and I took care of that."

She turned back to him then, her blue eyes shining with love. 'Thank you, Daddy." She threw herself into his arms and held on tight. He loved how strong she was, physically and mentally, emotionally and spiritually. He loved how tightly she held him, as if she'd truly missed him while she was off in Texas, Montana, Utah, and Canada.

Of course she had. He knew she had. Sometimes, though, he felt like she'd forgotten him, or that he annoyed her too much, or that she'd tire of his dad jokes, how he laughed too loud, or asked her boyfriends all the hard questions.

She stepped back. "Now. Where is this dog?"

"Right here," Amy said with a giggle.

A collective "aw" rose up from the crowd as they turned to see the puppy, who'd magically appeared on the picnic table. He tried to lick one of the empty plates with a smear of pink frosting on the edge, and Mike rescued it quickly.

"Oh, my stars." Gerty flew back to the table. "That is the cutest dog on the planet." She picked the German shepherd right up and cradled him in her arms. "Daddy, he's a black and silver German shepherd."

"I'm aware," he said calmly.

She let the puppy lick her face, pure joy radiating from her.

"Gross," Mike said good-naturedly, and Boone nodded at him.

"Agreed."

Gerty ignored them both and asked, "Where'd you get him?"

"Had a friend in Albuquerque with them," Boone said casually. "He shipped him up here with his son a few days ago."

Gerty met his eyes, challenge in hers. "A few days ago? Where has he been all this time?"

"At our house!" Amy nearly yelled. "Isn't he so cute, Gerty? Look at what his sweatshirt says."

She turned the dog over and read the dark gray sweatshirt. She grinned at her sister, passed her the wiggling dog, and embraced Boone again. "You're the best dad in the whole world," she said.

"Yeah, and an hour ago, you wanted to shoot lasers at me from your eyes."

She laughed, but she didn't deny it. As she stepped back, she surveyed her new horse and then her dog as it ran over to the horse. "I think my days just got longer."

"Sorry," Boone said, but he wasn't really apologizing.

"What should I name them?" she asked, and he turned, thinking he'd give his opinion if she really wanted it.

But she'd melted into Mike's side, and he said, "Whatever you want, baby doll."

"I think you should name the horse Mustang," Amy said.

Gerty laughed and said, "No, Amy. I'm not naming a horse Mustang."

"What are you gonna name it?" she asked.

Gerty took her hand and took her over to the horse as she said, "You have to listen to the horse," she said, her voice fading. "He knows his name."

Mike stayed next to Boone and asked, "Is that true?"

"Yep," Boone said, admiring his daughter. "Well, Gerty thinks it is. Some people just name their horses what they want." He gave Mike a smile and faced him fully. "Thanks for giving us a few extra minutes today."

"Sure, of course," he said easily. "I'm okay to steal her away this afternoon for a little bit?"

"That's Gloria's turf, but I think she's counting on it." Boone turned away from Mike, not sure why it bothered him that Mike was going to take Gerty somewhere. He knew his daughter was kissing Mike and had been for a few weeks now. Cosette had asked Mike if they could have Gerty and him for dinner that night, and he'd agreed without a problem.

Boone faded back to his wife's side and sat beside her. "You spoil her," Cosette said as she leaned into his chest.

"She loves animals," he said instead of defending himself.

"Any idea what Mike's got up his sleeve?" she whispered.

Boone turned into her and kissed the corner of her eye. "Nope."

"You didn't ask him?"

"I did not."

"Boone."

"They're adults," he said. "Aren't you the one constantly reminding me of that?"

"Constantly?"

Boone didn't want to argue with his wife. "No," he admitted. "Not constantly, but I know you've said it to me before."

"Maybe once or twice," she said.

"I'm trying to listen to you, baby." He grinned at her and laughed when she rolled her eyes.

"Daddy!"

He faced Amy as she ran toward him. "She's gonna name him Dusty! Dusty!"

"I hear you," he said to get her to stop yelling. "She's going to be the death of me," he grumbled under his breath.

"Funny," Cosette said. "I remember you saying that about another of your daughters, and now you can't get enough of her."

# CHAPTER

## *Twenty*

MIKE'S NERVES pounded at him the same way his heart did. He told himself not to glance over to Gerty again. He'd already done it three or four times, and she'd picked up on his anxiety.

"Where are we going?" she asked as he made another right turn.

"It's just...down...here." They'd been driving for about twenty minutes since leaving the farm, in the opposite direction from Ivory Peaks, and he hoped that wasn't too far from her job or family.

Just the fact that Mike had gotten her this gift spoke so much about the plans he had for his future. He'd loved growing up in Coral Canyon, and he wouldn't have objected to finding someone in that small, mountain town, getting married, and settling down in Wyoming.

At the same time, he'd always known his future sat in Denver, in a high-rise building, with a farm about an hour away. Hunter and his younger brother, Deacon, would run the farm where his father and theirs had grown up, most likely passing it to one of their children when the time came.

But that didn't mean that Mike couldn't buy a farm too. He rather liked the idea of having somewhere quiet to come home to—and retire too—when he was done with his time at HMC. If Gerty was there…even better.

He tried to swallow and couldn't, his throat the narrowest it had ever been. He had no idea how his gift would be taken, as it did imply certain things. He'd talked everything through with his father before he'd purchased the farm, and the sale had only gone through yesterday as it was.

His father's words came back to him as the road he drove on turned from paved to dirt. *If she doesn't want it,* he'd said. *Or it doesn't work out, Mike, then what? Do you want this farm and are willing to work it?*

The answer had been yes. He might see Gerty's ghost every time he came out here, but he knew ghosts faded, especially with enough therapy. He didn't want Gerty to fade from his life, and he was willing to give her the time she required from him. That hadn't changed, and he just needed to make sure she knew that.

An arch appeared, and Gerty leaned forward. "Big Ten Farm." She swung her gaze toward Mike. "What are we doing here?" She'd always been extraordinarily full of questions, and he'd forgotten that about her.

He gripped the wheel, his own frustration starting to rise. He and Hunter had come out this morning and tied a giant yellow bow around the barn, and the thought of telling his cousin that Gerty didn't want the farm…or him…made Mike ease up on the accelerator.

He could make something up, turn around, and take her back to Pony Power.

In fact, he probably should do that. The Lord would forgive him for the lie just this one time.

"These pastures are great," she said, her irritation with him thinly veiled in her voice. "My horses would love it here."

"That's great." He cleared his throat, the barn about to come into view. Two more seconds, and there it sat. He came to a complete stop and Gerty looked at him. He nodded out the windshield and waited for her to look too. When she did, he added, "Because this is your farm."

Silence filled the cab. Pure, complete silence.

Seconds clicked by, and Mike wasn't sure what kind of reaction he'd been hoping for. He knew with Gerty not to expect something, but he'd seen her explode to her feet when she'd pulled the collar out of her daddy's gift box.

"No," she finally said.

"Yes," he said. "Happy birthday." The words scraped his throat.

"Michael." She turned toward him, and he had no choice but to look at her. "Tell me you're lying and you didn't buy me a farm for my birthday."

He couldn't even smile. "My momma taught me not to tell lies," he whispered.

She made a strangled noise he wasn't sure was good or not, yanked on the door handle, and flew from his truck.

She slammed the door behind her, glaring at him—so she wasn't as happy as she was when her father had gifted her a dog and a horse—and stomped away in the wrong direction.

Away from the farm, not toward it.

"Lord." Mike didn't know what else to add. He'd prayed over this gift for a couple of weeks now, and never once had God told him not to buy it.

His door suddenly flew open, and Gerty stood there, her chest heaving. "That's it? You're just going to sit there?"

"I was asking the Lord to help me with you," he said calmly.

She yelled and slammed his door closed too. That got him to unbuckle, and he flew out of the truck and after her.

"Hey," he barked at her. She didn't stop or even slow down. He caught her quickly and grabbed her hand. "Hey. Can you calm down and talk to me like a human being?"

She pulled her hand away. "You can't just buy me everything I want."

"Why not?" he challenged. "Why the heck not, Gerty? Do you know how much two billion dollars is?"

She glared at him, but at least she wasn't marching anymore. She hadn't stopped though, and Mike kept pace with her. "Plus interest," he said. "For a decade. This—" He swept his hand toward the land—which he now owned. "—Is what I wanted to give you. I know you want your own place, and I can give it to you."

"I want to *work* for my own place."

"Trust me, honey, you're going to work this place," he

threw back at her. "It's a gorgeous piece of land, but it hasn't been taken care of in about five years." He slowed down, hoping she would too. She didn't, but she did detour off the road and over to the fence there.

Her shoulders lifted and fell as she faced the pasture and put one foot on the lowest rung. He gave her several long seconds and then joined her. Mike wanted to start throwing questions at her, Marine-style, but he held back.

When she didn't volunteer anything, he sighed. "Talk to me, Gerty."

"I don't know how."

"Why are you mad about this?"

"Because, Mike," she said, plenty of disdain in her voice. "You can't just buy people farms."

"Why not? This is exactly what HMC does for people." The fire inside him started to lick against his ribs, but he didn't want to fight with her. He drew in a deep breath. "Gerty, when I got my inheritance, I was given a very solemn charge to do something good with it. My Uncle Cy built a motorcycle shop—yes, it was what he wanted to do, but still to this day—and he's over seventy years old—he builds and donates a custom bike for a military veteran. He does good with his money."

"This is not the same at all," she said.

Mike didn't see the difference. "Hunter funded an equine therapy unit in Massachusetts before he even graduated from college. And he funded and helped his wife build Pony Power."

"Yeah, she's his *wife*."

Mike started to nod, sudden understanding filling his mind. "You think I'm buying you."

"No."

"You think you'll owe me something, then."

"Of course I will," she said. "And if you can't see that, you're delusional."

Mike dropped his head, trying to see it from her point of view. He'd known there was a possibility of her reacting this way, and maybe that said more than he'd thought. Maybe he'd brushed that thought from his mind because he didn't want to believe it. "This is what I want to do with my money," he said very quietly. "I want to seek out the quiet ones, the people who get overlooked in their families, those who have small dreams that are very big to them, and I want to make them come true."

His heart burned with the desire to do it. "I thought I'd start with someone I knew and cared about, because then they could help me see where I went wrong." He turned and faced her then, her displeasure smacking him right in the face. "I can see now I shouldn't have made it a surprise." He started to leave, and her arm shot out and grabbed his. He waited, his humiliation burning through his lungs.

"Mike," she said, and her tone was far gentler than before. "That all sounds so amazing. Really."

"Yeah, I believe you," he said sarcastically.

"Hey," she said, and he shook his head as a way of apology. "I just meant, with those other people, you'll be consulting with them on their dreams. Asking questions to see what they need and want, and then providing this amazing gift. I didn't get any of that."

"You don't trust me? You don't think I know what you'd like?"

She sighed. "That's not it at all." She released his arm and faced the mountains again. "This is...it's too much for a birthday gift, Mike. It would be one thing if it came from your foundation or whatever. This isn't that. This came from you."

"Yeah." He dared to slide his hand along her waist, and when she didn't bite or bark at him, he pulled her against his hip. "This came from me, to you, because I care about you and want you to have everything you dream about."

She stayed still next to him, almost unyielding but not quite. "Mike, it's too much for me."

"You think I'm too much for you," he said.

"You said we could go slow."

"That hasn't changed."

"How?" she asked, her voice pitching up. "You just bought me a farm for my birthday. How has that not changed?"

Another door opened in Mike's mind, and he had a very hard time not stepping away from her and leaving her right here on this farm she didn't want. She hadn't even gone around and looked at anything yet. He wondered if she even would.

"Gerty," he said calmly though his heartbeat thrashed against his ribcage. "You told me that you were imagining our life together, and it was you helping me in the morning before I drive into the city for work. And that I'd have to make that drive from our very own farm. Those were your words. 'Our very own farm.'"

"Yeah, but...."

"Did you not mean that?"

"I meant it."

Mike frowned, and he did drop his arm and step away from her then. "Okay, then, I'm gonna need you to explain to me why I *shouldn't* have bought this farm for you."

"It feels too fast," she said.

"You can live here as long as you want without me," he said. "That hasn't changed."

"It's too much."

He sighed and worked not to roll his eyes. Thankfully, he didn't. "Gerty, baby doll, listen. I have money. A lot of money. If we end up together, you're going to have to deal with that." He stepped closer and looked right into those blue eyes that had burned him in the past. She shrank away from him slightly, and he wasn't glad he could do that, but satisfaction sang through him that he could get a point across if he had to.

"So I guess I just need to know...do you not see us together anymore?"

# CHAPTER
## *Twenty-One*

GERTY LOOKED AT MIKE, really looked. Her eyes blitzed back and forth on his, trying to get a read on him. She didn't know what to say, but she knew precisely what she didn't want to do: hurt him.

Or lie to him.

Or lose him.

"I see us together," she blurted out, her voice too loud for this quiet farm. "I just...I like living sixty steps from you and coming over in the morning to help you with your dishes and make coffee and we talk and relax and—" She cut off because she'd run out of air.

Mike started to chuckle, which only made her mood darken. "Stop it," she grumbled, turning away from him.

"I won't." He put his arm around her and drew her back into his chest. His mouth came dangerously close to her ear. "I sure like you, Gerty. I'm seein' us together too."

"I can't get married right away," she said.

"I'm not asking you to marry me right away," he said. "I'm asking you to walk around this farm with me, and if you hate it, I'll sell it. I thought it would be perfect for you —and eventually for us—but if you really don't want it, I'll get rid of it."

She turned into him and buried her face in his chest. "You can't get rid of it."

He wrapped her up in his arms, and Gerty wound hers around him too. She clung to him like he was the only anchor she had in a stormy, thrashing sea.

"Why can't I get rid of it?"

"Because I already know it's perfect," she said.

"These fences need to be redone."

"Yeah, but the bones of the pasture are good." She stepped back, glad she hadn't cried. She still felt like she might, her chest constricting in that strange way it did when her emotions surged. She looked at him but had to look away as his powerful, adoring gaze was too heavy to hold. "I don't deserve a farm like this."

"Yes, you do," he whispered.

"I don't deserve a man like you."

"Also false." He gently brought her face back to his. "Gerty, you've been lettin' the darkness in. You've been listening to his voice, haven't you?"

"I'm trying not to," she said, her voice catching. Tears filled her eyes, and blast it, they came so fast, she couldn't blink them back. "I'm—" She cut herself off again, because she hated the pinched, nasally quality of her voice.

Thankfully and mercifully, Mike drew her back into his chest and held her while she cried. She wasn't even sure what she was weeping about. Losing James? Believing the things he'd said about her? This amazing birthday present from her clearly fantastic boyfriend?

All of the above?

Mike didn't ask her, and that only spoke to how well he knew her. It hit her then that some of the tears wetting his shirt were due to how well he knew her. He'd known she'd been ruminating on the cruel things James had said to her; he knew she'd broken her promise not to listen to them.

She drew in a deep, steadying breath and exhaled it out slowly as she stepped back. He gently wiped her face and leaned down and kissed each cheek. "I'm sorry," he whispered. "I didn't mean to make you cry on your birthday."

"It's not you," she said. "It's just…everything."

"Baby doll," he said. "Tell me what you want, and I'll make it happen."

She wished she could have him root out the insecurities in her life. She had so few of them, but the ones inside her head felt mighty and powerful. "I want you to show me the farm," she said. "Every barn, every pasture, the house, all of it."

"All right," he drawled like the cowboys she'd known in the rodeo circuit. "Remember, it's pretty rough."

"I think I can handle it."

He led her back to the truck, and leaned into her legs after she'd gotten in. He stood almost as tall as her sitting in his big truck, which he'd gone with his cousin to buy a few weeks ago, and gave her a smile. "I think you're the prettiest woman in the whole state."

She couldn't help smiling, though she did shake her

head. Gerty wanted to tell him that line was terrible and he shouldn't use it again, but she did like that he thought she was pretty. "Thank you, Mike," she said seriously, and she leaned down to kiss him.

She'd kissed him before. Many times, actually. This summer and others growing up. None of them had felt as meaningful as this kiss, on her thirtieth birthday, sitting down the road from the farm that could potentially be the land of her dreams. And he was the man of her dreams, and while all of it scared her to no end, Gerty reminded herself that she'd done a lot of hard things in her life.

He broke the kiss and leaned his forehead against hers. He said nothing, where some of her other boyfriends would've. She liked the silence and how much it said between them, and then he straightened.

"All right," he said. "Let's start with this front barn."

———

A COUPLE OF DAYS LATER, Gerty knocked on her aunt's office door, then entered the room at the back of the furthest stable. "Hey, Aunt Gloria."

"Come in, Gerty," she said, twisting in her chair to put something in a cabinet behind her. When she faced Gerty again, she wore a bright smile that made the lines around her eyes more pronounced.

Gerty looked up to her aunt in so many ways, and her words choked in her chest. She crossed the room in a couple of quick strides and sat down in front of Gloria's desk. Her aunt hated working indoors, but to run a training, riding, and therapeutic facility with as many horses as Pony Power had, there was some office work that had to be done.

"What's going on with you?" Aunt Gloria asked.

"I just…wanted to talk to you," Gerty said. Her hands twisted around one another, and she told herself to still them. They almost had a mind of their own, but she got them to stop. "Mike bought me a farm, Gloria."

Her eyebrows shot up. "He bought you a farm?"

"Yes." Gerty nodded. "It needs a lot of work, I won't lie. But the barns are good. The stables are sturdy. The farmhouse needs a lot of elbow grease, but it's otherwise solid."

Aunt Gloria absorbed everything Gerty had said, and Gerty didn't even know what she was saying. She hadn't meant to start with the farm. After she and Mike had walked through it all, him explaining things to her he'd learned on his tour before buying the place, she hadn't mentioned it to anyone.

Not Daddy or Mom, not anyone at Pony Power. She and Mike had talked more about it, but that was it. She hadn't said when she'd move in—or even if she'd be doing that. It was almost like the farm existed out there, and she could drive to it and walk around and no one would tell her she was trespassing. Because she wasn't.

"Okay," Aunt Gloria said. "Are you quitting here?"

"No," Gerty said with a shake of her head. "No, of course not."

Gloria sat back in her chair and folded her arms. "Running a farm is a full-time job, Gerty."

"Yeah." Gerty started nodding, and she looked down at her hands. "I really wanted to ask you about Uncle Matt."

"What about Uncle Matt?"

"I mean...." Now that Gerty was here, she had no idea why. She sighed, frustration building in her that she couldn't just talk like a normal human being. "Mike's really rich," she said. "I know Uncle Matt had some money when you guys got married. Did it...did it make you feel inadequate?"

Aunt Gloria sighed too, and Gerty dared to look up at her. She wore a puzzled look on her face, and she studied Gerty. "Honey," she said. "What are you really getting at?"

"I don't know." Everything inside Gerty came unhinged. "I just feel like I'm not good enough for Mike. For his money. He shouldn't be buying me farms, right? It's crazy. Who does that?"

Aunt Gloria eyed her for another moment and then she said, "Someone who cares a lot about you."

Gerty nodded. Mike did care about her, crazy as that may be.

"Baby," Aunt Gloria said. "I've known you for a while now, right?"

"Yes, ma'am," Gerty whispered.

"You're an amazing woman," Gloria said. "Whoever has led you to believe otherwise is dead wrong."

Gerty looked up and into her aunt's dark hazel eyes. "Has my daddy told you about James?"

"Yes," she said simply. "I lost something extremely important to me, Gerty, before I came here and met your uncle Matt. You're not alone in the way you feel or the way you've been treated. It's not fair, but you're not an island."

Gerty nodded, her next breath lodging in her throat. She didn't know what to say anyway.

"You and Mike seem good together," Aunt Gloria continued. "I know you need time, and I'll be struck dead right now if you haven't told Mike that." She grinned, and that helped Gerty relax.

"What about the farm?"

"What about it?" Aunt Gloria asked. "Do you like it? Want it?"

"Yeah." Gerty could admit that. "I'm not good without something to do, and it would give me a lot to do after work."

"Then do it," Aunt Gloria said. She leaned forward again, her smile kind and wise. "Honey, I don't know where you and Mike are exactly, but I see the way he looks at you, and I see the way you look at him. It's okay to fall in love with him."

Gerty nodded, because she somehow needed permission to fall in love with Mike. Even so, she wasn't sure she could do it right now.

"Gerty, you've got to lay down whatever you're carrying."

"I don't know how," she whispered.

"You go to God, and you give it all to Him," Aunt Gloria said. "He'll carry it for you, and you'll finally be free."

Gerty's eyes pricked, but she didn't let the tears fall. "I

haven't even been praying, because I don't know what to pray for."

"We've all been praying for you, Gerty-girl." She got up and came around her desk to crouch in front of Gerty. "You are loved, and not just by us here on earth. God loves you, Gerty, and it's time you started loving yourself."

One tear escaped, and Gerty swiped at her face. "I just feel so...unlovable." She looked at her aunt and let everything show. "It may sound stupid to you, but it's how I feel."

"It doesn't sound stupid to me." Gloria wrapped her in a hug and held on tight. "One thing I know, Gerty, is that God loves you, and He doesn't want you to feel this way. Maybe pray for Him to show you how he really feels about you."

"Okay," Gerty whispered against her aunt's shoulder.

"And let Mike take care of you," Gloria murmured. "He already knows you're strong, Gerty. You take care of him, and he likes that, but he wants to be a man too." She pulled back and nodded at Gerty. "Okay? They want to be men, and that means he wants to take care of you too."

Gerty studied her hands. "I want him to do that too."

"Then ask him to take you to the farm this weekend, and you two start to work on it together." Gloria gave her a smile that Gerty only caught the tail end of as she stood. "You're a good woman, Gerty. If you'd like to get in with one of our counselors here, let me know. Mike sees Harmon, and he's great with kids and adults."

Gerty got to her feet, her heartbeat settling now that

this was almost over. "I think I'm going to start with prayer," she said. "Go from there."

"Starting with prayer is always a good idea," Aunt Gloria said. "And if that doesn't work as quickly as you'd like, you can come back here anytime."

Gerty hugged her aunt again. "Thank you, Aunt Gloria."

"Of course," she said. "Take the highs with the lows, Gerty. I'd love it if my handsome, billionaire boyfriend bought me a farm." She gave Gerty a knowing smile and headed for the door. She opened it for Gerty and turned back to her, more serious than before. "But I know why it concerns you, and that's valid too. One thing I will say— don't stop talking. Don't stop talking to God, and don't stop talking to Mike. If you talk, you can work anything out."

"Talking." Gerty rolled her eyes. "The one thing I'm just *so great* at."

"You are great at it," Aunt Gloria said. "I thought we had a lovely chat just now."

"Because you can read minds." Gerty stepped past her and into the hall while Aunt Gloria laughed.

"I wish, honey," she said. "I wish."

Gerty waved at her and kept going, because she couldn't make a call back in this corner, and she needed to get in touch with Mike and find out what his weekend plans were.

She ducked outside and around to the back of the stable, where she drew in a deep breath, closed her eyes, and let everything around her go quiet. That took a couple of minutes, and then Gerty whispered, "Lord, it's me, Gertrude Whettstein. I'm real sorry I've been so quiet these past couple of months, but I just...don't know what to say."

Her stomach swooped, almost like she was riding a roller coaster, and Gerty swallowed to settle her nerves.

"I need to know where we are," she whispered. "I know You're probably mad I haven't been as faithful as I should've been. I want to do better. Can You let me know if I'm okay, and how to do better?"

Gerty had never had the booming voice of God fill her ears. She'd had pricks of thought over the years, and things that "rang true" in her heart. Something her daddy would say that made the hair on her arms stand up, and she simply knew it was true.

Right now, alone with only the wind and fences for company, Gerty kept her eyes closed and listened. With her ears and her heart and her mind all paying attention, the sweetest, softest feeling of love filled her.

And she knew—God loved her, even as silent as she'd been. Even as broken as she felt. Even as mean as she'd been to Mike when they'd first arrived at the farm.

She thought, *Apologize to Mike* and then *Keep working, Gerty. Move forward. Don't stand still.*

Her eyes opened, her tasks set by the Lord. "Thank you," she whispered. She looked up into the cloudless sky. "Thank you."

Gerty was very good with a task list, and she hurried to get to a place where she had enough service to make a call into the city.

# CHAPTER
## Twenty-Two

CORD RAKED out the last of the dirty straw in the stall, pitching it into the wheelbarrow in the aisle. In the next stall down, Travis did the same thing. And up at the end, Mike worked with them today too.

He marveled that the two men he worked with didn't have to work at all. They were both billionaires. Travis donated the entirety of his salary back to Pony Power, and Cord wasn't sure what Mike did. He probably simply worked for free. This was his uncle's farm and all.

"All done," he said a moment later, tossing his pitchfork into the wheelbarrow. "I'll be right back for y'all."

Travis yelled at him, and Cord lifted the heavy wheelbarrow, balanced it, and set off for the waste dumpsters. He didn't particularly like this part of the job, but he loved everything about Colorado. The wide, open skies, the cool breezes in the autumn, all four seasons, and the mountains which greeted him every single morning.

He dumped the waste and turned back for the stables. A woman walked ahead of him, her hand in that of a little boy. His heartbeat picked up speed, and not because he'd just exerted himself getting rid of the manure.

That was Jane, and he hadn't seen her around the farm yet today. She'd been working four days a week in the city, and then spending Fridays and her weekend here on the farm. She still lived in the big, gray house, as she was taking care of it for her parents while they were in Coral Canyon this summer.

Her younger brother, Deacon, lived there with her.

Today, she wore a light-wash pair of jeans and a bright blue blouse that had sleeves that waved in the air current as she walked. Her dark blonde hair had been pulled up into a ponytail, and he expected her to take the little boy into the arena where the ponies were already waiting. Two or three other children had already arrived, and sure enough, Jane took the boy in with them.

To his surprise, she didn't stay, but came right back out and latched the gate behind her. She turned, looked up, and paused as her eyes met Cord's. He told himself to keep on moving, because he did not want to get into any trouble with the boss's daughter.

"Morning, Cord," she said, her smile bright as she tucked her hands into her front pockets.

"Ma'am." He nodded at her, and while everything male inside him told him to stop and chit-chat for a few minutes, the rational side of him screamed at him to *keep moving. Do not stop.*

"Oh, I'm not even thirty," she teased. "You can't call

me ma'am." She stepped right into his path, and he had no choice but to stop. He could've mowed her down with the wheelbarrow, but that certainly wouldn't be good.

He looked at her, and she looked at him, and he had no idea what was happening. His blood seemed to fizz in his veins, and he'd never had this reaction to a woman before.

"I'm not fourteen anymore," she said.

"I can see that."

"Maybe you and I could try goin' to dinner." She raised her eyebrows, a clear question mark for her statement.

"I...I don't know about that, Miss Jane."

She stepped around the curved end of the wheelbarrow, those electric eyes locked on his. "I think we'd have fun."

"I'm not really into having fun," he said.

She cocked her head, her eyes narrowing. "What does that mean? I know you cowboys have card-playing nights and bonfires with each other. Those aren't fun?"

Cord didn't know how to handle her. Number one, he wanted to be the one to ask her out, and number two, he could never do that. So it was much simpler if he stayed out of her way and kept her out of his thoughts. He'd been doing a good job of it for the past several weeks.

Uh, a decent job.

Fine, he'd failed completely, but simply thinking about Jane didn't mean he had to act on those thoughts.

"I have to get back to work," he said, feeling stupid and slow. He started to push the wheelbarrow, and as he went past her, he caught the rosy scent of her perfume. He wanted to take a bite of her, swing her around as she laughed, and set her on her feet to kiss her.

In his mind, the image played out in full color, making Cord's pulse shoot through his body.

"I'm going to talk to my father," she said.

Cord stopped and faced her. "What about?"

"Us," she said.

"Jane." He dropped his head so his cowboy hat shielded her from his sight.

"What?" Her boots brought her closer, the crunching sound of her steps over the dry-packed earth.

He didn't quite know what, but he looked up just enough to see her under the brim of his cowboy hat. "Has it ever occurred to you that I don't need you to be in charge of me?"

She flinched like he'd slapped her across the face. Her cheeks colored and everything. "Excuse me." She turned on her heel and marched away.

"Jane," he called after her. She didn't slow at all, and Cord sighed out his frustration. His irritation at himself fired like a cannon through his whole body, and he pushed the wheelbarrow back to the stables while he cursed himself silently.

"There he is," Travis said with a smile. "That one's ready."

"Great," Cord said darkly.

Travis came closer. The man was in his mid-fifties now, and still just as good of a friend as he'd ever been to Cord. He'd gotten married and moved next door. He and Poppy had two kids of their own now, plus Steele when he came home from college, but Travis always had time for Cord.

He brought pizza over at least twice a month, and he and Poppy invited Cord to every Sabbath Day meal they had. As Poppy was the best cook Cord knew, he went willingly and often.

"What happened?"

"Nothing," Cord mumbled. He started to go into the stall Travis had raked, then paused and looked at his best friend. "Actually, I just ran into Jane outside." He looked over his shoulder, but he didn't see Mike.

"He got a call and left," Travis said. "Hunter."

Cord nodded, his heart in a knot. "She suggested we go to dinner."

Travis said nothing, and Cord couldn't read him in the shadows of the stable.

"She said she was going to call her daddy and talk to him about us goin' out."

"Okay," Travis said slowly.

"No," Cord said. "It's not okay, Trav. She's his daughter, and he made it ultra-clear to me that she's off-limits."

"When she was fourteen," Travis said. "She's not fourteen anymore."

"As she also pointed out to me," Cord said with plenty of disgust in his voice. "You think I don't know that? She's gorgeous, and smart, and everything I'm not. There is no way I'm going out with her, even if I wanted to, which I don't."

Cord had worked hard not to lie about anything,

because it came too easily to him. Everything sounded too true. This, though, rang falsely even in his own ears.

Travis didn't call him on it, though. "Maybe she's not off-limits anymore."

"Yeah, I'm sure the billionaire Gray Hammond would love his daughter to marry an ex-con." Cord rolled his eyes. "Don't say stuff like that, Trav. We both know it's not true."

"Just like you sayin' you don't want to go out with her." He took a step closer and leaned in, his deep, bass voice low as he added, "You're not the same man you were twenty years ago, Cord. It's time to let him go."

"I *have* let him go," Cord said.

"No." Travis shook his head. "You cling to him, and you use him any time you want to do something that will make you happy."

"I do not." Anger rose through Cord. "I know who I am, Trav."

"Yeah, so do I." Travis straightened and met Cord's eyes. "You're a really talented mechanic. You're a hard worker. You're a good man, and Gray Hammond knows that. We all know it—and Jane can see it too." He clapped Cord on the shoulder. "That's why she wants to go out with you."

Cord had never felt so conflicted. He couldn't organize his thoughts quickly enough to ask the questions streaming through him, because they only existed in pieces. Trav gave him a smile and said, "Call me when you're ready," and turned around. "I've got to go find Matt and help him with the mid-day feeding."

Cord couldn't even say, "Okay," fast enough, and Travis left the stable in silence. Cord spun away from the door as it banged closed. "He's wrong," he muttered. About what, Cord wasn't sure.

He felt like a good person, but only a few people knew who he'd been when he'd first come to this farm. Only Gray, Hunter, and Trav knew why he'd come in the first place. Only the three of them knew that he hadn't spoken to a blood relative in a decade and a half.

Leaning against the stall wall for support, Cord bowed his head and finally caught up to his thoughts.

"I want to go out with Jane Hammond," he whispered. "But that doesn't mean I liked her when she was fourteen. Does it? Will people think that?"

It didn't really matter what people thought, other than Gray and Elise. He had *not* entertained the idea of going out with Jane when she was younger, not even a little bit. He would be mortified if anyone thought that, most of all Gray.

He cleaned out the corner of the stall where Trav had raked the waste, forked in fresh straw, and moved down to Mike's stall. It was only half-finished, and Cord got the job done without complaint. Mike was a good man too, torn in a lot of different directions.

Because of his shoulder, he couldn't do a lot of the work Cord, Trav, and Mission did, and Cord didn't fault him that. He wouldn't want to be CEO of a huge family company, generations of Hammonds all watching him. He was nowhere near smart enough for that, for one, and for another, Cord didn't want the spotlight on him.

"That's another reason I can't go out with Jane," he grumbled. "If I do, everyone will be lookin' at us."

He pushed the full-again wheelbarrow toward the waste area, his mind churning. *What should I do? What should I do? What should I do?*

He'd already determined to stay away from Jane this summer. He'd assumed she'd move out, making that task easier, but she hadn't. She'd only crowded in closer, and Cord almost choked at the thought of her going out with anyone but him.

*Call Gray.*

The words came into his head in a loud, clear voice, and Cord actually groaned. "Really, Lord? I have to humiliate myself to go out with this woman?"

He couldn't call right now, because if Mike wasn't around, he had to get the horses out for the lunchtime free ride. Cord did that, the nagging thought to call his boss, his mentor, his father-figure still loud in his head.

He ignored it as he did his afternoon chores and then headed over to the mechanic shed to work on an old truck that wouldn't start. He'd asked Gray if he could use the shed and the tools on the farm to restore the vehicle, and he'd gotten permission.

"So maybe he'd give you permission to date his daughter."

There was only one way to find out, but Cord wasted his evening hours inside the engine, his stomach practically clawing itself out by the time he returned to his cabin. He put a pizza in the oven, showered, opened a bag of salad, and ate.

"It's too late to call now," he told himself as he went down the hall to bed.

The next morning, he went over to Pony Power, the same as he always did. Gloria and Matt handed out the day's assignments, and Cord accepted his and instead of taking his spot over by Travis, he positioned himself closer to Jane.

His heart pounded at him; his pulse shot lightning through his veins; his mouth had never felt drier.

"All right, everyone," Matt said. "Stay safe. Find us if you need us."

"But don't need us," Gloria said with a smile. Cord grinned back, because she said that almost every day.

The crowd started to disperse to get started on the day, and Cord moved to Jane's side. "Jane."

She looked over to him in surprise. "Morning, Cord," she said, glancing past him and then left and right. "Should we be seen talking to each other?" she asked in a mock whisper.

"Funny," he said in a deadpan. He cleared his throat, because he actually thought she was funny. "Listen, you haven't called your daddy, have you?"

"No."

He nodded. "Okay, good."

"Good? What does that mean?"

Cord leaned down, that infusion of rose to his nose making him feel strong and capable. "It means I'll handle it." He started to move away from her, but she caught him quickly.

"You'll handle it? Handle what?"

He cut her a look out of the side of his eye. "Askin' your daddy if it would be okay if I asked you out to dinner." He dang near tripped over his own feet, but the Lord was really watching out for him, because he didn't.

Jane fell back, and Cord turned and looked at her. "What?"

"You're going to call my dad and ask him if we can go out."

"Yes."

She blinked those blue eyes at him, pure shock in them. That melted away as she smiled, ducked her head, and moved her fingers as if tucking her hair behind her ear. It was all up in a ponytail, though, and Cord recognized the motion for what it was. She was flirting with him.

"Is that all right?" he asked, facing her fully.

Jane looked up, and their eyes met. Fireworks exploded in his stomach, and Cord sure did like this woman. "Yeah," she said slowly. "That's just fine."

He nodded, his jaw setting. He had to get himself under control before they went out, because he couldn't be showing her all of his feelings on the first date. If there even was a first date.

Besides, he still had an incredibly difficult phone call to make, and Cord had no idea how to have a conversation with Gray about his daughter.

# CHAPTER
## Twenty-Three

JANE LEFT her office in the city, ready for the weekend ahead. She loved math and numbers, because they made sense to her, unlike so many other things in her life.

Namely, the stunningly handsome Cord Behr. The past fourteen years had been kind to him, and he hadn't lost any hair and gained plenty of muscles working her family's farm.

Jane had minded her father and stopped flirting with the cowboys who worked and lived on the farm, and that had included Cord.

Hers had been an innocent crush, of which she'd had dozens from the ages of fourteen to probably twenty-two, when she'd graduated with her bachelor's degree in accounting.

She'd gone back to graduate school and completed that before starting at a firm in Colorado Springs. The environment hadn't been good for her, and Jane had called Hunter to find out if there might be room for her at HMC in the accounting department.

Of course there was, and Jane had started at the beginning of June, in a job she actually really liked, with a far better work atmosphere than her previous job.

The only problem was the long commute, but once her parents had gone to Coral Canyon for the summer, Jane had opted to stay out at the farm to help her mother take care of the house.

Deacon lived there too, but he wasn't exactly skilled in the domestic cleanliness department, and Jane would not allow her mother to return to a house that looked like a frat boy had lived in it for three months.

She'd moved to a ten-hour day and worked Monday through Thursday, taking a three-day weekend to spend time out in the country.

Growing up, she hadn't particularly enjoyed being so far from civilization, but now, she craved the quiet in a way her teenage self had loathed. She still loved the city, but she needed an escape every now and then.

She'd always liked cowboys, and she could admit that Cord was one reason she'd chosen to stay out on the family farm. He was simply delicious on the outside and so sweet on the inside.

She'd come on too strong last week, and Cord had said she'd call her daddy and talk to him about the two of them going out. Jane had never seen her father as angry as he'd been the night he'd confronted Jane about the incident in the gardening shed with Cord.

"You can't do that, Jane," he'd said, his voice rough and

cold. "He's a man, and you're a girl, and you could ruin someone like him."

Jane hadn't truly understood what he'd meant at the time, but she did now. To her, she'd been flirting innocently, and Cord had flirted back. He'd always been a bit of a flirt, even now, but Jane had never known him to go out with anyone.

He still hadn't asked her out, and she wondered if he'd called her father yet. Impatience built inside her, and once she made it to her car and had left the city behind, the country road in front of her, she dialed Daddy.

"Jane," he said in a much calmer, kinder voice than that fateful night years earlier. "What's up, sweetheart?"

Jane gripped the wheel, not sure how to start this conversation. "Hey, Daddy," she said, her voice a bit too chirpy. "How's Coral Canyon?"

"Wonderful," he said.

She knew he'd have moved there if not for the farm—for Hunter being in the role of CEO at HMC—and she wondered how long her parents would stay in Ivory Peaks after Hunter retired and Mike took over at HMC.

Probably not long.

Jane made small talk about the hikes around the area and about her job, and then the conversation dried up. "Listen," she said. "I was just wondering if you'd talked to…any of the cowboys at the farm? Lately?"

"Any of the cowboys at the farm?" Daddy asked, and that answered her question. In fact, she should've known that Cord hadn't talked to Daddy yet, because he would've called her if he had.

"What does that mean?"

"Nothing," Jane said quickly.

"Is there something going on at the farm I need to know about?"

"I'm sure there isn't," she said. "Matt would've called you."

"Right," he said. "But *you're* calling me."

Jane swallowed, her mind buzzing. She'd never held her tongue with her father, except for when he got really angry and passionate about something. He rarely played that card, and when he did, Jane calmed down and listened.

"I have to go," Jane said. "I'm driving, and I'm about to hit that dead spot outside of the city."

"All right," her father said, his voice cool. Jane suspected he'd call Matt the moment this call ended, and she sighed as she hung up.

She wished she had time to send Matt a text to spare him, but he'd simply tell Gray there was nothing to worry about, and that would be that. It wasn't like Matt knew about Jane's insane crush on Cord Behr. She was fairly certain Cord hadn't spoken about her to anyone— including her father.

She frowned as she drove, pressing harder on the accelerator to get her back to the farm faster.

She parked in the garage at the farmhouse and went inside. She didn't normally change and head out onto the farm within five minutes of returning from work, but today, she did.

Energy flowed through her as she went out onto the

front porch. She glanced over to Pony Power, but it was almost seven o'clock at night, and Cord had probably gone home a couple of hours ago.

She saw him very little during the week, but she managed to catch a glimpse on the weekends, especially when she attended church. He went every week and sat with either Mission, Travis and his family, or Matt and his.

Never her, and Jane couldn't believe she was jealous of her friends and neighbors. She could only dream about sitting next to Cord, inhaling the scent of his cologne, and holding his hand. She'd never held his hand, and surely it would be better than anyone's she had.

She'd had a fairly serious boyfriend during her senior year in college, but in the end, Kevin hadn't been the one for her. Him being on the rebound from his previous girlfriend hadn't helped, and they'd gotten married only six months after Jane had ended things with him.

"Calm down," she told herself as she went down the steps. She crossed the lawn and went around the house, between the farmhouse and the generational house, the back side of the farm coming into view.

The cowboy cabins sat to her left, the back yard and fire pit to her right. Sheds and barns, gardens and fields, spread before her, and she drew in another deep breath.

"You're going to let him ask you out," she said. She'd always been the one to initiate her relationships, and she'd always been the one to end them too.

"Once," she muttered to herself. "Just once, you're going to let the man ask you out first."

Yet her feet still took her toward Cord's cabin. Right up

the steps she went, and she knocked on the door. She could just see if he was home. Maybe talk to him about his weekend plans.

*No*, she told herself. She wouldn't do that. But she wasn't going to stay home when he was here and they could be together.

No one came to the door, and Jane turned around. She looked left and right and back left again.

The machinery shed. Of course Cord would be there, if he was still here on the farm. Perhaps he'd gone to town for dinner, or to get groceries, or some other errand.

It would be worth the walk over to the machinery shed....

Jane went that way, glancing at each cabin she passed, almost like she expected a cowboy to spot her and stop her. No one did, and Jane entered the shed, whose doors stood open.

Cord looked up from the engine of an old truck, surprise registering on his face for a couple of heartbeats before a smile took over.

That so wasn't fair, and Jane tucked her hands into her shorts pockets and waited as he picked up a gray rag and started wiping his hands. "Well," he said with plenty of teasing in his voice. The man really was a flirt, even when he tried not to be. "What are you doin' here?"

Jane had never been particularly tongue-tied around boys, but something about him made her lose her wits for a few moments. "I just wanted to talk to you."

He came closer, a touch of swagger in his step. "About what?"

"Nothing." She didn't wear her hair up in a ponytail in the accounting office, so she actually had something to tuck behind her ear right now.

"You came out here to talk about nothing?"

"I just…." Jane sighed, because she was who she was. "I wondered if you'd talked to my daddy yet."

Cord's face changed in a moment, moving from open and flirtatious to hard and closed off. "No," he said. "Not yet." He turned around and returned to the truck.

Jane watched him, her mouth shut but her mind moving faster than ever before. "I just—"

"You just want me to operate on your timetable," he said, throwing her a dirty look. "I'm not like you, Jane."

She snapped her mouth closed and blinked. "I don't want you to be like me."

"I need my job," he said, a hint of desperation in his voice now, hiding there behind the anger. "This farm is the only thing I know, and your father took…." He shook his head, his dark blue eyes flashing with danger. "I've been busy this week."

"Yeah," she said. "Seems like it." She lifted her eyebrows and looked pointedly at the truck.

He straightened and glared, one sexy hip cocked out. "Why can't you just let me handle this the way I want to?"

"I—" She had no answer, and therefore couldn't say anything.

"I'll talk to him when I feel ready," Cord said. "I just need some time to organize my thoughts."

Jane moved closer to him. "And what are those?"

He softened slightly. "I don't quite know yet. Like I said, I'm not like you, Jane."

"What does that mean?"

"It means you're quick, and I'm not."

"You're a smart guy, Cord."

He scoffed and shook his head. "I didn't even graduate from high school, so you're wrong there."

Jane straightened, not even realizing she'd been leaning toward him. "You didn't graduate from high school?"

"I got a GED," he said, bending over the engine again.

She watched him work for a few seconds. "I remember you getting this certificate."

"Yeah," he said to the inner workings of the truck. He sighed and stood up straight and tall again. He met her gaze, and wow, Jane would wait a long time for him to ask her out.

*Patience.*

It had never been her strongest suit, but she was willing to try. For Cord, she could wait.

She smiled at him, glad when he returned it. "Okay, Cord," she said. "Well, if you're around tomorrow afternoon, say around four o'clock, I'm going to be handing out cookies after our riding lessons." She turned and started for the door. "I guess that's what I wanted to talk to you about."

She turned back at the door and smiled in his direction.

"I like cookies, Miss Jane," he said, and while it wasn't a yes, she suspected she'd see him tomorrow afternoon.

# CHAPTER

## Twenty-Four

GERTY MADE the turn Mike had almost three weeks ago, glancing over to her father. He likewise looked at her, a wariness in his gaze.

"What is this place?" he asked.

Gerty took a breath and said, "This is my new farm, Daddy."

Daddy choked, as she expected him to. "Your what?"

"I'm going to need some help getting my stuff from Montana," she continued, glancing into the rearview mirror to see what her mom thought of what she'd said. "Will you guys go with me?"

"To Montana?" Mom asked.

"Yeah," Gerty said. "Most of what I own is in a storage unit there." The thought of returning to that state had her stomach in a knot, but she had to do it. It had been three weeks since her birthday, and she'd come out to this farm at least a dozen times since.

She'd spoken to Aunt Gloria, and she'd been praying every day and night since. She knew now that the Lord loved her, and that she wanted to live on this farm, fixing it up and getting it back to the place it deserved to be.

"How did you buy a farm?" Daddy asked. He folded his arms and trained all of his attention on her.

"I, uh, didn't buy it," she said. "It was a gift."

"A gift?" Daddy and Mom asked at the same time.

"Yeah." Gerty cleared her throat. "Don't freak out, okay?"

"I hate it when you start stories like that." Daddy sighed.

"Mike bought it for me for my birthday," Gerty said in a rush. "He's a billionaire, and he said he'd sell it if I didn't want it." She glanced over to her father, then back into the rearview mirror.

Mom wore a surprised look that held some horror in it, and Daddy gaped openly at her. "He bought you a farm for your birthday?"

Gerty nodded, her voice now lodged in her throat. "And I'm thinkin' that Dusty is strong enough to move now, and I'd like to move him over here." She focused on the road in front of her though there wouldn't be anyone out here. "I'd like to move out here and start fixing it up. You'll see, it needs a lot of work."

"Are you and Mikey going to live here together?" Daddy asked.

"Not until we get married," Gerty said airily. "If we get married."

"If?"

"We're dating, Daddy," she said. "I told him I needed to go slow, and that's what we're doing."

"The boy bought you a farm," Daddy said, his voice a bit too loud.

"First," Gerty said firmly. "He's not a boy. Second, I made sure he knew where we stand, even as I accepted the gift."

"Gerty," Mom said, and she glanced at her as the road went to dirt. "Are you sure about this?"

"Yes," she said just as quickly and firmly as she had correcting her father. "I'm not a kid anymore either, and I've been making sure I'm doing the right thing every step of the way."

"Shoot." Daddy turned toward the window, unrest streaming from him. But when he looked at her again, a hint of glassiness sat in his eyes. "You are a good girl, Gerty, and I trust you."

She grinned. "Thank you, Daddy. So you'll come with me? Well, me and Mike. He wants to go to Coral Canyon to see his folks, and I'd drive with him to Wyoming, then switch over to your truck for the rest of the trip."

She gave them a moment to absorb. "If you want. We can rent a trailer up there. Stop and see Grandma and Grandpa...and Momma. Eat at Birdie's." She grinned at her father then. "Come on, you can't say no to that."

"I'll have to talk to Matt," Daddy said, but that meant yes. "See if I can get time off work."

Gerty grinned and waited until she could keep the giggle out of her voice when she said, "All right, Daddy."

"I just texted Gloria," Mom said from the back seat.

"She said we can go any time except for the last day of the summer season, because she needs us for the party."

Gerty burst out laughing then, which covered up most of Daddy's grumbling.

"Come on," she said, giggling as she came to a stop in front of the farmhouse. "You want to go with me." She put the truck in park and twisted to look at Mom. "Or I know! Girls trip. Just me and Mom will go."

"No," Daddy barked. "Your mom can't drive all the way to Coral Canyon by herself."

"I'm sure I can," Mom said, grinning knowingly at Gerty. She didn't go many places without Daddy, and Gerty understood why. She didn't have the same past as her mother, and she understood why Mom stayed within her comfort zone. She didn't blame her for that, and Gerty realized she'd been on the go, letting the wind and a whim push her north and south partly to show Mom that it was okay.

She wasn't sure if she'd done that or not, but she had enjoyed her years away from Ivory Peaks. Now, though, as she looked at the old white house in front of her, she had the distinct feeling she needed to start putting down roots.

She'd been committed to moving onto this farm already, but this thought only solidified it. "This is right," she whispered, and Daddy reached over and took her hand.

She looked at him. "I've been trying to listen to God more than myself lately," she said. She nodded back to the house. "Moving in here is right."

"Seems so." He gave her a warm smile. "And Mike?"

"He's right too," Gerty said slowly. "For right now, for me. When I think about *not* being with him...." She exhaled and shook her head. "I don't know the future, Daddy, but right now and the foreseeable future, it feels right to be with him."

"We sure do like him," Mom said. "Don't we, Boone?"

"Yes," Daddy said, his voice a bit guarded. "We like him."

Gerty threw herself into his arms. "So you'll come with me to Montana?"

Her daddy held her tightly and said, "Just tell us when you want to go, baby."

"Next weekend," she said. "Can we go next weekend?"

Daddy chuckled and pulled back. "Tell me what time you want to leave."

"I'll let you know." Gerty squealed and opened her door. "Now, come on. Come see the farm." She slid from the truck and turned back. "And remember, it's rough right now, but I'm gonna fix 'er up."

She didn't wait to hear what her parents would say about her after she slammed the door. Surely they'd have *something* to say to one another, and she didn't want to hear it. If she gave them a minute, Mom would make sure Daddy didn't say anything too negative, though Gerty would hear it all later anyway.

She and Daddy didn't hold much back from one another, so when he joined her on the front porch and stomped his foot, she wasn't surprised when he said, "This needs to be rebuilt, Gerty."

"I know," she said gleefully. "Aren't you excited to do it?"

"Me?"

Gerty wrapped one arm around her father's waist and leaned into him. "Yes, Daddy. You're the best with horses, but you're good with a hammer and wood too."

"I think you have me confused with Mission," Daddy grumbled, but he'd come rebuild the front porch, Gerty knew.

She took a deep breath and said, "Okay, let's go inside." She opened the door, and it felt like she was opening a gateway to the next stage of her life.

An exciting stage she couldn't wait to embark on.

———

"READY?" Mike asked a week later.

Gerty climbed into the truck and dropped into the passenger seat. "I am, yes," she said. "I think my mom will have to go back to the house about three times." She grinned at him and leaned over the console to kiss him.

He held her face in one hand and took his time, and Gerty once again experienced the feeling of free-falling. "I'm excited about this trip, baby doll," he whispered.

"Yeah?" she whispered back as he pressed a kiss to the side of her neck. "It's an eight-hour drive."

"Then dinner with my folks," he said, and they both started to laugh.

"Yeah," she said among the giggling and chuckling. "It's a good thing I like you."

Mike captured her hand in his and twined his fingers slowly through the gaps in hers. "You do like me, don't you, Gerty?"

"Yeah," she said.

"You like me a lot, right?" He lifted her hand to his lips.

"Yeah," she whispered.

He looked up, the brim of his cowboy hat almost concealing those pretty eyes. "I like you a whole lot too."

"Yeah?" She felt sparkly from head to toe.

"Yeah," Mike whispered. "So much that it feels like I'm falling in love with you."

Gerty stilled, but she didn't let his words scare her into silence. "Have you ever been in love, Mike?"

"No." He drew in a breath, which broke the moment between them, and straightened. He gave her a quick smile and dropped her hand. He backed out of her parents' driveway and then looked at her. "You have, I know."

"Just the one time," she said quietly. She looked out her side window, her thoughts exactly where she didn't want them. "I think it'll be so much better to have that feeling for someone who feels the same about me." She offered him a quick smile. "Don't you think?"

"I would think so, yes," he said.

Gerty reached over and took his right hand in hers. "How's the shoulder today?"

"Feels good," he said.

"If you want me to drive, I can."

"I'll let you know."

Gerty nodded and let a few miles go by in silence

before she said, "Mike?"

"Hmm?" He looked over to her with his eyes hidden behind his sunglasses.

"I'm falling in love with you too," she said, the words so big in her too-small throat. "And I definitely think it feels different than when I was in love with James."

He gaped at her until the tires bumped over the warning strip in the middle of the road. Then he jerked the wheel to get the truck back in the lane. "Well." He cleared his throat. "That's good to know."

"Yeah, you wish you weren't driving right now, don't you?" she teased.

"I would like to kiss you," he admitted. "You don't want to kiss me?"

"Of course I do." Gerty pushed herself up and wrapped her arms around his neck.

"You're gonna kill us, Gerty." He laughed as she pressed several quick, little kisses all over the side of his face. They laughed together again, and Gerty had never experienced anything so comforting and exciting as being in the cab of this truck with Mike.

"And I'm not even the one driving," she quipped. She sank back into her seat and sighed happily as she looked out the windshield. "Do your parents know you bought me a farm?"

"Not exactly," he said.

"You didn't tell them?"

"I don't have to account for my money with my folks." He gave her a quick look and focused back on the road. "I sometimes do consult with my dad about things, like where I should invest or what I might do with my inheritance that will bless the lives of others, and I talked to him about this. Just not my mother."

"Are you going to tell her?"

"I'm going to start a foundation for this type of purchasing and donations," he said. "So, yes. I'll tell her, and then I'm going to sit down with Daddy and see what advice he has about getting the foundation set up."

Gerty nodded, but she couldn't fathom starting a foundation. "Are you going to run the foundation?"

"In the beginning," he said. "I think once I take over at HMC, I might not have time. See, Hunter runs a public outreach program too, using company funds, and I want to continue that." He smiled, and Gerty liked the softness of it. "My daddy started doing that," he added. "I don't want to let that die, though every CEO at HMC does things a little differently."

"Do you think you'll like being the CEO?"

"I think so," he said. "I don't hate it, at least, and there's a steep learning curve."

"I bet."

He reached over and twined his fingers with hers. "Both Hunter and my dad said it can consume me, and I need a plan to make sure it doesn't do that."

"You do?"

"My dad didn't even date until he retired from the job," Mike said. "He had us kids really late in his life, and I don't think he regrets it, but I think he does at the same time." He glanced over to her, his gaze holding longer on hers than before, despite the sunglasses. "I want a family sooner in my life than he had one. Hunt has four kids, and he's had them all while being the CEO."

"And his wife runs Pony Power."

"They have a lot of help," Mike said. "Hunt says it's a constant battle to leave work on time, balance his family life with his responsibilities, and not feel like a failure." He sighed, and his wasn't as happy as Gerty's had been.

A weight descended on her too, and she squeezed Mike's hand. "So you'll figure it out, day by day. Isn't that what you said you had to do on a mission? Figure things out, sometimes minute by minute?"

"Yeah," he said. "Day by day."

Gerty found herself hoping she could be at Mike's side, reassuring him of his choices—at work or at home—every day, and a smile started to touch her lips. Then she remembered that in order to do that, she and Mike would need to be married, and an inexplicable fear reached inside her chest and gripped her heart.

She frowned and looked away from Mike so he wouldn't see it. She'd thought about her wedding, of course. She'd had one practically planned already. She'd wanted to get married, but now, she suddenly felt like she didn't want to.

*No*, she thought as the landscape rolled by and they left Ivory Peaks behind. *You don't want to get engaged again.*

And she didn't. Her engagement to James had ended painfully, and she didn't want to experience any part of that again.

But how could she get married without getting engaged?

# CHAPTER
## Twenty-Five

MIKE ENTERED the kitchen of his childhood home, glad for the smell of blueberry muffins. "Momma." He stepped into her and wrapped her in a hug. "You made my favorite thing ever."

She laughed lightly and put her hands over his around her waist. "I just love having you home." She turned toward him, and he stepped back. He gave her a quick look, noting her sad-happiness, and stepped over to the cupboard to get a mug.

"You know I'm going to live in Ivory Peaks," he said. "I'm going to make my home there."

"I know." She nodded several times, looking worried. "It's where you belong." She gave him a smile, and that anxious air about her disappeared. "Your daddy's thrilled, of course." She opened the fridge and pulled out a carton of cream for him. "Sugar's there."

"I know where the cream and sugar are, Momma." He

smiled at her and poured himself a cup of coffee. "But thank you."

"Blueberry muffins?" Dad asked as he came into the kitchen. He pulled a sweatshirt over his T-shirt, and Mike wondered if he was really cold. Even early August in Coral Canyon could be warm, but Mike supposed a crispness already existed in the air here, especially in the morning.

"I have to have someone to cook for," Momma said, and she giggled as Dad wrapped her in a hug too.

"I'd take blueberry muffins any day of the week, my love."

"I know, but then you'd try to run with Gray." She gave him a knowing look.

"Fair point." Dad grinned and turned toward Mike. "Where's Gerty?"

Mike finished his sip of coffee. "I haven't seen her yet this morning." They'd driven to Coral Canyon yesterday, had dinner with her parents and his, and she was leaving with Boone and Cosette to continue the trip to Montana today without him.

She hadn't told him when they were leaving, but surely she wouldn't go without saying goodbye. Even as he thought it, he doubted, because Gerty could be sponta- neous and hot-headed sometimes.

*You've given her no reason to jump from the truck and stomp away*, he told himself. When he thought of her reaction to his birthday present for her now, it made him smile. Her reaction had been so Gerty.

"Smells good in here," Boone said, and Mike turned toward him.

"Coffee?" he asked, already reaching to get down two more mugs, as Boone's wife came down the hall right after him. She carried her overnight bag with her and set it by the corner of the wall that led into the foyer.

The house here in Coral Canyon was enormous, and Mike kept expecting his parents to tell him they were selling it and moving into something smaller. Fifty-five-plus communities and condos had been built in the center of town, and he held the opinion that they should move in there.

They'd said nothing about it to him, though, and he didn't want to bring it up while the Whettsteins were here. Not only that, but his parents had plenty of money to pay gardeners, housekeepers, chefs, and any number of people to help them maintain the house. Momma was also quite a bit younger than Daddy, but she'd never done much around the grounds. Inside the house, yes. Outside, no.

"Where's Gerty?" Boone asked.

"Haven't seen her," Mike said.

"It's not like her to sleep late." Boone poured in almost as much cream as he had coffee and looked up at Mike. They'd left their other two children with Matt, and Gerty had asked everyone at Pony Power to take care of Dusty, her rescue horse, and Max, her German shepherd.

Mike looked down the hall that branched to the right, where her parents had come from. He'd slept in his old bedroom, upstairs, furthest room down the hall. Gerty and her parents had been put up in the guest bedrooms on this level, his parents to the left off the main area of the house.

"I'll check on her," Cosette said, exchanging a glance

with Boone and then Mike. She started back down the hall as Momma put the platter of blueberry muffins on the island.

"They're hot," she said. "Butter's soft."

"Thank you," Mike said, but his attention suddenly wasn't on blueberry muffins. He'd just heard the front door open, and he started toward the foyer. He had further to go, and Gerty appeared in the doorway leading into the living room and kitchen before he could go investigate.

"Hey," he said, only mildly surprised to see her fully dressed, right down to her cowgirl boots.

She lifted a brown paper bag. "I got the bacon."

His eyebrows went up. "Bacon?"

"To go with the muffins." She smiled as she came toward him. He leaned down and kissed her quickly while she held the bag out to the side. Gerty kept going into the kitchen. "They sent two orders of the plain brown sugar kind," she said. "And two of the spicy-sugary kind."

She put the bag on the counter and started to open it. Mike watched as she pulled out two large to-go containers and popped the tops. Her father crowded in, as did Daddy. "I love the spicy-sweet kind," he said.

"You got bacon?" Mike asked.

"She's not in her room," Cosette said. "Oh. She's right here."

"She got bacon," Mike said.

Gerty looked at him then, and he wondered what she heard in his tone this time that she hadn't before. "I thought it sounded good," she said. "Your momma was talkin' about it last night, and I texted her when I got there, but she said she was making muffins. So I just got this instead of a full breakfast."

"You didn't need to get breakfast at all," Momma said with a smile.

"You barely eat breakfast." Mike met Gerty's eyes with plenty of questions streaming between them.

"I know." She stepped away from the countertop and to his side. "But my daddy loves breakfast." She nodded over to him. "And apparently, so does yours."

"You're trying to butter him up," Mike whispered.

"Of course I am," she whispered back.

"I hate whispering," Boone dang near yelled. "If you have something to say, just say it."

"Oh, please, Daddy," Gerty fired right back at him. "If you want to know, I just said I was trying to butter up you and Wes so you won't be so grouchy." She rolled her eyes and stepped away from Mike as both Momma and Cosette started to laugh.

"I don't need to be buttered up," Daddy said, his plate piled high with bacon.

"I do," Boone said. "I guess if that takes bacon, I'll accept it." He gave Gerty a grin, but she just motioned Mike to come join them. He did, his soul feeling lighter and lighter by the second.

"How did your shoulder fare with the drive?" Boone asked.

Mike automatically rotated it before he picked up a plate. "Pretty good," he said. "I almost asked Gerty to drive, but when I looked over at her, she'd fallen asleep." He grinned at her.

"For like, ten minutes," she said, alarm on her face. "I would've driven. You should've woken me up."

"We were almost here," he said. "And I value my life."

"Hey," she said as Boone started to chuckle. "I'm a good driver."

"No, baby," Boone said. "You passed your test. That doesn't make you a good driver."

She glared at him and then threw her napkin at him. "I bought you bacon, and this is the thanks I get?"

"Stop it," Cosette said, and quite firmly too. She shook her head. "I'm sorry, you guys. This is what happens when they leave the house together. It's embarrassing really."

"Hey," Gerty and Boone said together.

"I've been dealing with it for fifteen years," Cosette continued, her voice a kind of mock sad that made Mike grin even wider. "I'm the one who should be getting buttered up." She gave Gerty and her father a stiff glare.

"Don't you worry," Momma said. "I'm sure they'll treat you to a delicious meal once you reach Montana."

Silence draped the kitchen, and then Boone said, "Yeah, yep. Birdie's. Can't be beat."

Gerty reached across the table and covered her mother's hand. "Sorry, Mom."

Cosette grinned, and Mike sure did like how they interacted with each other. They loved her, and she loved them, and Mike appreciated how authentic they each were.

The very moment Boone finished his stack of bacon, he said, "We better get goin'."

A flurry of activity happened then, and before Mike

knew it, he stood on the front porch, Gerty in his arms. "I'll call you when we get there, okay?"

"Yeah," he said. "You'll be there three days?"

"Yep." She tipped up onto her toes and waited for him to be the one to lean down and kiss her. He did, taking his sweet Georgia time to taste her lips before he pulled away.

"Back here on Tuesday," she said. "Then we'll drive home Wednesday together." She stepped out of his arms, her smile beautiful and lighting up her eyes. "I'm sure I'll have some amazing stories to tell you."

"Can't wait." He watched her dash down the steps and get in the back seat of her father's truck, and he waved to all three of them before they continued around the wide circle-drive and left the property.

He turned back to the house, expecting to find his father there. Surprise filled him when both of his parents stood in the open doorway. "What?" he asked.

"You're in love with her," Momma said.

"Momma." He sighed. "Stop it. I am not."

"Close to," Daddy said.

"So what?" Mike asked. "Please, don't push me on this." He gave his father a look and then switched his gaze to his mother. "And don't put words in my mouth."

She shook her head and said, "Okay, fair enough."

"Daddy," Mike said. "I want to talk to you about some business stuff. When would be a good time?"

"Oh, boy," Momma muttered, stepping out of Daddy's arms and going back into the house.

Daddy wore joy and anticipation on his face. "How about right now?"

# CHAPTER
## Twenty~Six

GERTY LOOKED left and right as Daddy pulled up to
the one of three stoplights in Coldwater, Montana. A
sadness deep within her started to rise, and Gerty didn't
know how to swallow it back down.

She rode in the back seat, but Daddy's eyes found hers.
Tears welled and slipped down her face before she could
stop them, before she even knew why they'd arrived.

"Gerty," he said quietly.

"I'm fine," she choked out, a completely ridiculous
thing to say when she clearly was anything but fine. "Keep
going."

Since she just wanted this part of the trip over, Gerty
had opted to pass the small town where her momma was
buried, and where her maternal grandparents still lived,
and get her belongings moved out of the storage unit.

She needed this to be done.

She managed to ebb the flow of tears as Daddy accelerated through the light, and he turned into the storage facility before they reached the next corner.

Gerty had loved her mom before, but the fact that she didn't turn around and fire questions at her endeared her more to Gerty. She didn't reach back and pat Gerty's leg. She simply let her be, let her grieve the way she needed to, and let the silence soothe them all.

Daddy came to a stop outside of Gerty's unit, and they sat there. After a couple of seconds, he said, "Gotta talk, Bug."

"I don't know," Gerty said as a fresh wave of tears flowed down her face. "I just—I think I thought I was going to live here, you know? This was going to be my forever home, and it was ripped away from me."

She reached for the door handle and got out of the truck. Daddy stood there when she closed her door, and he folded her into his chest.

"It's not fair, Daddy."

"No, it's not." He stroked her hair and held her close to his heart, right where Gerty had always existed.

She'd wandered away, but she'd always been his. She'd explored who she was and who she wanted to be, but he'd always welcomed her right back here, to this place, right in the softest, most comfortable spot he could provide for her.

Gerty clung to him and sobbed, and sobbed, and sobbed. Daddy took it all from her, his own sniffling making Gerty feel guiltier than ever. He didn't need her drama and to take time off work for this trip.

She drew in a long breath that was enough to help her step back. "I couldn't have done this by myself." Gerty wiped her face and looked over the bed of the truck. Mom wasn't there, and Gerty twisted to find her silently weeping at the back corner of the truck.

"Mom, don't cry."

"I'm not." She looked up, her eyes wet. She gave Gerty a smile that lit the world, and Gerty flew into her arms too.

"Sh," Mom whispered in her ear. She didn't stand as tall as Daddy, and that meant she held Gerty almost about the head. "You do not let this man take any more from you, Gertrude." Her whisper felt like a shout in Gerty's soul. "Do you hear me?"

Gerty did hear her, and her voice reminded her of what Mike had told her two months ago.

*It's enough*, Gerty thought.

"I let him take so much from me," Mom said next, and Gerty knew who she meant. The man she'd been married to before Daddy. Mom had been abused, and she'd lived for over a decade in fear, keeping everyone at arm's length.

Daddy simply wouldn't let her do that, just like he never kept his opinions to himself about Gerty's choices, her current boyfriend, or anything else. He wasn't perfect, but he was perfectly him, and Gerty needed both him and Mom so much right now.

Mom finally let go, and Gerty looked right into her eyes. Mom cradled her face and nodded. "Now." She drew in a breath, which raised her slight shoulders. "We're here to clean out this part of your life, so you can move forward into a new time." She looked past her to Daddy. "Boone, let's do this."

"Yes, ma'am," he said.

Gerty let him and Mom get the storage unit open, the garage-style door squealing enough to make Gerty cringe. She turned her back on her parents and tucked her hands into her back pockets. That cocked her spindly elbows out to the sides, and she tilted her head back into the gorgeous Montana summer sky.

She did love this state. She felt like she belonged to the big sky, the wide open ranches, and the Rocky Mountains.

"All of that exists in Ivory Peaks," she whispered, the thought there in her mind and filling her mouth.

She couldn't believe she'd found Mike again. She couldn't believe he was going to be the CEO of his family company, and that she would be at his side.

"Maybe," she whispered, though the way their relationship was going suggested that she'd get to experience life with him.

City life had never been on Gerty's agenda. Her heart fluttered with a vein of panic, but a loud bang sounded behind her. She spun that way, her pulse now filled with speed and adrenaline.

"Daddy?"

"We're fine," he said from somewhere inside the depths of the unit. He appeared a moment later, anxiousness in his expression. "You're going to need to come help, baby."

"Yeah." She rounded the truck too, noting he'd lowered the tailgate already. "I'm coming."

She arrived in front of the storage unit and stopped, her eyes taking in the space. The last time she'd seen it, she'd barely been able to get the door closed and locked.

Right now, it was empty.

Mom came forward with what looked like a post that would go on a porch deck. Gerty recognized it immediately, and her thoughts that her daddy had unlocked the wrong storage unit dried right up.

She reached for the post. "This is from my headboard." The headboard that wasn't here. It went with the bed that didn't stand against the left-hand wall where she'd left it.

"There's nothing here," Daddy said.

"I can see that." Gerty turned around and tossed the post into the back of the truck. "Let's go."

"Go?" Mom asked. Gerty practically ripped off the door handle she pulled it so hard, and she got in the back seat while her parents looked at one another in bewilderment.

Foolishness raced through Gerty, tying her stomach in knots and kicking her anger into a new gear. She'd blocked James's number from her phone, but she knew where the Johnson Manor Ranch sat.

For it was going to be her home too.

She jabbed at her phone to put in the address, and by the time her daddy got behind the wheel, she had it ready for him.

She leaned over the seat and handed him the device. "Go here."

———

HALF AN HOUR LATER, Gerty slid from the truck once again. "Stay here," she said to her parents. She expected her mother to do so, but Daddy? No way.

Gerty wasn't surprised to find him standing at the front of the truck, his arms folded, glaring at the house where James supposedly lived. She'd be shocked if he didn't come outside to talk to her, because she'd inquired after him with the first person she'd run into on the ranch, and that had been his brother.

He'd been shocked to see her, but he'd stammered out that James lived in this cabin, and Daddy had dutifully driven them here.

Gerty had just collected the post from the back of the truck when she heard James's low chuckle. It had once made her warm from the inside out, and had always brought a smile to her face.

Not this time.

The hair on the very base of her spine stood up, and Gerty rounded the hood as Daddy said, "Gerty, I'm not bailing you out of jail."

She didn't respond as she threw the post as hard as she could. James, who had been coming down the steps, stopped. He didn't wear a cowboy hat, and he looked like he'd been asleep in the middle of the afternoon.

"You forgot this," Gerty yelled, not even stepping a toe of her boot onto his property. "Thanks for cleaning out all of that old stuff. I wish you'd have called, so I didn't have to drive all this way, but thank you."

He wore complete bewilderment on his face, and Gerty couldn't stand to look at him for another moment. She turned toward her father and stepped toward him.

"I'm going to wrap my hands around his throat if we stay for another ten seconds."

Daddy grabbed her hand and towed her around the truck. "Get in."

Gerty did, and Daddy slammed her door. She seethed, her chest rising and falling too fast. She didn't want to cry again, and she wouldn't. Not here. Not where James could remotely see her.

He stayed on his porch while Daddy got behind the wheel and drove away, kicking up dust into the still, dry air. Gerty refused to look anywhere but out the windshield until Daddy found the highway again, and then her shoulders fell.

"I'm sorry," she whispered. "Had I known...."

"Don't you dare apologize," Mom said from the front seat. "You do not get to take on his actions." She turned and glared at Gerty. "You will not."

Gerty nodded too, softening even more. She didn't cry, surprisingly, but she did turn to look out her window. Daddy increased the volume on the radio slightly, and he drove them toward her grandparents' house.

Gerty closed her eyes and prayed, feeling like she'd never prayed harder than she was in that moment.

*I didn't hit him with that post, Lord, but what am I supposed to do now?*

No immediate answer came, and Gerty didn't expect it to. God didn't speak to her like that, though she wished He would. He gave her bite-sized pieces of thoughts, usually in a very quiet voice, and sometimes spoken through someone else in her life.

*I want to do the right thing. What is the right thing to do?*

This time, the words, *Start over* came to her mind, and

she opened her eyes and turned back to her mother. "Mom," she said. "Will you make a list for me?"

"Gerty-girl, you know there's nothing I like more than lists." She bent to get a notebook out of her purse, and Gerty hadn't even doubted that her mother would have one.

"I need a new bed," Gerty said. "Sheets, and this time, I want the puffiest comforter in the world."

"Remember when I got you that butter-yellow one?" Daddy asked, his eyes kind and filled with hope as he looked at her in the rear-view mirror.

She gave him a smile, and that felt like a miracle to her. "Yeah, but I want it to be twice as puffy as that."

"Oh, boy." Daddy chuckled, further lightening the mood.

"And blue," Gerty said. "My favorite color is blue."

"Blue comforter," Mom said. "Sheets, towels, dishes." She listed the items off one by one as she wrote them in her notebook.

"I need hangers," Gerty added. "And a dresser and a nightstand."

"We'll buy it all," Daddy said.

"No," Gerty said as the sign for Saffron Hills came into view. "Grams gave me a bunch of money the last time I was here. Or she has an account for me. Some of Momma's money or something."

"What?" Daddy asked, his eyes creased with worry now. "Carrie can't do that. They barely have enough."

"They have plenty," Gerty said. "Gramps's investments

kicked up a notch this year. They said it would've been Momma's inheritance, and they wanted to give it to me."

Daddy pressed his lips together, and Gerty knew he'd bring it up with them. She didn't mind. If she couldn't afford everything, maybe she'd get some help from her parents. Or maybe she'd just keep working and saving, one day at a time, to rebuild her life.

*That's the right thing to do*, she thought. Rebuild her life one day at a time, and while James hadn't known it when he'd stolen everything out of her storage unit, he'd cleared the way for her to do exactly that.

And Gerty was going to do it.

She'd start with a brand new foundation, at a brand new farm—her farm. And if she and Mike could find a way to merge his city life with her country life, perhaps she'd have found her happily-ever-after where she'd least expected it—on the farm she'd never wanted to move to in the first place.

# CHAPTER
## Twenty-Seven

BOONE COULDN'T SEEM to let go of his mother-in-law. His relationships always felt so complicated, but just because Nikki had died over two decades ago didn't mean he could just leave behind Carrie.

He'd loved her like his own mother, because in a lot of ways she'd functioned as his mom. He'd never really had one of those to emulate, and he'd had to look to other women in his life for that example. Carrie had been the perfect addition to his life when he'd needed her.

"What happened today?" she asked, because she'd always been exceptionally skilled at reading the room. It didn't take much to see and feel the emotions streaming from Gerty, because she'd always worn everything right out on her face.

Boone honestly hadn't known what would happen at James's place, and he'd never been prouder of his daughter than he had been the moment she'd thrown that bedpost onto her cheating ex's lawn. He would've bailed her out, but he didn't want it to have to come to that.

The person inside him who wanted to be an exceptional father had had to warn her he wouldn't be there for her if she did something that would allow James to call the cops on her.

Thankfully, she'd handled it beautifully, and Boone really would purchase anything she needed. He finally pulled away from Carrie and looked her in the eyes. "You have an inheritance for Gerty?"

Her mouth tightened, which was Boone's answer. "It's not much, but we want her to have it. It would've gone to you and Nikki upon our deaths, and we don't need it."

"You sure?" Boone asked. He'd sold his and Nikki's house in Saffron Hills and it had been one of the most painful and most freeing things he'd ever done.

"I'm one hundred percent sure," Carrie said. "Now, someone better start talking about what happened today, and I think it better be you, Gerty-girl."

"Nothing happened today," Gerty said as she stepped into her grandmother's arms.

"The trailer is empty," Kyle said. The front door closed, and Boone moved over to him to say hello. "Why is the trailer empty?"

"Because we didn't have anything to pack up," Gerty said. "It was all trash, and I threw it all away." She smiled at her grandmother and then stepped over to Kyle before Boone could interject and embrace him. "Gramps, I've missed you so much."

Boone loved watching Gerty interact with Nikki's

parents. They'd go visit her grave tomorrow, and Boone already felt the drape starting to settle over his shoulders.

He could see his first wife so clearly, because Gerty was her spitting image. She also took after her grandmother, and Boone was never one to hold back the thoughts in his head.

"Have you guys ever considered moving to Ivory Peaks?"

A new kind of silence settled over the house, and as Gerty pulled away from her grandfather, even her eyes were wide as dinner plates. "That's the best idea ever," she said slowly.

"We could never," Carrie said.

"Why not?" Gerty rushed her. "Grams, I have the best farm on the planet, and there's a house there for you already."

"Gerty," Cosette said. She reached out and tucked Gerty's cornsilk hair behind her ear. "That house has a few holes in the roof."

"I'm going to fix it all up," Gerty said. "Daddy and Mike and Mission are going to help. Did you know he used to be a carpenter?"

"Not quite true," Boone said under his breath, though Mission was very good with a hammer and nails. He smiled at his daughter and faced Kyle and Carrie. "But there is a house there for you, and there are still seasons. They're just not as harsh as here."

"Nikki's here," Carrie said, her eyes filled with fear.

"Yes, and we'll bring you to see her anytime you want," Boone said.

"When's the last time you went to her grave without me?" Gerty asked.

"Gerty," Cosette chastised.

"I'm just saying," she started.

"Your tone is too harsh," Cosette told her, her dark eyes flashing. "Just say it nicely."

Gerty swallowed and nodded. She was an intense person, and Boone had no problem with her and Mike's relationship at this point. Gerty wasn't going to listen to him anyway. The girl had always been headstrong, and smart, and capable, and while she'd arrived at the house broken and quiet, she was very nearly right back to the spitfire of a woman who'd packed up everything she'd owned and gone to Austin for farrier school.

Who'd decided to learn barrel racing on a dare.

Who'd traveled the west with her truck, her horses, and her determination, grit, and wisdom.

A surge of love filled Boone, and he could only smile at his daughter. He blinked, and he swore Nikki was smiling back at him.

"Grams," Gerty said in a much kinder tone. "You and Gramps don't go see her without me anyway. Or Daddy." She tossed another look over to him, this one edged with anxiety. "She's okay here by herself at this point."

Carrie's chin shook, and she turned away from everyone. "Well, you're early, but it just so happens that I have a batch of cookies ready already."

Gerty stepped into Boone's side, and he drew her closer and kissed her temple. "Give her some time to come to terms with the idea."

"We need it to get that house fixed up," Gerty murmured, and then she stepped away from him saying in a much louder voice, "Grams, are those the white chocolate cranberry ones? I love those."

————

KEITH WHETTSTEIN SMELLED the evidence of the meeting he'd been invited to the moment he walked into the generational house. Uncle Boone looked over from the kitchen counter, where he hunched over something in front of him as if protecting it.

"Just me," Keith said, because Uncle Boone was planning something for Dad's birthday he didn't want his brother to know about. The whole thing had been sketchy in Keith's opinion, but he kept that to himself most of the time.

"Britt can't make it," he said. "Gloria is likewise preoccupied."

Uncle Boone faced him fully. "The new gelding?"

"He's not settling in at all." Keith sank onto a barstool, instant relief sliding down his legs and into his feet. He wanted to kick off these boots and put on a pair of slippers, but he simply reached for one of the sandwiches his uncle had put on the countertop.

Uncle Boone sighed and sat down too. "Fine," he said. "But this party is going to come together with only a prayer."

"My dad doesn't care about his birthday," Keith said.

"Yeah, but it's a big deal," Uncle Boone said. "You and Britt can help with the cake?"

"Yeah." Keith took a big bite of his sandwich and immediately regretted it. He wasn't sure how, but he'd forgotten about his uncle's penchant for peanut butter and honey sandwiches. Keith disliked honey with the strength of a raging wildfire. He gagged down the bite and got up to see what Gerty had in the fridge.

She wouldn't be living in this house for much longer, and then Gray and Elise Hammond would move into it. Hunter was retiring from his position as Chief Executive Officer at Hammond Manufacturing Company, and Mike would be taking over.

Keith and Mike were best friends, and Keith wasn't sure how he felt about Mike donning expensive suits and shiny shoes and working in the city. Keith had never been to HMC, but he'd seen the high rise during his time in the city for college.

Mike said he didn't mind the work, and now that he'd been there for almost three months, he felt more settled. Mike was smart—far smarter than Keith—and he'd no doubt pick up anything put down in front of him.

Keith swigged several swallows of milk straight from the carton, telling himself he'd pay his cousin back if Gerty got upset. She probably wouldn't, because Gerty didn't get too uptight about groceries. Cross her horse or her dog, and she'd pound down the door in the middle of the night.

Keith actually smiled just thinking about it. Mike seemed to be able to handle her, and in fact, he'd mellowed her a little bit. Or maybe she'd grown up and changed while she wasn't here on this farm.

Keith had only left for a few years of college, and then he'd returned. He'd gone to a junior college in the city and earned an agriculture degree. He loved this farm, and as he thought about Gerty and her new venture a few miles down the road, that familiar feeling of jealousy rose up inside him.

All he had to do was talk to his father, and he knew Dad would help him get started on a piece of land all his own. He'd also suggested that Keith do what he'd done— find someone who needed a foreman and run their farm. Dad and Gloria had done very well for themselves since coming to the Hammond Family Farm, and Keith wasn't so prideful that he thought he had to have his own farm or nothing.

He simply wanted *something* to happen in his life. The same thing day in and day out was starting to wear on him, and he couldn't wait to go to the horse auction this weekend.

Both Mike and Hunter were coming with him, and Keith returned to the counter, determined to push away his feelings of inadequacy. It wasn't exactly easy, not with both Mike and Hunter being billionaires. If they saw a horse they wanted, they could buy it, no questions asked.

Keith smiled as he thought of Molly and all the questions she'd actually have if Hunter brought home a horse from the auction. Buying horses was more her specialty, and Hunter the one who hugged her and told her she could buy whatever she wanted.

Unfortunately, Keith could not buy whatever he wanted, and after the meeting with his uncle to put together a ridiculously elaborate birthday party for his dad, Keith got behind the wheel of his truck and headed into the town of Ivory Peaks to get a few groceries.

He and Britt shared a cabin at the farm, and she wasn't a bad cook. His overprotective streak of her had never gone anywhere, and he loved his sister to his very core.

Instant shock filled him when he saw her exiting the single market in town with her hand secured in that of a cowboy.

*Keith* did the grocery shopping, so why did Britt have a plastic sack draped over her free arm? Why was she laughing with her head tipped back, her long, blonde hair spilling all the way to her waist?

Keith had lived in this town for almost seventeen years, and he didn't know the man she was with. How was that possible?

His truck shrilled a series of beeps at him; his seat rumbled; the automatic brake got applied.

Keith's adrenaline surged, and he tore his gaze from his younger sister to the windshield. A woman stood two feet from his front bumper, her green eyes wide with fear and surprise.

That quickly morphed into irritation, and she reached out and slammed her palm against the hood of his truck.

That unfroze him, and he launched himself out of the driver's seat. "I'm so sorry," he said. "Did I hit you?"

"Nearly," she said. "What in the world were you staring at?"

Keith looked past her to where Britt stood with the mystery cowboy. She looked absolutely terrified now, but she didn't scamper away. Britt didn't have a devious bone in her body, and Keith would fillet that man's muscles from his bones if he hurt his sister. Period. The end.

Frowning, he looked back at the woman. "My sister," he said, indicating her.

The woman turned, her thick, curly, dark hair swinging with the motion. Attraction fired through Keith, and he had no idea what the woman saw on his face when she looked at him again.

"Oh, sure," she said. "Britt and Lars."

"Lars?" Keith took a step closer to the woman whose name he had to know before she left. "Who's this Lars guy? Seems suspicious."

The woman laughed, and Keith reached to take the two bags in her hand. She looked at him, and a charge filled the air enough to make crackling noises fill his ears. She swallowed, a light in her eyes dancing that hadn't been there before.

"He's my older brother."

That still told Keith nothing. "Have you guys lived here long?"

"Our whole lives," she said.

"Then I should know you." Keith dipped his head closer to the woman's ear. "I feel like I wouldn't have forgotten about you."

"Then you're dead wrong," she said. "Because that's Lars Hansen, and I'm his younger sister Cara. You took one of my best friends to the prom. In fact, you dated her through most of high school."

"Cassidy?"

"Yeah," Cara said. "Everyone liked her best, and I was the one with the curly hair always hiding in the shadows."

Keith inched closer, his body wanting to be near hers. He pressed into the side of her leg. "I see you now, Cara."

"Do you?" she teased. "You nearly ran me over."

Keith grinned at her, the invitation to dinner on the way out of his mouth when Britt said, "Keith."

"I came to get the groceries," he said, refraining from saying, *The same as always.*

"Yeah." She swallowed and looked over to Lars. "This is Lars Hansen."

Lars grinned like a fool. "Britt talks about you all the time."

"Really?" Keith shook the man's hand, noting it was a good, strong shake. He had no idea how Dad would react to Britt dating Lars. She'd literally never dated anyone before. She'd gone on dates in high school, to dances and group parties.

This was clearly different. Lars shot Britt a sparkly look and said, "Are you going to tell him?"

Britt nodded. "Yeah, uh, Keith, he's my...boyfriend."

Lars looked absolutely thrilled, and he had such a good energy pouring from him that Keith couldn't help smiling too.

"That's great," Keith said. "When are you gonna tell Dad?"

# CHAPTER
## Twenty~Eight

MIKE SET the last folder to the side, ready to leave the office for the day. His shoulders ached in a way he hadn't felt since pre-surgery. In his head, he heard Hunter and his daddy telling him he couldn't work like this and expect to keep his health.

But his call with an executive in France had gone long, and Mike still had a report to file with accounting and then the promised proposals to send to the sub-contractors they used for logistical deliveries of perishable materials.

Mike hadn't even known they sent or received perishable materials, and when he'd admitted as much, Hunter had looked at him like he had four heads.

Hunt came from the labs at HMC and MIT, so of course he worked with things that needed to be refrigerated and preserved. Mike had learned then to phrase his musings as questions. Then he could learn what he needed to learn without seeming like he'd made ignorant assumptions.

By the time he left the office and started down the hall toward his secretary's desk, dusk had covered the city. That meant Mike would be returning to his cabin in the dark, and exhaustion pulled through him.

A sharp pain ran through his artificial shoulder, and Mike rotated it as he got on the elevator. He hit the button for the private, executive-level parking garage and pulled his phone out of his pocket.

An array of notification icons sat at the top of the screen, and Mike didn't even want to check them. But they couldn't stay there. They caused him a great deal of anxiety, and he started with the texts. Daddy, Hunter, and Gerty.

She'd sent four, and a twinge of guilt that he hadn't been checking his phone dove through him. She hated it when he didn't answer her, and she wouldn't call.

*Where are you? I'm at the truck rental, and they won't let me leave my truck here.*

He frowned at her first message, sure she'd meant to send it to someone else.

*I'm going to lose the truck. You must be in a meeting.*

Then she'd said, *Keith is coming to get my truck. Call me when you can, would you?*

She'd called too, and Mike started thumbing out a message to her. *Just leaving the office. I had that call with France this afternoon. Did you switch the date you were picking up the truck? I thought it was tomorrow.*

Gerty was moving into the farmhouse on her farm tomorrow. She, Travis, her daddy, and Mike whenever he had time, had been working on it for the past three weeks, and her bed had been delivered yesterday afternoon.

Mike had only seen pictures of the last several days of progress, because things at HMC had picked up considerably. Hunter said this was common in the fall, and Mike had wondered briefly how he could possibly have a family and be busy every fall. But he'd been too busy to worry about it.

Having a family wasn't the closest fire burning in his direction, and he and Gerty hadn't even started talking any more about marriage yet.

She'd gone to Montana to get her belongings, but James had stolen them. She'd been working like a dog at Pony Power, and then going out to the farm every afternoon and evening to get things livable for herself and her animals. She and her mother had been purchasing the items she needed to live on her own, as the generational house had been furnished.

He couldn't get his message to go through, and frustration pulled through him, only adding tension on top of his tiredness. When he stepped out of the elevator, Bobby rushed toward him.

"Sir," he said. "Your truck has a flat tire, so Trevor is prepping a company vehicle for you. We'll get the truck sent out to be fixed tomorrow."

"No." Mike slowed his step and looked over to the younger man. "That won't work. I'm not coming into the office tomorrow." Gerty was moving, and he'd promised her the use of his truck.

Even as he thought it, he reminded himself that Gerty

owned her own pickup truck. Her daddy had one. Every cowboy on the farm owned one. She'd also rented a moving truck, and surely she could make do without him.

Mike hated feeling indispensable, but he certainly was.

"I'm sorry, sir," Bobby said as the sleek, black, over-sized SUV rolled up to the curb, Trevor behind the wheel. "You can keep the SUV as long as you want."

That wasn't the issue, though Mike was sure he could never return the SUV and be just fine. He didn't see another solution, and he hadn't eaten and still had an hour's drive in front of him. "Okay." He tried to smile at Bobby. "Thank you, Bobby."

He nodded and smiled at Trevor and tossed his brief-case onto the passenger seat, where it would ride out to his cabin.

As he made the drive home, the roads became less and less busy. The noise inside his soul got louder and louder. On nights like these, he normally stopped and got some-thing to eat, but tonight, he didn't.

He was sick of eating out, eating in the truck, or eating alone.

As he drove past the brightly lit farmhouse where his aunt and uncle lived with Jane and Deacon, Mike realized he was lonely.

"Surrounded by people and lonely." He scoffed. That couldn't be right.

And yet, it completely was.

He pulled up to his house, noting that Gerty's truck sat out front. No lights illuminated his windows from the inside the way they did the other cabins on this lane, and he peered through the windshield as he reached to turn off the SUV.

He collected his briefcase from the passenger seat and got out, a sigh escaping from his mouth. He didn't see Gerty sitting on his front steps until she stood.

A smile filled his face quickly. "Hey." He hadn't exactly forgotten about her, but he had meant to call her on the drive. To be honest, he was sick of doing that too.

She didn't answer right away, at least not verbally. She did stick her hands in her back pocket, fanning out those elbows. Tonight, she wore a bulky sweatshirt that he still found incredibly sexy and a troubled look. "You didn't come help with the move."

"It's tomorrow," he said.

"No, Mike." She shook her head. "It was this afternoon. I told you over and over."

Mike shook his head, refusing to believe that he'd messed this up. "That can't be right."

"It doesn't matter." She started to brush past him, but Mike caught her arm.

"Hey." He didn't let her go, and even in the dim light, their eyes met. "It obviously matters. I'm really sorry. I thought it was tomorrow."

"France was waiting." She pulled her arm away and brushed at her eyes. Mike didn't know what to say or do, but an animal clawed at his heart. Gerty absolutely could not cry. He would do anything to make sure she didn't have to hurt.

"I swear it was tomorrow." He pulled out his phone to check his calendar.

"Mike, I changed it like, two weeks ago." She covered his phone with her hand. "You don't need to check it. It's done."

He looked up at her. "Did you eat?"

"Yeah," she said. "We all went out, like we planned."

Mike's chest felt so hollow. "I...don't even know what to say. I'm sorry. I really thought it was tomorrow." He sighed and sank onto the steps where she'd been sitting. "I even told the valets that I wouldn't be in tomorrow to get my truck."

Gerty didn't immediately join him on the steps, and that made his heart beat too fast in a bad way. "Why don't you have your truck?"

"It has a flat tire." He sounded wiped out, and he wondered if he could simply go to bed right now, no food necessary.

Gerty sighed as she stepped over to him and sat down too. She kept more distance between them than she usually did, and Mike didn't like it. He'd apologized, and Gerty would have to figure out how to accept it or not.

He reached over and threaded his fingers through hers. "I'm such an idiot for messing this up. I'm sorry." His whispers still sounded really loud in the quiet evening. "I have to get out of these clothes. Please come in?"

She gave him a look, softening right in front of him. "Fine," she finally said. "But I'm not cooking."

He gave her a soft smile and leaned toward her. "Okay," he whispered. "It's so good to see you."

"It's been a few days," she admitted.

"You've been busy at the farm." He got to his feet and

climbed the steps slowly, giving Gerty a chance to come with him.

She did, and they made it all the way inside before she asked, "What do you mean by that?"

"By what?" he started unknotting his tie. That done and Gerty still silent, he unbuttoned his shirtsleeves and peeled off his jacket. He laid it with his tie over the back of the couch, where it would stay until he had to do laundry —or until his momma showed up. So it would stay there for a while.

"Me being busy at the farm."

"I mean you've been busy at the farm," he said.

"You've been busy too."

"Completely," he said, pausing in his undressing. After all, if he went any further, he'd be revealing skin in front of his girlfriend. He peered at her. "What's wrong?"

"Is this going to be us?" she asked. "Meeting in the night, after days apart?" She folded her arms and cocked that sexy hip. "Because if so, I don't want it."

Mike blinked at her. "I'm not sure I'm following."

"You're going to work in the city."

"True," he said, feeling like he was playing a game of Twenty Questions with her.

"I hate the city."

Mike tried on half a smile, but Gerty didn't melt even a little bit. "You don't hate the city. You just don't want to live there."

"Right," she said. "And Molly and Hunter live there sometimes."

"No, they don't." Mike had seen the condo where

Hunter sometimes slept. Hunter. Not Molly. "They have a mansion in the hills of Boulder."

"Where she probably sleeps alone sometimes."

"Sometimes," Mike acknowledged. "Gerty, we've talked about me being the CEO."

"I know," she said. "I just guess—I guess I didn't realize what it was really going to be until today."

"Calls with France?" he asked, trying to be flirtatious. Again, she didn't budge. Mike sighed. "I'm sorry, baby doll. It was an honest mix-up."

"We're both busy," she said. "That's not going to change."

"Probably not," he said. "I know you, and you don't like being idle."

She didn't. She'd been working sixteen or eighteen hours every day to get the farm ready for her to move onto. If he wanted to see her, he went out there in the evenings, and he hadn't been complaining about it.

Irritation fired through him. "I'm going to go change."

She said nothing as he picked up his suit coat and tie and went down the hall. Mike should probably be looking for a house closer to downtown so he didn't have to drive so far after a busy, exhausting day.

At the same time, he wanted to be wherever Gerty was. "That's something," he muttered to himself, even if he was annoyed with her.

She'd literally just told him she hated the city and his job, when she'd known his job was in the city.

He'd gone at her pace. He wasn't going to bring up having her come live with him in the condo in the high rise, especially not with her farm. He'd assumed he'd be able to move in there with her.

As he pulled on a pair of sweats and a T-shirt, he wasn't sure about anything anymore. He half-expected to find his living room empty, and it was. Gerty, however, stood in the kitchen.

"You don't have to cook," he said.

"I'm not." She lifted the butter knife and started slathering spread onto a couple of waffles that had just obviously come out of the toaster.

"Gerty, we need to talk about us," he said.

"Maybe we are a little bit too busy right now. Maybe we need to find time for each other again."

He looked over to her, completely surprised to find her mouth hanging open. "What?" He hadn't said anything too horrible...had he?

He really needed to talk to Hunter more about how to balance his work life and his family life, because Hunt hadn't provided much detail about that. He'd said it was "hard," and Mike could see that already and he and Gerty hadn't even *started* talking too much about getting married.

He would, but he didn't think she was ready.

She sprinkled salt over the buttered waffles and carefully cut a triangle in the pair of them. "You think I work too much."

"Yeah," he said. "And I do too."

She pulled out her phone and pressed the button on the side of it. It chirped like she'd just gotten a message, but deep down inside him, he knew she hadn't.

"It's Daddy," she said. "I have to go."

"No." Mike moved to block her, the military side of him roaring to the surface. "Let me see what your daddy said. He can't need you somewhere."

She shoved her phone under her shirt, where her bra strap probably held it in place. Mike wouldn't be going after it there, that was for sure.

"Was it your daddy?" he challenged.

Gerty's eyes blazed with blue fire. "No."

"Who was it?"

She lifted her chin. "Someone in town," she said. "I ordered some straw for Dusty, and it's ready."

"Oh, so you're going to work right now."

"Yeah." She glared at him as she went past him. "You worked a million hours today. I can too."

He turned in time to watch her walk out the door and slam it closed behind her. Instantly, the military fight and alpha vibes inside him deflated, and Mike collapsed onto the couch.

"Now what?" he asked, but the empty, silent house had no answers for him.

# CHAPTER
## Twenty-Nine

GERTY SPREAD the straw inside Dusty's stall while the horse continued to snack on the autumn grass outside. He wouldn't come in here unless she made him, and Gerty simply lifted another section and kept working.

Work, she understood.

The hollow feeling inside her chest, she did not.

*You think I work too much.*

*Yeah. And I do too.*

"Mike does too," she said, as if that made her tendency to push herself to exhaustion better. As if the fact that someone else worked too much validated her drive.

"I'm not going to apologize for who I am." If she'd learned anything at all from her relationship with James, it was that. She was Gertrude Whettstein, and she had certain talents and abilities that others didn't understand.

So what if she'd been up since five o'clock that morning

to nurse Max as he'd eaten a little too much steak last night? She'd told Daddy to stop feeding him.

The move hadn't been easy on any of her animals, and a tension rode in the air that had Max on his feet, barking a few clipped warnings at something or someone.

For a moment, Gerty hoped it would be Mike. Of course he'd follow her and make sure she was okay.

James never had, but Mike wasn't James.

She definitely heard tires crunching over the dirt road beyond the stable, and Gerty straightened and tightened her ponytail. It was actually falling loose, and once that was done, she leaned the pitchfork against the wall and went to see who'd come to her farm.

Everyone she knew—minus Mike—had been on her property today, and it had taken less than two hours to get her moved out of the generational house and into the farmhouse here.

The porch had been shored up properly. The house had newly painted walls and refinished floors. The main stable and barn were ready for use.

She'd done nothing else with the land, the yard landscaping, or any other buildings. She didn't need them right now, and she could work on them over time.

September was sinking toward October, and the fall leaves had already started to appear in droves. Whatever she couldn't get done before the first snow fell would wait until spring.

Her heart wailed at her that she didn't want to wait until spring to make things right with Mike. They'd both been incredibly busy since her return from Montana. She hadn't told him about any of the personal revelations that she'd had there, because—well, they'd each been burning the candle at both ends. Mike had even stayed over at the downtown condo a couple of times.

Gerty liked that he could take care of himself now, though a piece of her had really enjoyed that she could be there for him in a way no one else could. She'd loved taking care of him, sipping coffee she'd made for the two of them together, and getting to see his struggles and pain. They'd talked about a lot of things in those moments, and Gerty's chest collapsed on itself when she stepped out of the stable and saw his company SUV there.

Of course he'd come.

He opened the door, and Gerty ran to him. She said nothing, because she didn't need to say anything. She was gangly and improper. She ran hot, and she walked out sometimes.

He caught her in his arms and buried his face in her neck.

"I'm sorry," she whispered. "I won't stomp out on you again."

He didn't say it was okay, and Gerty noted that. He held her tightly against his chest and pulled her ponytail through his fingers.

"I'm sorry I said you work too much," he said. "I said I did too." He pulled back and looked at her in the lamplight spilling from above the stable entrance. "We have to work on this together. It's not going to get any better, I wouldn't think, unless we do."

Though the lump in her throat felt like a baseball, Gerty nodded and said, "Okay."

"I feel like such a fool." He dipped his head and ran his lips along her jawline. "You moved in, and I wasn't here." He kissed the soft spot right below her ear. "I'm so sorry. Can you ever forgive me?" The hum of his words against her earlobe made her feel like melting butter.

"Yes," she whispered as she leaned back and took his face in both of her hands. "I have so much to tell you about Montana."

"Mm, yes, you've been very tight-lipped about it all." He closed his eyes and swayed with her, and Gerty let her eyelids drift shut too. The country stillness out here filled her all the way up, and she loved how peaceful and serene the mood felt now.

In the distance, Tennessee nickered, and that made Gerty open her eyes. "James had cleaned out my storage unit," she said. "He stole everything from me, and you know what?"

Mike stepped back, his eyes already searching hers. "What?"

"I don't care," she said. "I didn't care. I realized then that I didn't want *anything* I'd left in Montana, including him." Gerty wanted him to feel the weight of what she'd just said.

He absorbed what she said, his face giving away nothing. Gerty had always been good at saying what she felt, but only if she was upset or mad. Only if she was trading jabs with Daddy or telling her horses to chill out.

Things of the heart forced her into a corner, and Gerty didn't know how to deal with them. She didn't know how to organize the words, and Mike always did.

Tonight, however, he wasn't saying anything.

"Come see the house." She cleared her throat. "It's been a few days since you've been out here, and I got the backsplash in and all the handles on the cupboards."

She took his hand in hers, but he didn't move too far. "What about Dusty?"

"He'll keep." Gerty gave Mike a smile. "How was your call with France?"

"I didn't actually call the whole country." He ducked his head and used the brim of that very sexy cowboy hat to conceal his face from her.

She smiled too. "Do you like transitioning from CEO to cowboy billionaire?" Feeling flirty suddenly, she reached over and flicked the brim of his hat.

His hand flew up to press down the hat. "Yeah." He gave her a look out of the corner of his eye that was probably meant to tell her not to touch his hat again. "I like it."

"Are you going to do that every night when you get home from work?"

"I...probably."

"So our kids will get to see their daddy as a cowboy." Gerty stopped walking then and looked right at him.

Mike took her in and said, "Yeah," without missing a beat.

"And we'll all live together on this farm."

"I was hopin' you'd let me move in with you once we

get married, yes." He cleared his throat. "Gerty, are you—are you saying you're getting closer to that?"

She nodded and started walking again, the lights she'd left on in the farmhouse beckoning her home. "Yeah," she said. "After Montana, I feel like I'm getting closer and closer every single day."

He growled and stepped in front of her, sweeping her into his arms as she yelped and then giggled. He didn't hesitate in getting rid of the cowboy hat and lowering his mouth to hers.

He kissed her roughly for a couple of strokes, and all Gerty could do was hold on for the ride. What a ride it was until he softened and slowed, and she decided she wanted both with Michael Hammond.

The highs. The lows. The rough roads. The easy summer nights. All of it.

Absolutely all of it.

Now, she just had to figure out a way to say it in a way that would convince them both.

———

A WEEK PASSED, and Mike came home every evening. Sometimes Gerty waited for him on his front steps, and sometimes he showed up at her farmhouse in his suit and she fed him soups and sandwiches and pizza.

Then, he and Hunter went on a business trip to New York City, and she didn't see him for a week. When he got back, he had a mountain of work to catch up on in the office, and he stayed in the city.

October arrived, and with it, Gerty's absolute favorite time of the year. Autumn. Hay rides. Pumpkin carving. Apple cider. Straw bales and scarecrows and getting up before the sun, and working long after it went down.

Gerty loved farm life—everything about it—and she loved her work with the kids and horses at Pony Power. She still taught her horseback riding lessons, and she spent mornings on her farm now and worked from noon to six at Pony Power.

One evening, Gloria entered the administration lobby where Gerty was filling out her timecard for her mother. If she didn't, she wouldn't get paid, and Mom didn't make exceptions, not even for Gerty.

"Hey." Gloria smiled and waved as Gerty looked up. "I know you're headed out, but Red Velvet just threw her shoe and maybe pulled a tendon. The vet can't come until tomorrow, but can you come look at it and see if she can be shod again?"

"Sure." Gerty wasn't planning on seeing Mike that evening either, and as she followed Gloria down the hall and into the barn, she counted how long it had been since she'd see him, smelled him, kissed him.

Fifteen days.

Way too long, and Gerty suddenly had the best idea in the world. "Actually, Gloria?" She waited until her aunt had turned around. "I can't stay. I have something else I have to do tonight."

"Oh, sure." Gloria ducked her head as if embarrassed. "Sorry. You're just so dependable."

That was another way of saying Gerty worked too

much, but she didn't let it sting at her. There were seasons where she could work a lot. There were times when she shouldn't. She had the feeling this would be a lifelong battle for her, and right now, she needed to leave Pony Power on time.

So she did.

————

AN HOUR LATER, Gerty cursed under her breath as she once again couldn't find anywhere to park along the entire block where Hammond Manufacturing Company stood. "What are all these cars doing here?"

The only one still at work was Mike. Shouldn't all the employees be gone by now?

The clock on the dashboard read almost seven-thirty, and he'd texted earlier in the day to say he'd be staying at the condo again that night.

Gerty hadn't responded. They'd talked very little about a strategy to work less personally and to support each other in doing so in order to spend more time together.

Embarrassment attacked her again, as it had been for the past hour as she'd made the drive from country to city. Tears filled her eyes, and she simply wanted to go home.

"No." She shook her head and made a right turn into a parking garage. No matter what it cost, she'd do it.

Mike was not coming to her again.

She'd realized and already cried about the fact that he was the only one making any effort.

*He* always came to her. If he didn't, it was because he physically couldn't.

And she could.

A man in a dark suit approached, and he might as well have had spikes on his forehead. She rolled down her window, her voice already feeling pinched in her throat.

"I just need ten minutes," she said, though she wasn't sure if that was true. She knew Mike was the CEO, but she had no idea where his office was. She had no idea if she'd even be able to access the elevator he did.

She thought for at least the tenth time that she should call him. But he'd been sweet with her over the last several months with surprises and showing up wherever she was.

She missed him powerfully every time a new lesson started and he wasn't the one to bring her the horses. Or when she made her own coffee in the morning and sipped it alone. Or when she didn't get to kiss him goodnight.

Apparently fifteen days was her limit, and she wasn't going to let another hour pass without seeing him and telling him everything she'd learned in the past couple of hours.

"I know I can't park here," she said. "But I just need ten minutes to find my boyfriend and talk to him."

"This is private parking," the man said.

"Yes," Gerty replied. "I know. Is there any way I can get up to see Michael Hammond?"

The man's eyebrows went up. "You know Mister Hammond?"

Gerty cocked her head. "Is this the parking for HMC?"

She started scanning the little of the lot she could see, but she couldn't find Mike's truck.

"Yes," the man said. "The executive parking."

"So Mike is in his office?" Gerty swung her attention back to this man, her eyes dropping to his name tag. "Kevin, can you help me do something to surprise him? He's my boyfriend, you see, and I haven't seen him in fifteen days...."

# CHAPTER
## *Thirty*

MIKE HAD JUST PULLED a microwavable pizza made on French bread out of the oven when the phone in the condo shrilled out a ring.

Surprised, he dropped the food, and the pepperoni and sauce splatted on the floor while the tray clattered against the wall. Cursing, he turned away from the mess to find the phone.

He'd never even heard it ring before, though Hunter had told him if it did, it would be important. If he had to deal with another transportation issue, he didn't know what he'd say or do. It wouldn't be good, he knew that.

He missed his cabin in a way he couldn't describe and hadn't anticipated. He'd never minded the city, because it had a life force all its own. He liked how it never seemed to sleep, but now, all it did when he hadn't been sleeping was remind him how exhausting it was to be awake all the time.

He finally located the phone on the dining table for two and snatched it from the cradle. "Michael Hammond," he said, not really sure how to answer this phone. His secretary buzzed into his office all the time, and she simply said, "Mister Hammond?" and he'd answer to let her know he was there and listening.

"Mister Hammond," a man said. "It's Kevin in the parking garage. There's been an issue down here. Could you come down?"

Mike turned toward the kitchen, where he no longer had dinner waiting for him. Even when he had, it hadn't been exactly appetizing.

He rubbed his hand along his forehead, wishing he'd showered at the cabin, pulled on a pair of jeans, grabbed his cowboy hat, and gone to Gerty's.

He missed her so much, but she hadn't even responded to his text from earlier that day. She was probably mad he was staying in the city yet again, and he wanted to rage at her to join the club.

In that moment, Mike wondered if he could really be the CEO and keep Gerty in his life. The business trip, the endless work afterward, the transition that had started with Hunter moving files from his cabinets to Mike's....

It was all overwhelming in single pieces, and he'd been dealing with them all at the same time.

"Do I really need to?" Mike asked. "What happened?" It was *way* after hours, and surely he didn't need to go attend to something in the parking garage. Did CEOs even do that?

"There's been a break-in," Kevin said. "Your personal

vehicle was one of the cars broken into, and we want to make sure nothing is missing."

Mike's heartbeat accelerated with every word he said. "I'll be right down." He plunked the phone back into the cradle and turned to get on his shoes. He wasn't sure if he should get re-dressed in his suit and tie, and he decided against it. This wasn't an HMC issue; this was a personal issue.

He grabbed his phone as he left the apartment and he called Hunter while he waited for the elevator. "There's been a break-in in the parking garage," he said as he got on the car. "Is this normal?"

"Not at all," Hunter said, the frown in his voice surely mirroring the one on his face. "You're staying in the city again tonight? Or they just called you? Because you can tell them to handle things like that on their own."

"I'm here." Mike sighed as he leaned against the wall. He realized he hadn't pushed a button, so he wasn't going anywhere, and he jabbed at the button to get him to the executive parking level.

"I thought you were going home to Gerty."

"One," Mike said. "Gerty and I don't have a home together." His tongue felt too thick in his mouth, because he'd told his cousin too much about his feelings for Gerty. "Two, Diamond Transportation is being impossible. I was on the phone with them—with their corporate executive team, Hunt. A whole team—for over two hours tonight."

The truth was, Mike had been too tired to make the drive on dark, country roads back to the farm. He didn't have to spell that out for Hunter.

Hunt still sighed. "You haven't seen her for weeks."

"Three," Mike said. "I can manage my own relationships. Four, she didn't even text me back today."

He hadn't meant to put in that last item, nor had he meant for his voice to crack on the last word. Hunter said nothing, and as the elevator slowed, Mike said, "I'll call you later. Someone broke into my truck."

"Mike."

"I'm fine, Hunt." He ended the call, his military mode kicking on. The elevator stopped, but the doors didn't open. Mike closed his eyes and said, "Lord, I don't know how many more things You can throw at me before I start breaking."

*Just one more* came into his head, and Mike had often experienced that thought. When he'd been broken down in the desert, he'd wondered how much longer he could put up with the heat, the lack of fresh water, the constant noise from the other Marines.

*Just one more day.*

When he'd been in the hospital after his injury, he'd asked God how much longer he'd have to deal with his shoulder problems.

*Just one more* had been his answer. Whether that had been minute to minute, day by day, or month to month, Mike hadn't known.

He simply kept going for *just one more.*

"Fine," he grumbled. "But then I want a lot of blessings, please." His chest tightened, because he knew he didn't get blessings for doing something hard. It wasn't an exchange system between him and God.

He looked up at the ceiling in the elevator, finding it ridiculous and also fitting for HMC to find it mirrored. His reflection looked down at him, and Mike saw himself clearly for the first time in what felt like weeks.

Maybe since he'd gone to Coral Canyon while Gerty had continued on to Montana with her parents. Things had shifted between them then, and he hadn't realized it as quickly as he should've.

"Gerty doesn't stay quiet," he whispered. "Unless something's wrong. You have to make her talk."

He fumbled with his phone, ready to call her now and tell her he was on the way. She was an early riser and usually went to bed by nine or nine-thirty, but he had to see her.

Today.

He had to tell her something hard, and he wanted her to tell him all of her hard things. Every single one.

The elevator reached the ground floor, and Mike nearly muscled his way outside. Kevin met him there, a look of pure anxiety on his face. "Mister Hammond."

"I need a car," Mike said. "I don't care if it's mine." He glanced around, not really sure what he was looking for.

"We just need you to go through your truck first." Kevin handed him a pair of blue gloves that seemed like they belonged in a hospital. Mike reminded himself that HMC had two floors of laboratories, and they surely paid a pretty penny for the number of gloves they went through in a month.

He should know that number, but he decided he had time to learn it. He took the gloves, but he wanted to throw them in the trashcan. He certainly didn't put them on as he strode toward his truck.

If he didn't touch anything, he'd be fine. The truck sat in its usual spot, and he checked the tires as he approached. The back right one was brand new, thanks to a flat he'd gotten here in the garage too.

Mike had the sudden and horrifying thought that perhaps another Hammond didn't want him to take over at HMC. *Don't be ridiculous*, he told himself.

His grandfather's other children were very nearly all passed now, and their children were in their seventies too. Their children were either in their fifties and doing other things or didn't want the company. They probably had children too, but they likely weren't old enough to run the company. That was why Hunter had taken over in his mid-twenties and stayed as long as he had.

"It looks fine," Mike said. He entered the narrow passage between the truck and the wall and edged down it. It was a masterful feat he performed every morning when he arrived, because then he had to open his door and squeeze out too.

He opened the door, the rush of something foreign and floral hitting him straight in the nose. He blinked, trying to make sense of Gerty's scent in his truck.

Then he saw her sitting in the passenger seat. The air left his lungs and surprise took its place.

"Gerty."

"Hey, baby." She lifted her hand in a wave, and Mike took a moment to let the echo of her voice fill his ears. She had never called him *baby* before, but he really wanted to hear it again. And again.

He looked over his shoulder, didn't see Kevin, and got in the truck. He still held the gloves, and he glanced at them before tossing them in the back seat. "I don't think I need those."

Gerty giggled and shook her head. Mike practically climbed over the console he leaned so close, and he murmured, "I have missed you so much," right before he claimed her mouth as his.

She threaded her fingers through his hair and held him right where she wanted him, kissing him back exactly the way he needed.

"What are you doing here?" he asked between kisses.

Gerty kissed him again, and Mike was content to let her set the pace. She pulled away a few moments later, her chest rising and falling quickly with her breath.

"I missed you," she whispered. "And I was at Pony Power, and I thought—I have never gone to the city to see him. He always comes to me."

She looked up from underneath her eyelashes. "I maybe can't go to New York City with you, but I can—and I will—come see you here in the city when you can't make it to me. When you have to work too much, Mike, I won't. When I have to work too much, you won't. We have to make this work, because I do *not* want to ever go another fifteen days without kissing you."

Mike smiled, because when Gerty got talking, she *talked*. "So you came to see me, because you missed me."

She grinned back at him. "Yeah, that's about right."

"I told Kevin I needed a car, because I thought this one would have to be police evidence, and I just had to see you tonight."

Her bright blue eyes lit up. "Really?"

"Really." He ran his hands through her hair, which she'd taken out of its customary pony tail. "I—"

"I want a tour," she said, because what he'd been about to say was three little words that would change them once again. "Of the condo, of the company. Your office."

He chuckled and shook his head. He dropped his hands and settled into his seat. "The company is really big, baby doll."

"The condo and your office then."

He looked over to her. "Really?"

"Yes, really."

"Why?"

She tilted her head the way she did when Max did something she didn't like. The way she did when the answer was obvious to her, but the dog was still a puppy and didn't know better.

"Because, Mikey, this is where you work. This is where I'm going to come when you're working a lot, but we want to be together."

He shook his head. "Gerty, it's a long drive." He shook his head. "I'm fine making the drive, because I live out there."

"But you can't always come," she said. "You want this to work out between us, don't you?"

"More than anything," he whispered.

"Then I want to come to you when you can't get to

me." She said it so simply, like the sacrifices that needed to be made in a relationship belonged to both of them.

"Listen." She reached over and ran her fingers down the side of his face. He leaned into her touch and let his eyes close. He did love her, and he allowed it to flow through him freely. To experience it and bask in how warm and wonderful it felt.

"Right now, we're both working a lot, but I will not go a single day without seeing you because of work. James made it sound like it was my fault that we didn't work, but...."

Mike turned to face her, but she didn't wear any shame or pain on her face.

"I don't believe him," she said. "But that doesn't mean he wasn't right. You asked me to help us figure out this working situation, and here I am. I'm fixing what I don't like about today."

"You didn't answer me this afternoon," he whispered. "I thought you might be mad."

"I didn't answer because my riding lessons started at that same moment, that's all. Then I finished, and then I drove here."

Mike nodded, because Gerty didn't really have an inauthentic bone in her body. "Every single day?"

"Every single day, baby." She gave him a soft smile. "You either come to me on the farm, or I'll meet you at your cabin, or I'll come here. But if we're both in the state of Colorado, I want to see you at least once a day."

"Promise me that will never change."

"I promise," she said without hesitation.

Mike tucked her hair behind her ear. "I love you, Gertrude Whettstein."

Shock coursed through her eyes, and Mike pressed two fingers to her mouth. "You don't have to say it back. I just feel it so strongly right now, and I want to recognize it. I know it. I'm in love with you, and I want to see you at least once a day too. A lot more than that, but I get we have circumstances and situations that might mean it's once a day, in a truck in a parking garage." He slipped his fingers away from her lips, curious as to what she'd say to that.

"Kevin did say I could park here any time I wanted." She grinned at him. "Which is a good thing, because I circled this block three times before I finally pulled in here and begged him for ten minutes."

Mike laughed like she'd just told the funniest joke ever. "You two staged this, didn't you?"

"I had to get you down here," she said.

"Baby doll, if you'd texted me you were here, I'd been down here ten times as fast."

She laughed and as she quieted, Mike touched his lips to hers again. "Mike," she whispered against his mouth.

He didn't back up and give her much room to speak. "Mm?"

"I'm in love with you too." The words came out whispered, and Mike didn't immediately pull away and gape at her.

"I told you you didn't have to say it back."

"And when do I say something I don't mean?"

He did put enough distance between them then, so he

could see her face. A hint of redness rode in her cheeks, and she seemed almost embarrassed.

"Why are you blushing?" he teased.

"I just feel kind of dumb," she said. "I mean, with James and all. It was what? Six months ago when I was with him." She shrugged.

"And now you're with me," Mike said. "And we belong together, Gerty. We always have."

"We have, haven't we?" She smiled the most gorgeous smile at him, the light pouring from her absolutely angelic. "Now, come on. I want to see your condo and your office."

She turned to get out of the truck, but Mike stayed in his seat. "Lord, thank you for that woman."

He opened his door, so Gerty wouldn't squeeze down the passage to do it for him. "Bless me to deserve her every day for the rest of my life." He met her at the tailgate, tucked her hand in his, and said, "Now, I've never had anyone call me at the condo, so the ring scared me. We may or may not have a mess upstairs."

Gerty looked at him with wide eyes. "What kind of mess?"

"The pepperoni pizza kind of mess."

# CHAPTER
## Thirty-One

GERTY STEPPED out of her farmhouse to the cold bite of wind. October had become November, while it hadn't snowed yet, she was sure it would today. The sky foamed with angry clouds, and she best get her outdoor chores done quickly so she could return to the house for breakfast.

She liked hot meals, and she'd put oatmeal in the crock pot last night so she could make cream of oat cereal this morning. Her younger siblings were coming this weekend for a sleepover, and Gerty needed to get to the grocery store to get the food she needed to keep them all happy while their parents went to a show in the city.

She and Mike had seen each other every single day, even if only for a few minutes, since she'd driven to the city over a month ago. Every time she thought of him, a huge sense of love and security overcame her, and she let it warm her from top to bottom as she hurried down the steps, Max at her heels.

She fed and watered her horses and made sure all the doors were secure before returning to the house. When she got within ten yards, the scent of sausage met her nose. She expected to find Daddy or Mom or both of them in her kitchen, fixing breakfast for her. Daddy had come out once a couple of weeks ago, after Gerty had mentioned to him that she thought she'd marry Mike within the next year.

They'd exchanged their I-love-you's, but Gerty still didn't want to rush into another engagement. In fact, she didn't want to get engaged at all. Mike knew that, but Gerty also hadn't told him she absolutely wouldn't wear his ring before she became his wife.

Daddy had said, "You need to tell your mother," and Gerty had. Mom did want to know, because she'd wanted to be more involved in the plans for Gerty's non-existent first wedding, but she'd been too far away.

Gerty had told her she didn't want anything fancy. In fact, she wanted to marry Mike right there on the farm, with just their families and friends in attendance. She'd need a dress, but she'd seen the suits Mike wore to work, and he already had the wardrobe.

Every time she thought that, she reminded herself that the man was a cowboy billionaire, and his family probably had standards for how they got married. She hadn't attended Hunter and Molly's wedding, but she'd sat through a dinner with Uncle Matt and Aunt Gloria as they told the story of how they started dating.

Apparently, Uncle Matt had told Gloria at Hunter's

wedding that he wanted to dance with her—and only her —that night. They'd been married in one of the fanciest locations in Denver, with hundreds of people in attendance, and Gerty wondered if she'd have to do that too.

She wasn't great in heels or with putting on appearances, but her boyfriend was going to be the CEO of the largest corporation in the city. That came with certain responsibilities, and Gerty told herself she should probably schedule a time to talk to Molly. What she hoped the woman would tell her, Gerty couldn't even guess at.

She already knew the challenges that came with a schedule like Mike's. She wanted him, and therefore, she could deal with his schedule.

She stepped into the house and bent to get off her muddy boots, calling, "I'm back."

"Good," Mike said, and Gerty's head jerked up. "I was just about to come looking for you."

He wore jeans and a dark brown leather jacket, with a belt looped around his waist, and the sexiest cowboy hat in the world perched precisely on his head. He lifted a pan from the burner and turned toward her. "Eggs are done, and they're terrible cold."

That was when she noticed he wasn't wearing a shirt under his jacket. She could only stare at his chest, as it had been a while since she'd been to his cabin to help him get dressed. He hadn't been lifting weights since his surgery, but the man still had muscles from the waist up that made Gerty swallow hard.

"You're staring," he whispered, and Gerty blinked out

of her stupor. Somehow the man stood right in front of her now, a gentle yet knowing smile on his face.

"You're not wearing a shirt," she said.

"I needed your help this morning."

Gerty regained her full awareness and cocked out her hip. "So you show up in a leather jacket—which is totally hot, by the way—and make breakfast?"

He grinned at her. "Yes, ma'am." Mike put one hand on her hip and swayed with her while he kissed her in a thorough way that still left her wanting more.

"Where's your shirt?" she whispered against his mouth.

"Somewhere around here." He kissed her again, and Gerty slid her hands along his ribs to his back. The leather kept plenty of his body heat close to his skin, but her hands were cold from the work she'd done outside.

"You're freezing." He shivered, and that made Gerty giggle. She felt so girly and feminine around Mike, and she sighed as she looked up at him. The moment changed, but it also remained soft and meaningful.

"The eggs are going to be cold."

He nodded, his grip on her body going nowhere. "One hundred percent cold." He slid his hand along her hip and into his pocket. "I know you don't like jewelry."

Gerty's pulse jumped at her. "I wanted to talk to you about that."

He lifted his eyes to meet hers. "About your dislike of jewelry?"

She shook her head slowly, wishing God would just put

the words she needed into her head, preferably in the right order too. *Please*, she prayed.

"About us getting engaged," she said.

Mike let a blip of surprise slip across his face. "I wasn't going to propose."

"Ever?" she teased.

His smile was so sexy and so perfect, and Gerty wanted to kiss it away. As she did, she felt something hard in his hand as he pressed it against her back.

"You can't just kiss me when you don't want to talk," he whispered, and his voice came out hoarse.

"It sort of works sometimes."

"Not this time." He stepped away and held up a necklace. "I know you don't want to wear rings and bracelets and watches and all that. But what about something like this?"

The silver chain caught on the light in the kitchen, and Gerty admired the simple cowboy hat charm at the lowest point of it. "Is this—?"

"Can I just say it?" he asked, an edge in his voice.

Gerty swallowed, glad the words went down easily. "Yes, please."

"Of course I want to have an engagement," he said. "My parents want that. I imagine yours do too. I know you'd prefer something small for the ceremony and wedding, and that's just fine. I was just—"

"Is it?" Gerty asked. "Having something small?"

He tilted his head, and that made his jacket shift, showing more skin along the zipper of his coat. "Yes," he said in his crisp, CEO voice. "Why wouldn't it be?"

"You're an important person in the community," she said. "Hunter and Molly had a huge wedding downtown."

"Does that sound like me at all?"

"No, but...it doesn't sound like Hunter either."

"Hunter is quiet," Mike admitted. "He loves fishing and crossword puzzles. But he's far more social than I am. Molly's family was also well-known in the community."

Gerty slipped back into his arms, and he draped the chain around her neck. He tugged her ponytail out of the way so the cool metal sat against her skin, and Gerty liked it. She liked it, because it came from him, and she swore she could feel the imprint of his touch on it, and now on her.

"I don't want a big wedding," he whispered as he pressed his cheek to hers. "I want to see you in a pretty dress, with your momma and daddy and siblings. All of your horses will be lined up, of course, and Max can walk you down the aisle."

Gerty smiled against his face, but he didn't. "My daddy would never allow that."

"Mm, probably not." He took a breath. "I know you want to do it here on the farm, and I'm good with that. This is going to be *our* house. *Our* life together."

"It just makes sense for us to start it here," she whispered.

"I have a lot of uncles and cousins," he said. "I'd like them here, and that requires a little bit of a lead time."

"So like, can we get married next weekend?"

Mike pulled back and searched her face. "You're not kidding."

Fear bolted through Gerty, and she shook her head. "I want to be yours. I want to marry you. I just…." She sighed and looked away. She kept the blinds closed back here, and she couldn't see outside to anything that might have soothed her.

"You don't want to be engaged," he said.

"I'd like to skip it."

"That's why I bought the necklace."

She brought her eyes back to his. He smiled and reached up to smooth back her hair. "I know you, baby doll. I know you don't want to be engaged, but I want to have something official where when people ask, I can tell them, yes, we're getting married."

She reached up and touched the cowboy hat. "So this is like the diamond ring."

"Sort of," he said. "I mean, I didn't get down on both knees and ask you to marry me."

Her eyebrows went up. "You want to do that?"

"Yes," he said simply.

Gerty backed up to give him room, but he chuckled and shook his head. "No, baby doll." He took both of her hands in his, and foolishness ran through her. "I want to ask you to marry me very close to the wedding date."

He kept his eyes trained on their joined fingers too. "So I was thinking—if you agree—that we count the locket as our pledge to each other to get married. It's not an engagement. We pick a date. We tell our families. We start planning the wedding, and then sometime really close to that date, I'll ask you to marry me and give you a ring."

Mike allowed some time for the things he'd said to

settle into the kitchen, and only then did he look her in the eyes. "What do you think?"

Gerty knew exactly what she thought. "I think you're the sweetest man in the whole world." She tipped up onto her toes and pressed a kiss to his lips. "I think you're perfect for me. I think I need to figure out how to print that picture you took of us a couple of weeks ago in our Halloween costumes so I can put it in this charm that I didn't know was a locket."

He grinned at her, and she returned it. "I think I need to talk to my mom and get started on a dress."

"We can pick a date this morning," he said.

"Yes," Gerty said, wondering what it would feel like to say that same word to him when he did ask her to marry him. When she stood across the altar from him and said she'd be his wife.

Gerty looked around her kitchen as if a calendar would manifest itself and she could circle the date she'd become a Hammond. That didn't happen, and she looked back at him. "Couple of questions."

"I'd be shocked if you didn't have any," he teased.

She half-rolled her eyes. "One, can I see the ring before you propose?"

"Mm, no." He didn't qualify the answer. Didn't explain why. He simply told her no, and while it brought a flash of irritation to her gut, Gerty calmed herself quickly.

"Fine." She couldn't pretend to be mad at him very well, and she broke down into laughter as he stood there with that stoic smile on his face.

"What's the second question?" he asked.

"Where's your shirt?" She scanned the room for it and found a wad of fabric draped over the back of her brand-new couch. "You're distracting me with that broad chest."

When she picked up the shirt, she discovered it was really two T-shirts, and she dropped one back to the couch as she caught the other one. Mike pressed in behind her and took it from her. "This one's yours." His deep voice made her cells tingle in anticipation, but she stayed still as he shook out the shirt and she read it.

She burst out laughing, and she picked up the second one. His was black and said, *She's mine* with an arrow pointing to the side. Hers was a light blue—she detested white T-shirts—and said, *He's mine* with an arrow pointing the other direction.

"Let's put them on right now," she said.

"Like I said," he said. "I needed your help."

"I'll bet you did." Gerty turned into him and very slowly, she reached up and pushed his jacket off his shoulders. He stood there, doing absolutely nothing to help her, though his shoulder was very nearly better now. He still did physical therapy and saw his doctor often, but his range of motion was good, and he was almost pain-free.

Her eyes tracked along the scars on his shoulder, and she ran her fingertips along them. She cut her eyes over to Mike's, but he'd closed his. He breathed in, almost like he was trying to memorize her touch.

Gerty sure did like the affect she had on this man, and she ducked her head to get the T-shirt and help him into it. But she grabbed hers first. "Keep your eyes closed," she whispered.

"Why?" His eyelids fluttered.

She watched him while she stripped off her sweatshirt and pulled the T-shirt over her head. With it all pulled down so she was covered, she said, "Okay, right arm." She slid the sleeve of that arm up while he lifted it slightly, and when it was in place, she pulled the shirt over his head.

He usually took over here and lifted his left hand to get the other half of the shirt on, but today, he didn't. "Left hand," she prompted, and he did it. She tugged the hem down so it covered his belt, and then she stood back.

"Okay. Eyes open."

Mike complied, and Gerty cocked her hip and grinned at him. His face split into a smile, and he caught her around the waist. They both laughed as she collapsed into his arms.

"I love you, baby doll," he whispered.

She managed to say, "I love you too," before he kissed her. Gerty hadn't just gotten engaged, but she and Mike had done something far better.

They'd promised themselves to each other, and she knew without a doubt that Michael Hammond kept his promises.

*Six Months Later*

MIKE FLIPPED OPEN the ring box for probably the twenty-fifth time. He knew what sat inside, because he'd looked at Gerty's engagement and wedding ring every day for the past three months.

She hadn't seen it once—but she would tonight. His parents had been in town for a week now, staying in a cabin on Uncle Gray's farm.

Hunter had transitioned the Chief Executive Officer position over to Mike on January first, and he'd then moved his family into the farmhouse where he'd grown up with his father.

Jane and Deacon had moved into Hunter's sprawling mansion closer to the city, and they both had a commute now.

Jane opened the door and entered. "She's here."

Mike slammed the lid closed and took a deep breath. He wasn't worried about Gerty saying yes to his proposal.

He wasn't worried that she didn't want to marry him. He wasn't worried that she wouldn't show up in only three more days for their wedding.

Her grandparents had narrowly escaped a late spring storm in Montana to be here for the wedding, and they were staying in the house Mike had been working on with Gerty's father in every spare moment he'd had in the past six months. They'd live in that house come summertime, once they got everything in Montana packed up and moved down here.

Gerty literally didn't have anything left in Montana, and Mike couldn't wait to start their life together here in Ivory Peaks, the city of Denver, and the Rocky Mountains.

Jane brushed her hands along his collar. "You look great. Your mother and mine have been cooking up a storm. Everything is perfect."

"Thank you, Jane," he whispered.

"If you don't come out in the next couple of minutes," she continued as if he hadn't spoken his gratitude. "Your sister is going to say something she'll regret." Jane's blue eyes caught on Mike's, and they said so much more than her voice did.

"Opal wouldn't ruin this for me."

"Not you," Jane said meaningfully again. "Your momma hasn't said anything to her about her now-former doctor boyfriend, but unfortunately, my momma didn't get the message."

"Oh, boy."

"It's damage control out there," Jane pulled her hands back. "Got the ring?"

Mike held up the box. "Got the ring." Mike forced a smile to his face, and he rolled his shoulders. Only a flicker of pain, a whisper of it and then gone.

He felt overly hot, but that was because unbeknownst to Jane or anyone else, he wore two shirts. Nonetheless, he followed his cousin out of the bedroom and down the hall to the big living area in Hunter's mansion. It was the biggest space they owned, and the wind had kicked up here in Colorado too.

Hunter stood at the counter where Mike had seen him several times, a drink in his hand and his head thrown back as he laughed with Uncle Cy and Mike's father.

Daddy saw him and immediately put down his glass of orange juice. "There he is."

Mike hugged his father, though he'd been out here twenty minutes ago. "Everyone's back?"

"Your momma just got here," he said. "She has the cake out in the garage."

Everywhere Mike looked, he saw Hammonds. Daddy's four brothers were here. Their wives, and all of their children. Every single one, and Mike couldn't help but send up a prayer of thanks for the goodness of his family.

Gerty's grandparents and her uncle Mike visited with Uncle Colton, and her siblings sat with Hunter's kids and Matt's kids, their cousins.

Jane stood by the hallway that led into the foyer, and she suddenly turned and signaled to everyone in the room.

The noise went down in a wave, with only the youngest not understanding until it was too late that he was supposed to quiet down.

Boone moved past Jane first, and then Cosette. Gerty came last, and she paused to take in the crowd gathered there.

She'd known this was a dinner with Mike and his family, and she'd met all of them over the holidays, which they'd spent in Coral Canyon, at the Whiskey Mountain Lodge and Mike's parents' house.

She surveyed the crowd, and Mike stepped forward, the ring box gripped in his hand. Gerty wore fairly normal attire for her. Her patchwork jeans were a step above those she wore around the farm. Her blouse tonight didn't have sleeves, and it billowed in pretty pink, purple, and blue flowers.

"Baby doll," he said, and her eyes locked onto his. She took a step toward him before he asked her to, and he added, "I need some help with my shirt," as she approached.

She scanned him from head to toe. "Looks mighty fine to me, Mikey."

A couple of people twittered with laughter, but Gerty's mouth barely twitched upward. He grinned, because he loved the woman in front of him so very much.

"Go on," he said, nodding down to the buttons on his shirt.

"In front of everyone?"

"Yes, ma'am."

Gerty heaved a sigh, really putting on a show, and reached to start unbuttoning his shirt. She started at his collar, and she quickly undid the buttons while Daddy and Mike's uncles catcalled.

When her daddy whooped, she burst out laughing. Her face was still bright red by the time Mike pulled his shirt out of his jeans and ripped it open.

"You're wearing our shirt," she said, searching his face.

He held up the ring box. "I think it's time we got engaged, baby doll."

An eagerness entered her expression. He opened the box to let her finally see the ring, and she gasped and brought both hands to her mouth. "Mike."

"It's two pieces," he said into the silence that had fallen after his show of ripping off his shirt. "This piece doesn't have any gems, and you can wear it while you work on the farm. When we're just goin' to church or horseback riding, you can fit this piece onto it."

The second piece acted like a wrap-around flower, with a massive, round diamond making up the "bloom" of the flower.

Gerty stared at it, her eyes wide, and Mike held up his hand when her younger sister started to say something.

"Do you like it, baby doll?"

She finally blinked and looked up at him. "I love it."

He got down on one knee and held up the ring. "Gerty, I love you with all I have in my heart, and all I want is to be with you forever. Will you marry me?"

Gerty shook her head in rapid-fire nods. "Yes." She laughed and launched herself at him. He managed to snap closed the ring box and catch her, all her long limbs wrapping around him. "Yes, baby, yes. I'll marry you."

The crowd of family lifted the roof with the noise they made with their applause and whooping. Whistles and yeehaws surrounded them as Gerty fluttered kisses across his face.

With her balanced on his single knee, he finally took her face in both of his hands and brought her mouth to his.

Somehow, amidst the chaos, he managed to kiss her properly for about two seconds before someone pulled them apart.

"Put the ring on, Uncle Mike," someone said, and one of Hunter's little girls handed him the diamond ring.

Gerty stepped away from her daddy and turned back to Mike. She gave him the flirtiest smile as she held out her left hand.

He slid the diamond band onto her ring finger and then lifted it to his lips and kissed it.

*Ah's* and *Oh's* filled the air, and then Jane handed Gerty her shirt. She pulled the tee he'd made for her months ago over her blouse, and they positioned themselves properly so that his momma and hers could snap pictures of their official engagement.

"Dinner," Aunt Elise called, and food always stole the attention from Mike when he needed it to.

"Three days," he whispered into Gerty's ear. "I'm going to be yours in three days."

She looked up at him. "I love you, Mike. I can't wait to be yours."

"I love you too, Gerty."

———

Read on for a sneak peek at the next book in this family

saga & Christian Romance series, **HIS SIXTH SWEETHEART**, to find out how things will progress with Jane and Cord....

*Preorder it today by scanning the QR code below with your phone!*

## Sneak Peek! His Sixth Sweetheart, Chapter One:

JANE HAMMOND STOOD in front of the mirror in her parents' bathroom and clipped her hair back. She'd slept in rags meant to make her golden locks curl, and boy had it worked. A little too well, and Jane had already complained to her mother about how "poodly" she looked.

Momma couldn't do anything about it, and she was super involved with helping her best friend's son get married today.

Jane loved Mike as if he were her brother. They were only a couple of years apart, and because Momma was best friends with his mother, she'd spent a lot of time growing up with him. They shared a lot of the same characteristics, but Jane wore everything she felt and thought on the outside, while Mike had learned to cage it inside him.

She caught herself staring at nothing again, and she jerked back to attention. Her heart beat a little too quickly for a few seconds, and then she tried to tame one more lock of hair by pinning it out of her face too. With most of the curls on the back of her head, Jane decided she could leave the bathroom and not die of embarrassment.

Her heels clunked on the old wood floor in the generational home, and she expected to find her father nursing a cup of coffee and reading something on his device at the kitchen table. He didn't disappoint, because the lawyer in him did everything exactly the same every single day.

Jane wanted to scream with his routines, because she didn't like doing the same thing every day. She wouldn't eat the same food for breakfast; she wouldn't get ready in exactly the same way; heck, sometimes she even drove different roads to work, just to have some variety in her otherwise completely, utterly, horribly stale life.

"Hey," Daddy said with plenty of admiration in his voice. "It's beautiful, Jane." He set aside his device and smiled at her with all the fatherly love a man could possess.

Jane sighed, her shoulders slumped as she finished the walk to the table.

"Oh, boy," Daddy said. "Your cousin is getting married in an hour. You better straighten up before then." He didn't say it unkindly, but he'd known Jane for all the years of her life—almost three decades now—and she needed a firm hand. A strong voice. Someone to tell her when she was acting like a child or irrationally, when, unfortunately, she did both sometimes.

Since starting at HMC last year, she'd gotten better. Or so she thought.

"What's eatin' at you?" Daddy asked when Jane said nothing.

Sometimes Momma had cornbread biscuits on the table for breakfast, but today wasn't one of those days. Gerty and Mike had chosen an eleven-thirty ceremony time, so they could feed everyone lunch, have an early afternoon dance, and be done by three.

Mike had gotten them airplane tickets to Spain or France for a river cruise, and that only made Jane's jealousy double. She wasn't exactly jealous. Not really.

"Daddy," she said carefully. She'd been waiting for Cord Behr to ask her out for months now. That dream had started to dry, wither, and die, but Jane still held onto the very last root with everything she had. If he'd even so much as sprinkle a drop of water on it, her hopes of going out with him would spring back to life.

"I'm sittin' right here," he drawled.

"I can't get my thoughts right." Jane put her face in her hands, then remembered that she and Molly had spent a significant amount of time that morning doing their makeup. Jane loved Molly more than she could describe, as the woman had been like a second mother to her once she and Hunter had gotten married years ago.

Jane babysat their kids sometimes, and with her mood being attached to literally everything in her life, she sometimes came home from that weeping and wondering and begging God to let her know when she'd be able to start building her own family.

"Remember how you used to tell me how impatient I was?"

Daddy cocked his head. "I was not expecting that."

Her daddy *had* often told her she needed to learn to be patient—and Jane had taken that to heart. She'd worked and worked on accepting that not everything happened exactly when she wanted it to. It sure seemed as if the Lord wanted her to keep learning that lesson, but Jane wasn't sure why.

Had she not been patient enough?

With her job? With the men she dated? With herself?

*With Cord?* whispered through her mind. She would not ask her father about him. Not again. She felt certain Cord would never speak to her again if she pressed the issue on him.

"I feel like I've been working so hard to be patient," Jane said. "I'm trying to find someone to marry, but it just doesn't seem to be working out."

Daddy reached over and covered her hand with his. Jane pulled back on her emotions. "I feel like I'm patient at work when I'm waiting on others to do their job so I can do mine. I'm patient with the time it takes to truly change my mind and heart, and while I still think it's slow, I'm doing it."

"Yes," Daddy whispered. "You are, Jane. I've seen it." He gave her another warm smile. "This is just about finding a boyfriend?"

"Not all of it." Jane exhaled heavily again and looked past her father and out the window. She could see the roofs on a couple of cowboy cabins—Cord's included. He lived alone now, and he'd been working the farm for just over fifteen years.

"But yes," she said. "All of it. Having someone to share my thoughts with, the things I don't understand, the things I love, the things that bother me…I want that." She met her father's eye again, and he nodded slowly.

He'd aged well, probably because of the amount of exercise he did. The man loved to run, and he'd even done the Boston Marathon in his mid-forties, before he'd married Momma and started having more kids.

Silver lined his temples now and salted his beard and mustache. Momma kept his hair trimmed, and the shortest of it didn't seem to hold as much darkness as it once had. He was a powerful presence in any room he entered, and especially so in his midnight-black suit, the dark blue tie already knotted precisely around his neck.

Jane wore a deep blue dress that matched his tie, and since she was ready an hour before the wedding started, she was probably more like her father than she wanted to admit.

The Hammonds were never late, she knew that. In fact, if she showed up fifteen minutes early to a family brunch, she'd be the last one there. It had driven her to the brink of madness in her mid-twenties, but now she simply expected to get jazzed for showing up *before* the agreed-upon time but after everyone else.

"I know you do, sweetheart," Daddy said. "You'll get it."

She managed a smile in return. "You look like the cat who ate the canary."

"I'm just thinking of who's coming to this wedding,"

he said. "Mike has a lot of friends. Friends from Wyoming. Friends in the military. Friends from HMC."

"I work at HMC too," Jane said in a deadpan. "Trust me, there's no boyfriend material there."

Daddy laughed, and that lightened Jane's heart. "I'm just saying," he said amidst the last of his chuckles. "Say yes to everyone who asks you to dance at the wedding. That's all."

"No one is going to ask," Jane said. Before Daddy could protest, the front door opened, and both of her younger brothers entered the generational house.

Deacon, the youngest of Daddy's younger boys, entered. "Morning," he said. "Look who I found lurking on the porch."

Tucker came inside rolling his eyes. Jane jumped to her feet to go say hello to her brother. The brother she hadn't seen in seven months. "You're here." She realized as she said the words how very much she sounded like Momma.

Tucker laughed as he wrapped his strong arms around Jane. "You sure do look pretty," he said, far more rodeo cowboy twang in his voice than necessary. Still, that was the circle Tucker ran in, and she couldn't expect him to turn it all off when he came home.

"Hey-oh," Hunter said as he came inside. Jane could see so many memories with him in it. He'd been fifteen when she was born, and he'd been the very best big brother in the entire world. He'd held her and read books to her. He'd helped her with her spelling words while he worked on a crossword puzzle.

He'd started two charitable foundations and run the multi-billion dollar company for seventeen years.

Jane felt like a complete failure next to Hunter. He grinned with the force of gravity and opened his big wingspan as if gathering all of his chicks to keep them safe from the stormy weather ahead.

"My brothers and my sister." He could command a room too, but he did it in a much quieter way than Daddy did.

They all moved into Hunter, because he was the sun, and they all revolved around him. Jane wanted a man like him in her life. Someone who was so good, and so giving, and so smart. Sure, she had a type—and that was blonde-haired, blue-eyed cowboys—but she could stand to dance with a dark-haired man if she had to.

*Maybe at the wedding*, she thought, and that single thought, no matter how farfetched, buoyed her up enough to bring a smile to her face.

———

AN HOUR LATER, Jane walked down the aisle with her arm tucked through Tucker's. She carried a small bouquet of seven flowers in blue and white. Her gown flowed around her feet with every step.

Gerty and Mike had a hobby farm and dozens of acres of land about ten miles south of Jane's family farm, and they were getting married there today. She'd come to help string streamers and strings of lights through the rafters of this old barn.

Someone had swept the floor clean, and every available surface glinted with soft lights, pretty white flowers, and accents of blue in the punch bowl, the centerpiece vases, and the bow ties all the men wore.

After she'd handed her few flowers to Mike to create one big bouquet, she couldn't help glancing over to the men's side of the altar, where her brothers stood. Keith Whettstein waited over there too, as he was a good friend of Mike's and had been working on the farm since he moved to Colorado with his father.

Britt Whettstein stood on Jane's side, but she kept smiling at her boyfriend only three rows back. Jane worked not to roll her eyes, because Britt was the nicest person ever. She wasn't super smart, but she worked hard and she tried hard, and given her limitations, she functioned in society very, very well.

Hunter stood almost on top of Mike, barely leaving room for even a breath of space between them. She wasn't sure if it was to keep Mike in place, but it seemed to be working if it was.

The rest of the wedding party arrived, and Jane didn't see Cord. Mission, Matt, and Vince had all made it down the aisle and taken their places as best men. Gerty's younger siblings had arrived, and thanks to Amy, plenty of white rose petals now littered the aisle.

The music kept droning on and on. Gerty didn't appear in the doorway of the barn, and Jane started to fidget. She glanced over to Molly, who wore wide eyes filled with concern.

Momma sat with Daddy in the front row, and even she

straightened and twisted to look behind her, as if the problem with Gerty's arrival would be standing in the doorway.

Just when Jane was about to snap, the music changed. It pitched up in volume and speed, as the wedding march piped into the barn.

Gerty appeared first, a glowing smile on her face. She was radiant in every single way, and Jane swore she saw a halo of white light around her entire person.

Her daddy was a big, burly man, quick to laugh and tell jokes, and absolutely terrifying if he thought hew as being lied to. Not that Jane had done a lot of lying in her life. A few little white lies here and there, but nothing serious.

She sensed a presence behind her, and sure enough, the warmth from someone's body melted into hers. She held very still, because someone had just put their hand on her waist and leaned into whisper something in her ear.

"You look ravishing," he said. Jane would know that voice anywhere, and shivers scattered through her whole body at the nearness of Cord Behr. The fact that he was up there in front of everyone, on the wrong side of the altar, whispering in her ear, felt scandalous all on its own.

She glanced over to Daddy, but he'd stood and was facing the back of the barn, where Gerty still waited with her daddy.

Oh, this Cord Behr was as smart as he was good-looking.

His hand started to slip away, and Jane wanted him to stay more than she cared to admit. "You and me are dancin' today," he said. "With you in that dress, if we don't, it'll be a real shame."

She twisted enough to look at him to see if he was joking or not. He could tease a lot, and he was Colorado's biggest flirt. He wore a smile to go with his sandy hair and those gorgeous eyes. Jane had lost herself in them many times, and she blinked so she wouldn't do so again.

He gestured between the two of them. "Me and you. Dancing. Later."

She nodded, and he turned and ducked around the back of the altar to take his place between Travis and Mission. That put him in a spot where she could admire him from afar, which was what she'd been doing for the past fifteen years.

Gerty reached the altar, and her father leaned down and pressed his lips to her cheek before handing her over to Mike. The two of them looked at each other, and it was like they'd turned into small children experiencing the magic of Christmas for the very first time.

If that was what it felt like to get married, Jane wanted it even more. Mike and Gerty had been friends in their teens. They'd even dated a little bit.

*All in God's timing,* she thought, which was a phrase she used often with her life coach. Gerty and Mike hadn't been ready to be standing here in front of the altar fourteen years ago. They were now.

The ceremony started, and Jane watched Cord. His words tumbled around in her head, ringing and making her excited in one breath and absolutely terrified in the next.

*You and me are dancin' today. With you in that dress, if we don't, it'll be a real shame.*

Could she really dance with him here, in front of everyone? She wanted to, and she couldn't wait until the music started again and men and women filled the dance floor.

Cord caught her staring, and the corners of his mouth twitched upward. Jane smiled at him too, wondering if he'd talked to Daddy about the two of them dating. Daddy had not been happy with it when she was younger, but a common theme around the house these days was that Jane wasn't a little girl anymore. Or even a teenager.

She was a grown woman, with a college degree, a good-paying job, and a place to live, eat, and sleep. So what if it was Hunter's sprawling mansion that she and Deacon could barely keep up with?

Right now, it was all she had, and Jane considered leaving Coral Canyon…for good. Businesses everywhere needed accountants, and Jane wouldn't have any trouble getting another job.

Then she looked at Cord. She couldn't leave town—or him—without knowing if they had something good or not.

*Me and you. Dancing. Later.*

She gave him a weak smile, but he caught it, doubled it, and grinned back at her appropriately.

Jane's impatience kicked in then, because she really just wanted to dance.

*Sneak Peek! His Sixth Sweetheart, Chapter Two:*

CORD BEHR COULDN'T BELIEVE what he'd whispered in his boss's daughter's ear. He immediately amended the thought, because Gray Hammond wasn't his boss anymore. His son, Hunter, was. And Cord and Hunter were really good friends, especially now that the man spent every day on the farm where he'd grown up.

Cord didn't understand everything about the legal stuff, but he didn't have to. Gray and Elise had moved into the generational house, and Gray had officially retired from running the farm. Hunter, Molly, and their children had moved into the farmhouse, and Hunter now ran the farm while Molly maintained her rule over Pony Power.

Matt was still the foreman of the farm, but he was pulling back more and more. The farm had needed a full-time foreman, because Gray didn't want to put in the work, but Hunter was only in his mid-forties, and he could do a lot more than his father. Not only that, but Matt had just turned fifty-five this year, and he couldn't do as much.

Now that Cord was forty, he understood how his body couldn't quite do everything it once had.

He sure couldn't look away from Jane right now, even when he told himself to do it. He could admit he'd waited to talk to Gray once he'd learned that the man would be retiring. Then Gray couldn't fire him.

*Hunter knows about you too*, he thought, and his stomach flipped the way it always did when he thought about others knowing about his past. He wasn't sure why he thought starting anything with the quick-witted and super-smart Jane Hammond was a good idea. She'd demand to know everything about him and probably needle him until he told her.

He finally ducked his head, a smile coming to his lips. Jane had backed off when he'd asked her to. He'd learned months ago that she just needed a firm hand, and she'd responded well to it.

She'd even texted to apologize later.

The minister finished up the ceremony, and Cord looked up and brought his hands together along with everyone else as Mike tipped Gerty back and kissed her. They both laughed, so that didn't last long, and then they faced the crowd that had gathered in Gerty's barn for the wedding.

Cord whistled through his teeth as the couple separated to hug their families. Mike enveloped both of his parents in one embrace while Boone gripped his oldest daughter tightly. Cord sure did like Mike and Gerty, as they'd always been kind to him.

Mike had been out on the farm less and less since becoming CEO. He still had a cabin there, but everyone would be moving his stuff to Gerty's farmhouse while the two of them were off on their honeymoon. He'd been spending more time in the city, as apparently, the CEO had an apartment there, or at the house where Jane and Deacon now lived.

Cord had never been to either place, as he had no reason to leave the farm for much more than gas and groceries. That didn't take him out of the sleepy, beautiful town of Ivory Peaks though his parole no longer forced him to stay within city limits.

He wasn't on parole anymore, and for a brief moment, he wondered if he had to tell anyone about his former misdeeds at all. Then Mike faced him, and he spread his arms and hugged the man. "Congrats," he said as Mike chuckled and then moved on to Mission and Travis.

Cord stood out of the way—something he was very good at. He was used to being an observer, and that was the way he liked it. The last thing he wanted was any spotlight on him at all.

Dancing with Jane would put an incredibly bright light on him, and Cord swallowed as he drifted further out of the way.

"Ready?" Trav's voice made Cord snap out of the place he'd just started to fall into. The man had saved Cord more times than he knew, and Cord nodded. God knew, and

Cord knew, and he thanked the Lord every single evening and every single morning for Travis Thatcher.

"Yeah." Cord's voice sounded like it had been shattered. "I'm ready."

Gerty and Mike had wanted simple and small, and that meant they'd asked their friends to help them with this wedding and all the activities included in it. The barn had been ready when he'd arrived this morning, but he, Travis, Mission, and Keith had volunteered to move the chairs from the rows and to the tables, which were all set up and waiting on the fringes.

Some of them would have to be moved inward, but for now, they slipped away from the congratulations still happening, and as Cord reached the wall of the barn to pull a table out, he turned back to see where Jane was. Standing with her mother, her arm around Elise's waist, as they both smiled at Mike. The two of them were close—both Jane and her mother and Jane and Mike—and the last thing Cord needed was anyone looking more closely at him.

Michael Hammond had unlimited resources, and if he didn't like something Cord did to Jane, he could literally destroy Cord. That went against everything Cord knew about Mike, but still, the threat lingered in the back of his mind.

"You're awfully quiet," Trav said, and Cord looked at him.

"Sorry. Just thinkin' about something."

"Yeah? What?" Trav picked up the other side of the table and waited.

"I don't want to talk about it," Cord said.

Trav usually let things slide, so Cord wasn't surprised when he didn't push the topic. Part of him wished he would, but the four of them, along with a few guests, hurried to set up the chairs around the tables and get everything positioned correctly. The wedding guests continued to mill about, and the caterers set up a buffet at the back of the bar in record time.

Bree Hammond checked with them, and only a minute later, the luncheon began. Gerty and Mike had not assigned seats anywhere, but Jane's table had filled with her family. Her siblings and her cousins, and she fit with all of them. She definitely had the lightest complexion and the flaxen hair while everyone else had been dealt dark genes from the pool. But she still fit.

Cord hadn't had a family the way she did in a long, long time. He couldn't help watching her and wondering what it would be like to be a Hammond. He'd been thinking about that for almost fifteen years, and it always made him smile.

Gray had taken him under his wing, and Cord had, in essence, become a Hammond. The thought of doing anything to upset Gray made him physically ill, and a lot of his decisions in life had stemmed from how Gray would react or what Gray would think.

He'd counseled with the man many times on things over the years, and Gray had always been kind and thoughtful in his advice.

The ringing of clinking glasses filled the air, and Cord looked up to the head table. Mike stood, and he reached his hand out to Gerty to do the same. She did, and Cord smiled at her reluctance to do so. She didn't like the spotlight either.

He was surprised she'd worn such a traditional wedding dress, because he'd never seen the woman wear anything but jeans and tank tops. Lace covered the dress from shoulder to hem, and the top did look like a skin-tight tank top with wide straps. The skirt flared at the waist and fell in full layers to the floor, with the tips of her cowgirl boots only showing when she walked.

Right now, she stood, beaming up at Mike as he spoke into the mic. "Sometimes the Lord leads us to right where we need to be, at exactly the right time." He lifted his glass. "To my wife!"

Several cowboys yelled, "Yeehaw!" and many more people took a drink of their champagne. Cord didn't drink, so he didn't reach for his water glass.

"Your turn," Mike said, grinning at Gerty like this was a fun game. Gerty sure didn't think so, and Cord leaned forward as if he'd need to pay extra-close attention to what she'd say.

"All of my horses have tried to tell me that Mike is trouble," she said into the mic. "But I went and fell in love with him anyway." She pulled the mic away as Mike tried to take it from her. "Because he's perfect…." She faced him again, and he no longer tried to get anything from her. "For me. He's perfect for me." She turned to the crowd. "To my husband!"

Another round of cheering and clapping rose into the air, and as that tapered off, Bree took the mic from her new daughter-in-law. "We'll be moving the tables to the sidelines again for the dancing. Feel free to move your chairs around, grab some more dessert from the buffet, and join us on the dance floor after the couple has their first dance."

Cord tried not to look for Jane, but his eyes roamed the barn anyway. She looked up from her phone and latched directly onto his gaze, making his mouth turn to sawdust. Her hair had been curled and fell in gorgeous, soft waves down her back. Her bare shoulders dared him to touch them, and a buzz started inside his bloodstream he hadn't felt since he was a teenager with his first crush.

Jane was so much more than that already, and Cord was tired of fighting his feelings for the woman.

At the same time, he immediately started looking around for Gray, and he wasn't hard to find at the next table over, where he sat with his brothers and their wives. He wasn't concerned with Cord or Jane at all, his attention on one of the twins as they talked about something.

"Come on," Trav said, and Cord got to his feet to move the tables again. They pulled chairs out and set up short rows between tables, and then the lights in the barn turned off. All the sparkling lights that had been hung in the rafters leant light to the space as Mike led Gerty out onto the dance floor.

Cord smiled as he took his new wife into his arms, because there was something sweet and wholesome about Mike and Gerty. Cord knew everyone had their problems, but in that moment, with the low lights and the romantic song, it sure did seem like everything with the two of them was absolutely perfect.

He wanted that level of comfort with a person. He wanted someone to know everything about him—all of his flaws and issues—and love him anyway. He wanted someone to love.

"All right, folks," a man said. "Please join the couple on the dance floor." Another slow song started, and Cord tucked his hands into his pockets to hopefully wipe off some of the sweat. He felt like he was back in junior high, with the boys on one side of the gym and the girls on the other.

If he'd ever gone to a junior high dance, that was. Which he hadn't. He'd spent his time doing much less savory things, and that alone kept his feet rooted to the spot. Trav led his wife out onto the dance floor, as did all of Mike's uncles, his daddy, and his brother.

Keith danced with Jane, and Cord swallowed back the urge to go swat his hands away from her waist. Keith hadn't dated anyone in a while either, and one look at him and Jane told Cord they were nothing more than friends. Nothing electric flowed between them, and in fact, Keith seemed to be looking for someone else.

Cord only had eyes for Jane, and after the song ended, he worked up his nerve to get closer to her. He did, and as another song started, he reached out and caught the tips of her fingers in his. "Hey."

She faced him and slid her fingers further into his when she saw it was him. "Hey." A shy smile filled her face, and she ducked her chin. "I wasn't sure if you were really going to ask me."

"It's the second dance." Someone bumped into Cord

from behind, and he took that as a a sign to stop taking up so much space. "Do you want to dance?"

"Yes, sir." She folded herself easily into his arms, and all the tense parts of Cord relaxed.

"It was a nice wedding," he murmured. His eyes drifted closed, and he took in a long inhale of Jane's hair and skin. She smelled soft and floral, with a hint of something crisp among the more powdery notes.

"Yeah," she said. "It was."

Cord wasn't great at small talk, but he'd learned a few things over the years. "How's work?"

"Oh, work is work," she said. "I've actually been thinking about getting a new job."

Cord frowned, but he didn't open his eyes. He could almost feel his way around the dance floor, what with every sense on such high alert. "You have? Why?"

"My life is just so…boring," she said.

"Mm." Cord leaned his head closer to hers, though he was practically touching her already. "I bet we can spice it up."

"Yeah?" she whispered, the word still plenty challenging. "How are *we* going to do that?"

Cord smiled, glad to see her sassy side hadn't died in the past several months. "I think we can start with dinner."

"Are you asking me to dinner?"

"Yes, ma'am."

Jane pulled back, and Cord opened his eyes as he let her. She searched his face, and Cord didn't like the open scrutiny. He ducked closer to her again, skating his cheek along hers. "Stop it," he whispered.

"Stop what?"

"Looking at me like that."

"How do you want me to look at you?"

"Like you're not judging me."

"I wasn't," she started, but her defense pretty much died there.

He chuckled softly, his mouth right at her ear. He wanted to taste her skin so badly, but he told himself he wouldn't do it here. This was date zero, and he absolutely would not kiss her now, in public, though the wedding was small.

"Are you going to say yes?" he asked.

"Yes," she whispered.

"Good," he said. "So this next weekend." He pulled back and looked at her again, his eyebrows up in the silent question mark he hadn't included in his tone.

She nodded, and then flinched mightily when Gray barked, "Cord."

Cord dang near jumped out of his skin too. He switched his gaze to Gray's. "Yes, sir."

Gray frowned like it was the only thing he knew how to do. "Can I talk to you for a second?" He looked back and forth between Cord, Jane, and back to Cord, his displeasure only deepening as it boiled and rolled into near-tangible thunder. "Now."

———

*Preorder it today by scanning the QR code below with your phone!*

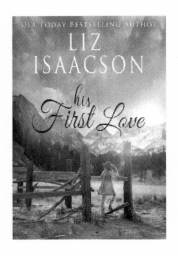

**His First Love (Book 1):** She broke up with him a decade ago. He's back in town after finishing a degree at MIT, ready to start his job at the family company. Can Hunter and Molly find their way through their pasts to build a future together?

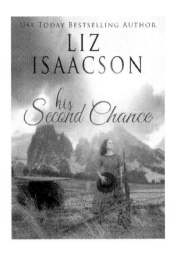

**His Second Chance (Book 2):** They broke up over twenty years ago. She's lost everything when she shows up at the farm in Ivory Peaks where he works. Can Matt and Gloria heal from their pasts to find a future happily-ever-after with each other?

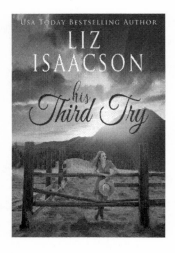

**His Third Try (Book 3):** He moved to Ivory Peaks with his daughter to start over after a devastating break-up. She's never had a meaningful relationship with a man, especially a cowboy. Can Boone and Cosette help each other heal enough to build a happily-ever-after...and a family?

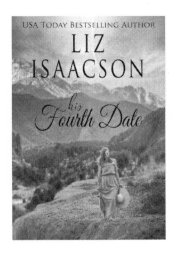

**His Fourth Date (Book 4):** Their relationship has been nothing but loose goats, a leaking roof, and her complete humiliation after he pays her mortgage so she won't lose her farm. Travis wants to go back in time and start over with Poppy, but he doesn't know how. Can a small town speed-dating event get their second chance off on the right foot?

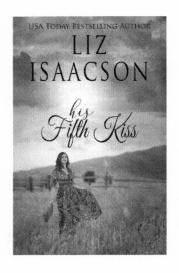

**His Fifth Kiss (Book 5):** They once had a few summers together. Now, Michael Hammond is back in town after a devastating injury overseas. He's looking to reset and recover...not to fall in love. But with Gertrude Whettstein also back at the farm, can Gerty and Mike make their second chance romance into a happily-ever-after?

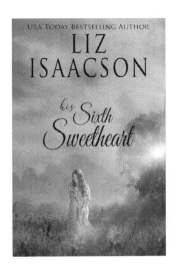

**His Sixth Sweetheart (Book 6):** She's had a crush on him for decades. He's finally in a place where he feels ready to date the boss's daughter. Can Cord and Jane take their relationship to the next level without getting burned?

**Her Cowboy Billionaire Birthday Wish (Book 1):** All the maid at Whiskey Mountain Lodge wants for her birthday is a handsome cowboy billionaire. And Colton can make that wish come true—if only he hadn't escaped to Coral Canyon after being left at the altar...

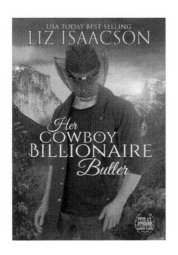

**Her Cowboy Billionaire Butler (Book 2):** She broke up with him to date another man...who broke her heart. He's a former CEO with nothing to do who can't get her out of his head. Can Wes and Bree find a way toward happily-ever-after at Whiskey Mountain Lodge?

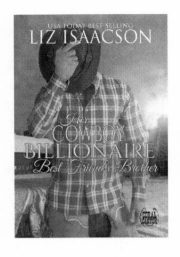

**Her Cowboy Billionaire Best Friend's Brother (Book 3):** She's best friends with the single dad cowboy's brother and has watched two friends find love with the sexy new cowboys in town. When Gray Hammond comes to Whiskey Mountain Lodge with his son, will Elise finally get her own happily-ever-after with one of the Hammond brothers?

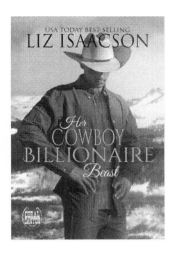

**Her Cowboy Billionaire Beast (Book 4):** A cowboy billionaire beast, his new manager, and the Christmas traditions that soften his heart and bring them together.

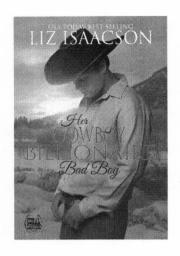

**Her Cowboy Billionaire Bad Boy (Book 5):** A cowboy billionaire cop who's a stickler for rules, the woman he pulls over when he's not even on duty, and the personal mandates he has to break to keep her in his life...

# Books in the Christmas in Coral Canyon Romance series

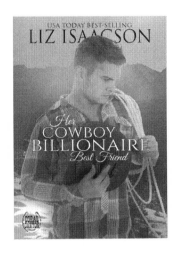

**Her Cowboy Billionaire Best Friend (Book 1):** Graham Whittaker returns to Coral Canyon a few days after Christmas—after the death of his father. He takes over the energy company his dad built from the ground up and buys a high-end lodge to live in—only a mile from the home of his once-best friend, Laney McAllister. They were best friends once, but Laney's always entertained feelings for him, and spending so much time with him while they make Christmas memories puts her heart in danger of getting broken again…

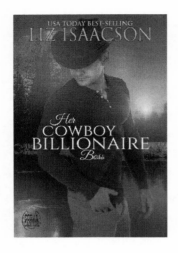

**Her Cowboy Billionaire Boss (Book 2):** Since the death of his wife a few years ago, Eli Whittaker has been running from one job to another, unable to find somewhere for him and his son to settle. Meg Palmer is Stockton's nanny, and she comes with her boss, Eli, to the lodge, her long-time crush on the man no different in Wyoming than it was on the beach. When she confesses her feelings for him and gets nothing in return, she's crushed, embarrassed, and unsure if she can stay in Coral Canyon for Christmas. Then Eli starts to show some feelings for her too…

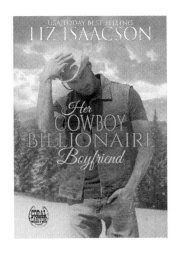

**Her Cowboy Billionaire Boyfriend (Book 3):** Andrew Whittaker is the public face for the Whittaker Brothers' family energy company, and with his older brother's robot about to be announced, he needs a press secretary to help him get everything ready and tour the state to make the announcements. When he's hit by a protest sign being carried by the company's biggest opponent, Rebecca Collings, he learns with a few clicks that she has the background they need. He offers her the job of press secretary when she thought she was going to be arrested, and not only because the spark between them in so hot Andrew can't see straight.

**Can Becca and Andrew work together and keep their relationship a secret? Or will hearts break in this classic romance retelling reminiscent of *Two Weeks Notice*?**

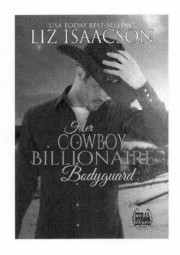

**Her Cowboy Billionaire Bodyguard (Book 4):** Beau Whittaker has watched his brothers find love one by one, but every attempt he's made has ended in disaster. Lily Everett has been in the spotlight since childhood and has half a dozen platinum records with her two sisters. She's taking a break from the brutal music industry and hiding out in Wyoming while her ex-husband continues to cause trouble for her. When she hears of Beau Whittaker and what he offers his clients, she wants to meet him. Beau is instantly attracted to Lily, but he tried a relationship with his last client that left a scar that still hasn't healed…

**Can Lily use the spirit of Christmas to discover what matters most? Will Beau open his heart to the possibility of love with someone so different from him?**

**Her Cowboy Billionaire Bull Rider (Book 5):** Todd Christopherson has just retired from the professional rodeo circuit and returned to his hometown of Coral Canyon. Problem is, he's got no family there anymore, no land, and no job. Not that he needs a job--he's got plenty of money from his illustrious career riding bulls.

Then Todd gets thrown during a routine horseback ride up the canyon, and his only support as he recovers physically is the beautiful Violet Everett. She's no nurse, but she does the best she can for the handsome cowboy. **Will she lose her heart to the billionaire bull rider? Can Todd trust that God led him to Coral Canyon...and Vi?**

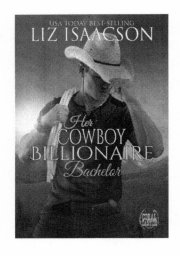

**Her Cowboy Billionaire Bachelor (Book 6):** Rose Everett isn't sure what to do with her life now that her country music career is on hold. After all, with both of her sisters in Coral Canyon, and one about to have a baby, they're not making albums anymore.

Liam Murphy has been working for Doctors Without Borders, but he's back in the US now, and looking to start a new clinic in Coral Canyon, where he spent his summers.

When Rose wins a date with Liam in a bachelor auction, their relationship blooms and grows quickly. **Can Liam and Rose find a solution to their problems that doesn't involve one of them leaving Coral Canyon with a broken heart?**

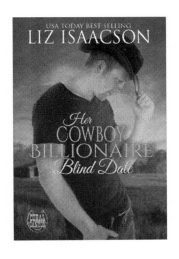

**Her Cowboy Billionaire Blind Date (Book 7):** Her sons want her to be happy, but she's too old to be set up on a blind date...isn't she?

Amanda Whittaker has been looking for a second chance at love since the death of her husband several years ago. Finley Barber is a cowboy in every sense of the word. Born and raised on a racehorse farm in Kentucky, he's since moved to Dog Valley and started his own breeding stable for champion horses. He hasn't dated in years, and everything about Amanda makes him nervous.

**Will Amanda take the leap of faith required to be with Finn? Or will he become just another boyfriend who doesn't make the cut?**

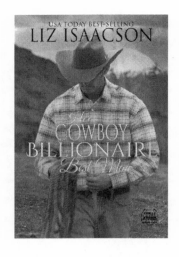

**Her Cowboy Billionaire Best Man (Book 8):** When Celia Abbott-Armstrong runs into a gorgeous cowboy at her best friend's wedding, she decides she's ready to start dating again.

But the cowboy is Zach Zuckerman, and the Zuckermans and Abbotts have been at war for generations.

Can Zach and Celia find a way to reconcile their family's differences so they can have a future together?

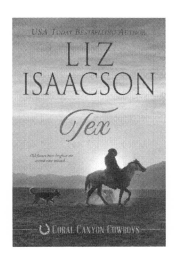

**Tex (Book 1):** He's back in town after a successful country music career. She owns a bordering farm to the family land he wants to buy...and she outbids him at the auction. Can Tex and Abigail rekindle their old flame, or will the issue of land ownership come between them?

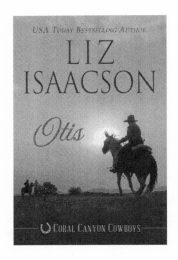

**Otis (Book 2):** He's finished with his last album and looking for a soft place to fall after a devastating break-up. She runs the small town bookshop in Coral Canyon and needs a new boyfriend to get her old one out of her life for good. Can Georgia convince Otis to take another shot at real love when their first kiss was fake?

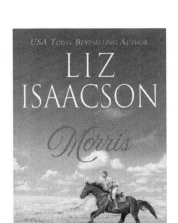

**Morris (Book 3):** Morris Young is just settling into his new life as the manager of Country Quad when he attends a wedding. He sees his ex-wife there—apparently Leighann is back in Coral Canyon—along with a little boy who can't be more or less than five years old... Could he be Morris's? And why is his heart hoping for that, and for a reconciliation with the woman who left him because he traveled too much?

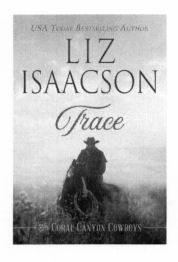

**Trace (Book 4):** He's been accused of only dating celebrities. She's a simple line dance instructor in small town Coral Canyon, with a soft spot for kids...and cowboys. Trace could use some dance lessons to go along with his love lessons... Can he and Everly fall in love with the beat, or will she dance her way right out of his arms?

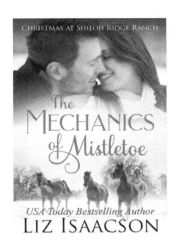

**The Mechanics of Mistletoe (Book 1):** Bear Glover can be a grizzly or a teddy, and he's always thought he'd be just fine working his generational family ranch and going back to the ancient homestead alone. But his crush on Samantha Benton won't go away. She's a genius with a wrench on Bear's tractors...and his heart. Can he tame his wild side and get the girl, or will he be left broken-hearted this Christmas season?

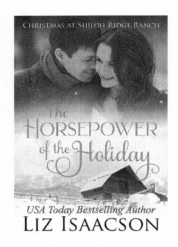

**The Horsepower of the Holiday (Book 2):** Ranger Glover has worked at Shiloh Ridge Ranch his entire life. The cowboys do everything from horseback there, but when he goes to town to trade in some trucks, somehow Oakley Hatch persuades him to take some ATVs back to the ranch. (Bear is NOT happy.)

She's a former race car driver who's got Ranger all revved up... Can he remember who he is and get Oakley to slow down enough to fall in love, or will there simply be too much horsepower in the holiday this year for a real relationship?

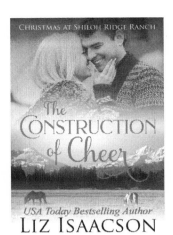

**The Construction of Cheer (Book 3):** Bishop Glover is the youngest brother, and he usually keeps his head down and gets the job done. When Montana Martin shows up at Shiloh Ridge Ranch looking for work, he finds himself inventing construction projects that need doing just to keep her coming around. (Again, Bear is NOT happy.) She wants to build her own construction firm, but she ends up carving a place for herself inside Bishop's heart. Can he convince her *he's* all she needs this Christmas season, or will her cheer rest solely on the success of her business?

**The Secret of Santa (Book 4):** He's a fun-loving cowboy with a heart of gold. She's the woman who keeps putting him on hold. Can Ace and Holly Ann make a relationship work this Christmas?

**The Harmony of Holly (Book 5):** He's as prickly as his name, but the new woman in town has caught his eye. Can Cactus shelve his temper and shed his cowboy hermit skin fast enough to make a relationship with Willa work?

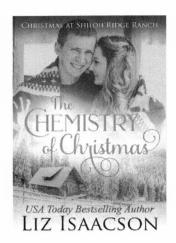

**The Chemistry of Christmas (Book 6):** He's the black sheep of the family, and she's a chemist who understands formulas, not emotions. Can Preacher and Charlie take their quirks and turn them into a strong relationship this Christmas?

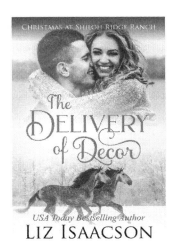

**The Delivery of Decor (Book 7):** When he falls, he falls hard and deep. She literally drives away from every relationship she's ever had. Can Ward somehow get Dot to stay this Christmas?

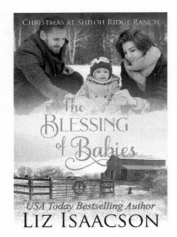

**The Blessing of Babies (Book 8):** Don't miss out on a single moment of the Glover family saga in this bridge story linking Ward and Judge's love stories!

The Glovers love God, country, dogs, horses, and family. Not necessarily in that order. ;)

Many of them are married now, with babies on the way, and there are lessons to be learned, forgiveness to be had and given, and new names coming to the family tree in southern Three Rivers!

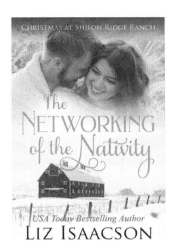

**The Networking of the Nativity (Book 9):** He's had a crush on her for years. She doesn't want to date until her daughter is out of the house. Will June take a change on Judge when the success of his Christmas light display depends on her networking abilities?

**The Wrangling of the Wreath (Book 10):** He's been so busy trying to find Miss Right. She's been right in front of him the whole time. This Christmas, can Mister and Libby take their relationship out of the best friend zone?

**The Hope of Her Heart (Book 11):** She's the only Glover without a significant other. He's been searching for someone who can love him *and* his daughter. Can Etta and August make a meaningful connection this Christmas?

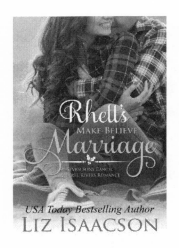

**Rhett's Make-Believe Marriage (Book 1):** She needs a husband to be credible as a matchmaker. He wants to help a neighbor. Will their fake marriage take them out of the friend zone?

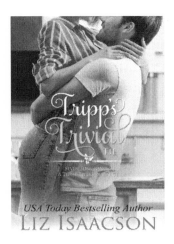

**Tripp's Trivial Tie (Book 2):** She needs a husband to keep her son. He's wanted to take their relationship to the next level, but she's always pushing him away. Will their trivial tie take them all the way to happily-ever-after?

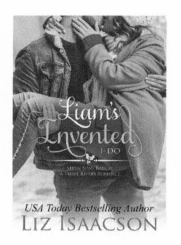

USA Today Bestselling Author
LIZ ISAACSON

**Liam's Invented I-Do (Book 3):** She's desperate to save her ranch. He wants to help her any way he can. Will their invented I-Do open doors that have previously been closed and lead to a happily-ever-after for both of them?

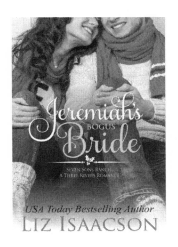

**Jeremiah's Bogus Bride (Book 4):** He wants to prove to his brothers that he's not broken. She just wants him. Will a fake marriage heal him or push her further away?

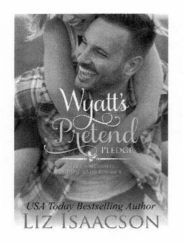

**Wyatt's Pretend Pledge (Book 5):** To get her inheritance, she needs a husband. He's wanted to fly with her for ages. Can their pretend pledge turn into something real?

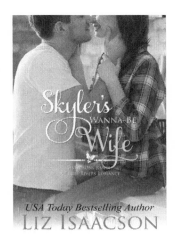

USA Today Bestselling Author
LIZ ISAACSON

**Skyler's Wanna-Be Wife (Book 6):** She needs a new last name to stay in school. He's willing to help a fellow student. Can this wanna-be wife show the playboy that some things should be taken seriously?

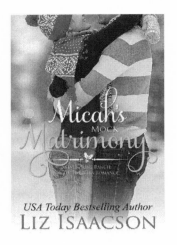

USA Today Bestselling Author
LIZ ISAACSON

**Micah's Mock Matrimony (Book 7):** They were just actors auditioning for a play. The marriage was just for the audition – until a clerical error results in a legal marriage. Can these two ex-lovers negotiate this new ground between them and achieve new roles in each other's lives?

# About Liz

Liz Isaacson writes inspirational romance, usually set in Texas, or Wyoming, or anywhere else horses and cowboys exist. She lives in Utah, where she writes full-time, takes her two dogs to the park everyday, and eats a lot of veggies while writing. Find her on her website, along with all of her pen names, at feelgoodfictionbooks.com.